SATAN'S LEGIONS

Book Two: **Friendship**

by

Philip G. Brown

Published by Swanford United Books
Please contact:
swanfordunited@aol.com

ISBN 978-0-9932461-4-2

Acknowledgements

I'd like to thank my copy-editor Jane Hammett, an Advanced Professional Member of the Society for Editors and Proofreaders, for her sterling work on my books.

I'd like to thank Evesham United FC for permission to use the cover photograph of their excellent youth team, which also played the part – in my imagination – of the team in my books.

There is an index of characters at the back of the book.

1: Saturday, 25th May. 9.15 a.m. 15 Leighton Lane.

JACK

Jack picked up the phone in the kitchen and dialled.

"Hello, is that Mrs Huntley?"

"Yes... who is that?"

"I'm Jack Moseley, Mikey's brother. I was wondering if we could bring him over to visit Mike?"

"Is Mikey still angry, Jack?"

"No, he just wants to see his friend."

"Mike's still scared about what happened. He thinks Mikey hates him."

"Oh no. In fact, he said it wasn't really Mike's fault."

"He's a very forgiving little boy then, Jack."

"He's all right, I suppose... for a pest. So is it OK if we wheel him over?"

"Of course. We'll be in until around lunch time."

***

2: Saturday, 25th May. 9.45 a.m. Fruit and Flower, Swanford high street.

ROBERT

"Young man, there's another young man gesticulating at you through the window."

A slight colour rose in Robert's cheeks and a smile threatened to override his serious shop-assistant face. "Sorry ma'am," he said to the lady customer, thankful that Mrs Annesley was still glued to her accounts book in the storeroom.

"Just these," said the customer shortly, a smartly dressed woman whose hands looked as if they'd never scraped a potato in their life.

Robert carefully put each item on the scales, but could have guessed to the ounce what they weighed.

"Why do you charge for the carrot tops?" she asked, while behind her Jack took a furtive step into the shop.

"Er, I suppose I could knock ten pence off, ma'am..."

"No matter."

"That'll be £2.40 then, thank you, ma'am," he said, placing the three brown paper bags into the Asda bag-for-life that she offered him.

The woman gave him the exact money then marched out, sniffing disdainfully at Jack as their paths crossed.

"Hello, carrot top," he whispered. "Could I have a very large banana, please?"

"All in good time, *sir.*"

"Where is Mrs A?"

"You're fortunate, *sir,* she's in the counting house, counting out her money."

"Hi, Robert!" shouted Mikey, having wheeled himself into the shop, while Dan paced up and down the pavement outside, like a soldier on sentry duty.

"Jesus, pestilence!" hissed Jack, "not so loud!"

"You're coming to my house on Monday," said the little boy. "Jack ripped up your card."

"Am I? I am... did he?"

"Yes, it was a very naughty thing to do."

Robert gave Mikey a sideways look. "Not like telling tales, then?"

The little boy's face fell.

"Yes, that caught you, didn't it?" said Jack.

Mikey looked up at his brother, then hung his head. "Are we still going to Mike's?"

"Maybe, if you say sorry for telling tales."

"Sorry... I'll be good from now on."

"Huh!"

"What time do you want me on Monday?" asked Robert.

Jack cocked his head on one side. "All the time," he murmured.

"I heard that," said Mikey.

"Early – about ten, if that's all right? Everyone will be there in the evening."

"Hurry up," chided Mikey, almost running the wheelchair into a trio of customers as he made for the door. "Dan, come and push me!"

"You're a pest, pest!" Dan's voice floated through the shop and Jack smiled ruefully.

"You are lucky, you know," said the American.

"They're your brothers too now," Jack said.

Robert smiled. "You'd better scoot, otherwise our luck will run out."

"I love you," Jack mouthed and turned to go.

"I'll make sure you get your banana delivered on Monday, *sir*."

The English boy grinned, but didn't look back.

Robert continued to gaze towards his boyfriend until his eye was caught by a flash of sunlight. Whereupon his whole field of vision seemed to fill with the white reflective glare of a transit van, coming too close and too fast.

"Jack!" he called. "Jack!"

But his voice was drowned out in the roar of the engine.

The van shrieked as the wheels mounted the pavement. It seemed to gather more speed as it aimed for where Dan was standing with Mikey. It hit the window, sending fragments of safety glass showering into the shop, before careening off and hurtling away down the high street.

***

3: Saturday, 25th May. 10.15 a.m. Folly Farm.

<u>ALAN</u>

Derek dragged Alan from the van and slapped him round the head. "How are we going to explain this away to Dad, you stupid little shit?"

"I don't know!" cried Alan, trying to defend himself by flailing his arms.

"Well, *I* know, because you'll be the one doing it, fucker."

"Stop it, please, Derek!"

But his brother wouldn't stop, and punched him in the stomach and then between his legs, flooring him instantly. Alan writhed on the ground, screaming and holding himself.

"Now, you cunt, I'm going to teach you a real lesson..."

Alan curled into a ball and whimpered as he heard his brother unbuckling his belt. Then his clothes were ripped from his body. "No, please, Derek... no!"

The first blow caught his bare thigh, the second his back, the third his stomach, then the blows just rained down on him until he could no longer move, no longer speak, no longer think...

***

4: Saturday, 25th May. 10.15 a.m. Fruit and Flower, Swanford high street.

<u>JACK</u>

Mrs Annesley was in the shop, giving details of the incident to a policewoman, while workmen, who had already arrived to board up the window, crunched through the glass underfoot. The sounds percolated through to the stockroom, where the boys waited on packing cases for their turn to be questioned.

"What did Mum say?" asked Dan quietly, touching a deep scrape on his chin.

"You mean, besides having a screaming fit?" answered Jack. "No, she was OK really. She's on her way."

Dan leaned forward. "I saw who it was."

"I think we all know," Jack replied.

The boy shook his head. "I don't think you do. It was Alan Henderson..."

Robert looked from one brother to the other. "You mean the little blond guy?"

"It was him for definite. I noticed the van because it was tearing down the high street so fast that I sort of sensed it was a danger. Then I saw the driver at the same time as he saw me. That's when he swerved towards us."

"Was there anyone with him?"

"Not that I could see."

"I thought you had to be about fifty in this country before you were allowed to drive," said Robert, who had imagined being able to get a licence when he turned sixteen.

"Just like you have to be fifty in your country before you're allowed a drink?" countered Jack.

"I'm bored," said Mikey. "Can we go to Mike's now?"

"What shall we say to the police?" asked Dan.

Jack noticed how pale his brother was and how his hands were still shaking, even after half an hour. "You saved Mikey's life, that's what I'm going to say." He smiled. "You fool!"

That at least got half a grin out of Dan.

"Makes you wonder how he managed to miss you," said Robert.

"I don't know the answer to that. I was pushing Mikey away as fast as I could by then. All I saw was this white streak flying by, about a foot from my left ear, then I tripped and fell and the wheelchair hit the wall."

"Why would he do it though, LB?"

"I thought you might ask that," said Dan, shamefaced. "To be honest, I have kind of been bullying him during the past few weeks."

Jack regarded him. "Was that something to do with us?"

Dan nodded, looking down at the floor. "He's been off sick for a fortnight..."

"In that case, I don't think we should mention any names," said Jack. "Just say it was a white van."

"But the guy is a maniac," said Robert. "He should be locked away."

"It's not as simple as that," said Jack.

"I want to go to Mike's," insisted Mikey.

A constable lifted the yellow tape, allowing Pamela Moseley access to the shop. Mrs Annesley regarded her.

"All ruined," she said, "but at least no one was hurt."

Pam surveyed the damage, thinking that it didn't look as bad as she'd imagined after Jack had phoned her. "Where are they?" she asked.

Mrs Annesley gestured towards the back of the shop.

"We shall need to speak to the boys before they leave," said the policewoman. "And they may all need counselling after such a shock."

Pam narrowed her eyes at her. "I'm taking them home," she said, brooking no argument. "You've got our address, if you need to speak to them."

"It's Mummy," cried Mikey, moving his wheelchair forward.

Pam strode into the stockroom, bending to give her youngest a kiss and a hug, then stood for a moment, gazing at the rest of her brood. "I don't know what I'm going to do with you all," she said briskly. "It's just one thing after another with you lot."

"Sounds like you're blaming the victims," said Jack.

She locked eyes with her eldest son, communicating how she was really feeling, and there were hugs all round after that; even Robert got one.

"I think I'd like to go home," said Dan.

"I want to go to Mike's," said Mikey.

"Michael Moseley, there is no way you are going to Mike's today. I shall phone Mrs Huntley and see if we can arrange something for tomorrow."

"I'd better start seein' what I can do to tidy up the shop," said Robert, rising from his packing case.

"You'll do no such thing. You'll come home with us, and get some hot sweet tea inside you. Then we'll see about getting you back to your family."

"Yes, ma'am!" said Robert, feeling as if he should salute a superior officer.

***

5: Saturday, 25th May. 12.30 p.m. At an undisclosed location.

<u>ALAN</u>

From far away, a voice was mocking him. "Alana! Alana Henderfag! When are you going to grow a dick instead of sucking other people's?"

"I've killed you, Dan Moseley," he shouted back. "You can't hurt me – you're dead!"

Two policemen took him and bundled him into a van. The back doors slammed, the engine started, a siren wailed. The vehicle moved off and, though his eyes were closed, he could see patterns of light and shade constantly repeating, as if they were travelling down a tree-lined avenue.

He floated upwards through layers of consciousness and, as he ascended, the pain became steadily worse and the hum of an engine grew louder. He tried to open his eyes, but his eyelids seemed stuck together. He was lying face-down inside the vehicle, bouncing along a twisting road. The metal floor felt hard against his bare skin. It was making him feel sick. He was sore all over, but the worst of it was coming from between his buttocks.

He felt behind him. There was a sticky wetness there, then his fingers touched something hard and not of himself. He drew his hand away and forced his eyes open. Bright red blood covered the tips of his fingers. Nausea overcame him. His eyes rolled up. The black roof of the van suddenly became the floor as he tumbled over and over into unconsciousness.

6: Saturday, 25th May. 9.15 p.m. 14 Edward's Lane.

DI DAVID RAINS

The Detective Inspector stood in the twilight on the doorstep of Councillor John Henderson's house, waiting impatiently for an answer to his ring. His gaze fell on the election poster for the United Kingdom Majority Party candidate, which was propped sideways against the wall in the driveway and, after weeks of service, showed signs of decrepitude.

At last the door was opened by an attractive blonde woman wearing a high-necked, sleeveless green dress set off by a silver rope necklace.

"I'm sorry to keep you waiting," she said. "I was making drinks for the others."

"I'm Detective Inspector David Rains," he announced, entering the hallway. "I don't think I've seen you here before, have I?"

The woman looked over her shoulder as she led him down the passage. "I'm Cynthia, Councillor Henderson's new personal assistant."

The Detective Inspector was tempted to reach out and feel one of her buttocks, which looked mouth-wateringly firm in her tight-fitting dress, but he resisted and merely raised his eyebrows. "I suppose these days the party can afford to give its faithful servants a few perks."

Cynthia opened the lounge door and allowed him to pass through. The room was already occupied by three other individuals, two of whom he knew well. The third was Lawrence Hyde, whose face adorned the poster outside and who had recently been narrowly defeated by Sarah Heath in the Woolgrove constituency at the general election.

Councillor Henderson spoke from his large armchair. His words were laced with a chilly sarcasm. "Good evening, David. I'm sorry to have to call you out so late on a Saturday night. Do take a seat and help yourself to a drink."

"Thank you," he answered meekly, nodding at Police and Crime Commissioner Kenneth Anderson, who was sitting in the other armchair.

"Cynthia, would you see to my wife's needs before you go? Thank you for all you've done tonight." This time there was no hint of sarcasm in the Henderson voice.

"It's a pleasure, Councillor," said the woman in the tight green dress, who quietly closed the lounge door behind her.

"I can see you'd like to get your hands on that, David," said Kenneth Anderson.

The detective glanced at John Henderson to see how he was reacting to such a suggestion, but as usual the councillor's face was a mask.

"She's very attractive," he said non-committally.

John Henderson gave a low chuckle. "You'd like to fuck her, wouldn't you?"

"Well, I—"

"Let's get down to business," interrupted the councillor. "Hyde, the party has decided to give you another chance, should anything untoward happen to Ms Heath in the near future."

"Is that likely?" he asked.

It was the Police and Crime Commissioner's turn to chuckle. "We have plans for the wishy-washy Ms Heath. She seems incapable of grasping the fact that the days of her liberal sort of politics are at an end."

John Henderson fixed the prospective candidate in his mesmeric gaze. "You only need a couple of hundred of her voters to change their minds for you to become a Member of Parliament. Does that give you a clue as to what you need to do?"

Lawrence Hyde blinked. "My coffers are dry. We spent every penny—"

"Then I advise you start saving for that rainy by-election day," said the councillor, and he reached inside his suit. "To start you off, here's a donation from the party's most generous sponsor, Burnoco Oil."

"But I think we've reached our legal limit," stammered the prospective candidate.

"Legal, Mr Hyde? Legal? You sound as if you don't want to become a Right Honourable gentleman. We're doing God's work. And *He shall supply all your need according to his riches in glory by Christ Jesus...*" Councillor Henderson threw the envelope at Lawrence, who caught it awkwardly. "Now run along, I have other business to attend to."

When the prospective UKMP candidate for the currently non-vacant seat of Woolgrove had left, John Henderson turned to the Detective Inspector, his expression altogether more malign. "Are you aware of the incident that happened today in the high street?"

"Only in passing. White van, hit and run, wasn't it? I saw it on the news."

"Don't I pay you enough to keep your eyes and ears wide open?"

"Yes, but it's Saturday..."

"When you're on my payroll, you're working twenty-four hours a day, seven days a week, making sure that all police business involving this family is taken care of."

"OK, sorry. What do I have to do?"

"In this instance, nothing, except to take the file to the nearest incinerator and burn it."

Detective Inspector Rains nodded slowly. "Was it Derek?"

"No, it wasn't Derek. It was my youngest son..."

David sat back on the sofa in surprise. "You mean Alan? He was driving the van?"

"Yes, and it seems he's becoming an even bigger liability than that brat Stewart."

"In what way?"

Kenneth Anderson took a drink from his glass of whisky and soda, and gave a sardonic laugh. "The worst way."

"My youngest son has been spoiled by his mother," clarified John Henderson. "He has always been strange, and now I suspect he has turned into a queer."

"Oh, nasty," said Detective Rains. "How do you know?"

"Nothing a child of mine does escapes my attention."

"I take it he's not here, then?"

"He has been removed to the country for treatment by our partners."

"Haven't there been objections?"

"If you mean his mother, she only knows that I have him and that if she starts misbehaving his fate will be sealed – and so will hers..."

"What will happen to him if he isn't cured?" asked David tentatively, his heart beating a little faster as he imagined his own fate if he crossed Councillor John Henderson.

"If he doesn't become *normal*, I shall make money out of him, then either have him killed or sold off to the highest bidder, and by then his mother will be in no position to intervene."

"Have another drink, David. You seem to have gone a little pale," said the Police and Crime Commissioner.

Councillor Henderson took a second envelope from his inside suit pocket. "This is for Inspector Hammerton; his membership of UKMP is enclosed. I'm pleased he made the right decision."

Detective Inspector Rains took the envelope, feeling its weight, and his mouth watered.

"We are all pleased with Arthur," said Kenneth Anderson. "By becoming one of us, he's helping to keep Swanford a decent place to live in."

***

7: Sunday 26th May. 9 a.m. The Baptist Church, Westbury Avenue.

ROBERT

One of Pastor Fisher's innovations was to have piped organ music playing softly in the background as the congregation entered and exited the church. Another was to lead the service dressed in a suit rather than clerical garb, though so far neither had improved overall attendance.

The Crittendens took up their usual places in the third pew, just in front of Patty and Edith, who were there, as ever, in their Sunday best. One of the reasons Robert still enjoyed coming to church was listening to the two old ladies whispering to one another before proceedings commenced. He smiled and nodded at them, and they politely returned his greeting.

A middle-aged couple entered the church, he in a lounge suit, she in a canary-yellow knee-length dress and matching hat. To a ripple of conversation they walked down the aisle to the vacant front pew. Once seated the man turned and smiled, offering his hand across the vacant pew.

"Good morning, Frank, I hope you are well – and you, of course, Maybelle."

While she merely smiled at him, Robert's father raised himself off his seat and took the offered hand. "Fine, thank you, Councillor, I'm pleased that you and your wife could make it. I hope it will become a regular occurrence."

"Oh yes, we must all keep the faith."

"How is the new election shortlist coming along?"

"We're going to give Hyde a second chance. If Ms Heath doesn't come on board she'll soon find her days in politics are numbered."

Frank turned. "And this is my son, Robert. Robert, this is Councillor Henderson, a very important man in this town."

The boy half stood. "How do you do, sir."

They shook hands and the councillor gave him a curt nod and for a moment eyed him with a penetrating gaze through his thick-lensed spectacles. This was the first time Robert had seen Stewart Henderson's father in the flesh, and he was struck by how exceptionally powerfully built the man was, especially when compared with his son. There was also something darkly attractive about him that was both disturbing and disconcerting. It was as though the man had made some immediate and subtle connection with him just through a look and a handshake. He forced himself to avert his eyes, noticing that, in contrast to her husband, Mrs Henderson made no attempt to take part in the exchanges, not even offering a greeting of her own.

The music ceased; a signal that the service was about to begin. The congregation rose as Pastor Fisher emerged and stood by the altar, smiling benignly. "Friends, let us sing a song of victory to get us in the mood. 'Stand up, stand up for Jesus, Ye soldiers of the cross'!"

During the hymn, Robert's thoughts drifted to the following morning, when he would meet up with Jack. He had already told his parents that he was going to see if Mrs Annesley needed any help clearing up in the shop. This was not a complete lie, because he intended to do just that, but for only a short while.

Fifteen minutes passed with his mind elsewhere, though he had been able to sit and stand on cue, like a driver on autopilot.

"My goodness!" cried Edith in a small voice, which nonetheless carried round the church. "I didn't know that..."

Robert was brought out of his reverie as the pastor turned his attention to the excited old lady. "That's because you are a true Christian, madam, and not steeped in the ways of the Devil. Satan's sexual demons often prey on people by performing carnal acts through nightmares and erotic dreams. They can lure the vulnerable into promiscuity, and even homosexuality..."

Robert glanced around him. His parents were rapt, Patty and Edith were staring as if transfixed, while many others in the congregation shifted uncomfortably.

The pastor's voice softened. "Yet even the most sinful can be redeemed through the goodness of our Lord Jesus Christ. You see, Satan's demons are cowardly creatures that shudder and shake before the light of our Lord. They cannot remain in the body of a soul that calls out to Jesus for succour and salvation. When the Holy Spirit enters, then demons flee away."

***

8: Monday, 27th May. 8 a.m. The high street, Swanford.

JACK

Jack rested his bike against the wooden board that now covered the right-hand window of Fruit and Flower, knowing full well that this inspection of the crime scene was just a tactic to postpone his main reason for being out so early on a bank holiday Monday. The police still hadn't been round to interview them about the incident, which he found strange, but anything involving the Hendersons seemed peculiar.

The shop wasn't yet open and the police tape still fluttered across the entrance. He peered inside, noticing the glass chips strewn across the floor. It was odd that Alan had been driving the van in the first place, odder still that he had appeared to be alone in the cab, and completely baffling how a thirteen-year-old could have kept control of the vehicle even after mounting the pavement and hitting the window. He hadn't even left any skid marks.

Delaying his real mission no longer, Jack wheeled his bike slowly along the high street, rehearsing what he was going to say to Mr Ray. This would be the first time he'd been to the newsagent's since he had stormed out so many months ago. His mother had told him about the postcard in the window asking for a paper boy, and his need to start earning cash again had overcome any anxiety he felt at having to enter this particular lion's den.

He propped his bike by the drainpipe and sheepishly entered the shop. There were two customers already inside and he hung back until they had gone, whereupon he sidled up to the counter.

"Hello, Mr Ray."

"Jack my boy, it has been a long time and no see. What can I do for you on this May morning?"

"I'm sorry, Mr Ray, for what I said."

"It was a very misfortunate incident."

"And thank you for telling Mrs Chambers about me."

"Credit where credit is due, Jack my boy. The lady is one of the old school. She was born in Calcutta in '32, you know..."

Jack cleared his throat. "Er, I saw the sign in the window... and I was wondering... if there was any chance of applying?"

Mr Ray's moustache bristled. "Well, Jack my boy, the position is for a responsible person to take up the p.m. round and delivery of the weekly freebies. But things have changed in this vicinity, and to answer the application question I shall have to defer to my number-one son."

Jack's heart sank. The round described was the one Sandip used to do and, if the decision was his, then he stood no chance. Mr Ray disappeared through the door at the back of the shop, reappearing shortly with a small, studious-looking boy with short black hair. Though there was a distinct family resemblance, the boy as yet had no sign of a moustache.

"Do you know my number-one son, Sourajit, Jack my boy? He goes to the same good school as you – not that den of iniquity down the road."

"Are you Dan Moseley's brother?" the boy asked, his voice melodiously deep.

"That's me," said Jack brightly. Dan Moseley's not so famous brother, he thought.

"He is a very good footballer and not a bad cricketer for an English boy," said Sourajit. "Next year I will be in Year Eight and shall follow in his footprints." He looked up at his father, nodded affirmatively, then retired once more to the back of the shop.

"It seems, Jack my boy, that you have the necessary approval rating and have been hired. When my number-one son comes of age, he is going to be an astute player on the business scene. Already he knows his onions."

"Thank you. When would you like me to start?"

"Tomorrow p.m."

"How is the pay?" asked Jack tentatively.

Mr Ray gave him a broad smile. "The same generous terms and conditions."

"OK. May I ask a question?"

"Certainly, Jack my boy, but please hurry because a customer is about to make a purchase."

"What happened to your former number-one son, Sandip?"

Mr Ray frowned and shook his head sadly. "I expect at this moment that lazy good-for-nothing dipshit will be lazing in his bed, smoking one of my hard-earned cigarettes. But tomorrow he will be up at five to deliver the morning papers, Jack my boy."

***

9: Monday, 27th May. 5 p.m. 15 Leighton Lane.

<u>DAN</u>

Dan and Sophie were in the kitchen sorting out yet more drinks and salad for the barbecue, when there was a loud knock on the door. Max and Mandy stood, arm in arm, on the doorstep.

"Hello," said Max, looking through Dan. "The life and souls of the party have finally arrived."

Without comment, the boy stepped aside to allow them to enter, and as Mandy passed she jabbed her finger at him. "Are you looking out for your brother now, instead of acting like a cunt?"

Dan went red and Sophie came up and grabbed his arm protectively. "Why are you talking to him like that?" she demanded.

The bigger and brighter girl glided passed imperiously without deigning to answer.

"Yes I am, and yes I was," said Dan emphatically, calling after her.

Mandy half turned and gave him a sideways look. "Then perhaps one day you might actually become a half-decent human being, and not just a piece of eye candy."

Max stopped short. "Manners, don't I provide enough eye candy for you?"

"Maxxy, you can never have too much eye candy..." The pair walked on into the hall, where Mike Hartley was trying to make Mikey dizzy by spinning him round in the wheelchair.

"Again!" cried Mikey.

"Oh God!" said Max. "It's the two little wooden boys together."

"What do you bozos think you're doing?" asked Mandy.

"Just playing," said Mike, a mad gleam in his eye.

"Does that include ripping up the carpet?" enquired Max with a self-satisfied simper.

Mikey looked over the side of his wheelchair and his smile disappeared. Mike had already dropped onto his knees and was trying to smooth the carpet back into position.

"Come, Manners, let us leave the sawdust brains to their fate."

"You two better get that sorted," shouted Dan. "Mum will be here in half an hour."

"I want to wash that hag's mouth out with a Brillo pad," said Sophie. "And why didn't you just flip her off?"

Dan gave her quick kiss on the lips. "Whatever you think of her, Soph, she's usually right." He grinned. "Especially about the eye candy."

"Conceited," she replied and eyed him quizzically. "How come you're back to your old self today?"

***

10: Monday, 27th May. 5.45 p.m. 15 Leighton Lane.

<u>PAM</u>

The barbecue was in full swing when Pamela Moseley arrived back home. The smell of burned meat was wafting over Swanford, as were the sounds of teenage revelry, which included loud music blasting out of speakers borrowed from Sam Crabtree at the Jewel Café.

Jack and Robert were standing in matching aprons doling out burgers, hot dogs and chicken legs to a continuous queue of hungry mouths, while Dan and Sophie had replenished the drinks and sides and had joined Justin, Freddie and their girlfriends around the plastic garden table. Charlie and Barbara were jawing with Max, while Mandy had taken Stewart aside so he could tell her all his news. Meanwhile, Mikey and Mike were still trying to figure out how to reattach the hall carpet to the floor.

"Michael Huntley! Who gave you that hammer?" demanded Pam. "And what have you done to my hall carpet?"

The boy stared at her in panic.

"It wasn't Mike's fault; we were just playing," answered Mikey.

"I shall speak to you later, young man," his mother said. "Meanwhile Mike, you can give me that hammer and take Mikey out into the garden. And try to stay out of trouble!"

Pam held the back door open for them, then made a beeline for the organisers. "Hello, Robert," she said modulating her voice above the din. "I thought you were a guest and here you are doing all the work."

"Half the work," corrected Jack. "Why have you got a hammer in your hand?"

"Have the neighbours complained yet?" she asked, sticking a finger into her left ear.

Jack grinned. "I sent Robert round to sweet-talk them. Seems to have worked so far. We said we'd finish at 7.30 on the dot."

"By which time they'll all be deaf anyway. I took this hammer off mad Mike Huntley. You should see what those two monkeys have done to the hall carpet."

"Mum, can Robert come round tomorrow? We've got a lot of revision to do."

Pam saw their eyes meet and their faces light up conspiratorially. "You don't normally ask when you have friends round to revise," she said suspiciously.

"Oh, Robert likes to keep his parents informed, and I mean all day, for meals and everything," said Jack hastily.

"Hmm, well, I'm taking Mikey to the hospital to see if he can be fitted with crutches in the morning, and so we won't be back till who knows when."

"Mikey will be just like Tiny Tim in *A Christmas Carol*," said Robert and, on seeing her bemused expression, he added, "It's a book by your English writer Charles Dickens."

"I know," said Pam, not wanting to be lectured on English literature by a boy, especially an American boy. "I'm not ignorant, you know, Robert. I've seen the film..."

Jack sniggered.

"Is Stewart here?" Pam asked, regaining her poise.

They all peered around through the smoke and saw him chatting animatedly to Dan. Both boys walked over. Stewart withdrew a slightly crumpled letter from his back pocket and handed it to Pam. "It's from my mum," he explained. "I don't know whether Jack has said anything..."

Jack made a face and shook his head.

"Thank you, dear," she said, eyeing her eldest son suspiciously. "And how are you getting on in Basingstoke?"

He smiled. "I'm happy."

"Stewy might be coming back to Swanford," said Dan.

"My mum has gone to see a lady about becoming a live-in carer on Westbury Avenue."

Pam nodded attentively, but her thoughts were on the topic that had been uppermost in her mind for most of the day. "Stewart, have you heard anything about your younger brother?"

The boys all exchanged glances. "No – well, not for a while."

"I was told in the post office that his dad is removing him from the school because of bullying. In fact, very serious bullying..."

Dan blushed.

"What sort of serious bullying?" enquired Jack.

Pam frowned and she lowered her voice. "Sexual..."

"Who told you that?" asked Dan, his voice going up half an octave.

"Someone who knows one of the school governors. Councillor Henderson is causing a stink, so I'm informed."

"I wouldn't believe anything he says," stated Stewart flatly.

Pam was taken aback by such a forthright condemnation of his father. "Well then, what can be done about it? We don't want the school getting a bad reputation."

"Nothing," said Stewart. "He'll get what he wants, as always."

"Would you like anything to eat, Mrs Moseley?" asked Robert. "We had hoped to be able to offer fish, but I'm afraid the fleet failed to catch anything."

"Ha, ha," said Dan.

"Not even a minnow." chimed in Jack. "Strange – someone I know was boasting about catching enough trout to fill the freezer."

"Don't tease," said Pam, and turned to her middle son. "Oh, darling, wasn't it a success?"

Dan made a face. "Don't tell Freddie, but I was bored out of my mind. All we got were damp butts through sitting on wet grass all day. I told Justin that we should have gone swimming instead."

Pam looked warily at the offerings on the grill. "What do you recommend, then?"

***

11: An undisclosed date and location.

ALAN

It was dark, but he had seen flashes of bright light, as if he had been caught in an electrical storm. A strange bed, in a strange room, with a strange smell. He lifted his head off the pillow. Next to the bed, a tall, deeply set window had bars across it. Bleary-eyed, he felt as if he had just smoked one of James Edison's roll-ups, but at least the soreness had lessened. Sleep furled him in a cloak of blackness...

A grey dawn light. The window wasn't barred after all, but was like a window in a church, where tiny panes were set in strips of lead. Oh, but he was urgently in need of the toilet! It felt like his guts might explode if he didn't find one soon. He lifted his body off the thin mattress and gasped with pain. It was worse, far worse, than when he had woken earlier. More carefully, he swung himself into a sitting position on the edge of the bed. His pyjama top was thick and scratchy and the buttons chafed his skin. He discarded it, for the first time seeing the dark welts that covered most of his torso. He stood up and had to steady himself on the cupboard beside the bed, noticing that there was a Bible on it. The striped pyjama bottoms were tied at the waist with a cord and stretched beyond his feet, but he didn't want to be naked so he pulled them up, bunching the cloth into one hand. Walking was painful too. There were belt marks even on his toes and, he knew, on the undersides of his feet as well.

Light from the window illuminated two doors. One was locked, but the other opened into a bathroom with a black-and-white tiled floor. But where was the lavatory? This only contained an old-fashioned bath and a wash bowl. Desperate now, he made for the door in the far wall. Here it was! He dropped his pyjama bottoms and sat down on the wooden seat. But now he was in position, he found it difficult to open himself up. He strained, gasping and moaning for release, and when it eventually came it felt as if the whole of his insides would pour out of him.

Afterwards, he felt relief, but also a deep soreness, and he sat for a while, allowing himself to rest while he calmed down, before the next ordeal. He was afraid to wipe himself, knowing what he might find on the toilet paper. But what was this toilet paper, anyway, hanging on a metal roller? It was shiny and hard and translucent, like tracing paper. And then he noticed there was no handle to flush, just a pipe. He looked up, seeing a tank above his head with a chain hanging down. He pulled it and water gushed into the toilet bowl, splashing his bottom. He decided to wash himself in the bath, but even that was difficult because his joints were so stiff and any movement caused pain.

Sunlight streamed through the open door as he watched the dark, bloody water drain down the plug hole. It had been cold, and there had been only a bar of hard green soap to wash himself with. Now he found there was no towel. He stepped out onto the cold floor, retrieved his pyjama bottoms and went back out into the bedroom.

He dried himself on the pyjama top and was reassured to find no blood when he rubbed himself gently between his buttocks. His testicles too were particularly tender and might have been slightly swollen. He dabbed them carefully, noticing with surprise that a few blond hairs were starting to sprout at the base of his penis. His feet remained wet because it was too painful to stretch out to dry them.

Alan looked out of the window, shielding his eyes from the sun. It had no casement and so couldn't be opened, but the room was high up, overlooking a large expanse of grass with trees beyond. What little of the building he could see – a red-brick edifice – seemed to confirm his belief that he was being held in some sort of detention centre.

A key turned in the lock and the door opened. A woman came into the room carrying a tray. "What are you doing out of bed?" she said, the varnished floorboards creaking under her feet. By this time, the boy was halfway back under the blankets.

"I went to the toilet," he replied.

"Sit up," she ordered, "and straighten your pillow. Where's your pyjama top?"

The cast-iron bed frame groaned as he did as he was ordered.

"I dried myself on it," he said.

She set the tray down across his knees. There was a bowl of cornflakes, a glass of water and a boiled egg with two slices of toast. He was hungry and hadn't realised.

"Is this prison?" he asked.

The woman's unsmiling face regarded him. "The Old Rectory."

The words meant nothing to him. "You mean juvie?"

"The doctor will be along shortly, so hurry up and eat your breakfast. I have work to do."

She left, locking the door behind her.

He drank some water, then started on the cornflakes. There was no sugar. His swollen lips made eating a slow process, and he found it hard not to dribble. The boiled egg was something of a novelty for him, and he had to remember to break the top off with the teaspoon. There was no butter on the toast, and no knife to cut it into soldiers, but he ate it anyway, noticing that there were two pills on the plate. He picked one up: *Aspirin* was written across it. He swallowed both with a drink of water.

Afterwards, he felt a little better. If he was a prisoner, they weren't going to starve him, and at least Derek wasn't there to hassle him.

***

12: Tuesday, 28th May. 7.45 a.m. 15 Leighton Lane.

PAM

Roger Moseley savoured the quiet that was breakfast time on a school holiday. "Peace, perfect peace," he said, spreading an extra-thick layer of marmalade on his toast.

"Listen to this, Rog," said Pam, who had put on her reading glasses to study the letter that Stewart had given her the previous evening.

"That's a rare sight," he answered.

"What?"

He pointed to the cheque that lay by her plate. "Someone sending us money. How much is it?"

"One hundred pounds – and it's not for us, it's for Jack."

"Jack! Who'd want to send him a hundred pounds after the way he's been behaving for the past few months?"

"Listen!" ordered Pam.

Dear Mr and Mrs Moseley,

I am Stewart Henderson's mother, and this letter is to thank you for the kindness you have shown my boy, but also to express my gratitude to you for having brought up such a wonderful son as Jack.

Without him, Stewart would not have been able to cope with the hardships he's had to face in the past six months. Now, thanks to Jack, not only is his life back on track, but my life is also so much better. I am overjoyed to be reunited with Stewart.

Stewart has told me that Jack was having his own problems during this period, which makes it all the more

24

remarkable that he was able to take my son under his wing and pull him through. It was he who suggested contacting me and, at no small personal risk to himself, found the means to do it. Your younger son, Dan, also played his part in ensuring Stewart's safety.

Although Jack insisted that he didn't want the money back that he gave to Stewart to see him through, I feel I must repay at least part of it.

The only other thing I can do is to thank him once again for the friendship he showed my son in his time of greatest need.

And for that we shall always be in his debt.
Yours sincerely,
Anne Waverly.

"Always be in his debt," repeated Pam, shaking her head.

"My son Albert Schweitzer," said Roger.

"And the things we said, and accused him of..."

"We weren't to know, were we? He never tells us anything!"

"Who never tells you anything?" questioned Dan, padding into the kitchen and sitting at the table.

"Is it normal, dear, to wear only your boxer shorts to the breakfast table?" asked his mother.

"Do you want me to take them off?"

"Don't be cheeky," said his father. "Just because you're on holiday..."

"Chill, Dad," said Dan, pouring out a bowl of Crunchy Nut Cornflakes then drowning them in milk. "What did Stewy's mum say in her letter?"

"Only that your brother is a saint," answered Roger, "something your mother and I are somewhat sceptical about."

"You never see it, do you?" crunched Dan, spraying droplets of milk out of his mouth.

"Don't speak with your mouth full, dear," corrected Pam.

"Don't see what?" enquired Roger.

Dan swallowed, put down his spoon, wiped his mouth with the back of his hand and looked at each of his parents in turn, as if they were naughty children. "You don't understand Jack; you've never understood Jack. Jack is the best of the best..."

"I think you're being a bit unfair on your parents, dear. We both love your brother very much."

Roger huffed. "Excuse me, sonny Jim, but I seem to remember you were telling us not so very long ago, like last week, to keep your brother away from you or you would do violence to him."

"That's because I needed to grow up," said Dan.

"So all that feuding between you was your fault?"

"Yes, entirely."

Roger looked at his wife in exasperation. "He's got him under his thumb again!"

"Won't you be late for work, dear?" said Pam soothingly.

"Hey," said Jack, entering the kitchen in just his boxers. "Mikey's dry."

Roger got up and began to search for his briefcase. "I suppose you worked that miracle as well?"

"He says he wants a double cheeseburger with Coke for breakfast as a reward."

"Over my dead body," said Pam.

Roger picked up his briefcase from where he had left it the day before. "I shall probably be late home – there's an important union meeting tonight."

"Oh goodness, what now?"

"More reorganisation, more privatisation. Parks and Recreation, and there's rumours about social services, would you believe?"

"We can't afford for you to go on strike," said Pam flatly.

"You haven't told Jack off for only wearing his boxers," said Dan.

"That's because he hasn't sat down for breakfast yet, dear," smiled Pam.

Jack sat down next to Dan and reached for the Crunchy Nut Cornflakes. "Mum, Robert can only stay for an hour or so this morning, so I've kind of rearranged our revision for Friday, if that's OK..." He began to slice a banana onto his cereal and, not waiting for a reply, turned to his brother. "We need to talk, LB; will you still be here at nine?"

The younger boy nodded. "No worries – I'm not out till ten thirty-ish."

"You see," said Roger, giving his wife a kiss on the cheek, "we're just like servants used to be in Victorian times: invisible except for receiving and obeying orders."

Pam squeezed his hand and nodded towards their eldest son. Roger huffed again, then sighed. "Jack!"

The boy looked up. "Yes, Dad?"

"You're a credit to the family."

***

13: Tuesday, 28th May. 9 a.m. 15 Leighton Lane.

DAN

"Be careful!" exclaimed Mikey, imitating his mother.

"Shut up, pest, or I'll drop you over the banisters," replied Dan.

Pamela Moseley watched anxiously from below as her youngest son was manoeuvred downstairs, flinching each time his broken leg bumped against the wall. "Do you think I should call Jack—"

"No!" cried Dan, "I can do it. He's just a little baby..."

"Bloody," murmured Mikey so that only his brother could hear.

There was a knock at the door. "Come in!" yelled Pam.

Robert appeared in the hall. "Good morning, Mrs Moseley..." He looked up. "Do you need help there?"

"No!" shouted Dan.

"I want Robert to carry me," said Mikey.

Dan reached the bottom of the stairs and lowered his brother none too gently into the wheelchair. "There you are, pest, I hope that's the first and last time."

Pam breathed a sigh of relief. "Thank you, dear. But I don't think he'll be able to go up and downstairs on crutches."

"I will," said Mikey. "Push me, Robert."

"Bossy," replied the American. "Mrs Moseley, there's a taxi outside. I told the driver you'd be along directly."

"Thank you very much, Robert, and you know you're welcome here any time, don't you?"

"That's very kind of you, ma'am. I'm just sorry I can't stop today."

"You know, I wish my family were as polite and well-mannered as you, Robert," said Pam.

"Yeh, well, you brought us up," responded Dan.

Five minutes later the boys watched from the kerb as the taxi headed off up Leighton Lane. "And don't come back!" shouted Dan, then he turned and grinned at Robert. "How's the veggies?"

Robert furrowed his brow. "I got the impression that Mrs Annesley is thinking of shutting up shop."

"Really?"

"She wasn't specific, but I think the window might have been the final straw."

"That's bad news then, and just when Jack's got his old job back."

"She told me to come in next Saturday as usual, but after that..." His voice trailed off.

"Listen," said Dan. "I've got a little job to do, but I'll be back in about twenty minutes. It'll give you and Jack time to have a make-out session before the meeting. He's been in the bathroom for about an hour getting ready for you."

Robert blushed. "You English boys are so forward."

Dan clapped Robert on the arm then sped off down Leighton Lane. When he reached the corner with Knowles Road he stopped and looked round. Remembering where he had thrown Alan Henderson's skateboard was not as easy as he had thought it would be. The raised gardens stood behind low walls and most had been planted with a further screen of yellow privet.

The first house he tried had no one in, and a cursory look around proved fruitless. At the second, a girl in her late teens answered, listened indifferently to what Dan had to say, shook her head and closed the door on him.

"Oh yes, I found it under the rhododendron," said the old gent at the third house. He stepped onto the path and beckoned Dan to follow. Shortly they were standing before a glossy-leaved bush some three feet in diameter strewn with lavender-coloured flowers. "I keep it thriving, despite the soil," he said proudly. "Seaweed extract, that's the secret."

The boy nodded, hoping the lecture wouldn't go on for too long. "Have you still got the skateboard?"

The man beckoned Dan to follow him once again and this time they went up by the side of the house to a well-kept shed. "They're a woodland shrub, really," he continued, unlatching the door. "That's why I planted it under the lilac." He waved for Dan to go inside. "Terrible for suckers, lilac, but a lovely show, I always think, and it sets the rhododendron off grand."

The skateboard was propped up against a deckchair, and a cursory inspection revealed no damage. "Thank you very much," said Dan with a wide smile.

"I was going to give it to my grandson if no one claimed it. Are you good at it?"

"Actually, I'm hopeless. This belongs to a friend of mine, and he's awesome." He was quite aware that calling Alan a friend and an awesome skateboarder stemmed from a guilty conscience, especially after what his mother had told him at the barbecue.

The elderly man lifted an eyebrow. "Awesome, is it? We used to reserve that word for gods and monsters."

***

29

14: An undisclosed date and location.

<u>ALAN</u>

The doctor's been, but he was not like Dr Howell at the health centre. The first thing he asked me was *do I want to be free of the demon of homosexuality?* I think he was accusing me of being a fag and so I didn't answer and that annoyed him. He told me that *if I continued to pursue a perverted lifestyle, I should expect to be beaten up, but that was as nothing as the punishment I would receive in the afterlife when I was consigned to hell.* He said my only salvation was to read the Bible and come to Jesus Christ.

Another man was there with him, but they never said a word to each other. This one was dressed in white coveralls, like he'd just come from the hospital, except I think he was more like a guard, because he stood by the door with a hard expression on his face. I suppose he was meant to frighten me – which he did.

I had to take all my clothes off and just stand there while the doctor examined me. He listened to my heart and looked into my eyes and ears, then he felt my balls and pressed his finger on each side and asked me to cough. Then he asked me how long I'd been *indulging in homosexual practices*. This time I told him straight that I wasn't a fag, and asked him if I'd killed the boy in the wheelchair. I don't think he knew what I was talking about, and so I guess the police haven't told him.

He asked me *if I'd passed a stool* since I'd been there, which I eventually worked out to mean had I done a pooh? His next question was *did I pass any blood?* and when I said yes he made me get on the bed on my hands and knees with my legs spread. He put on a pair of vinyl gloves and smeared some sort of ointment on his finger. When I saw what he was going to do, I started to cry because I knew it was going to hurt. He told me to shut up, as I'd brought all this on myself, and I felt like a real fag then.

Almost as soon as he pushed his finger up there, my head started to spin and my heart began beating real fast, like I was on acid or something. He told me he'd come back tomorrow to administer a second dose, and that in the meantime I should read the Bible and let the Holy Spirit enter my heart – because if I didn't I'd never be free of the demon.

Later the woman came back with a towel, a toothbrush and a spare pair of pyjamas, but she didn't say anything.

***

15: Tuesday, 28th May. 9.40 a.m. 15 Leighton Lane.

JACK

There were two light taps on the door.

"You can come in, LB, we've finished *making out*."

Dan entered with a smirk on his face and a skateboard under his arm.

"You found it!" said Jack.

"Yeh. I had to listen to ten minutes of *Gardener's World* from an old buffer in the process, but here it is, no worse for wear." Dan propped the board up behind the door and sat on the bed next to Robert. "So, what's up?"

Jack punched some numbers into his phone, which was already attached to his speakers, and shortly the image of Stewart Henderson appeared before them. On his lap was his half-brother Alex.

"Just a sec, Stewy, I'll adjust things so you can see us properly."

Jack propped the phone on his chair and went to sit on the bed with the others. "How's that?"

"OK, but the backlight from the window is casting you all in shadow."

Jack frowned. "You've been reading too many of those photographic books." He altered the angle of the phone again. "Is that better?"

"Some," answered Stewart critically, "but it would be better if you had some front fill lighting..." He smiled. "Just joking. I've got a small person here who wants to say hello. See there, Alex, that's Uncle Jack, Uncle Robert and Uncle Dan."

"Hi, Alex," they chorused.

"Has your mum heard?" asked Dan.

"Yeh, she got the job! We're moving on the 19th June; that's a Wednesday."

"Brilliant," said Jack. "Will you need any help from three strong lads?"

"Probably. I'll let you know." Stewart grinned at them.

"What about your mocks?" asked Robert.

Stewart's grin faded. "I've got to take them when I get back. So, while you're all out having a good time, I'll be slogging away in a classroom on my own."

"Have you been sent work?"

"Mum collected a box full from school, but I know I'm going to fail everything anyway."

"Stewy, you're just as bright as any of us, it's just that you don't concentrate."

"I don't see the point."

Jack leaned towards his phone. "What happens when you want to go to uni to do a photography course and you haven't got the grades?"

The boy blinked and his eyes lost some of their focus as his mind began to work on possibilities he had never considered.

"Whoa!" said Dan. "See that? My brother scores a screamer from thirty yards."

"I will try to revise, but there's a lot going on," said Stewart at last, half-committing himself.

"So, to the main point of this call," said Jack. "I thought Dan and Robert needed to hear first-hand what you've got to say about your brother, Stewy. Especially if they're going to become involved."

"That sounds ominous," said the American.

"I know you don't like Alan," began Stewart, "and I know what he tried to do to Dan, but after what your mum said last night, I'm sure they've started to hurt him… and once they start they won't stop."

"In other words," said Jack, "he needs our help."

"And I want to," added Dan, "but I don't see how. Alan's not like you, Stewy. He doesn't know Jack or Robert, and he thinks I'm his number-one enemy."

"I'm just asking you to look out for him, if you get the chance. The trouble is, I'm not going to be there for three weeks, and by that time who knows what will have happened to him?"

"We'll do what we can, but it may not be very much," said Jack.

Stewart nodded, set down Alex and told him to run along. Then he focused on the screen once more. "I've made a decision to tell them what was done to me." He blushed.

"That's really brave of you," said Robert.

"Are you doing it for Alan?" asked Dan.

Stewart shrugged. "Half for him, half to get it off my chest."

"Who are you going to tell?" asked Jack, more downbeat than the others.

"It's all right – not the police, that's for sure."

"But who, Stewy?" pressed Jack.

"Mum's going to make an appointment for me to see a counsellor when I get back. Apparently it takes two to four weeks after a referral, so I'm going to see the doctor this Thursday."

"Have you told your mum what happened?"

"I don't think I can do that, Jack, but I would like to tell you, if that's all right?"

"Of course. When?"

"Now. I've been working up to it…"

"See you again, Stewy," said Robert, tapping Dan on the arm as he rose. "I was thinking of buying a bike, since I'll be a hundred before I'm allowed to drive a car in this country. Maybe you could show me what's what, as you English say."

"No probs," said the younger boy. He waved goodbye at the screen then they both left, closing the door behind them.

"Hey, Stewy, I wish I was with you in person," said Jack, mentally preparing himself.

Stewart looked away from the screen. "I don't know where to begin..."

"Do you remember Mr Colt talking about stream of consciousness in writing?" said Jack.

The boy's face went blank.

"No worries – just let it all hang out..."

***

16: Tuesday, 28th May. 10.20 a.m. 15 Leighton Lane.

<u>ROBERT</u>

I suppose they get it from their mom, but I've noticed all the Moseley boys are very welcoming. There's no formality with them and once you've been accepted, you kinda just fit in. Dan showed me his bike, told me how much it was and where he got it from, then said he'd go with me to the retail park to help me choose if I wanted.

Then we went back to his room and he showed me his collection of cups and shields most of which are for soccer, or football as he calls it. He said that Jack had told him that I was a good swimmer and when I said I'd swum the 100 metres in a minute, he was impressed. What isn't so impressive is the fact that I've not done any proper swimming for six months, which is probably why I've been putting on weight. After the exams, maybe I should put that right.

Jack came in and looked pretty down, as you might expect. I could tell he'd been to the bathroom to rinse his face, because his hair was wet, which probably meant he'd been crying. He said that Stewy was a wreck at the end, and he wished he'd been there with him, rather than on the end of a Skype call.

It surprised me when Jack said that Stewy wanted Dan and I to know what had happened to him, so that we would understand what Alan Henderson might be going through. I guess he was aiming that at me, because I wasn't too keen on helping that villain. If I'd been in the States I'd have probably said he deserved whatever he got, and left it at that. But things seem to be different here: instead of clear blacks and whites, everyone deals with the grey in-betweens.

Derek and John Henderson were the ones involved, and even the English would have to agree they are unadulterated monsters. It started with them knocking Stewy about, then it progressed to beating him. There wasn't a pattern at first, just that they would get fuelled on drink and drugs once or twice a week and lay into him on the slightest pretext. Later, it became more ritualised. They would take him somewhere blindfolded, strip him naked and beat him, usually with belts. When the marks began to be noticed at school, they stopped the beatings and instead tied him over a chair and forced objects up his backside. Only after he ran away – and then recaptured – was he physically raped. He never knew which one did it, not only because he was tied and blindfolded, but also because they began to drug him so that he was only half-conscious. They also made him inhale something which he said kind of loosened him up. This happened four or five times before he finally escaped.

I had to give Jack a lot of love when he found us, because he was totally drained, then Dan held him real tight. It's real swell to see those two so close again. They're not just brothers, but true friends as well.

My faith has been badly dented recently, but I don't believe I'll ever become an atheist. Although none of the English people I'm close to go to church and hardly any of them are true believers, they still feel like good Christian folks to me, though I don't think Pastor Fisher or my dad would agree. The fact that I cannot share with my parents the most important part of my life makes me sad, but it also makes me mad, because I believe that our Lord Jesus Christ would love a person like Jack Moseley, almost as much as I do.

***

17: Tuesday, 28th May. 11 a.m. Pear Tree Cottage, The Ropewalk.

ROBERT

Maybelle Crittenden was sitting in the lounge, idly turning the pages of *The Garden* magazine, when Robert arrived, breathless after running – or, rather, trotting – all the way from the Moseleys' house. Easing off his shoes, he wriggled his toes to cool his hot feet then made for the lounge.

"Sorry, Mom," he gasped, slumping down into the armchair next to the fireplace.

"You are half an hour late, Robert."

"I know; I shall have to get a bike."

Since their falling out over Auntie Una and the revelations about his father, relations between mother and son had been strained and an unnatural formality existed between them. Robert felt that his mother was least to blame for their troubles and wanted to take a leaf out of the Moseley manual and apologise to her.

"Mom, can't we be friends again, please? I'm sorry I spoke harshly to you about Auntie Una."

Maybelle cast aside her magazine. "Robert, your daddy and I have been so worried by your behaviour recently. You were always the most dutiful and respectful son, but since we got to this benighted country things have gone steadily downhill. Even your trip back home didn't shake off that devil within you – in fact, it seemed to make it worse. I don't know what possessed you to have anything to do with those *Latins*. They are not family!" Maybelle stopped and collected herself.

"Well, now I've got that off my chest, perhaps this day will mark a new beginning. I accept your apology. "

Robert listened to all his mother had to say, allowing all the reproach to wash over him, then when she had finished he sat up. "Mom, thank you. I've got some revision to do this morning, but I could help you with the garden this afternoon, if you'd like?"

"That would be very helpful, dear. Those bramble roots are so deep I haven't the strength to get them out."

"I've got a feeling I may be looking for another job in the near future."

"Has Mrs Annesley given you notice?"

"Not yet, but I think the window accident has put it in her mind to close up."

"I don't expect those little two-bit stores can compete these days."

"And I was thinking of taking up swimming again; they've got a twenty-five-metre pool at the leisure centre."

"It's your father saying that I overfeed you that's put that idea into your head, isn't it?"

"No, Mom, I just do far less exercise here than I used to in Tyree."

"Well, hon, if you're going to get a bike and go swimming regular, then you're gonna need a job – because we can't afford it, that's for sure."

***

Robert glanced at his Mickey Mouse alarm clock. Ten past ten. He switched his phone on, meaning to dial Jack, but then he saw that he had received a text and an email. The text was from Rosa Miller in Tyree.

HRU & how is your sexy boyfriend*? Pls, pls, pls send photo and make me jealous. RM.*

His reply was similarly worded.

Hi, R, Hope UR well. I'm fine & so is J. Lots happening, not all good. Exams nxt wk. Will send photo ASAP. RC.

The email was from Tom Sanchez, the first he had received since his visit.

Hello Robert,
I am sorry to have not replied sooner, but Abuela and Susie have both been ill. Just a bug, I think, but made worse for one by her age and the other by asthma.
I have been tearing my hair out, trying to figure out what to do for the best, but things are a little more settled now.
Barney has been running wild both at home and in school. He has been caught fighting, but it is not all his fault, because they tease him about his hair.
Susie's birthday is on Dec. 28th and Barney's on Aug. 20th.
All the best,
Tom

Robert replied immediately.

Hello Tom,
I was really sorry to hear about Susie and Grandma Sanchez. Give them both my best wishes.
Tell Barney to wear his hair with pride.
I'm on holiday from school this week, but because I have exams next week I am stuck with having to revise. Life in England is full of surprises – some good, some not so good.
Will email again soon,
Robert

The American felt deflated after the news from Tom and was in two minds whether to speak to Jack or just send a text. In the end, his heart won out.

"Hey," said Jack.

"You OK?"

"Yeh, better now I'm speaking with my boyfriend instead of having to cope with a certain pestilence."

"What's Mikey been up to?"

"Oh, Nana Moseley gave him a DVD of *Treasure Island* and naturally he dragged me down to watch it with him. Nan told him it was a film about a man with a crutch."

"Is that the Bobby Driscoll one?" questioned Robert.

"Yeh, only I would have said it was more the leering, eye-swivelling pirate one."

"Did he like it?"

"Oh God, yes! I feel another obsession coming on – which is probably why Nan gave it to him."

"Why would she do that?"

Jack chuckled. "Because Mum and Nana Moseley think they're in a competition for world domination. Therefore they like to throw spokes into each other's wheels."

"Now, ain't that something..." commented Robert.

"Families, eh?"

"Talking of which, I've patched things up with my mom; did a bit of gardening for her this afternoon."

"Wish I'd been there in the shed with your lovely feet..!"

"One-track mind, Jack Moseley."

"How's Friday shaping?"

"Good! They're both going to this church thing in the country."

"Didn't they ask you to go?"

"No, and they're quite cagey about it."

"Secrets all round, then."

"I wish it didn't have to be like this, Jack. I'm finding the lies and half-truths are coming far too easily."

"I haven't thought about telling mine. What would actually happen if your parents found out?"

There was a long silence, before Robert spoke. "I would never be able to see you again, Jack."

***

18: An undisclosed date and location.

<u>ALAN</u>

I've just had fish and chips for dinner, which wasn't bad. The food is the best thing about this place. No one answers my questions properly, so I still don't know where I am or when my trial will be. I think it's Wednesday, but I'm not sure. The doctor came again this morning, but I'm not going to talk about that any more, except to say my bum is a bit better, though it's still painful when I go to the toilet, and I still can't reach my feet properly.

I'm getting so bored. I tried reading the Bible, like Dad used to do. This one's different because it's in English instead of that old-fashioned language. There were bookmarks everywhere and at every one there was a passage about why being a fag will get you sent to hell. I tried to find that bit about the fag boys and the Stone of Ezel, but I couldn't. Maybe that part isn't in this version.

I wasn't going to mention the dream I had last night, but it's been on my mind because it was quite nice and I wish I hadn't woken up. Dan Moseley wasn't dead and we were sort of like best friends. He asked me to go swimming with him at the leisure centre, and when we got there we had the whole pool to ourselves. I was kind of watching him from the edge of the pool because he could swim really well, but his foot got stuck in some weed and I had to dive in and rescue him. When I pulled him out, we were on the bank of a river and he smiled at me and then I woke up and I was sorry I'd killed him.

The woman's name is Mrs Warner. She's just been in to fetch my tray and tell me that I can go out for a walk in the grounds. She brought me a pair of slippers – size six – which, unlike the PJs, fit just right. Perhaps she measured my feet while I was asleep. I expect the place is surrounded by a fence with barbed wire and searchlights so we can't escape. I say *we*, but I don't even know how many others there are in here.

19: Thursday, 30th May. 10 a.m. 15 Leighton Lane.

JACK

The first mock mathematics GCSE paper was five days away, on 4th June, the Tuesday they went back to school. The day after, they had English literature, and Jack was quietly confident that he had it covered. *Coriolanus*, *Ozymandias*, *Under Milk Wood* – and *Animal Farm* because it was the shortest book on the list. He was still mulling over whether or not to give Rameses II some credit for having half a statue left on the lone and level sands – unlike Shelley did in his poem – when the volume of music coming from his brother's room suddenly increased by half as much again, which meant that Justin Walker had arrived.

Jack put his head round the door, which was already ajar. "Hey," he said.

"Is it too loud?" shouted Dan.

Jack waggled his hand which meant *it's OK, but yes it is really,* and Dan turned down the amp by two notches.

"Spoilsport," said Justin with a smile.

"Is Freddie coming over?" asked Jack.

Dan shook his head. "Gone to see his granddad in hospital."

"I wanted a word..."

"Serious?"

"Alan... Have you said anything to Justin? Because he needs to know."

Dan shook his head again and turned off the music.

"Are you talking about Alana Henderfag?" asked Justin with a grin.

Jack gave his brother a helpless look.

"Just, your re-education begins here." Dan took him by the shoulders and guided him backwards to the bed. "Now sit, listen and learn," he said.

"Am I ready for the heavy?" asked Justin, seeing their expressions.

"As you'll ever be," replied Dan, and he sat by his friend and told him about the skateboard; the incident with the van; the removal from school, and Stewart Henderson's request for them to help his brother.

"Jeez!" said Justin. "You Moseleys lead exciting lives. And Alana was actually driving a transit, on his own, by himself?"

Dan nodded. "And there are two more important points..."

"Shoot, man."

"One, this is top secret, and I mean you can't tell anyone – not Kate, not your mum or dad, not Coach Brennan, nobody."

"I get it... and two?"

"We're not going to call him Alana Henderfag ever again, got it?"

"Gee, man, this *is* heaviness. It was just a joke."

"Not to him," said Jack.

"OK, OK, I surrender. Lead me to the firing squad."

Jack took a deep breath. "Talking of which, I want to put something to you both. It's just a suggestion, but it might be worth the trouble in the long run."

"Oh!" said Dan, looking worried. "Is this new to me?"

Jack grabbed a chair and sat facing them. "Just be calm and think about it."

"OK, we'll have a go."

"When you get back to school on Tuesday, I think the three of you should go to Ms Lane and tell her what you did to Alan."

"No way!" responded Justin. "We'll be suspended."

"Why?" asked Dan, his face losing its colour. "You know what a hard-nosed crab she is."

"LB, we're dealing with serious shit here. The Hendersons have a lot of friends in high places, but Ms Lane, as far as I know, isn't one of them—"

"But Jack, you can't make us," interrupted Justin.

"I know I can't, and I don't want to. It's up to you—"

"Then it's got to be no!"

"Hush, Just," chided Dan, "let's give Jack a chance to explain."

"We know already, LB, that the Hendersons are violent stop-at-nothing bastards who used to beat up Stewy regularly. Stewy thinks this is now happening to Alan, and he's decided to report them for what they did. But that's in the future and we don't know how it will pan out. Meanwhile, the Hendersons are looking for someone to blame for what they've done to Alan, and that's why his dad has taken him out of school and accused people at school of bullying him sexually. So, what happens if Alan rats on you? What happens if he's asked why he tried to run you over?

You won't just get the hassle for what you actually did, but for whatever the Hendersons have done to him as well. And that will mean not just suspension, but being expelled – and maybe even prosecution."

"But it's not fair," said Justin, horrified. "It was just a joke! They'll stop me going to the Academy." He put his head in his hands. "I can't believe this."

Dan looped his arm around his friend's shoulders. "It's OK, Just, we'll talk it over with Freddie, but whatever we decide to do, and whatever happens, I'll take the blame. After all, I started it."

***

20: An undisclosed date and location.

ALAN

43

Why do I keep dreaming about Dan Moseley? This time, he was in hospital and I went to visit him, but they told me he was already on the operating table because his heart had stopped. So I ran down all these corridors, but I couldn't find him and I was in a panic. Then I saw him from high up and they were just going to open him up, and I shouted for them to stop because I could do a better job. And then I was at Silverstone, in the pits, wearing orange mechanics' overalls, which were too big for me, and I had a box of tools for servicing an F1 car, and there were all these other mechanics around me. Dan Moseley was lying on a trolley that had racing-car wheels under these bright lights with just a sheet over him, and he was asleep and looked really nice and peaceful. And a nurse asked me if I was ready to begin, and although I didn't know what I was doing, I said yes and the trolley shot away...

There isn't a mirror in my room, not even in the bathroom, but there is one in the hall downstairs. Everything about this place is so old-fashioned, like my great-nan's house before she died. My right eye is still puffed up, but the left one is almost back to normal except for the yellow colour. My lips are about half the size they were, which means I don't dribble so much, but the gash on my nose, where he caught me with the belt buckle, has had a stitch put in it by you-know-who because it's still a bloody mess and when I wake up in the morning there's blood all over my pillow.

After breakfast, I went for another walk in the grounds, but my legs won't carry me far. I can't even climb the stairs without stopping to rest a couple of times. I'm not sure if it's Thursday or Friday. The house is really big, and there's millions of windows and chimneys, but I still haven't seen anyone else my age. Perhaps there aren't that many young criminals any more. Here's a funny thing: I hadn't noticed there was one of those old-type fireplaces in my room until I saw the chimney from outside.

There's a concrete path leading from the back door of the house all the way down to a walled garden. It has an S-shaped curve and I'm thinking it would be an ace place to skateboard. I didn't go down, though, because I was afraid I might not be able to get back up, that's how weak I am. I suppose my board is still at Dan Moseley's house, or perhaps his parents have burned it, knowing it was mine. It's too late now for both of us, but if he'd have asked me, I would have let him have a go on it.

When I got back to my room, Mrs Warner was waiting for me. She said that guests would be arriving soon and that she had been ordered to lock me in until they had gone. After my walk I usually have a little sleep anyway, till you-know-who comes, but I suppose they have to take precautions with prisoners, especially murderers like me. Mrs Warner left me a tray with some cheese and pickle sandwiches wrapped in cling film, a strawberry yogurt with a plastic spoon and a glass of orange, which she said would tide me over until the evening.

I was woken by the sound of expensive car doors being slammed. When I looked out there was a line of them on the driveway. I counted eighteen, though there may have been more out of sight. Three Jags, two Audis, five Mercs, four BMWs, one Bentley, one Cadi XTS, and – wow! A Rolls-Royce Phantom II Continental, in two-tone maroon and brown. This one was a 1934 model, I think, and must have been worth at least 100K. The Phantom II was one of the first British cars to have synchromesh gears. I love old cars almost as much as I love F1. If I had pencil and paper, I would draw it.

I had not long since eaten my sandwiches when the door was unlocked, and this guy came into the room. He said his name was Peter, and he asked me what mine was. I thought about lying and telling him it was Jayden, but then I began to suspect that it might be a trick, so I told him my real name. Then he said that he was going to exorcise my demon. This kind of freaked me out because I thought it might be connected with what you-know-who does with the ointment...

This one's a real geeky type, though, tall and skinny with an Adam's apple which bobs up and down when he speaks, and big teeth which look as though they've never seen a brush. Then there's his glasses, which have thick black frames and the lenses are covered in a film of dust and grease so I can't see his eyes properly.

We sit facing each other on these hard wooden chairs and after five minutes I'm having to shift round because my bum's still tender, but he thinks it's because the demon is getting agitated. The sessions always start the same way:

"Alan, have you been reading your Bible?"

"A bit," I say, which was true the first time.

"Do you see what your lifestyle will mean for you, unless you change?"

"I'm not a fag," I tell him every time.

By the end of the first session I realise I'm not afraid of Peter, and his being there helps to pass the time, even if he does talk rubbish.

There's long shadows over the driveway as I watch the cars leave one by one. I'm quite hungry, as it's been hours since I had my yogurt. Funny thing is, I'm stuck in this room for most of the day and you'd think I'd put on weight, but just the opposite is happening for some reason. Maybe it's because I'm not getting sweets and fizzy drinks and double helpings.

I suppose I'll never become world champion F1 driver now, but if I did I would buy a Rolls, just like the one out there. I'd need to build up my strength, though, because it doesn't have power steering, and I'd have to learn how to double declutch before I could change down into first gear.

I've just seen my dad's car, a bronze Volvo S80, head off up the drive. I know it's his from the number plate. Surely he must realise I'm here? Perhaps he wasn't allowed to see me and was just checking up that the place was OK.

It's nearly dark now. All the cars have gone and I've had nothing to eat. I may as well get ready for bed, even though I'm not really tired. The sky is dark blue and there are no clouds, just a few stars. I've no idea what time it is, but if I was at home I would never be going to bed this early, not even on school days, but there's nothing else to do.

46

Mrs Warner brought me a tray. She put the light on and nearly blinded me. It was just a ham salad with two slices of bread, but there was a slice of that pink and yellow cake with marzipan around it, and a cup of tea, though it was a bit stewed. I think she saw that I was upset, so she started going on about not having a moment's rest because of all the visitors, and I was lucky to get anything, and that she wasn't at my beck and call. Then she stopped suddenly and gave me a strange look because I was acting like a real fag and had to wipe my eyes. So I told her I'd seen my dad's car, but he hadn't been to see me.

When she came again to collect my tray, she stayed and straightened my bed and plumped my pillow while I cleaned my teeth. Then she tucked me in, like Mum used to do, and I felt a bit better.

***

21: Friday, 31st May. 12.15 p.m. 15 Leighton Lane.

PAM

Pam arrived home from her shift at the post office to find Dan drinking a glass of milk in the kitchen.

"Hello, dear, is everything all right?"

"Yeh."

"Where's Mikey?"

"In the lounge."

"Are Jack and Robert here?"

"Yeh."

"I'll put some soup on."

"Not for me, thanks – I don't have time."

"But you must have something to eat."

"I'll pick something up at the leisure centre."

"Is that where you're going?"

"I've got an important meeting with Justin and Freddie."

"You sound just like your father with your important meetings."

"Where's my trunks?"

"Where they always are – in your drawer."

"What about a towel?"

"Where they always are, dear, in the airing cupboard."

"I should be back by five."

"I expect your father would like to have his important meetings in the swimming pool."

Dan smiled. "It's not a crime to mix business with pleasure, is it?"

Pam studied him. "Something happened yesterday. You were very moody..."

"Well, whatever, I'm sorted now."

"Hi!"

Pam put her hands on her hips to address her youngest son. "Michael Moseley, why are you walking around with just one crutch, and what is that thing on your shoulder?"

"You're confusing him, Mum; little babies can only deal with one question at a time."

Mikey narrowed his eyes at his brother. "Dan drew me a treasure map."

"That was nice of him, dear..."

"On the glass table top!" added Mikey, triumphantly.

"Shut up, pest!" Dan turned to his mother. "I'll wash it off when I get back."

"You'd better..."

"Pieces of eight," said Mikey, nuzzling the object on his shoulder.

"What are you doing, dear?"

The little boy lowered his voice as much as he could and closed one eye. "By the powers, I be teaching my parrot to talk!"

Dan chuckled. "It's surprising what you can do with a toilet roll, a coat hanger and some poster paint."

"What's got into you two?"

"Guess what, Mum? It's goodbye *Pinocchio*, hello *Treasure Island*."

"Whatever was Nana Moseley thinking about giving him that old DVD?"

"Why not?" answered Dan. "It is a kids' film, for kids."

"She knows that Mikey's always been very imaginative in the way he responds to things."

"Very camp, you mean."

"Daniel Moseley, I will not have you speaking like that!"

Mikey balanced on one leg and pointed his crutch at them. "By thunder! There'll be no killin' till I gives the word..."

"Another couple of watches and he'll have memorised the lot," laughed Dan.

"Oh dear!" exclaimed Pam and a moment's silence fell. "Are you sure your brother and Robert haven't gone out? They're very quiet."

"I expect they're hard at it," replied Dan with a blink and a smile. "Revision, I mean."

His mother gave him a searching look.

"Gotta go." Dan darted from the kitchen, knowing he had been indiscreet.

"Can Mike come round this afternoon?"

"No dear, he can't." Pam drew out two tins of Heinz tomato soup from the cupboard, still mulling over her middle son's curious turn of phrase. Before opening them, she went to the sink where she carefully wiped the tops, a habit she'd learned from her mother. "Wash your hands, then get a packet of rolls from the bread bin."

"What am I, a slave, or something?" retorted Mikey, imitating one of his brothers' favourite expressions.

"Do as you're told, dear," said Pam, emptying the contents of the tins into a saucepan.

"See ya," cried Dan, rushing past them.

"Daniel Moseley, I want a word..."

"No time, Mum – I'll miss the bus." He wrenched open the door and sped off down the path.

Pam continued to stir the soup until it started to simmer, at which point she turned down the heat, doing exactly as the instructions stated.

"This is the ship's galley, isn't it?" said Mikey, thoughtfully. "Where I do all the cooking for the officers."

"Do something useful, will you? Go to the bottom of the stairs and shout for Jack and Robert to come down."

"They're asleep in bed..."

"What do you mean, *they're asleep in bed*?"

Mikey realised he had said the wrong thing and put a hand to his mouth.

"Michael Moseley, answer the question!"

"I wanted to show Jack and Robert my parrot."

"So you went upstairs on your crutches?"

"Yes," squeaked Mikey, a blush spreading across his face.

"And you sneaked into Jack's room..."

Mikey nodded, expecting the world to fall in.

"...and they were *asleep*?"

"I didn't wake them. I came straight out," he said quickly.

Pam tried her best to maintain a calm exterior, while inside she was going through a fevered overload of emotions.

"Am I in trouble?" asked Mikey, his lips beginning to tremble.

"Lay the table, dear, I won't be a moment," she said, gritting her teeth. "And don't touch that pan..."

Oh no! Oh please not that! Help me. I must know. What if he is? What if they are? Anger welled up, then panic, then blame. It was Robert's fault; it was her own fault; it was Roger's fault; it was Jack himself who was responsible for this crisis. The family wouldn't survive such a catastrophe!

Pam rushed down the hall and started up the stairs two steps at a time. But as she neared the top, her pace slowed. Realisation dawned that she was too stressed, too uptight, for this sort of confrontation, and would only make matters worse. She began to take calming deep breaths and relax her upper body, as she had learned once in yoga classes. At the top she held on to the banister to steady herself, to relieve some of the tension. Then she tiptoed along the landing. There was no sound. Mikey had left the door ajar. Her hand trembled as she pushed it open.

Both boys were fast asleep, their breathing soft and regular. Jack's head lay on Robert's bare chest, as if listening to his heart. His left arm was stretched out, exposing a tuft of dark armpit hair. Suddenly Robert gave a little gasp and his eyes opened. Pam froze. The American blinked a few times, then smiled sleepily and kissed the top of Jack's head. His eyes closed once more and it was Jack's turn to smile as he snuffled and snuggled in close to Robert. Pam shut the door quietly and went back downstairs.

Mikey had laid the table to the best of his seven-year-old ability and was sitting quiet and miserable, his toilet roll parrot still on his shoulder. Pam came up behind him and hugged him. "And how is my beautiful boy?" she asked.

"I'm sorry I went upstairs on my crutches and into Jack's room without knocking," he said. "Am I grounded?"

"Not this time, darling," she said.

"Why?"

"Because sometimes when you do the wrong thing, you're also doing the right thing."

Mikey looked up at her and smiled. "Are you feeling better now?"

"You're quite a wise little fellow sometimes, Michael Moseley," she said.

"Are Jack and Robert coming down for dinner? I want to show them my parrot."

"I think we'll give them another ten minutes," she answered. And me, she thought, by which time I shall be cool, calm and collected and will behave as if nothing has happened.

"Would you like to see my treasure map?" asked Mikey.

"Good idea, dear," said Pam. A welcome distraction, she thought.

***

22: An undisclosed date and location.

<u>ALAN</u>

I woke up in a cold sweat this morning because I had been dreaming about Dan Moseley and the boy in the wheelchair. They were side by side on slabs in the mortuary and their skin was cold and bloodless and sort of greenish, and they had scars running down the whole length of their bodies where they'd been sewn back up after the post mortem. The thing is, as I stood there watching them, I knew that they were going to open their eyes and get off the slabs, like the walking dead.

I was glad it was light when I woke up and I could look out the window, but I was still a bit scared when I went to the bathroom, in case *they* were in there.

Mrs Warner gave me scrambled egg for breakfast, which I'd never had before. I was a bit suspicious at first, but it was nice, and there was butter on the toast as well. She lent me an umbrella for my walk because by then it was tipping it down.

Sometimes I think I'd like to live here, then at other times I'm bored out of my mind. I think about my dad's car last night and I wonder what my mum's doing and whether she's worried about me. If she is, I expect they'll have prescribed her more Valium. Perhaps she doesn't know I'm here. I expect she does, though, because the police will have told her what I did.

On the doorstep I pulled up my PJ bottoms and bunched them at the knees to stop them getting wet. I left my slippers off as well and walked in my bare feet, which meant keeping to the grass, but I didn't mind. There was no wind and the umbrella kept most of the rain away, but I didn't stay out long because I was getting cold, my PJs kept slipping down off my knees, and my joints were starting to ache.

When I got back, Mrs Warner had me sit in the hall while she dried my feet, which is still difficult for me. Then she asked if I wanted anything to read. I thought she meant an F1 mag or maybe a comic, but she took me to this room where the walls were lined with smelly old books. I asked her whether there was anything on cars and she went round the room and pulled out this ancient wedge called *The Practical Motorist's Encyclopaedia* by F.J. Camm. It was the first time I'd laughed for weeks. Mrs Warner wasn't very impressed till I explained that a 'cam' opened and shut the valves in a car engine.

Later, Peter went through each of those bookmarked passages in the Bible and when I started the five-minute shift-around on my chair, he smiled, showing me his big yellow teeth, and told me my demon was getting worried, and that if I'd just accept Jesus I could be rid of it. Then he asked if I had any questions, so I gave him this long list starting with: Did I kill the boy in the wheelchair? Followed by: what day is it; how long will it be before my trial; can my mum visit; does he think they'll send me to an adult prison; can I have a handheld Nintendo?

He didn't give me one straight answer to my questions, not even down to telling me what day it was. I've got a feeling he thinks my demon is trying to trap him, and that any answer that doesn't have the word *Jesus* in it will undo all the work he's done.

***

23: Saturday, 1st June. 5 p.m. Fruit and Flower, Swanford high street.

ROBERT

Mrs Annesley gave Robert a wage packet, the first time for weeks that he had not received his money direct from the till. "Such a shame, you've been a very good worker, and if you need a reference..."

The American saw both regret and relief in the eyes of his employer. "Thank you, ma'am, and I'm sorry to be leaving."

Curiously, the shop had enjoyed its best week of trading for many months, probably due to the notoriety caused by the transit van, but overall the business was failing and the window was still boarded up because Mrs Annesley had no insurance to cover the cost of replacement.

One more reason to dislike Alan Henderson, thought Robert, closing the shop door and giving Mrs Annesley a valedictory wave with his umbrella. It had been raining for most of the day, and the roads and pavements were awash with water. On the way home he phoned Jack, who was still on his paper round, to tell him the bad news.

"Bummer."

"Yeh, I don't know where I'm going to find another."

"Hey, I'm meeting the gang in the Jewel later, do you think you'll be able to come too?"

"Sorry, Mom's cooking this huge reconciliation dinner and then they want to talk to me about the church meeting they had yesterday."

"OK, pudding..."

"Jack!"

"But I love rubbing your little belly mound."

"It's so embarrassing. I must get that bike and start swimming again."

"I'm practically swimming now. I'm sure Mr Ray will get complaints about soggy papers. Hey, what about going to the leisure centre tomorrow?"

"It's Sunday, Jack."

"Damn! I'd love to see you in a pair of Speedos."

"How did you know I wore Speedos?"

"I just hoped..."

"I might be able to go Monday."

"Ooh, let me know. Shall we invite everyone?"

"Why not? There's safety in numbers."

"Good news: Dan says that Justin and Freddy have agreed to see Ms Lane with him."

"Alan Henderson is making a lot of trouble for us."

"That's because he's a troubled kid."

"You're soft in the head, Jack Moseley."

"Talking of trouble, Dan told me that he almost let our cat out of the bag with Mum."

"Oh, Jack, that's terrible. That really scares me..."

"Don't worry, he beat a hasty retreat and when he got back it had all been forgotten."

"We really gotta keep this under control, you know."

***

Frank leaned back in his chair and closed his eyes. "Maybelle, that meal was fit for a president, though there are some presidents who I would not give house room to."

"It was delicious as always, Mom," added Robert.

"Well, I am glad you men enjoyed it, because I'll be serving it as leftovers for the next three days."

The table was still littered with the remains of roast turkey, walnut stuffing, mashed potato, creamed onions, swede and carrot mash, hot rolls – in fact, everything that would normally be served on the fourth Thursday in November across America.

"Son, I'm very pleased you apologised to your mother; it was the manly thing to do. I think it goes without saying that the passing of your aunt means a clean break with the past and all that went with it."

Robert nodded, the implication being clear. *Don't have any further contact with Tom Sanchez and his family.* Another part of his life that needed to be kept secret.

"Dad, did Mom tell you that I'm thinking of taking up swimming again?"

"No, but I think it's a good idea. A healthy mind and a healthy body are two sides of the same coin."

"Robert *has* a healthy body, dear," said Maybelle, suspecting oblique criticism.

"Not as healthy as I'd like, Mom, I can't run a yard without feeling pooped."

Frank chuckled. "When I was your age we'd spend every available minute of the summer down at Silver Lake."

"Looks like it'll have to be the leisure centre for me, and that'll mean a bus ride until I can afford a bike."

"Such a shame that Mrs Annesley had to shut up shop," remarked Maybelle.

"As it's an inset day I was thinking of going tomorrow to see what it's like."

"But what about your exam revision, dear?"

"First exam is math on Tuesday. I'm up to speed on that, but I'll have the morning to study anyway."

"Inset days!" huffed Frank. "If they need inset days, it ought to be for Bible study so that teachers are taught right from wrong. Then they just might be able to stamp out the perverted behaviour that we've heard about recently."

"We and other like-minded parents are hoping to instigate a few changes at schools in this country over the coming months, Robert."

"Now, Maybelle, let's keep that side of things under wraps for the time being."

Robert looked from one parent to the other. "You wanted to talk to me about the meeting you had yesterday."

Frank straightened up. "Yes indeed, son. Do you remember me taking you to see Archbishop Benn at the Old Rectory some three months ago, after you had the altercation with that Moseley boy?"

"Yes, sir..."

"Well, it was there that the conference was held. Some very important and influential people both locally and nationally came together because we all share the same concern about the moral decay of this country over the past twenty-five years. Now that at last there is a government which has a righteous outlook, our church and members of other Christian denominations have decided to invest time and capital in promoting the Biblical way of life. Pastor Fisher and myself were representing our church. Substantial sums of money are available for this missionary work, and we hope our cause will attract many decent people from all walks of life."

"Do you give them money, Dad?" asked Robert.

"I am always pleased to give what I can, Robert, but it is Burnoco which is very generous in its support for our cause. And because their UK home is here in Swanford, this town is especially important to them. Call it a prototype, if you will – an exemplar for others to follow. It may not be obvious yet, but we, and those like us, already hold many of the reins of power on the council and soon that will extend to the London legislature as well."

"But how did you get people to vote in the way you want?"

Frank and Maybelle chuckled together. "Propaganda and money, son, that's what wins elections. Make them afraid and offer them salvation, just like our Lord God. Remember the parable of the sower: *And when he sowed, some seeds fell by the wayside, and the fowls came and devoured them up: but other fell into good ground, and brought forth fruit, some a hundred-fold, some sixty-fold, some thirty-fold.* We provide the good ground to those that support us, and the fowls to those who don't.

"We have over three hundred MPs in the UK Parliament who are willing to endorse our cause, and a near majority in the Lords too, including a number of bishops. Unfortunately, the member for the Woolgrove constituency is not inclined to support us, and so we shall have to make sure that she comes round to our way of thinking or force a by-election..." Frank paused and beheld his son's questioning expression. "I can see you are a little shocked by my candour, son. But to do God's work it is necessary to use all means at our disposal."

"But I don't see what this has got to do with me. I'm not even old enough to vote..."

"Do you remember Archbishop Benn's words to you, when you sat at twilight in his parlour?"

"You mean about becoming a Christian soldier?"

"Exactly, Robert, exactly! Pastor Fisher wants you to lead the youth wing of our movement. If you are agreeable, and I trust you will be, I shall inform him, and he will arrange an induction course for you. First, let me say that it will be nothing like the disaster with Pastor McKellan. That was a real wake-up call."

"But my exams?"

"Do not worry, your role will not begin until the summer holidays. Meanwhile, as each day passes, we shall be removing the square pegs and inserting our round ones into various holes. It is time to mobilise a Christian army against the forces of secularism, atheism, socialism and the scourge of homosexuality."

"Isn't it exciting?" said Maybelle. "You, me and your daddy are going to fix this old country good."

Frank Crittenden stood up and offered his hand. "So, Robert, what do you say?"

"Of course, sir, of course I'll do it... but I don't know how." Robert rose too, and shook his father's hand, thinking that he and his father were a perfect pair of hypocrites.

"You will know how soon enough, son. This is a new order, a new beginning, and you will be there at the forefront of our great crusade."

***

24: An undisclosed date and location.

ALAN

I'm not going to say much about last night's dream, except Dan Moseley and I were in it together and it was the faggiest thing ever. It had seemed all right at the time, but when I woke up I knew it had been a nightmare and I shouldn't have enjoyed it at all!

Can doctors tell if you've had a wet dream? And, if so, can they tell what it was about? This morning, just to be on the safe side, I had a bath and changed my pyjama bottoms. Luckily I'm not so achy today and can actually bend my legs and dry my toes. My brother Ben was always bragging about his wet dreams. He'd be having massive sex with a girl and wake up to find he'd produced gallons of jizz. Sometimes he'd even show me his boxer shorts where he'd wiped it off and then he'd try to put them over my head, which was gross. I only managed a few drops, so perhaps I'm not so much of a fag after all...

When you-know-who came for his visit, I was worried about the you-know-what, but I needn't have been. He didn't even examine me today, except to take a close look at the stitch in my nose. He told the nurse to take it out the day after tomorrow, which must mean he's not coming anymore. Hooray!

I've been reading *The Practical Motorist's Encyclopaedia* by F.J. Camm. There's no photos in it, only drawings and diagrams and loads and loads of writing. If I had been around then, I could have done all the illustrations with no trouble. A lot of the basic stuff hasn't changed at all, it's just that nowadays there's more electronics under the bonnet and the engines are mostly transverse. The weirdest thing about the book, though, has nothing to do with F.J. Camm; it's what someone's written on the first inside page: *To Alan, A very happy Christmas, 1954.* I showed it to Mrs Warner, but she didn't twig until I told her my name is Alan. She gave me another of her strange looks then.

When I went for my walk, I took the book with me and read for a while, sitting on a bench in the sunshine overlooking the garden. If this is prison, I can think of worse things.

Peter didn't come today and so I guess even he has a day off. This meant that I got really bored and so I searched again for the story of that fag boy in the Bible who hid behind the Stone of Ezel, but I still couldn't find it. The only thing that saved the day from being a complete downer was that I had a roast dinner. I love roast dinners, especially when the meat is really tender, and there's mashed and roast potatoes and the

Yorkshire pudding soaks up the gravy. I even ate the cauliflower. I was really stuffed by the end because there was rhubarb pie and custard for afters and the pastry was real melt-in-the-mouth. When Mrs Warner came in to collect my tray I told her it was the best dinner ever and she smiled at me, which she's never done before.

As I got ready for bed that night, I felt quite excited, but then I forced myself to think about other things because I didn't want to have to change my PJ bottoms again.

***

25: Monday, 3rd June. 3 p.m. Prestleigh Leisure Centre.

JACK

Prestleigh Leisure and Fitness Centre was a blue glass-and-steel edifice with two pools: a six-lane twenty-five-metre swimming pool and a kidney-shaped leisure pool. On a school holiday or at weekends the noise was deafening, as it echoed off every shiny surface. So it was on this day.

Max and Jack had climbed the twelve metres or so to the upper deck, where they were about to embark on their fourth race down the pair of flumes that wound around the inside building before disgorging their occupants helter-skelter style into a small pool at one end of the leisure pool. On each occasion, they stopped to look through the window of the café, where Mandy was sitting alone at a table by a pillar with a book and a banana milkshake. Both boys also took the opportunity to appraise their reflections in the glass. Max was tall and spindly and already had a knot of black hair in the centre of his chest, something which Jack was envious of, while he in turn had a classic V-shaped torso, which Max hankered after, but would never attain.

"Manners is still ignoring us," said Max.

"I think she wants your company," replied Jack.

Max waved at her, to no effect. "She may as well have stayed at home or gone to the Jewel. The drinks are much better there anyway, and cheaper."

"OK, one more race and then you can go and kiss and make up."

"Very well... If you remember, it is two-one to me, even though I had to deal with that pair of revoltingly squelchy children the last time."

Jack went to look over the barrier to see if he could spot Robert and Dan below in the twenty-five-metre pool. His thoughts strayed to the fetching pair of black Speedos that his boyfriend had been wearing, though he had been a little disconcerted by the matching bathing cap.

"Why did you allow your brat to accompany us?" asked Max, leaning on the rail beside him.

"He wanted to race with Robert."

"I think it's very odd bringing a younger sibling to one of our meets. You'll be inviting him to the gym next, or even the Jewel."

"Yeh, I might do that, and bring Mikey as well."

"Oh God, no!" cried Max. "How strange that in *its* current embodiment *it* should have swapped a wooden head for a wooden leg."

Jack backhanded his friend's arm. "Look lively there, Maxxy, ye lily-livered land-lubber, cos it be my turn to ride the faster flume."

***

"So what was the fuckin' point?" asked Mandy a good half hour later, after allowing Max just a kiss on the cheek.

"You don't understand the male need for competition, Manners. You see, even though the score ended even, during our little contest the testosterone was coursing through our bodies in a most positive and pleasing way."

"Bullshit," she replied.

Max grabbed a chair from another table and signalled to Charlie and Barbara to move round so he could sit next to his girlfriend. Meanwhile, Jack sat opposite with a paper cup of the leisure centre's tasteless tea in front of him. "Everyone prepared for tomorrow?" he asked.

"Shut up, Moseley," said Charlie. "This is a no-one-mentions-exams afternoon."

"You just did," observed Max.

"Only to make the point," insisted Charlie.

"Maths does my head in," said Barbara. "Factorising quadratic equations, I just don't get it."

"Babs!"

"Shut up, Charlie, we can talk about exams if we want."

"At least it'll all be over in a couple of weeks," said Jack. "My main worry is staying awake long enough to write about Henry II and his barons."

"I'm afraid it's chemistry for me," said Max. "It doesn't make sense that three of this and two of that make four of one and half a dozen of the other..."

"Ooh, two sticks of eye candy," interrupted Mandy, putting down her book and waving, just as she hadn't done to Max.

Jack turned in his seat to see Robert and Dan standing close to the window in their bathing costumes, big smiles on their faces. He smiled back and raised his eyebrows.

"Nice bods," said Barbara.

Max leaned over to Charlie. "Don't worry, they're just trying to make us jealous."

"And succeeding," said Charlie, gritting his teeth.

"Moseley, what's that fuckin' thing your boyfriend's got on his head?"

"All Americans wear them in competitions," replied Jack.

"I think it's sexy," said Barbara.

Charlie cleared his throat and Mandy picked up her book and began to read again.

Dan pointed at Robert and put up seven fingers, and then at himself and put up three fingers. "Not bad," mouthed Jack.

Charlie cleared his throat again.

"We're just going to have one go on the flumes," signalled Dan.

The two boys hurried away and Jack turned back to his drink. Charlie cleared his throat for a third time.

Mandy lowered her book. "Masefield, will you fuckin' well shut up? You sound like some old lag on one hundred snouts a day."

"But he's a queer," said Charlie, staring wildly and pointing across the table, "a bloody queer."

Jack looked up, suddenly aware that he was being talked about. "What's the matter with you?"

"He just admitted it. A fucking shirt-lifter. I thought there was something not right about those two."

"Charles, get a hold of yourself," said Max, levelly.

But Charlie shot to his feet, scraping back his chair. "I'm not staying here!" He glared at Jack "I cannot believe you!" His shout echoed around the cafeteria. Then he stalked off towards the exit, and with a sigh of exasperation Barbara rose from her seat and went after him.

"What was that about?" asked Jack, worried.

"I'm afraid that Manners made an ill-advised remark and you didn't appear to notice, so engrossed were you with your beau."

"Oh fuck," said Jack, going red.

"Moseley, you and the Yank are so fuckin' obvious that only the blind, the dim and those that don't want to see, like that cunt Masefield, wouldn't know that you two were together."

Jack looked at Mandy and then at Max. "How long..."

"I'm afraid what Manners lacks in subtlety she makes up for in perceptivity. We have been following your ups and downs for months."

"Jesus!" said Jack. "You know what will happen if this gets back to Robert's parents?"

Mandy got out her phone and began to text furiously.

"What are you doing, my sweet?" asked Max.

She threw the phone down in front of him.

Masefield, if you grass them up I will personally rip your balls off.

"Press send for me, will you Maxxy?"

Max did as he was told, then showed Jack the text.

***

"We did one thousand metres altogether," said Dan, accepting a cup of hot chocolate from his brother with a smile.

"Your brother is very competitive," yawned Robert. "I was ready to quit after five hundred."

"That's because you'd won all the races up till then."

"Have a drink," said Jack, putting a cup of coffee in front of the American. "I've got something to tell you."

Robert looked across the table at Mandy and Max, who were gazing delphically at him. "Where's Charlie and Barbara?" he asked suspiciously.

"Crittenden, we know you're a homo," said Mandy, "so get over it."

The American sputtered, and coffee sprayed from his mouth. A blind panic seized him. He needed to get away as fast as possible. He got up, sending his chair falling backwards, but Jack grabbed hold of him, took him in his arms and held him tightly. "It's all right," he soothed, "you're with friends. You're with me." He gave the American a kiss. "And I love you."

Robert allowed himself to relax into Jack's body, putting his head on his shoulder. "I'm scared," he whispered. "I don't know where I'm going."

Dan picked up the chair. "I'll get something to wipe the table."

"Thanks, LB."

"The church wants me to be the leader of a youth group, and it's all about rooting out people like you and me. I hate all this lying, all this uncertainty. I don't know how much more I can take..."

Jack gently manoeuvred the American back to his seat. "It's because you're so honest. Now sit, and take it easy. Put your mind in neutral for a while."

As Robert dropped listlessly into the chair, Max breathed a sigh of relief. "Well, Manners, your intervention was a triumph of subtlety and tact, if I may say so. I'm sure the Foreign Office will be in touch directly to recruit you to the diplomatic corps."

"Crittenden has got to learn that there's more to life than his fucked-up parents and his even more fucked-up church."

"That's all very well, Manners, but we are all only fifteen years old, still under our parents' thumbs, and to add spice to the mixture, Robert is in an alien country."

"What's that about aliens?" enquired Dan, returning with enough kitchen paper to wipe every table in the café.

"Oh good," said Max. "We're back to teenage speak."

Dan finished wiping and stuffed the wad of paper into the nearest bin. "Robert, shall we have a quick look at the bikes in Halfords before we go?"

The American looked at the boy. "You're trying to cheer me up, aren't you?"

Dan sat next to him and slung an arm round his shoulders. "That's what brothers are for."

Mandy left off her straw for a moment to look across the table. "Since when did you become so fucking nice, Moseley junior?"

"Since I got to know you, Mandy," said Dan quick as a flash.

Jack laughed. "Good one, LB."

"Touché," murmured Max, impressed despite himself.

Mandy blew Dan a kiss across the table.

"Manners, please, save your kisses for me!"

Robert turned to Dan. "What you said means a lot to me," he said quietly. "I lost my own brother when I was ten to meningitis. He was seven and I loved him very much."

65

The table went silent. Jack took his boyfriend's hand and, squeezing it gently, looked at his brother. "You've done good there, LB. That's a difficult one for Robert."

Mandy noisily sucked the last of her milkshake out of the glass. "Crittenden, can I give you two pieces of advice?"

"Sure, Mandy. I need all the advice I can get."

"Right, decide if your man over there is worth the hassle, and if he is, fight for him. And that means forsaking all others and being faithful to him. And if he isn't worth the hassle, you'd better fuck off, and the sooner the better."

Nobody moved, nobody spoke, but beneath the table Jack felt a hand grip his arm and begin to caress him tenderly.

"Are you still with us, Crittenden?" asked Mandy after a spell.

Robert continued to stroke Jack's arm with a rhythm that seemed to match their beating hearts. "I guess..."

"Second piece of advice, then. Read what Larkin says about parents and act accordingly."

"Philip Larkin is a poet – er, was, I mean," prompted Max, seeing his baffled expression. "And a librarian."

Mandy pushed her glass into the middle of the table and began to fiddle in her home-made woollen handbag. "Maxxy, it's time you and I made tracks, and as for you three," she said, looking up, "hadn't you better fuck off to Halfords? Otherwise Moseley will miss his paper round and Mr Ray's number-one son will be on his back, all four feet nothing of him."

***

26: An undisclosed date and location.

<u>ALAN</u>

It's funny not having a watch or a clock. I don't think there's a single one in this house. My body seems to have got used to getting up when the sun rises and going to bed when it sets. That's all right at this time of the year, but what happens in the winter? I'll be going to bed at four o'clock in the afternoon! When you're in a detention centre waiting to go on trial, do they add that time on to your sentence? I wonder how long I'll get? At least they won't hang me like they used to do in England, or give me an injection to make my blood boil, or shoot me like they do in America. It's still dark outside now, so I think I'll go back to sleep. I haven't had any dreams yet – well, none that I can remember.

When I woke up later in the morning I felt disappointed. I suppose dreaming about Dan Moseley makes him seem alive and means I can pretend I haven't killed him. I know it's weird, but I have these funny feelings about him, even though he's dead, and I don't mean the feelings I had in my *gross wet dream*! I wonder why I never had any proper friends at school? Everybody seemed to ignore me or hate me. Perhaps it was because I used to hang out with my older brothers and never needed anyone else. Do friends come to you because they like you, or do you have to go and make friends because you like them? How come the one friend I'd choose to have above all others is the person I killed? I'm not sure if that makes me a saddo or a psycho – probably both...

After my walk I went back to my room and Peter was there a bit earlier than usual. He was agitated and pacing round and round as though I was late, which I wasn't because we don't have any set time. We sat down and, instead of the usual questions, he asks me straight out if I'd been having dirty dreams about boys, and I'm gobsmacked because I'd been found out, even though I'd had a bath. I began by stammering and stuttering that I didn't have dirty dreams, but I was quaking in my boots and my face was burning and he leans in and says, *Demon, we found the stains of sin on this boy's pyjamas.* And I'm thinking either I must have produced a lot more than I'd thought, or he must have been searching through my PJs with a microscope.

Then he springs up and pushes my shoulders hard. I topple backwards still in the chair, hit the back of my head on the floor, and wrench my back. Meanwhile, he has pulled out this cross from somewhere, his pasty face has turned pink, and he's standing over me slobbering spit and shouting: *Out, demon, out!* And I realise he's a complete nut job. He brings the cross down close to my face and I'm still entangled with the chair. I kick out and accidentally catch him on the arm and he goes berserk and starts hitting me on the nose with the cross while reciting 'Our Father, who art in Heaven,' like we used to do in primary school. I manage to roll off sideways and make a dash for the door. I slam it shut and turn the key just as he throws himself against it. Now, he's locked in and I'm locked out.

Mrs Warner arrives to see what the row is about, and finds me flaked out on the landing, holding my head, blood streaming from my nose, while Peter is banging on the door for all he's worth. Then the big man arrives. Big as in charge and big as in fat. Just climbing the stairs makes him out of breath. He's got a dog collar on and Mrs Warner starts to bow and scrape and call him *Archbishop*. At the sound of his voice, Peter calms down but when the door is unlocked, he comes out, all shaky and pale, and stares at me like a mad thing and says: *I almost got it out of him.*

My legs feel wobbly and Mrs Warner helps me to get back into bed and gives me a wet flannel for my nose, then you-know-who is summoned, but he's not too impressed and just re-stitches my nose, hands me two paracetamol and tells me to take two more before bedtime.

I have a little nap after all that and, because it's a nice day, Mrs Warner lets me out for another walk. I sit on the bench and read some more of *The Practical Motorist's Encyclopaedia*. I gen up on loss of compression, which means the engine loses power usually because of bad seals in a cylinder. I wish I had a car to practise on, especially a really old one which has a starting handle and a running board, like that 1934 Rolls-Royce Phantom.

Tonight's supper is absolutely scrummy. Fried egg and bacon with crispy fried bread to soak up the yolk, chocolate cake and ice cream for afters, and a cup of tea with sugar. Oh boy!

**

27: Tuesday, 4th June. 10.45 a.m. Swanford Community School.

DAN

Because of exams, morning assembly on the first day back at school was for Years Seven to Nine only. Perhaps this was why no mention was made of Alan Henderson's removal, or the reasons for it. Except for the cognoscenti, his absence, if noticed at all, was put down to a continuation of his time off through sickness, and very few teachers and even fewer pupils cared if he was there or not.

Dan Moseley, Justin Walker and Freddie Hall rarely went into the administration block and had never been inside the two rooms given over to the school's equality counsellor. There was a notice on the outer door which said *Please knock and enter* and *frappez avant d'entrer, svp* and *Bitte klopfen und geben,* which they did, finding themselves in a small waiting area with four chairs, a water cooler and a low table on which were a selection of tatty council magazines.

The sign on the inner door merely said *Ms H.E. Lane,* with no instructions as to what to do. Dan knocked, more determined than the other two, but received no reply.

"She's not in, let's go," said Freddie.

"Maybe we should give her five minutes," proposed Justin.

"I'm staying," stated Dan.

Freddie went to the window and put his arms flat on the sill. "We'll miss our break, and all for the sake of whiny Henderfag."

69

"Don't be a div, thunder pants." Dan hoped the mention of an old and hated nickname would have the required effect on his friend.

Justin smiled. "Have you seen what her initials spell?"

"Do you mean HE or HEL?" laughed Dan, sitting on the edge of the table.

"And what are you finding so funny?" asked Ms Lane, bustling into the room in a cloud of chiffon and an armful of folders. "And why are you sitting on the table? Don't you know what a chair is for?"

Dan shot to his feet. "Sorry Miss." They all turned to face her.

Equality counsellor Mrs Helen Edith Lane knew that she had a problem with adolescent boys. She was not as naturally sympathetic to them as she was to girls. Her worst professional outcomes had been with male teenagers, and in the early years of her career she had been duped several times by boys who hoped to get a rise out of her in order to gain some kudos with their peers. It was her own fault, she knew. She had a lack of empathy with this strange sub-species which meant she could not read their characters as well as she could females. Now, here were three boys of the very type that caused her most aggravation, larking about in her office.

"Well, what do you want?" she asked brusquely. Her mood had not been helped by the meeting she had just attended of the school governors, of which she was one of the staff representatives. The subject had been the homosexual bullying of Alan Henderson, and she had found her own position under fire.

A letter from Councillor Henderson had been read out about the treatment suffered by his son, which stated that the school had preferred tolerance and political correctness over traditional morality and family values. When the paragraph was read out espousing a return to Christian precepts as the basic ethos of the school, several of the foundation governors had been vociferous in their support, as had the newly appointed authority governors. Others had mentioned the

70

decline in the reputation of the school if the newspapers got hold of the story – and that an inspection by Ofsted would be sure to follow.

Ms Lane had pointed out that the police had only been in touch to tell them that an incident had occurred and that an officer would be attending at some future date. She also mentioned the parents of the two pupils allegedly involved, who had contacted the school to try to find out what had happened. The two sixth formers concerned had never been in trouble before, they were in the middle of their exams and their lives were about to ruined – all with no substantial evidence.

This cut no ice with the meeting, and when she quoted the Equality Act 2010 to the gathering, she herself had been attacked for being too interested in the rights of minorities rather than the good of the school as a whole.

"That particular piece of legislation will not remain on the statute book for long," said one of the new governors. The headmaster, as ever swayed by the loudest voices, had told her, though in more diplomatic language, to get her act together or face the consequences.

"We are in a new political orthodoxy, Ms Lane," he had concluded, "so get with it."

"May we have a word with you, please, Miss?" asked Dan.

Ms Lane really disliked pupils calling her 'Miss', but she was too tired to argue the point. "What about?"

"Er, Alan Henderson."

Her brow creased into a frown. "You're Jack Moseley's brother... Daniel, isn't it?"

Dan nodded, surprised that she knew of him. "Yes, Miss."

"You'd better come in, but I hope for your sakes that you're not wasting my time. And bring two chairs."

The boy's exchanged glances as Ms Lane marched into her office, which was a very small, windowless room. Dan and Justin picked up a chair each and followed, finding her already seated behind her desk. There was no sign of a computer screen, and the only piece of electrical apparatus visible was a heavy-duty fan which whirred on a filing cabinet behind her.

The boys sat in line, fidgeting nervously as she appraised them. "Do you want me to make a record of this visit?" she asked.

The three looked at each other again. "Er, I don't know," said Dan, feeling a bead of sweat trickle from his armpit.

Ms Lane was disinclined to take notes, because she was weary after the governors' meeting and was doubtful that the boys had anything relevant to say.

"Let's keep it informal, then. You're Justin... of Woolgrove Wanderers Football Academy fame?"

"Yes, Miss, Justin Walker."

"The school has been in correspondence with your prospective club. Category one, the highest ranking."

"Yes, Miss."

"Perhaps one day when you're established you can come back to your old school and give the pupils a pep talk?"

"I suppose so, Miss." Justin was taken aback by the degree of knowledge Ms Lane had on him.

"Not to worry – we're probably getting several years ahead of ourselves." She turned to the third member of the trio. "I'm sorry, I don't..."

Freddie was put out that he did not have the same fame or notoriety as the others. "Freddie Hall."

"Ah, yes. Your sister was Megan?"

"Yes, she's at uni now." Freddie was glad to get at least some acknowledgement via his family.

"Well, what do you know about Alan Henderson?" She addressed Daniel, as he appeared to be the leader.

"He's been taken out of school, hasn't he Miss, because he was bullied?"

Ms Lane gave a non-committal nod.

Dan took a deep breath and continued. "It was us who bullied him, but I was the worst..." The story unfolded while the equality counsellor listened, but said nothing. When Dan concluded with the tale of the skateboard, she continued to sit silently, and the sound of the fan seemed to grow very loud in their ears.

"What else?" she said at last, confused about why they would make such a candid confession.

Freddie was puzzled, but the others less so.

"That's it, that's what we... I did," stated Dan. "And it was wrong and we're sorry."

They shifted nervously in their seats, waiting for the repercussions. Ms Lane thought long and hard, uncertain of their motives and not certain that this was all they knew. At last she took a stab in the dark. "Who advised you to come and see me?"

Dan was taken aback by the question and tried to hide his blush by pretending to mop his brow with his hand.

"Well?"

"I can't say," he replied.

"Why?"

"It seems the wrong thing to do." He met her gaze squarely this time. "We took the advice, but the decision was ours."

Justin nodded in agreement.

"But what advice did you take that made you want to come and see me?"

"We didn't want to," said Justin, "but we needed to get our side of the story straight."

Our side? Ms Lane was more confused than ever now. "Do you expect someone else to tell a different story?"

Justin was about to speak again, but Dan waved him down. "We've told you all we *know*," he said flatly. "All we *know*."

"Are we going to be punished?" asked Freddie.

"Don't keep us in suspense, Miss," pleaded Justin.

Ms Lane put up her hand to stop them. "I'm not thinking about punishments at the moment. Daniel, do you need to speak to me alone?"

He shook his head. This was getting strange. "No," he said. "The three of us talked it over. Justin and Freddie know as much as I do."

It occurred to Ms Lane that the boys might be playing games with her, bringing back memories she would have preferred to forget. Still, none of them seemed the duplicitous type and Daniel appeared to be trying to tell her something important that she ought to know, but could only find out if she gained his trust.

"How did you know Alan had been taken out of school by his father?"

Dan thought back to the conversation he'd had with his mother at the barbecue.

"Mum told us."

"Why would she tell you that?"

"Because Stewart was with us..." Almost before he'd said it, Dan felt he was falling into a trap.

"Stewart Henderson," she said quietly.

"I'm not saying any more about that," he said, angry with himself. "As I said, what we did to Alan was wrong and we're sorry, but we didn't do anything else."

And that's the crux of the matter, thought Ms Lane. I believe what they say, but I'm sure they know something else *was* done – and maybe they might even know who did it.

"Please, Miss, we're missing our break," said Freddie.

"I think you can go, Freddie, and you too, Justin, if you want."

"You can't lay this all on Dan," said Justin. "We're all guilty."

"It's all right Just, I don't mind."

"Freddie, you may go. I want a few more words with these two and then they'll join you. They will inform you of the reparation, I expect."

Freddie looked blank.

"Punishment," clarified Ms Lane.

Freddie rose and looked down at his friends. "I'll see you later," he said.

"We'll bring you the bad news," said Dan.

Ms Lane waited for Freddie to depart and then she waited a little longer. Dan and Justin exchanged looks, not understanding what was going on. Their equality counsellor appeared to have gone into a state of inertia.

"Right!" she said abruptly, slapping the table and making them jump. "I have to break this deadlock." She swivelled in her chair, unlocked the second drawer of her filing cabinet and, after a moment's search, drew out a thin folder. Between the cardboard sleeves was a facsimile of the letter sent by Councillor Henderson to the school, along with three photographs printed on A4 paper. She took out one of the photographs and laid it before the two boys, not taking her eyes off their faces.

Justin turned away, but Dan kept his gaze on it, becoming more upset the longer he looked. Ms Lane whisked the photograph off the desk and returned it and the folder to the filing cabinet. Then, from the upper drawer, she drew out three plastic cups, a tray and a bottle of Robinson's lemon barley water.

After fetching water from the cooler in the outer office, she set two cups of squash in front of the boys and made one for herself.

"You've missed your break," she said. "And I'm sorry for upsetting you."

Dan took a sip. "Where is Alan now?"

"In a sanatorium somewhere."

"Who took the photo?" asked Justin.

"A doctor. There are two other photographs that show he was sexually assaulted, but I'm not going to show you them."

"Derek Henderson did it," said Dan, "him and his brother, John. I know that as much as you know that Alan is in a sanatorium and a doctor took these photographs."

Ms Lane smiled to herself. For once she had got her psychological insights into the boys right. "And Stewart Henderson?"

"That's up to Stewart," said Dan, swallowing the last of his drink.

Ms Lane scribbled on a piece of paper and turned it for the boys to see. "Put that number in your mobiles, but don't associate it with my name. If you or a friend has any information you want to pass on, or you need assistance, call me. This is a can of worms, and if you are not careful it may cause you problems."

When they had done as requested, they started to get up, but Ms Lane waved them down. "You know this school has a very strict anti-bullying policy, don't you?"

"Yes, Miss," they chorused.

"And you picked on Alan because you thought he was gay?"

"It'll never happen again," said Dan. "I had some issues at the time, but that's in the past."

"Very well," she said. "What about you, Justin?"

"No more bullying, that's a promise."

"Good, but the penance for your cruel and flagrant abuse of Alan Henderson must be severe and fit the crime."

Their faces fell. Justin stared down and held his forehead, visions of the Football Academy receding into the distance. Dan half-shut his eyes and looked away. No more than I deserve, he thought.

"Do you know Noah Marshall?"

"Er, I've heard of him," said Justin. "He's not my type."

"Befriend him," said Ms Lane. "That is your penance, but it is also an opportunity to show who you really are."

"He's in Year Nine," said Dan.

"Being in the year above does not make him ineligible for friendship."

"Why?" asked Justin.

"Because I fear what might happen to him. There are two boys at this school who are facing police questioning about the Henderson case on no other basis than their sexuality, and they were always discreet about who knew about them, until that business over the gay bar in Victoria Street. Noah is the only other openly gay boy in the school, and he's only that because it is somewhat difficult for him to hide. Thirteen hundred pupils in this school and three openly gay boys. It's nearly as bad as your Association Football."

Dan thought about his brother and Robert, of Alan Henderson, and the photograph Ms Lane had shown them of his bruised and bloodied face, and then thought of Noah Marshall. The narrow-chested, blue-streaked-hair-hanging-over-the-right-eye, swishy kid with the big snub nose, cupid's bow lips and high-pitched voice that everyone joked about. They would never live it down. Just speaking to him would mark them for life.

"Cruel and unusual punishment," said Dan.

"And where does that saying come from?" asked Ms Lane.

"I don't know; I heard it somewhere."

"It's American, isn't it?" said Justin.

"It's in the 1688 English Bill of Rights, before the United States was even a twinkle in Washington's eye and a hundred years before the Eighth Amendment."

"Can we go now, Miss?" asked Dan.

"Yes, you may, but I'd still like to know who gave you the advice to come and see me."

Dan smiled "It wasn't Noah Marshall, that's for sure."

Ms Lane was feeling a little better now. Her view that the school faced dark times ahead remained, but she had taken heart from what she considered to be a most unlikely source: namely, two adolescent boys. "Who is taking your next class?"

"Mrs Parkin, Miss. Spanish."

"I'll phone and tell her you'll be ten minutes late."

***

The friends walked down the corridor and away from the administration block, not quite understanding all that had happened, but feeling relieved and rather adult.

"She was talking about the two sixth form boys, wasn't she?" asked Justin.

Dan nodded his head.

Justin laughed. "Noah Marshall – is she serious or what?"

"We are going to do it, aren't we?" said Dan seriously.

Justin looked hard at his friend. "What is so different about you these days?"

"Better or worse?" asked Dan.

"Better, really; you're kind of more together."

Dan eyed his friend. "Are you with me on this, Just?"

"Why not? But Freddie will think we're joking."

"We've just been allowed a look over the fence, you know."

"What do you mean, wise owl?"

"A look into Teacherland."

Justin glanced at his watch. "We've got five minutes."

"In that case, I'm just going to look in on Jack, if I can."

Justin nodded. "Well, be careful. Interrupting an exam is a capital offence. I'll see you in Parkey's Plaza."

***

Dan dashed to the nearest stairs, which against all the rules he ascended three steps at a time, made a left, took a prohibited shortcut through the library and raced down the grey-tiled corridor to the music room. Through the glass pane in the door he could see the rows of Year Ten pupils bent over the first of their mathematics papers. Jack was sitting on the far side by the window, not writing at the moment, but reading a question, one elbow on the desk and his wrist pressed against his mouth in concentration. Mr Joseph, the only black teacher in the school, was invigilating and, fortunately, was engrossed in a book. Dan stepped back one pace and began to wave furiously, hoping that Jack would catch the movement out of the corner of his eye.

"Excuse me, young man!"

Dan jumped two inches off the floor. "Oh, sir, you scared me!"

Mr Colt walked up to the boy and spoke sternly. "It's Mr Moseley the younger, if I'm not mistaken?"

"Yes, sir," said Dan. Why does everyone know who I am? he thought, going very red.

"I hope and pray that those semaphoric gestures were not sending mathematical clues to your brother, Mr Moseley."

"Oh no, sir, I was just trying to attract his attention."

"And why, in the middle of an important examination and when you are already late for your next class, was there such urgency in making this contact?"

"I just wanted to tell him that everything was OK, sir, in case he was worried, and that I would see him at dinner. And actually, sir, I'm not late for my class because Ms Lane gave us a ten-minute let-off."

"Ah, I see! So you have been in the hands of the redoubtable Ms Lane. Well, I can understand why Mr Moseley the elder might have been worried."

"Are you going to give me a detention, sir?" Dan hung his head. He knew that an hour's detention would mean an inquest at home and the probability of missing football practice that night. Suddenly, he felt a lot less like an adult.

Mr Colt frowned. "As I am taking over from our esteemed geographer Mr Joseph for the last half hour of this examination, I shall give you a choice in that matter."

"OK, sir," said Dan, feeling very depressed.

"Either you can do a detention, or I can pass on your message to your brother."

The boy blinked several times then, as comprehension dawned, he looked up and a grin formed on his face. "Oh, sir, thank you, sir."

"Seeing the Moseley smile is always worth a little give and take," said Mr Colt. "Now, run along or your ten-minute dispensation will have expired, and Mr Moseley..."

"Yes, sir?"

"Don't do it again."

***

28: An undisclosed date and location.

<u>ALAN</u>

I dreamed I was at Dan Moseley's funeral, saying sorry to his friends and family, and we were all sad, but – strangely – no one was angry with me. When they were lowering the coffin into the ground, I noticed it was upside down and stuff was falling out, and it was all the spare parts for a car engine, so I threw myself onto it, to try to turn it round the right way. That's when I woke up. I guess I'm as crazy as Peter. As soon as my trial is arranged, I'm going to plead guilty and get it over with quick.

I hear a car pull up outside. It sounds familiar. When I look out, my dad is standing on the driveway, talking to the archbishop, and Peter's there too. I'm glad Dad's come back for a second visit because it must mean he hasn't forgotten me, but I am a bit worried about what Peter might say to him about you-know-what. I wish Mum had come to visit as well, but at least Derek isn't there.

Mrs Warner comes in and says I can pack up and go. I can't figure this out. It's not what I expected and I'm suddenly scared and don't want to leave, not just because of Derek and what might happen to me, but because I actually quite like it here.

"But I haven't had my breakfast," I blurt out. I see her look hard at me and then her expression suddenly softens from stony to understanding, and I feel like crying. She comes over and gives me a hug and then I can't stop myself crying and I know that I'm really just a big baby. And she tells me I'm one of the nicest ones she's had, and that I can keep the book if I want. She calls me an innocent, which means she doesn't know that I have faggy wet dreams and I'm a murderer.

As we drive out of the detention centre, all I've got on are my pyjamas and slippers, and my only other possession is *The Practical Motorist's Encyclopaedia.* I notice that there's no barbed wire or searchlights, and the gates are wide open. Maybe they're electronic. Dad hasn't said anything to me, not even hello. I can tell he's annoyed. He probably had to put up loads of money to bail me out.

After about five minutes he gives me a stern look and says, "You've caused me more trouble than you're worth."

I answer: "What's the date of my trial?"

And for some reason, just saying this makes him angry and he belts me across the face with the back of his hand and calls me a shit-shover. I'm dizzy and see stars and can't focus my eyes and there's a lot of blood again. The shock of it makes me cry out because my dad has never hit me before in my life and has hardly ever sworn at me. Now I know how Stewart must have felt.

"Stop squealing like a girl," he yells at me. "Or you'll get another!"

"Sorry," I reply and it comes out like the faggiest whimper.

"You will be," he says in this low voice which frightens me more than being hit.

Then he grabs my book off my lap and throws it out of the window...

***

29: Wednesday, 5th June. 7.30 p.m. 15 Leighton Lane.

<u>PAM</u>

"This is nice," said Roger, taking a sip of wine and relaxing into the settee.

Pam moved closer to him. "Hmm."

He slipped an arm around her back. "We should do this more often."

"Hmm," replied Pam in a slightly less agreeable tone. This little oasis of togetherness had taken two days of military-style planning to prepare for. The elder boys were at Nana Moseley's installing her new Blu-ray player while Mikey had been allowed a very special mid-week sleepover with his best friend, and new crew member of the *Hispaniola*, Mike Huntley.

"The wine and the dinner are making me quite, mmm, you know..." he said.

"Sleepy?" suggested Pam. Well, don't drop off just yet, she thought, smiling at him and dabbing him playfully on the nose.

"It's not our wedding anniversary, is it?"

"If you'd forgotten our wedding anniversary, we wouldn't be snuggled up on the sofa like this."

"That's true. But I do suspect some ulterior motive."

"Roger, how could you think such a thing?"

"I've got it!" he said, sitting bolt upright. "It's another man, isn't it?"

"Yes, it is... Mr Pullin from the post office."

"Oh, lord!" he exclaimed, taking a swig from the wine glass and settling back into the sofa. "But doesn't the Zimmer frame cramp his style?"

"He's very athletic on it – and the tricks he can do with his false teeth!"

They chuckled together and then for a few moments enjoyed each other's company in silence.

"Roger..?"

Ah, here it comes. "Yes, Pam, my dearest one."

"What if I were to tell you that there might really be another man in our lives?"

"What?" he said, a look of horror on his face. "You're not
—"

"Good heavens, no!"

"Tell me, then."

She altered her position so she could look at him directly, and took a deep breath.

"What if I were to tell you that one of our sons is *gay*?"

"Oh, lord! Which one... Oh, it's obvious. How do you know?"

Pam sat up "Well..."

"It's that American boy, isn't it?" Roger said, before she could say any more. "Are you sure?"

"Yes and yes."

"God! First they come over and steal our women. Now they come over and steal our boys!"

His wife smiled. "I'm a bit surprised. You seem quite relaxed about it."

"No, I'm not." He took another gulp of wine. "I just haven't taken it in." He looked at her. "Did he tell you?"

"No."

"How do you know, then?"

"Mikey."

"Mikey told you!"

"He gave them away, quite innocently actually."

"So, the super-grass told you, and what did you do?"

"I peeped in on them."

"Oh, for God's sake, you didn't catch them at it, did you?"

"Roger!"

"What, then?"

"They were wrapped in each other's arms, asleep."

"Naked?"

"Bare-chested, but the duvet was pulled up."

"Post coitus, I suppose," he said with a grimace.

"I don't know, but they looked... so beautiful, Rog. Jack had his head on Robert's chest and his expression was so content, so happy. So different from how he's been over the past months."

"So, what are we going to do? Whip them, forbid them to see each other, send Jack for psychiatric counselling, or get out the *rainbow* banner?"

"What do you think, Roger?"

He drained his glass, took a deep breath, then shook his head. "Let's not make a fuss about it. He'll tell us when he's ready. Hopefully, he'll tell you and spare me the embarrassment. Anyway, one out of three's not bad, is it?" Then his eyes glazed. "I'd forgotten about Mikey! He likes all that kind of gay stuff, doesn't he... and what's the latest, acting like Robert Newton in *Treasure Island*? Talk about flamboyant. Next thing, he'll be asking us for a pair of ruby slippers. At least Jack was never like that."

"Rog, Mikey's only seven! Give him a chance. And at least he'll have a good role model in his older brother."

"And what about Dan – how is he going to react when he finds out that his brother is *one of them*?"

"Oh, he knows. I know he knows. Have you forgotten already that horrible tension there was between them?"

"Do you think it was about *that*?"

"It makes perfect sense."

"So why are they now as thick as thieves, even more than they were before?"

"I think Dan has learned a lesson. Haven't you noticed? He's matured a lot in the past few weeks. He listens more, he thinks more, he's less selfish."

Roger thought for a moment. "Now you come to mention it, Coach Brennan said almost the same thing at practice last Tuesday."

"Well, there you are then. All our children are lovely. We're very lucky." Pam closed her eyes, allowing all the tension that had built up over the past couple of days to slowly drain away. Then she tipped the last of her wine down her throat.

Roger massaged the back of her neck. "I never thought I was grown-up enough to be a parent. I still don't, really."

"Then let's hope we can learn from this, and if any of our children start having problems, for whatever reason, we can do a bit better than we did by Jack, letting him struggle on his own for all those months."

"About this American boy, Pam?"

"His name's Robert."

"Sorry, but what about *Robert's* parents? They're going to be severely hacked off, aren't they?"

"I think that may be an understatement. I had a quick look at some of their church's Old Testament, hellfire and damnation websites."

"You've been preparing all this for days, haven't you, buttering me up?"

"Yes, I have."

"You're a very devious woman, Pamela Moseley." He grinned at her.

"You know that's Jack's grin as well, don't you?"

"And you're still at it, appealing for your son through our shared genetic inheritance."

"*Your* son, Roger, and don't you forget it."

"What if Robert's parents start getting rough, and disown him or accuse us or Jack of corrupting him?"

"That's why we have to support each other and both of them!"

"Both?"

"There are no half-measures in this, Rog. We've let Jack down once and now we have this new government promising an anti-gay crusade they'll need our support even more."

Roger frowned. "The government *you* voted for."

"That's between me and the ballot box."

"You like him, don't you? Robert, I mean?"

"Don't you?"

"I hardly know him. I've usually been out with Dan when he's been here."

Pam laid her head on her husband's shoulder. "He's gorgeous, Rog. Not just how he looks, but his lovely manners and personality. I know exactly what Jack sees in him."

"Jesus! First she fancies a geriatric old codger at the pension counter, now she's got the hots for her son's fifteen-year-old boyfriend."

"Do you mind that there are so many men in my life?"

"Actually," said Roger, "it's beginning to make *me* feel rather randy."

"Ooh, is it?" Pam said, putting her wine glass down.

"Yes, it is, and since this is one of those very rare occurrences where we are alone, I'd really rather like to do it now, here, on the carpet."

"Oh, come on then, Rog, fuck me like I was an old trollop..."

***

The front-page story in the *Swanford Mail* on Thursday 6th June read:

Fury Over Assault
Exclusive By John Little

A thirteen-year-old boy has been the victim of a horrific series of sexual assaults, and the perpetrators are believed to be pupils at his own school. So says Detective Inspector David Rains, who is leading the investigation into accusations of homosexual bullying at Swanford Community School. Two of the school's sixth form pupils are in police custody and are awaiting further questioning.

The assaults are said to have taken place during the latter half of May and to have occurred on school property.

Neither the victims nor the alleged perpetrators can be named for legal reasons, but the father of the thirteen-year-old said that his son had been withdrawn from the school and he had sent a strongly worded letter to the headmaster. He said that the accused, as well as having to face the full force of the law, should also undergo treatment for their homosexual condition.

A spokesperson for the school said that the pupil concerned had been absent for some time due to sickness, and they were monitoring the situation carefully and would cooperate fully with the police enquiry.

A half-page advertisement in the same issue of the *Swanford Mail* read:

The Demon In Our Midst

Concerned Citizens of Swanford. This is for you.

The homosexual lifestyle has been indulged for the past fifteen
years.
Have you noticed the increase in licentiousness in our town?

The flaunting and promulgation of sinful activities
And, worst of all, the criminal acts perpetrated on our youth.

If you are concerned, and particularly if you are a concerned
parent, come join our service at
the Baptist Church, on Sunday 9th June at 9 a.m.

If you support the new government's initiative to curtail this
unnatural practice, don't keep it to yourself. Arise, awake!

*Swanford Mail reporter John Little will be at the service,
after which he will write a feature which will appear in next
week's *Mail*.*

We are a friendly, family-orientated church that believes in
Biblical truth, the sanctity of traditional marriage and a strong
Christian response to sexual immorality.

***

30: Sunday, 9th June. 8.50 a.m. The Baptist Church,
Westbury Avenue.

ROBERT

The Crittenden family arrived in good time, expecting
there to be a larger than usual congregation. They were right.
The church was already half full, and there was a frisson of
excitement as they took the places in their usual pew. It was a
brighter, more colourful place too. New high-wattage lanterns
gave out a warm, welcoming glow, and vases of summer
flowers scented the air. Gerald Fisher had recruited a five-
piece band – two guitars, percussion, saxophonist and
keyboard – to provide the music, and they were playing quietly
as the parishioners entered. "This is more like it," Frank
whispered to Maybelle.

Directly across the aisle from the Crittendens, Police and
Crime Commissioner, Kenneth Anderson, and three
councillors were sitting together with their spouses, studying
their hymn sheets. Just behind them, *Swanford Mail* reporter
John Little was already taking notes. Next to him sat a
photographer with a Nikon camera, and occasionally the two
would lean towards each other to converse in whispers.

Robert recognised a number of fellow pupils who were
attending for the first time with their parents. The eldest was
Patrick Johns, the head boy, who often did the readings in
assembly. His navy-blue suit perfectly matched his black hair
and pronounced stubble. A small girl of strikingly similar
looks, but without the stubble, sat next to him. The only one he
knew well enough to speak to was Lucas Spriggs, a Year Ten
pupil who, though not in the same class, regularly crossed his
path in PE and rugby.

Just before nine o'clock, John Henderson arrived,
walking down the aisle with his wife and three of his boys.
There were murmurings throughout the church as people
noticed the imposing figure, and some gasps as they spotted
Alan Henderson making slow, listless progress, sandwiched

between his brothers John Jnr and Ben. All were smartly dressed in suits and ties, but bunched up and just visible below Alan's trouser turn-ups Robert noticed a filthy pair of striped pyjama bottoms. The councillor nodded solemnly at Frank and Maybelle before taking his seat in the front pew.

The music stopped and Pastor Fisher appeared, attired in a powder-blue suit and striped tie. The congregation rose and the pastor smiled benignly at them. "Friends, I would like to welcome you all to our Family First church, where we don't stand on ceremony. Please be seated." He gestured with both hands. "It is a joy to see so many new faces here today, especially the shining, innocent faces of our young boys and girls. Today you will hear some harsh words spoken and witness the terrible results of Satan's demons, but remember – with the love of our Lord Jesus Christ we shall fear no evil. Now, let us sing a rousing traditional hymn, 'Guide Me, Oh Thou Great Jehovah, pilgrim through this barren land'..."

Robert turned his head, expecting to see Edith and Patty in the seats behind him, but instead there was a young couple, the woman carrying a sleeping baby. Quickly he scanned the rest of the pews in case these newcomers had usurped their usual place, but there was no sign of them.

Ten to fifteen minutes passed, and some of the assembly began to get restless as they were not used to the order and ceremony of a church service. Then Pastor Fisher started his sermon.

"The Christian world, by and large, does not understand that we are in a continuous spiritual war: a cosmic struggle between good and evil. It began with Adam and Eve and their experience with Satan, and continues to this day. But we have such a namby-pamby idea of Christianity that we think being a Christian just means being a 'nice' person. We are not alarmed by sin, we do not fear sin, instead we are beguiled by it. We look on it as a little thing, fit only for the child within us. Whereas it is a huge behemoth waiting to swallow us whole!

"Christians from other generations knew there was a cosmic struggle going on for their souls, and they prayed fervently that they would be delivered. We have lost that sense of struggle, my friends, and we need to renew our faith, put on God's armour and take up the Sword of Truth and take the fight to Satan's Legions!

"Councillor Henderson, I would ask you to come up to the altar and bring your son Alan with you so that the good people of Swanford can see what the allies of Satan, these so-called *gays*, have done..."

Robert watched the councillor stand and lead his son by the hand up the steps to where the pastor was standing. There were gasps of horror when Alan turned to face the congregation, revealing his swollen and battered features. A flash bulb went off. The boy blinked and shuddered, then suddenly, painfully, he ran to where his mother was sitting in the front pew and tried to pull her up. His voice quavered, no real words coming out, just a series of moans and whimpers. But Lisa Henderson would not budge.

"The poor boy," said Pastor Fisher, projecting his voice throughout the church. "We cannot show you the injuries that have scarred his body, even to his most private parts. But now you see how the demon of homosexuality works, for it has even tried to enter his soul." He turned to the councillor just as John Henderson Jnr guided Alan back to his seat. "Can you describe your anguish at this terrible crime?"

Councillor Henderson stood straight, gazing through his glasses at the rapt congregation, and once again Robert felt his dark magnetism as the large man began to speak. "It is a well-known fact that the homosexual element recruit new members – vulnerable children – to their aberrant lifestyle. My views on the subject are well known. These perverts took revenge on me through my youngest son, first by trying to recruit him, then, when he wouldn't succumb, by getting pupils at his school to beat and sexually abuse him. The same thing happened to my son Stewart. who was forced to move to another town to avoid further sexual violence."

"What about the police?" someone shouted from the congregation.

"I cannot complain about the Swanford police and our excellent Crime Commissioner, but their investigations are hampered by red tape and regulation. I know that in the ranks of the officials in this town there is a homosexual element working against the common good, the moral majority. The sooner we are rid of the so-called European Convention on Human Rights, and the 2010 Equality Act is repealed, the sooner we shall be able to deal with these degenerates."

There was a scattering of applause throughout the church as the councillor retook his seat. Pastor Fisher held up his hands for them to desist. "Friends, I know that you will have been as shocked as I was at the treatment meted out to this poor boy. But now, in God's church with God's help, we shall set his soul on the road to recovery. We shall bow our heads in our weekly prayer and ask our Lord Jesus Christ to heal Alan of his wounds and in time to make him spiritually whole again."

"Dear Father in Heaven, we beseech you to bless us and keep us in the week ahead. Let us pray for those in foreign lands who suffer in your name; let us pray for the poor in spirit, and the sick in body or mind. In particular, let us pray for this unfortunate boy in our midst who was tortured by depraved homosexuals, who are possessed of Satan's demons. And thank you, Lord, for delivering him from their immorality back into the safe and loving arms of his family. Guide us away from sin and into the fellowship of the Holy Spirit. We ask this in the name of our Lord, Jesus Christ. Amen!"

The congregation responded with their 'amen', and Pastor Fisher bowed his head in acknowledgement. "Friends, immediately after the service the ladies of the church will be serving refreshments in the vestry. In addition, for those of you who may be interested, we have our very own John Little from the *Swanford Mail* here, who I know is anxious to hear your views on our service. I also know that John has brought along a photographer, and if you would like your children to appear in next week's *Mail*, stay behind after the service for a group photograph. Now, we will sing our final hymn before the blessing, and let us show Satan that he has no place in our church, no place in our town, and no place in this world by raising the roof. Let us sing 'Go, tell it on the mountain'."

***

Robert was feeling ever more alienated both from his parents and his church. Until recently he would have accepted all that had been said in the service without question. Now, he saw not only hypocrisy and distortion of the truth by those he had always trusted and looked up to, but also an incitement to violence couched in Christian language aimed against himself and the person he loved. His love for Jack was not inspired by demonic possession, he was convinced of that, though he was so indoctrinated into the teaching of the church that even this had to be thought over and intellectualised.

As did the idea of helping a violent thug like Alan Henderson, whatever excuses Jack and Dan made for him. It was, if not anathema, at least bitter waters for him. Even the injuries the boy had suffered did not move him particularly, because he had brought them on himself. But he had made a commitment to help, and help he would.

After the service, it was clear that the Hendersons were intent on leaving as quickly as possible. John and Ben spearheaded their exit with Alan between them, walking in measured steps up the aisle while the councillor and his wife brought up the rear. Though the congregation was mostly gathering on the north side in order to be near the vestry and the refreshments, a number wanted to commiserate with the family, not to mention cast prurient eyes over their abused son.

On the pretext of going to chat with Lucas Spriggs, Robert left his parents and followed. At the entrance, the councillor had no choice but to pause while eager well-wishers offered their condolences and shook his hand while his wife stood stony-faced and unresponsive by his side. He told his sons not to wait, and they wormed their way through the small throng, taking Alan firmly by the arms.

The Ford transit was situated a number of parking spaces along outside the church, only a few yards from Church Lane. Taking a chance, the American ran in a straight line towards it, dodging the gravestones, and arrived at the boundary wall before the Hendersons had reached the lychgate. Hidden from view by a holly tree, he jumped down onto the pavement and squatted behind a red Fiat Punto just one space away from the van.

Not long afterwards he heard approaching footsteps and then Ben's voice, close by. "You're in for it now, you stupid shit. Derek will murder you."

"Your mummy won't be there to protect you, either."

A slap and a cry from Alan was followed by the sound of one of the back doors of the van opening.

John's voice. "You go and wait in the front. I'll deal with the fag."

Ben's voice: "What are you going to do to him?"

John's voice: "Never you mind."

The back door slammed shut and there was a short hiatus. Then Robert heard more footsteps approaching and prayed it wasn't the owner of the Punto.

Councillor Henderson's voice. "Where are they?"

Ben's voice. "In the back."

Councillor Henderson's voice. "Look after your stepmother."

The front passenger door opened and the back door reopened.

Councillor Henderson's voice. "What have you done with the suit?"

John's voice. "In the locker."

Councillor Henderson's voice. "Give the bugger what for as we drive. Don't gag him. I want his mother to hear."

The front passenger door slammed shut.

John's voice. "Are we taking her home first?"

Councillor Henderson's voice. "No, my car's at the farm, we'll drive straight there. That'll give you ten minutes to get him ready.

John laughed. "Ready for the big show!"

The back door slammed shut.

As the Ford transit made a three point turn out of the parking space, Robert crawled around the Punto and onto the pavement, where he couldn't be seen as it drove off. Then, dusty, sweaty and still trembling with fear, he sat for a while, thinking up lies to tell his parents when he got back inside the church. Now he fully understood why Jack and Dan wanted to help Alan.

*

31: Monday, 10th June. 12.05 p.m. Swanford Community School.

<u>JACK</u>

In the main hall, Mr Colt sat in his invigilator's chair, stroking his chin, while before him stood two anxious pupils. The English language examination was over and the completed papers were neatly piled on his desk. Marking was a chore, but a chore that he quite enjoyed, if truth be told. It seemed to him that English, more so than maths or science, gave him a privileged insight into the souls of his charges.

"I hope your concerns did not affect your ability to complete the examination paper."

"I don't think so, sir," said Jack.

"And you won't, I hope, let any of this intrigue interfere with your revision?"

"No, sir," said Robert.

"It must be apparent to you that I, along with the majority of my colleagues, know a good deal less about what is going on in this school than some of its pupils."

"Andy Venables and Adam Ellis were caught in a shakedown of that gay pub, the Orange Lounge on Victoria Street. Do you know it, sir? It's just a shell now."

"I'm afraid, Mr Moseley, my knowledge of the gay scene is limited to what you tell me," said Mr Colt with a smile, "and I have had no personal connection with either of those two boys, as they were not in my class."

"We think their names were on a police list and they're being used as scapegoats," said Jack.

"They are innocent, sir, that's what we wanted to tell you."

"But you wouldn't have told me unless you expected me to do something about it."

"It helps that another person knows," said Robert.

"A problem shared is a problem halved," added Jack with a smile.

"If you wish, I can at least pass on this information to the redoubtable Ms Lane?"

"Yes, sir. Dan says we can trust her."

"Mr Crittenden, do you believe your parents or your church know the true nature of the Hendersons?"

Robert gave some consideration to his reply. "The honest truth is, sir, that I don't know, but I would like to think not. They are probably blinded by their own prejudices."

"It does not, of course, excuse their culpability," said Mr Colt, almost to himself.

"When Stewart tells his counsellor what really happened to him that should sink them," said Jack.

"Maybe, maybe – and it would certainly help to get corroboration from the youngest Henderson."

"We hope to work on that," said Robert.

"Boys, I am not a pessimist at heart, but there are times in the affairs of man when the tide of public opinion turns against enlightenment and takes the easy option of ignorance and prejudice. This change is most often predicated on fear, and those that manipulate this most basic instinct for the enhancement of their own power, wealth and position are playing a most dangerous game."

"Are you telling us to watch our backs, sir?"

"That seems to be the appropriate vernacular, yes. At all times."

"Thank you for giving us the chance to talk, Mr Colt," said Robert.

"Hmm, it seems we live in interesting times, eh boys?" Their teacher rose stiffly and began to gather up the examination papers. "Now to your task, for which Mr Harris, our esteemed PE instructor, will be duly grateful."

Mr Colt walked slowly towards the exit, while the boys set about folding and stacking half of the hundred or so tables and chairs on which the students had taken their examination, in order to clear a space for Year Seven basketball practice that afternoon.

"If we get this done quickly," said Jack, "there'll be time for a snog in the storeroom."

Robert paused and eyed the English boy. "That is quite an unseemly phrase," he said.

"I am feeling quite unseemly," admitted Jack. "We haven't had a grope for four days."

"A grope?"

Jack nodded slowly, trying to hide a grin, while Robert scanned the hall and its purlieus for interlopers.

***

Charlie Masefield had hardly said a word to them since their falling out at the leisure centre, and though they still gathered together at their usual table the atmosphere was uncomfortable for all. After a week of this, even Max was finding it difficult to jolly things along, while Mandy – when not glaring at Charlie – had her head buried in a book.

Thus, after they had eaten, Jack and Robert were glad to get out of the canteen and walk to their prearranged destination, the bench on the edge of the cricket pitch. A rendezvous that was far enough away from the school to have their mobile phones switched on without incurring the wrath of the rule-makers. High in the near-cloudless sky the sun shone down, casting shadows so foreshortened that they were hardly there at all. Jack held his jacket by the loop, letting it hang over his shoulder, while Robert carried his neatly folded over his arm.

"Could Stewy tell you anything useful when he rang?" asked the American.

"When he was driven to this place, which must be the farm they took Alan to, he said the van always turned in to the right."

"That should halve the number."

"He said that he wasn't even aware that the family owned a farm."

"Are you looking forward to meeting Mrs Chambers?"

"I don't know, eighty-three-year-olds? I don't think we'll have much in common."

"It was kind of her to offer to put Stewart up."

"Well, it's only three days before they move, anyway."

"What time is his train due?"

"Ten fifteen... Hey, look who's there!" Jack waved at the distant figure of a girl who had emerged from the trees at the edge of Woolgrove Wood and was hurrying back towards the school.

"And look who's there," said Robert, pointing to a boy who was sauntering diagonally towards their bench, having come from the same location.

***

When they reached the bench, Dan was already seated, fidgeting with his smartphone. "I've been waiting ages," he said.

"Ages as in a minute," said Jack, "since we were watching you and Sophie making out under the trees over there."

"Peeping toms," said the boy. "Still, I can understand it. I expect you were wanting a few tips on technique."

Jack sat down beside his brother and nudged him with his shoulder. "I expect Mr Peebles was watching you too, through his binoculars."

"Ugh! Do you think he wanks off on it?"

Robert frowned disapprovingly, which was just what Dan wanted. He looked up at the American with a grin on his face and tapped the bench next to him.

Robert took up the offer and sat down, primly draping his jacket over his knees. "You English boys take crudity to the next level."

"Sophie seemed in a hurry to get away from you," observed Jack.

"It's just her period," replied Dan, nonchalantly.

"Oh God! At least that's something we gay boys don't have to worry about."

"I don't even know what it means," admitted Robert, and when he saw the two brothers open their mouths to explain, he put up his hand. "And don't want to, thanks all the same!"

Dan showed them his phone screen, on which was an aerial view of Swanford. "I put two circles around the town at six and eight mile radii, to correspond to a ten-minute drive, then, given the direction the van was travelling, eliminated all but the south-west quadrant. That gives us twenty-three farms."

"That's a lot of farms!" said Robert.

"Yes, but then I excluded all those that did bed and breakfast."

"Good thinking, LB."

"That left twelve. Then I took only those with entrances on the right-hand side of the road travelling from Swanford and we're in luck – that left only four; Yew Tree, Orchard, Bridge and Folly Farm, which also has a stables."

"I don't think Stewy mentioned horses – in fact, he couldn't hear much at all."

"I've looked at them on Street View, and I think we can discount Orchard Farm."

"Why?"

Dan showed them a picture of the beautifully restored and appointed farm with its swimming pool, gazebo, solarium and neatly trimmed lawns, all set behind electronic gates.

"I see what you mean. Celebrityville."

"The others are pretty much what you'd expect, so Justin and I will go and recce them over the next week."

"This is brilliant work, LB."

"So, the big day is set for Sunday 23rd," mused Robert. "But I hate to think what might happen to him between now and then."

***

32: Tuesday, 11th June. 10.35 a.m. Swanford Community School.

DAN

Assembly's finished early as it's still only Years Seven to Nine attending, so I thought I'd get some water at the drinking fountain before break. There's three of these in an alcove just outside the canteen and they're usually pretty busy, but as luck – or bad luck – would have it, the only other person there this morning is Noah Marshall.

I don't think anyone would believe he's a Year Nine, because he's not only a lot shorter than me, but also really skinny – he has no muscle and no fat. Which makes his head seem all the more funny, really, because it is, like, oversized for his body, or is his body undersized for his head? Whatever, it sort of looks like his head is as wide as his body.

As soon as he sees me he brushes his hair down, then flicks it so that it's just covering his right eye. I hadn't noticed before, but it's got dark blue streaks in it and it's very gay. He's hovering, I can see that, which may mean he's either waiting for someone or wanting to avoid someone.

"Hi," I say and bend to take a drink.

He kind of sighs back at me and I notice he's trying to hide his hands, which makes them all the more obvious. The skin on the backs and between the fingers is all dry and shiny red, and I know it's eczema, because I've had it and I still get the odd patch here and there especially on my forehead. I've got a tube of Betnovate which I keep in my bedside drawer, just in case.

"You've got eczema," I say, which isn't the greatest opening line to say to someone you don't know, especially as skin problems are a really sensitive subject in my age group. I see his blush and look of horror. "I get it too," I add quickly, and this seems to relax him.

"What do you use?" he asks after a pause, and his voice isn't level but seems to rise and fall for no reason.

"Betnovate."

"I haven't tried that; my doctor gives me Synalar-N."

"When I was twelve I had it in my scalp and I was given Synalar gel. That was the worst time with it. My mum gave me a number-one clipper cut. I think I've got seborrhoeic eczema, which is different but the same, if you know what I mean."

Noah smiles. "It really makes me itchy. I want to scratch and scratch and scratch."

"They made me wear a pair of gloves taped on with Elastoplast."

He peers at me through his one visible eye. "There's no sign of it on you."

"No, I haven't had any since last winter. It seems to come and go without reason."

He shows me the back of his left hand, which is really red and scabby. He's trembling a bit, so I hold his fingers. It's not catching. "You've been scratching this," I observe.

"Sorry, Doctor," he replies and we both laugh. "Noah," he says and holds out his right hand.

"Dan, Dan Moseley."

"Ouch!" he says when I grip his hand to shake, and he's not joking because his own grip is quite girly.

100

"Why are you shaking hands with him?" says a voice behind me. I turn and recognise Logan Atkins and with him is his friend Jacob Lively. They may be in Year Nine, but they're so low in the pecking order that I'm not afraid of them.

"What's it got to do with you?" I ask.

"It's since they became good church-going Christians," says Noah. "They're doing God's work."

"You know he's a homo, don't you?" Jacob asks me.

"A what?" I counter.

"A homo, a homosexual."

"What does that mean?"

Jacob looks at me to see if I'm being serious, then he takes a step forward and whispers, "It means he wants to put his thing up your rear end."

"Is that what they teach you about at your church?" I ask. "Putting your things up boys' rear ends?"

I hear Noah chuckle and Jacob goes so red that his acne looks like it's about to spontaneously combust.

"He's probably one of them, as well," Logan says, giving me the evil eye.

"You'll have to ask my girlfriend about that," I reply. Yeh, I know that's a pretty overused phrase, but it is true in my case.

"They can turn you into one of them, if you let them," warns Jacob and I laugh in his face. "Does your church give you perches to sit on as well? Because you sound like two, fucking, squawking parrots." Actually, I'm getting angry now which is not good.

"Dan," says Noah, "chill, they've been brainwashed."

"Shut up, Marshall," says Logan. "We aren't done with you."

Jacob slaps his friend on the arm. "Let's get out of here before we're infected too."

The two of them sidle away and except for the noise from the canteen all is silent again.

"Is that why you came here, to get away from them?" I ask.

"Something like that. I have been getting a bit more hassle than usual."

I nod, then realise I haven't got anything more to say to him. "Well, I'll see you around."

"See you, and thanks for being there. At least I don't feel so alone now."

I turn back to him. "You're not alone, Noah. Listen, if anything serious starts happening come and talk to me or my brother Jack. Do you know him? He's in Year Ten."

Noah shakes his head and I can see he's wondering what's going on, so I try to lay it on the line. "Those two jerks we just dealt with are amateurs. There's worse than them, and because you're openly gay there's a chance you may get involved."

Now he looks twice as worried and his expression makes me laugh. "Noah!" I say. "It's OK, honestly, just... you know..."

"Keep calm and carry on?" he suggests, and his head appears to have blown up like a balloon on his little shoulders.

"Yes, exactly!" I give him what I hope is a reassuring grin, then toddle off to find Justin, feeling pretty chuffed with myself.

***

33: Tuesday, 11th June. 5 p.m. 34b Savoy Flats.

NOAH

The Savoy Flats where I live are just off the high street. 'Savoy' makes them sound posh, but they're anything but. Some people call them the Allfours, because there's four four-storey blocks, with four flats to each storey, interconnected by walkways. They form a square and in the centre is supposed to be the communal garden, but it's more like the communal rubbish dump. People throw their bin bags, old mattresses and

TVs out of the windows. The dustmen come once a year and clear it. That's the week the rats go on their holidays.

The flats used to belong to the council, but they were sold off to a private company about twenty years ago. What's strange about this is that the council now pays this company to take their tenants they can't house anywhere else. So we've got our share of addicts, head cases, disabled people, long-term sick and those with a condition known as general malaise.

I live with my dad in this uplifting environment. Fancy that – a girly gay boy living with his dad and not his over-protective outrageous mother. According to my dad, my mum got sick of him when I was three and went to live with a bank clerk on the Prestleigh Road. They were never married, anyway. I keep promising myself that I'll find out exactly where my mum lives and call in for a visit. "Hi, Mum, I'm your son Noah. You left me when I was three and now I'm a fourteen-year-old effeminate homosexual." Cue for celebrations. On second thoughts, maybe I won't bother.

Everyone at school has known for years that I'm gay – well, a year in July actually – so why have Logan and Jacob started to hate me now instead of just ignoring me like they have done in the past? I've seen others giving me dirty looks too, as though I've just been wiped off someone's shoe. Hey, folks! I'm still the same boring, ugly, forgettable Noah I always was. There was one compensation today: Dan Moseley. Why does my heart flutter when I say that name? Dan Moseley. He may only be in Year Eight, but he has everything a boy desires. Even *I* know he plays football. I wonder what he looks like in his kit? More to the point, I wonder what he looks like without his kit! Trouble is, one swallow doesn't make a summer. I'll probably never talk to him again. Sigh...

At school there's an area of the canteen which I call the wasteland. This is the part just beyond the potted palms and trellis. There's five square tables all in a row, occupied by the least popular pupils in each year. Naturally, I fall into that category. There are some even more unpopular than me, but that's because they either smell or are sociopaths. I sit with

Anne Marie Leonard and Paul Sharpe. I think out of school they are full emo types, whereas at school they're just miserable gits wearing as much black stuff as they can get away with. Anne Marie is always moaning to me that she would have been better off in a boy's body, but the way she looks at Paul Sharpe, and he at her, makes me think differently. Sometimes they make me feel like the original gooseberry fool. I suppose she could want to be a gay boy, but I don't think Paul Sharpe would fancy her/him then. The thing is, I don't fancy either of them, Anne Marie because she's a girl and Paul Sharpe because he's just too much hard work.

My dad is a barber – not a hairdresser, a barber. He cuts the hair of doddery old men and charges them a fiver. He also cuts mine and charges me nothing. I like the way he cuts my hair. He does it exactly as I want, with a long fringe covering my right eye, and short back and sides. The fringe is my fashion statement, but it's also there so I don't have to see my face in totality when I look in the mirror. Of the many faces I see each day, mine is the most stupid. I'm fourteen and have got a snub nose like a two-year-old, except it's big. Once I looked up *lips* on the internet to see who had them like mine. The only person I could find was this film star from a hundred years ago called Clara Bow. Only I don't need any lipstick to make them that shape.

Now, about my head. As you may have heard, it's big – that is, it's big in relation to the rest of me. No, I'll be truthful and say it's big anyway. It's like Humpty Dumpty before he had a great fall. Recently, though, I've noticed that my hands and feet are also getting ridiculously large compared to my body. I've decided I'm turning into the Creature from the Black Lagoon. Any day now, I expect to wake up and find I've grown gills.

Anyway, as I said, my dad is a barber, which means we've got no money. Once he showed me a paper which said that his occupation is the lowest-paid in the country. Typical! The rent for our measly two-bedroom flat on the top floor of block three is £330 a month. And measly is what my bedroom is. I have a single bed, a desk and a cupboard, all left over from World War II, and I have to edge in sideways. We had to alter the door so it opened outwards. The kitchen is full of antique appliances that behave as they want, not as we want. The living room is separate – that is, separated by a door – and is a riot of mid-twentieth-century furniture. It is also lit by a fluorescent lamp. It's not a straight one, though, like you'd see in a chip shop; it's circular. That doesn't mean the light is any better, and I hate it. It makes the room look cold and the people in it have their skin turned the colour of vampires. But the bathroom is the worst; it's got black mould growing up the wall in one corner. This is because it hasn't got any windows and relies on an extractor fan that is so full of dust it doesn't whirr, it coughs. If I had any friends, how could I possibly invite them in and not be embarrassed by all this luxury?

As well as the flat rent, my dad has to pay £180 per month for his shop. Which isn't a shop at all. It's two rooms in a slummy house on Victoria Street. That's the street that had a gay bar on it, before the council closed it down as a danger to public morals. I've heard that two sixth formers from school used to go there, but I haven't found out who they are. We keep our bike in the back room of the shop, along with various boxes of razor blades, combs, gels and condoms which no one ever buys because they can get them for half the price at the supermarket. I keep telling Dad to have a grand sale, but he won't. I expect the condoms are way past their 'best before' date. We've got no car, obviously, and we can only afford one bike. I ride it to school most days then cycle back to the shop and walk home from there. Our dad only uses it when he thinks he needs to do some exercise, which means hardly ever.

Our dad is forty-one years old and yet he acts like the old pensioners whose hair he cuts. He has to wear glasses, because if he didn't there'd be body parts all over the floor of his shop. When he comes home he takes them off and then stumbles around for ten minutes trying to find them. He's also bald – well, he's got some hair, mostly grey, round the back and sides. At least he isn't one of those men that hide their bald patch by swirling what they've got left onto the top of their heads. That is so naff. What if I go bald by forty-one? I'll really look like Humpty Dumpty then. Oh my God! If I don't find someone to love me soon I'll be over the hill and into terminal spinsterhood.

Which brings me on to my other problem: eczema. Dan Moseley was really nice to me about it, but what he doesn't know is that I haven't just got it on my hands, but in my groin area as well. Oh yes, to add to my problems, Noah has an itchy, red, flaky groin. Time to run for the hills, folks! When I first noticed it, I thought it might help to shave my pubes. It's not as though I'm Chewbacca down there anyway, but no, no, no, never again! It made it twenty – no, a hundred – times worse. I only did one side and the itch was so bad it gives me the shakes just thinking about it. My dad made an appointment for me at the docs and so with a red, partly hairless groin and an even redder face I went down to the health centre.

Fortunately I saw no-nonsense Doctor Clarke. She just drew on a pair of rubber gloves, gave me the once-over and prescribed Nizoral Anti-Dandruff shampoo and more Synalar-N. Shampoo for my pubes? I thought she was joking, but she told me it's all hair and to get a grip. They've grown back now anyway, and it's just a low-level irritant at the moment.

***

34: Thursday, 13th June. 6.30 p.m. 15 Leighton Lane.

PAM

Pam laid the latest edition of the *Swanford Mail* in the centre of the table, hoping that it would lead to a conversation with Jack. Under the headline *Bashed by Gays! Exclusive by John Little* there was a half-page full colour photograph of Alan Henderson's face, barely recognisable because of his injuries and the Photoshop enhancement.

The garden gate banged shut and Pam watched her eldest son wheel his bike up the garden path. He's going to drop it just by the kitchen door, she thought, then frowned as she heard the inevitable clatter.

"Hello dear," she said as he came into the kitchen. "Have you ever tried propping your bike up instead of just letting it fall?"

He blinked at her. "What's for tea?"

"Quiche and salad."

Why doesn't he tell me he's gay?

"Hmm, quiche again. You ought to see what they've done to number 41."

"I will see, won't I, on Sunday?"

Jack kicked off his trainers. "You're not going to come in, are you? That would be so embarrassing."

"You don't think I'm going to drive you all the way to the station and back and not say just a quick hello to Mrs Chambers, do you?"

"But I know what one of your 'quick hellos' is like – they last for hours. In fact, Mrs Chambers is so old she'll probably be dead by the time you've finished saying hello."

"Don't be ridiculous, dear."

Why doesn't he tell me he's gay?

"Better get changed then. Dad not home?"

"Another meeting, that's all he seems to do these days."

Jack went to the sink and filled a glass with water. "LB not in?"

"In his room, but he's got company..."

"Sophie?"

"Sophie, yes..."

Why doesn't he tell me he's gay?

"Has he been issued with the extra-strength condoms?"

"Don't be rude, dear."

"It's not rude. You know what these young people are like..."

"Hi!" said Mikey.

107

"Avast there, me hearty pest, isn't it about time you got rid of that plaster cast?"

Mikey looked up at Jack, then at his mother, then back at Jack. "What's extra-strength condoms?"

"Oh, they're things you put on your..."

"Jack!" said Pam. "Tea is nearly ready, go and get changed."

Don't tell me you're gay now, whatever you do! Why ever did I put that awful picture on the table?

"Mum..."

"Yes dear?" *Oh, here it comes. I shall have to clench my teeth and keep smiling.*

"When does Mikey have his plaster off?"

"I'm taking him next week to see the consultant, and he might be put in a half-cast."

"Good!"

"Why do you say *good* like that?"

"Because his cheesy feet stink."

Mikey giggled.

"They most certainly do not!"

Mikey sat on a chair and lifted his leg into the air. "Jack, come and smell my cheesy feet."

Jack swallowed the last of the water and put the glass in the washing-up bowl. "Don't be disgusting pest, or I won't buy you a parrot for Christmas."

"Jack! You haven't promised him a parrot, have you?"

"I think I might have done, actually..."

"I want a green Amazonian," said Mikey, who had been on Wikipedia.

"Mikey, we cannot afford to look after a parrot, Jack cannot afford to buy a parrot, you are not having a parrot."

"He could have a stuffed one."

"Yeh!" agreed Mikey.

Jack glanced at the *Swanford Mail*. "Why have you put that stupid newspaper in the middle of the table instead of in the bin where it belongs?"

"Are you going to the gym tonight, dear?"

"Of course I'm going to the gym, what else would I be doing on a Thursday night?"

"Well, don't forget next Monday."

"What?"

"You know perfectly well what. Your father and I are going out for a little celebration."

"Oh that! How many years is it? A century?"

"Twenty happy years."

"So I've got to suffer by staying in and looking after your afterthought."

"Mikey is not an afterthought. Why don't you invite Robert round for tea or something?"

"Yeh!" cried Mikey.

Jack pretended to have a fit. "Because, Mother dear, Robert's parents think we are all spawn of Satan, which means he has to lie every time he leaves the house, which he doesn't like doing..."

"Am I a spawn of Satan?" asked Mikey.

"No, you *are* Satan. Now, grab your crutches – sorry, crutch – and I'll carry you upstairs so we can have some fun annoying LB and Sophie until teatime."

Mikey nodded vigorously, and held up his arms.

"You'll do no such thing, Jack Moseley."

Jack hoisted Mikey into his arms. "Don't worry, we'll be the souls of discretion..."

***

35: Thursday, 13th June. 6.45 p.m. 15 Leighton Lane.

JACK

"Lower away there, matey," said Mikey at the top of the stairs.

"We're not going to disturb LB; that was just to wind Mum up," said Jack, setting him down.

A voice came through Dan's open door. "It's OK, Jack, there's not much going on in here."

Mikey hopped across the landing and into the bedroom. Jack followed.

"Where's Sophie?" the little boy asked, looking round, perplexed.

"In the bathroom."

The toilet flushed and a moments later Sophie meandered in and collapsed onto the bed, a pillow clutched to her stomach. She groaned.

"Did you take the ibuprofen?" asked Dan.

The girl nodded. Mikey hoisted himself onto the bed beside her and put an arm around her waist. "Sophie's ill, shipmates."

"I'm not ill, darling," she replied, "it's girl problems."

"Then I be glad I'm not a girl," said Mikey, opening one eye wide and closing the other.

"You're the nearest thing to a girl in this house," said Dan.

Mikey pointed his crutch at Dan. "Arr, if I 'ears any more of your sauce, I'll clap 'e in irons."

"What a precious he is," laughed Sophie.

"What a show-off, you mean," said Jack.

"He's making me feel better anyway... a bit."

"Does this happen every month?" asked Jack.

Sophie shook her head. "Not normally quite as bad."

"You haven't noticed my latest dartboard, have you?" said Dan, pointing to a picture cut from the *Swanford Mail* which was pinned to his real dartboard.

Jack walked over to study it. "Robert told me about this. Do you know any of these dickheads?"

"Jack swore," said Mikey.

Dan came to stand just behind his brother. "I had a run-in with Logan Atkins the other day. He's the one with his hair combed forward, wearing the blue sweater. The boy standing next to him with the terrible acne is his best friend Jacob Lively. They're both in Year Nine."

"The other Lively," went on Sophie, "is Joanna, but you should recognise her, Jack, she's in your year."

"Yeh, I recognise her by sight," he replied, "she's Jason Spriggs' girlfriend."

"Jason Spriggs knocks about with Ben Henderson – at least, at school they do," said Sophie.

"That figures," remarked Jack. "I can tell even on a photograph that Lucas, the younger Spriggs, is creeping around Patrick Johns."

"Patrick Johns is hot," said Sophie. "All the girls think so."

"The one I know best," stated Dan, ignoring the comment, "is Harry Lewis. He's in my year – that's him, the tall one with short fair hair, and the smaller lookalike is his brother Adam, who's in Year Seven."

"Then that must be their older sister," said Jack, pointing to an attractive girl with long wavy hair. "I think her name's Sarah; she's in the lower sixth."

"Jack, if your friend Robert goes to this church, why isn't he in the photo?" queried Sophie.

"Because he's got more sense than to want his picture in this comic."

"My parents are thinking of going next Sunday," admitted Sophie.

"Why?" asked Dan.

Sophie shrugged. "Dunno. I doubt if I'll go, but a few of the girls were talking about it."

"Tea's ready!" shouted Pam from the bottom of the stair.

Sophie groaned and hugged the pillow even closer. "I'll have to give it a miss, Danny. Sorry... I'll just stay here and have a little sleep, if I can."

***

<u>ROGER</u>

Jack walked into the kitchen dressed only in a towel, with water still dripping off him from a shower. "Dad?"

Roger looked up nervously from his breakfast cereal. "Hello, Jack, there's plenty of toast if you want it."

"Dad, where's Mum?"

He's looking a bit furtive, thought Roger. I hope this isn't going to be the moment. He's caught me on the hop and his mother isn't here. *Help!* "She was called into the post office. Someone's off sick."

"Dad... I..."

Oh, lord! He's hesitating. It must be. It must be. "Aren't you going to be late for your paper round?"

"My round's in the afternoon."

Damn! Of course it is. What am I going to say? It would be far better if he told his mother. I'm not in to this confessional, heart-on-sleeve, reality TV type dramatics, like Pam is. I know, I shan't look at him. He may chicken out. I'm not ready!

"Dad..."

God, I suppose it must be taking him an awful lot of courage to do this. Doesn't he know that he's my son and I love him? "Why don't you go and get dressed and—"

"But Dad!"

"Jack, it doesn't matter. I know... your mother knows. We're happy for you, don't worry, we'll support you and Robert in any way we can. OK?"

Did I do it right? Just be calm. Eat some more cereal, like everything's normal and you're really relaxed about it, even though my hand's shaking and I can hardly hold this spoon. Oh God! Why is he looking at me like that? Why has he started shivering? Why is he just wearing that towel? And is that water or are there tears in his eyes?

"Jack, I told you, why don't you go and put some clothes on, before you catch a chill?"

"Dad, that's what I was going to tell you. There aren't any clean clothes in the airing cupboard."

Father and son looked at each other for a long moment, then Roger put down his spoon, got up from the table, walked over to Jack and took him in his arms. "Let's go and find some, then, shall we?"

***

37: Saturday, 15th June. 11 p.m. Pear Tree Cottage, The Ropewalk.

ROBERT

That's my phone vibrating. It must be Jack. Who else would phone me at this hour? Talk of the devil...

"Hello Jack, guess who I was just thinking of?"

"Er... Patrick Johns?"

Ah, this is going to be one of those conversations the English like, where you make up some stuff, the ruder the better, and it all has double meanings but doesn't actually mean anything at all.

"How did you know?"

"I've seen the way you look at him when he's doing those Bible readings in assembly."

"You know I'm a sucker for those dark-haired types."

"Am I a dark-haired type?"

"You might be."

"And did you say... you're a sucker?"

Uh-oh, I know where this is going and he's making me blush, even though no one can see me.

"Are you blushing, Robert Crittenden?"

"Oh Jack, stop it..."

"I'd like to, though, wouldn't you?"

"Oh God, Jack..."

"Go on, say you would.."

"Maybe. I don't know!"

"Are you as excited as I am, just thinking about it?"

"I'll ring you back in five minutes."

***

"Jack?"

"I was unseemly, wasn't I?"

"Very."

"Good, though."

"Hmm, that's as maybe..."

"I love it when you're all stern and buttoned up."

"Jack!"

"Sorry... Actually, I've got something to tell you."

"What?"

"Now, keep calm and take it easy..."

This can only mean one thing and I'm panicking already.
"Go on..."

"My parents know about us, but it's OK..."

"OK! How can it be OK? You didn't tell them, did you,
Jack?"

"No, my dad *told me* this morning. He was really nice
about it."

"But how? Not Dan?"

"Mikey."

"Mikey!"

"Ssssh! That sounded way too loud."

That was too loud, but fortunately Dad's in the shower
and Mom's downstairs in the kitchen sorting out menus for
next week. Jack was just telling me how Mikey sneaked into
his room that day we were in bed together. This is getting mad.
Like a leaky bucket with more and more holes in it. One day
all this is going to blow up in my face. I know it would be
better for me to confront my parents before they learn about it
from some other source, but it won't be easy like it has been
for Jack. He seems to be blessed. His mom even wanted to

invite me over on Monday. I wish I could, but I mustn't think about that...

"OK, I've calmed down a bit."

"Good."

"You're not going to hit me with any more bombshells, are you?"

"No; it was Stewy's birthday today so we all took him to the Roxy and then the Jewel."

"I wish I'd been there."

"I wish you had been. Stewy practically wet himself when Mandy gave him a card."

"That boy needs to lower his sights."

"Ahh, he's really cute, you know, when you get to know him, and not half as thick as people think."

"I'll take your word for it."

"Are you set for tomorrow?"

"Yeh, it shouldn't be a problem."

"And you've got Dan's number?"

"Jack, you're the worrier on this. My job's easy."

"Dan and Justin are doing the first recce tomorrow; they may even get two done."

"Which two?"

"Yew Tree and Folly Farm, they're about two miles apart."

"I still don't really understand why Dan is so determined to help Alan Henderson after what he did."

"Robert Crittenden, I just don't get why as a practising Christian you don't understand the word *forgiveness?*"

Well, he's just put me in my place there, and of course he's right. I'm going to have to do some serious praying.

***

38: Sunday, 16th June. 3.30 p.m. 41 Westbury Avenue.

PAM

Even though I can only imagine what it was like before, I can tell they've done a top-drawer job on the house. This sitting room is very comfortable, and so tastefully decorated. All the furniture and carpets are new, the windows are huge, and there are French doors, all double-glazed. It smells of fresh paint and there's some lovely William Morris design wallpaper, which would look overpowering in a small room, but in here it just suits. I think there were only coal fires in the house before – for goodness' sake, what a drudge for an elderly lady, especially in winter – but now the whole place is centrally heated. The old mantelpieces have been kept, however, and those real-flame gas fires installed. Either side of the chimney breast are a matching pair of solid walnut bookcases. I don't know whether they are custom-made or not, but they fit perfectly from wall to ceiling and the shelves must contain a thousand books between them.

I suspect that Mrs Chambers is a woman of considerable means. She was in the Colonial Medical Service and then became a GP, and her husband had a very swanky photographic business. There are quite a few examples of his work around the house. They're all in black and white, even the landscapes, and beautifully framed. They're not really for me, though, but Stewart loves them, I know that because he'll notice one and just stare at it for the longest time.

He is a funny little boy, Stewart – well, I say little. He's fifteen now and almost as old as Jack; it's just that he seems so young in comparison, though he must have a lot of grit, knowing what he's been through. I'm not sure I like seeing the grown-up Jack. When we were coming up in the car and they were chatting in the back, it was as though he was a completely different person. I probably don't know the half, because I could see both of them through the mirror sometimes glancing at me and abruptly shutting down the conversation. Obviously Stewart is fully aware that Jack is gay and Robert's his boyfriend, and he seems rather to revel in it. I'm still not quite able to use that word – boyfriend – without feeling odd, but I expect I'll get used to it. I suppose I shouldn't have been eavesdropping anyway, not that I understood half of what they were talking about. Stewart treats Jack like some wise old uncle. It may be that's how Dan sees him as well. Perhaps this is the real Jack, and the stroppy teenage boy that Roger and I know is only a small part of him. Heaven knows what he and Robert get up to...

Mind you, they are still boys. Both Stewart and Jack had to have a go on the stair lift and I must say I wouldn't have refused a turn myself. I think I would call Mrs Chambers formidable – I hardly dare call her Elspeth – she's very tall and bony and I guess she was a real beauty in her day. At eighty-three it's not surprising she has a bit of a stoop, but she's still able to bustle around on those new hips, though she soon gets tired and flops into her chair; it's the type that tips you in and tips you out. One of those would suit me down to the ground. She's got to manage on her own until Wednesday, although she will have Stewart with her and she's not going to starve because the fridge and freezer are stacked out with food, mostly from Marks & Spencer, I noticed.

While Elspeth is entertaining me with afternoon tea – lovely old country-rose bone china service – the boys are upstairs. I hope they aren't getting into mischief. I think Anne Waverly has definitely fallen on her feet coming here. She seems a very friendly person, if a little driven. There are five bedrooms, a bathroom, box room and a separate toilet. The biggest one has been transformed into a lounge for them, and both she and Stewart have their own bedrooms and the box room has been made up for little Alex. I call it a box room, but it's probably bigger than Mikey's at home. That leaves two guest bedrooms, both at least the size of mine and Rog's. Do I sound like a jealous cow? I have to confess, I might be a bit.

The kitchen must have been enormous, like in a country house, because it still seems spacious compared to our poky one at home, yet half of it has been converted to a separate utility room. It's like the engineer's deck of a spaceship, because it's all white and most of the household controls are in here.

Oh, I just must mention Mrs Chambers' – Elspeth's – bedroom. It was the huge front room and I suspect it was never used much. Now it has a fully en suite bathroom. It's one of those with a door in the bath, a tiled floor with a drain in the centre, handles all over the place and even a toilet seat that lifts you off. What will they think of next?

Her bed is a four poster with red drapes. I could see she thought it a ridiculous extravagance, but an enjoyable one nonetheless. It certainly made our old Silentnight seem superannuated. The bay window has tinted glass so no one can see in – not that they would anyway, because the trees in the front garden practically hide the house, and the curtains are electronically operated. Well, they're made of such heavy material you'd need to be Mr Universe to draw them.

I think I should be going now; I can see Elspeth's ready to nod off. Maybe I'll just wash the cups. Jack said he'd walk home, which means those boys are plotting again. I haven't seen them for an hour or more. They're exploring in the cellar. I know they would think me an old witch if I barged in on their territory so I'll forego the pleasure, though I am tempted.

***

39: Sunday, 16th June. 4.15 p.m. 41 Westbury Avenue.

<u>JACK</u>

I'm looking at Stewart and he's grinning at me, because he knows how embarrassed I am. Are all mothers like mine? Talk about nosey. Anyway, she's gone.

We've been down in the cellar for the past hour or so, to be out of the way. This is where the workmen put all the stuff they didn't throw into skips. There's plenty of floor space, but I'm practically bumping my head on the ceiling and there's just one light bulb. Stewy has found all that darkroom equipment from upstairs and a box of old photographs together with their negatives – that's a word he's taught me. He wants

118

to take them and store them somewhere else so they don't go mouldy, which is probably wise because it has that earthy, musty smell down here.

I forgot that we'd lose phone reception in the cellar, so when we got back up I found three messages waiting. The first was another one from Robert about geography revision, so I texted him back saying I'd ring tonight. Hmm! And two were from LB, so I'm going to ring him now.

"Hey, LB, sorry. We've been hiding from Mum in the cellar."

"Jack, it looks like Folly Farm. The Hendersons' white van was poking out from behind the house."

"What's the place like?"

"A slum. Justin brought his binoculars, so we didn't need to get too close. Everywhere's overgrown and I don't think there are any horses in the stables. In any case, there are holes in the roof. I guess they hire the place out to riders, because there's a paddock with fences."

"What about the house itself?"

"I wouldn't want to live in it."

"Well, it looks like we're on for next Sunday, then. Did you get the text from Robert?"

"Yup, I assume it was the same as yours: *Church full. Alan and John not present.*"

"If that happens next Sunday, we should be OK."

"It'll be a doddle, just like today. We're at Larch Farm now. We met up with some of the team to do a bit of swimming and some lazing around."

"Good one, LB. I'll see you tonight, back at the ranch."

"How's Stewy?"

"Here he is, find out for yourself..."

"Hello, Dan. I'm OK. Thanks for the card. You should have come last night, we had a great time."

"You know what they're like at the Roxy with their fifteen rules. It'd be too embarrassing to get barred."

"I had to show them my ID card before they'd let me in. Hey Dan, they've done this place up really well. You can come over any time, you know."

"That'd be good. Don't suppose you're looking forward to tomorrow?"

"No way. They're sending a taxi to pick me up, otherwise I think I might chicken out..."

Stewy hands back my phone and says he wants to confess to Mrs Chambers about his occupation of her house. He wants me to be there too, which is fair enough. The only trouble is, he wants to do it now!

So here we are, hovering outside the sitting room as the old lady calls it, and Stewy is getting up the courage to knock. When he finally does, there's a pause before we get a 'hello, come in', and we enter to find Mrs Chambers sitting bolt upright in her chair, having probably just woken from a nap.

"Come in, boys, there's no need to knock on an open door. Help yourselves to the cakes. I bought them specially and they need eating up."

Well, that's an offer we can't refuse, but once we're sitting on the new sofa, I have to shove a plate under Stewy's nose to stop him from dropping crumbs all over the place.

"Mrs Chambers, I lived in your house for a few weeks while you were in hospital," Stewy blurts out, going very red and nearly choking on his cream horn.

To her credit, the old lady doesn't flinch or show any reaction, except I think she might be slightly amused by the performance. I was not quite sure how much Stewy's mum had told her about his recent past, and now it seems she hasn't told her very much.

"You know, I thought it was strange how, from the moment you walked in, you seemed to be familiar with the layout of the house. Were you party to this intrusion, Jack?"

I nod, but before I can say anything Stewy's speaking again. "Jack was only helping me; it's not his fault. It's not Mum's fault either – she knew nothing about it. Are you going to send me away?"

"I very much doubt it, Stewart, but I should be very interested to learn the motive for your curious behaviour."

"It's a long story, Mrs Chambers. Have you seen last week's local newspaper?"

"I may have, but I'm afraid I would classify much of what I find in the media these days as instantly forgettable tittle-tattle. Though I do recollect seeing a picture of an unfortunate boy on the front of last week's paper who had been the victim of an assault."

"That's my brother, Alan," says Stewart.

"Gracious!" exclaims the old lady, picking up her spectacles from the occasional table. "Jack, would you mind fishing the edition out of the magazine rack over there?"

I hand the copy of the *Swanford Mail* over to her and she holds it up, looking first at the picture, then at Stewart, and finally back at the picture. "I see very little resemblance," she says. "Not that you can tell much from these manipulated photographs."

"How did you know it had been altered?" I ask, to which Stewart gives me a sideways look.

"It's a very shoddy job, especially with all the new techniques they have now. In my husband's day it was often done with no more than a fine sable brush and Indian ink."

Of course, that makes me feel a fool because I'd forgotten that photography was such a big part of her everyday life. "Sorry, Mrs Chambers," I say. "I'm being a dunce." And Stewy gives me a wry smile, as if agreeing with me.

The old lady waves the apology away and continues to scan the paper. "Bashed by gays, exclusive by... My fourteen-year-old son was the victim of a homosexual attack, alleged his father, who cannot be named for legal reasons... How interesting. You know, the press are always able to print a story the way their proprietor wants it."

I trade a glance with Stewart, and it's clear he doesn't understand the remark any more than I do.

"Mrs Chambers, Alan was assaulted by my brothers, just as I was, and that's why I left home and hid here. My dad knows what's going on as well and is just trying to shift the blame onto gay people, because he hates gays. Oh, and Alan is thirteen, by the way."

"And where is your brother now?"

Stewy looks at me and I look at Mrs Chambers. I don't know if I trust her enough to give away our plans or the reasons for them – after all, only four of us know the whole story and, in my opinion, the fewer the better. It also strikes me that she is a good listener, which is an excellent way of getting more information out of a person than they would normally divulge, whether for good or ill.

"Could Alan come to stay with me for a little while?" asks Stewart. "He wouldn't be any bother, you'll hardly know he was here."

Wouldn't be any bother? You'll hardly know he was here! If this sounds far-fetched to me, what must it sound like to her? But clearly this has been Stewy's plan all along. It's also a fact that I had given no thought to what would happen to Alan once we got him away from his brothers.

"You didn't answer my question," says Mrs Chambers.

Stewart turns to me. "What shall I say?"

"Whatever you think is best," I reply and, feeling I'm copping out, add, "I'd go for it."

"Mrs Chambers, will you promise me you won't speak of this to anyone, not even my mum?"

The old lady takes off her glasses, and her eyes, which usually look quite dim, have a sort of gleam in them. "I shall give you my word, on one condition..."

We both nod our agreement and she continues: "From this moment on, I want you to call me Elspeth. If you call me Mrs Chambers again, I shall ignore you."

Stewy gives her one of his cute smiles. "Elspeth... Jack, Dan and Robert are going to rescue him next Sunday."

"Hope to..." I correct.

"I see." She stares at us as if gauging our sanity. "This is all quite a lot to take in at once. Shouldn't the police be involved in something so serious?"

"We don't trust the Swanford police," says Stewart.

I expect an eighty-three-year-old brain needs more time to process information than a fifteen-year-old one, because there's quite a long pause before she speaks again. "Jack, perhaps you would be kind enough to make us all a fresh pot of tea while Stewart explains himself in some more detail?"

It takes me about ten minutes to do a job which normally takes a minute. I'm not used to teapots or milk jugs, but at least Mum laid out the cups on a tray when she washed up. When I return, Stewy and Elspeth are chatting more conversationally and he already has permission to sort through the box of old photographs. I put the tray down beside her on the occasional table and allow her to do the honours. I can see that some of her fingers are a bit gnarled and she has liver spots all over the backs of her hands. Mum has about half as many, but she's always complaining about how old they make her feel.

Elspeth hands me a cup and tells me to help myself to sugar, which I do. I take a quick look at Stewy to see if he's OK, and he appears to be more relaxed now. After we've settled down the old lady turns her attention to us again.

"Boys," she says, "I lived in Aden for five years from 1946, which I know must be the equivalent of ancient history to you, but what Stewart is telling me brings to mind my time there, rather than my subsequent life in a pleasant market town in England."

That sounds to me like she doesn't believe what we're saying, or at least thinks we are exaggerating, but Stewart's mind is clearly on a different track to mine. "You were a doctor, weren't you?" he asks.

"No, not at that time. They didn't employ female doctors in the Colonial Medical Service. I worked as a nurse under my father from 1949. He was a medical officer in the Indian Service and was transferred to Aden after the war. I was interested, he encouraged me and from the age of seventeen, I was on the wards of the Civil Hospital. Patronage was everything in those days, and it didn't take long before I was on the payroll."

"So, you were a nurse and not a doctor?" Clearly Stewy has a bee in his bonnet about this.

"I was everything. Conditions were appalling, equipment was limited and you had to muck in and do your best. Then in 1951 my mother died and my father thought it would be best if I had some proper training, and so I was sent to England. Maybe he had an inkling of what was to come in the colony. I was almost twenty and had never lived in the home country. On my father's recommendation, I got a place in the Royal Free in London, where I stayed for eight years."

"And then you were a doctor!" Stewy states triumphantly.

She smiles at us. "That's right, I was a general practitioner and opened a surgery in Hampstead, where my husband had his photographic business. But Jack, you have a rather quizzical look on your face."

"I was just wondering if you believe what we've been telling you."

"Of course I believe you, and you must do whatever you see fit."

***

40: Monday, 17th June. 12.40 p.m. Swanford Community School

DAN

Sophie and I have just arrived in the canteen. She's feeling better, by the way, so much so that we've been doing a bit of lip-mashing in the dug-out. There's so much more freedom for us lower orders now the upper years are doing exams. Better still, the canteen is only half full because the Year Ten mock geography GCSE was delayed because Mr Joseph is off sick today and they had to find another teacher to stand in.

I see that Justin and Kate are already sitting at our table, and he's just given me a knowing – you've been to the dug-out – look. Meanwhile, Freddie is near the front of the line, probably taking all the best portions. Today, the choice is between chilli with rice (or diarrhoea and grit, as I call it), or vegetarian macaroni cheese (or cheesy vomit, as I call it). Sophie doesn't like me calling food diarrhoea or vomit because it puts her off, which is why I've shortened it to d & g and cheesy v, which even most of the dinner ladies accept as standard ordering terminology.

Suddenly, the level of background chatter falls away and everyone's watching this line of people weaving between the tables, reading aloud from these little black books they are holding. Since a picture of these people is currently occupying my dartboard, I have a good idea of what they're about. And I'm right. They've worked their way beyond the trellis and have gathered round the table occupied by Noah Marshall. I guess they must have spotted that he was on his own today and not sitting with his pseudo-Goth friends.

"Can you get me some d & g and a choco brownie?" I say to Sophie and hand her my tray.

"Where are you going?" she asks and I look at her as though it's obvious.

As I saunter across the canteen, I nod at Justin. Most people have gone back to eating their dinners, but some are still viewing the little gathering with mild curiosity. I look round for prefects, who are supposed to supervise the canteen during lunch, and notice our head boy, Patrick Johns, and two of his assistants sitting not three tables away, doing absolutely nothing.

The penalty for homosexual acts is death to both parties. They have committed a detestable act, and are guilty of a capital offence. They are reading this in unison from their copies of the bigot's Bible, or whatever it is. The ringleader is Sarah Lewis, Year Twelve, and she's with her younger brothers Harry and Adam. Naturally, my two old friends Logan and Jacob make up the quintet.

Meanwhile, Noah is sitting there doing his best to ignore them, but even so five people standing around you inferring that they want you dead is going to have an effect on your appetite and may just worsen your eczema as well.

"Hey, Noah, there's a space on my table," I say.

He looks up at me through his one visible eye and I can see he's on the verge of tears, and it's not because of them, it's because someone has come to help him, and I'm willing him not to give in and cry in front of these morons. So I give the morons what I hope is a withering look then go round and pick up his side plate with a choco brownie on and his carton of milk, and tell him to bring his dinner. The trouble is, they're getting louder and have decided to shuffle into a tight circle round us. We're both effectively trapped now, and I want to lash out at them, when suddenly Justin's there by my side, and so are Jack and Robert and Max and Mandy, and Noah and I are practically borne aloft and taken to our table.

Then Mandy turns on Sarah Lewis. "What do you think you're doing, you silly cunt?" She says it loud enough for the whole canteen to hear, and by now everyone knows something interesting is going on and all eyes turn her way.

Immediately Sarah's smiley face freezes, the chanting stops and her band of disciples look to her for leadership.

"Mandy Simpkins, that's enough!" The commanding voice of Patrick Johns has issued an order from over yonder, but Mandy is not one to be easily cowed. She goes up to the prefects' table, puts her hands flat on the Formica and bellows, "Johns, you're a fucking disgrace. You're supposed to be head boy of this school, head boy for every one of its thirteen hundred pupils, not for some cult homophobic fucking church with fifty members."

We're all clapping now. Patrick is red in the face and very angry, but doesn't know how to handle the situation. To be honest, if I were in his position, neither would I.

Then it's all over. Someone, probably a dinner lady, has summoned the headmaster and with him is Mr Wilkinson, the deputy head, Coach Harris and Ms Lane. In they sweep. Sarah and her disciples quickly disperse like ripples on a pond, and the two main protagonists are asked politely to follow the teachers' group to the headmaster's study.

I get up and call out to Ms Lane, but she puts up her hand to stop me, then walks quickly over to our table and says *'muchas gracias, señor'* to me in a quiet voice, which has never happened to anyone before in the whole history of the school. Justin and Freddie just glance at me, but Kate's and Sophie's mouths drop open in amazement. Noah gives me a puzzled look, but then we all settle down again to eat.

"Noah, you've got a really big head," says Sophie out of the blue. I never realised she was such a master of tact.

He flicks his fringe away from his visible eye and looks at her. "Our dad told me that my mum's cervix was stretched as tight as a drum when I came out. He said I only weighed five pounds, but four pounds of that was my head, and it was like giving birth to a rugby ball."

Well, that made us boys laugh, and the girls too, but I think they were crossing their legs as well at the thought. It broke the ice and we all began talking about how much we all weighed when we were born, et cetera, and we kind of forgot what had gone on before. And now I hope Noah sits with us again, because he's pretty good company, even if he is a Year Nine.

***

41: Monday, 17th June. 5 p.m. 34b Savoy Flats.

NOAH

My dad says he's glad he's got a gay son because it makes him feel more masculine. Is that a compliment? He's had three or four girlfriends, as far as I can remember, but once they've crossed the threshold of this dump they don't last long. It could be me, though. They see what my dad's genes produce and they bolt for the door.

Dan Moseley is becoming my knight in shining armour and is a really nice bloke too. I wish he was gay, 'cos I could really go for him. His friend Justin Walker is hot too, but not quite as dishy. Fancy them wanting me to sit with them. That business with Ms Lane was a bit strange, though. What was that all about? I don't know if I'll have the courage to go up to their table tomorrow and just sit down. Maybe I should wait for another invite. But why be such a wuss about it? They can only tell me to sling my hook? I only wish there was someone else my age who was gay; I'd have more confidence then. I wouldn't care even if they looked like the back end of a bus. I can see the lonely hearts advert now: Creature from the Black Lagoon seeks Back End of a Bus Man for friendship and maybe more...

I don't know what Anne Marie will say when she gets back from being off sick and finds I'm not sitting in my usual place. I expect, if Paul Sharpe is there, she probably won't even notice. Paul Sharpe never sits with me when Anne Marie is absent. I've no idea where he goes, but it ought to tell me something, really.

My dad isn't the most dynamic person in the world. He spends all day clipping hair then comes home, has tea, and sits in front of the TV until it's time to go to bed. I think that's his idea of the perfect day. He's not a bad dad though, as far as it goes, and I know he loves me, because quite often he'll come and give me a hug out of the blue. He gets hold of the back of my big head with one hand and puts the other round my waist and sort of draws me into him. I pretend not to like it, but I do. He always asks, *How is my best boy today then?* I usually answer by saying, *Geroff me!* But he knows I don't mean it and I put my arms round him and squeeze and I can smell the brilliantine on him.

As a gay boy I am expected to be fashionable, but that's difficult on £3 a week pocket money. That's why I've got lots of beads and bangles and not much else. I did save up all of March's and some of April's pocket money, and my dad doubled it as my birthday present, for this really cool sweater: it's charcoal-grey with red horizontal stripes in the midsection.

Recently, I've been hoarding again, this time to buy this awesome sleeveless vest for the summer that I saw in Mars Colony. That's a shop in the retail park, only it's so small it's little more than a cubicle. The vest is £16 and if I save for just one more week, Dad will give me the rest, otherwise he says the summer will be over. It's divided vertically, red on the right side – you might have noticed that I like red – and horizontal stripes on the left in navy blue and white, though each of the stripes has a different gold pattern stitched into it. It goes just perfect with the navy blue shorts with the red hems dad got me from Matalan. They were on sale for £6 and were a real bargain.

Despite being dirt-poor, our flat is always warm, there's breakfast and tea every day, and on Sundays we go to Wetherspoon's for dinner. It's become a bit of a ritual, that has. It's dead cheap at Wetherspoon's and the food's good. I expect that's where most of the child allowance goes. Before we go, I always have my best bath of the week. I do try to be clean, despite eczema and the mouldy bathroom. I lie there in baby bubble bath with the water just above my nipples – I hate my nipples because they remind me of tiny red suction cups. I try to press them in, but they always pop out again. I used to think they were filled with milk, but that can't be true, can it? Anyway, I lie there listening to music on my headphones and I go into a dream and it's really relaxing until the water gets cool and my skin crinkles. Then I have to make sure my finger and toenails are just so. They're much easier to cut when wet. Not too long and not too short is how I like them. I used to bite my fingernails, until I realised everyone thought I was a disgusting skank, so I stopped. There was this boy in junior school who used to bite his toenails too, which is over-the-top gross.

While I'm having my bath, Dad gets out the Henry and hoovers the whole flat. It's as regular as clockwork; we're both creatures of habit. And it's the same at the shop. Last thing every night, he has to make sure that there isn't a single hair left on the linoleum before he comes home. That's about six o'clock. I usually have tea ready for him then, which is the least I can do, I suppose. Afterwards, I wash up before starting my homework.

Weekday breakfast is Dad's job. He gets up half an hour before me, has a wash and shave ready for work, then wakes me up. I am a badass sleeper, and while I'm dressing, all bleary-eyed and making myself look beautiful – ha! ha! – he's doing two mugs of tea, cereal and either a boiled egg with toast or bacon butties. Yum!

Can you tell I'm quite happy at the moment, despite being under a fatwa from Sarah Lewis and her Christian brothers? I wonder why…

***

42: Monday, 17th June. 6.30 p.m. 15 Leighton Lane.

JACK

I'm back from my round and it's nearly time for Mum and Dad to go out to their twentieth wedding anniversary celebration. They're going to Grange Farm, which is a swanky-ish restaurant on the Sheepway, that's the road that runs up by the cemetery where Stewy first met his mum. I think they have the meal, then there's some sort of last-century cabaret where the geriatrics can get up and Zimmer-frame the night away.

Monday is the bargain day of the week, which is why they're going tonight and not tomorrow, which is the actual anniversary. I know we haven't got masses of money, but I think they ought to go out and enjoy themselves a bit more. They both seem to work pretty hard and probably deserve to get away from us more often.

"So, you're deserting your children. Leaving us home alone, like *bad* parents," I say as soon as I get in. "Not that I want you to feel guilty..."

"Don't worry, you won't," Dad replies, taking the lead for once because Mum is still fiddling with her face.

"Have you been generous and left us some scraps of dry bread and a some cheese out of the mousetrap?"

"Just the dry bread," says Dad. "It's in a dog bowl under the sink."

"Where's LB? Sweeping the chimneys?"

"If we had any, yes, but he's actually in his room doing his homework."

Mum is still looking at herself in the small mirror by the door. "Do I look all right, dear?" she asks me.

Actually, she looks really nice for a mother, so I'll be generous with my comments. "You'll do, I suppose."

"Hi Jack!"

It's my nemesis, Long John Mikey. "What do you want, pest?"

"Mummy and Daddy say you're looking after me tonight and I've got to be good."

Cue obnoxious behaviour all night.

"Will you play a game with me?"

"No."

"I'm Jim and you're Israel Hands and you have to chase me up the rigging to the crow's nest. You throw a knife at me and miss. Then I blow your brains out with my flintlock pistol, and you fall into the sea and sink into Davy Jones's Locker..."

"No."

Mikey hops one step nearer. "We can do it once before you get tea..."

"Have a lovely time, dear, and we should be back about 11.30, but don't wait up for us. Your father's got half a day off tomorrow, so we can have a lie in. It's best if you set the breakfast things before you go to bed. Mrs Huntley will collect Mikey at quarter past eight, so make sure he's dressed and ready with his gym kit and has cereal and a piece of toast and a glass of milk. And don't forget to wake Dan if he oversleeps again."

I have not agreed to any of this. "Gym kit! He's on crutches."

"Crutch," says Mikey.

"He still has to do exercises, dear."

Dad opens the door. "Night then, Jack. Thanks for helping out..."

And out they go, and I'm left with all the jobs for the next fifteen hours and a pest smiling up at me, waiting for me to get into my Israel Hands character. Do you ever feel as though you've been stitched up? It's a good job it's an exam-free day tomorrow.

When I've had a wash and changed into shorts and granddad style, long sleeve T-shirt. I come back downstairs and look in the fridge. There are three plates of ham salad with some leftover quiche all done up in cling film and a lemon cheesecake. They must have had a half-price offer at Tesco. Still, that's not so bad, and I get them out and put them in our usual places on the table, along with cutlery, glasses and a carton of orange juice. I butter some slices of bread which I put on a plate in the middle, along with squeezy bottles of tomato sauce and mayonnaise, then I stand back to admire my handiwork.

All this time, Mikey's been hovering reasonably patiently nearby, so at last I give in. "Right then, Jim lad, will 'e fetch me that bottle o' rum, so a man can take the edge off 'is thirst?"

"Come and get it, dirt bag!" he shouts, being quite free with his script when he wants to be. And off he scoots down the hall and into the lounge. When I get there, he's balanced on the settee with his toy pistol. I kneel behind the settee, which passes as the rigging, make some *arring* noises, climb up and put my head over the parapet. Mikey is by now completely in character and is shaking with fear. "One more step, Mr Hands, and I'll blow your brains out!" he squeaks.

"Now then, Jim lad, you wouldn't shoot this old sea dog, would 'e?" And I'm slowly drawing out the kitchen knife which I've hidden up my sleeve. As soon as he sees it, Mickey screams like a girl and fires – too soon, really, but I drop the knife and clutch my face and fall backwards into Davy Jones's Locker. But it's not over, because I've thought of an addition to the normal script. Mikey peers tentatively over the top of the settee and I turn slowly, until I'm looking up at him and then my eyes open, for I am now zombie Israel Hands. "Time to feast on the flesh of little Jim 'Awkins, sez I!"

Mikey squeals. "No, no, Jack, stop it!" He lies down on the settee, flailing his arms and kicking his legs, including the broken one. I drop over the settee almost on top of him and start to tickle him and slobber on his face, while he shrieks and laughs and is barely in control and I'm hoping he's managed not to wet himself. "Arr, that be nice flesh. I shall eat it all 'cept for them disgustin' cheesy feet..."

"Help me!" Mikey hoots.

Then another voice intervenes. "Jack... Jack!" I look up and see LB in the doorway. "Phone... Elspeth."

I go through to the kitchen, where the house phone is kept on the wall, trying to remember that I am no longer zombie Israel Hands.

"Hello, Elspeth?"

"Jack, I'm sorry to disturb you – it sounds as if you were having fun..."

"Sort of..."

"I found your number in the phone book."

"Sorry, I should have given you my mobile number. Is everything OK?"

"Tell me, is Stewart with you?"

"No."

"Oh dear. You see, he hasn't returned from his meeting, and I am getting rather concerned. All the council offices will be closed by now."

"Weren't they supposed to bring him back by taxi?"

"Yes, he was collected this morning at ten o'clock as arranged, and the driver said he would return as soon as the meeting was over."

"Just a moment. Dan's with me now – I'll get him to ring Stewart on his mobile."

LB dials up and waits. "It's gone to voicemail. What's happened?"

"Stewy hasn't returned from his meeting."

"Jeez! I'll try again..."

"Hey, Stewy, it's Dan. If you're there, give us a ring, OK?"

"Sorry Elspeth, we've drawn a blank here."

"I shall have to call his mother."

"OK. I don't think it's wise to call the police, unless we really have to."

"I understand. If I hear anything further I'll let you know."

"Likewise. I don't suppose you can remember the name of the taxi firm?"

"I'm afraid not; the driver had an identification badge round his neck, but I took no notice."

"OK. I'll speak to you again shortly."

I run upstairs and get my phone in case I've had a message, but there's nothing.

When I get back to the kitchen my brothers are both at the table, waiting.

"No luck?" says LB.

I shake my head.

"Jack's worried," says Mikey.

"Yeh, worried that you haven't washed your dirty paws."

He looks guilty, so I pick him up and lower him onto the low stool by the sink. "Soap and water."

He frowns, then commences – after a fashion – to wash. "You managed not to wet yourself when we were playing, then?"

Mikey nods solemnly and I give him a hug and the towel to dry his hands and shortly we're all sitting around the table having tea. The phone rings. It's Elspeth again. She's tried getting through to Anne Waverly's phone, but it's continually engaged. I can tell she's on edge and I don't blame her. Being eighty-three and all alone in that big house with Stewart having gone AWOL must be daunting. I remind her, as casually as possible, to keep the doors and windows locked.

***

It's eight fifteen now. We've finished tea and I'm about to wash up. LB is doing the honours with Mikey tonight, which means a sponge bath and a story before bed. He's better at the former than me, but not as good at the latter because he doesn't do character voices, especially as it's the complete and unabridged version of *TI*.

My mobile goes off. It's a message:

Urgent! Come to Woolgrove Wood alone ~ SH.

Woolgrove Wood is the little wood on the far side of the school playing fields, where Robert and I went on our first day. I try ringing Stewy without success and so I send a message.

RU OK?

There's no reply. I'm not sure what to do, and run upstairs to talk to LB.

"I shall have to go – alone if I have to," I say.

"Jack, what did Mr Colt say to you and Robert?"

"I know – but I can't ask Robert, I can't ask Max or Mandy because they don't have transport. You can't go because of Mikey..."

"I can look after myself," comes a little squeak, from someone who's lying on a plastic sheet in just his underpants and a plaster cast.

"Don't be ridiculous," I say and then address Dan. "In any case, you need to make sure everything's secure here, just in case..."

He nods thoughtfully. "OK, I've got an idea. I'll phone Justin, see if he's up for it."

"It may be risky," I say.

"He knows practically everything already, Jack, and Woolgrove Wood is only a stone's throw away from where he lives."

"I trust him, LB, but would he trust me if he knew..?"

"Best not go there now. Tell him when the time is right."

Justin is at home and has been earning extra pocket money credits by mowing the lawn. When Dan explains about the message from Stewart, he's ready to jump on his bike and head for the woods. It's all a bit too gung-ho for me, so I insist he meets me at the junction of Edward's Lane and Knowles Road to talk strategy.

***

43: Monday, 17th June. 8.30 p.m. Edward's Lane.

<u>JACK</u>

A pair of grey baggy shorts, off-white drawstring T-shirt and sandals all sprinkled with dust and grass clippings is not a great fashion statement, but Justin is one of those loose-limbed, well-built boys who looks smart whatever he's wearing.

"Old man," he says with a grin.

"Steep hill," I reply as I arrive breathless and sweating.

I show Justin the message that is supposedly from Stewy, and make it plain to him that I don't know what we might be getting into, but he seems quite relaxed about it all and I wonder if this unflappability is what makes him such a good footballer.

We lock our bikes together around a lamp post and set off on foot up Edward's Lane. Strangely, this is the first time I've ever been out alone with Justin. It's not far to a dirt track on the left which will take us down between the houses to the perimeter fence of the school playing fields. There's a ditch too, but that's easily jumped, and the fence is either hedge or posts with two bars of wood. Beyond the rugby and cricket pitches, silhouetted against the setting sun is Woolgrove Wood, looking much darker and more sinister than I have ever seen it before.

We turn right along the track, which now runs parallel to the playing fields, but immediately pause as there's a Ford Focus police car about fifty yards ahead. It's facing away from us and has stopped where the track has become too narrow for it to go any further. On our right, behind a mass of brambles, six-foot-high fences hide the back gardens of the houses on Edward's Lane. Some have gates, but most don't, and I wonder if the Hendersons have one.

A large man out walking with his Labrador comes towards us and has only just enough room to get between the car and the brambles without being caught on the thorns. Clearly annoyed at the standard of parking, he's in no mood to start a conversation with two teenagers. On the other hand, the dog, which is not much more than a puppy, comes bounding up to us and Justin squats down and strokes it, something I'd never do. The man gives us a cursory nod as he passes, then whistles for the dog to follow.

By this time, I've had a good look round. The car is empty and there is no sign of any police. We press on until the track, which is now just a path, ends at the banks of School Brook. I don't think that's it's official name, but that's what everyone calls it. It's just above ankle-deep at this time of year, some fifteen feet wide, and babbles along quite swiftly. It runs along the north side of the playing fields and then sweeps south, bordering the west side of Woolgrove Wood where Robert and I had to... wash... ahem!

Justin and I climb over the fence. There's no one about, but here we are at our most exposed. We hope that Mr Peebles hasn't got his binoculars out, though the groundsman's house is way over at the front of the school, about a third of a mile distant. We trot across the field and enter the wood through a gap. It suddenly seems very dark and much cooler, and though our eyes quickly become accustomed to the gloom, I realise it won't be long until sunset. Neither of us thought to bring a torch.

There are no paths so we pick our way as silently as possible through the sparse undergrowth. Justin taps me on the shoulder and signals for me to listen. I hear nothing but the song of a blackbird marking its territory high in one of the trees. Then, as we approach the glade in the centre of the wood, I see articles of clothing scattered among the tussocks of grass. Lying face-down, there is a naked body, in almost the same spot as Robert and I lay together,.

I stop and look at Justin. This is quite terrifying. The body appears very white in the half-light, and it is undoubtedly Stewart Henderson. I move towards it, hoping to see signs of life. A sock, a trainer and a ripped pair of underpants lie on the ground before me. With relief I see he's breathing, but barely, and his wrists have been bound behind his back. Justin remains on the edge of the glade, and I begin to wonder whether it was wise to bring him.

Stewart's eyes are closed, and his lips are slightly parted, with a bluish tinge. I'm not sure why he's unconscious, though, because there are no obvious injuries on his head or body. I stroke his hair and whisper his name, but there is no reaction. There is nothing for it but to phone for an ambulance.

Then Justin cries out. I look round and see two uniformed policemen in the glade. One is advancing towards me; the other is restraining Justin. I think about running, but almost as soon as I have risen to my feet, he has grabbed hold of me and is forcing me back down into a kneeling position. I recognise him, even though the last time we met he was wearing a business suit. It's the officer with the jowls who assaulted me in the headmaster's office.

He pins my legs with his knees, draws my hands together and cuffs them behind my back, then grabs me by the neck and forces my head down until it is touching the ground.

He puts his mouth close to my ear and whispers, "We told you to come alone, Moseley. Now we have to deal with that little boy you brought with you." He slaps me across the head.

"Stewart needs an ambulance," I say.

"No, he doesn't, but you will. We're going to make an example of you, queer boy. Here's the story as we'll tell it to the gentlemen of the press: *The suspect, Jack Moseley, injected his victim, Stewart Henderson, with heroin then attempted to rape him. Unfortunately, Stewart died, and a post mortem is to be carried out to determine the exact cause of death.* What a juicy story!" He laughs. "If you try to get up or make a noise, I'll kick you from here into next week."

He releases me and beckons the other officer to bring Justin over.

"And who are you, sweetheart?" he asks, brushing himself down.

"We had nothing to do with this..."

"Shut up and answer the question."

"Justin... Justin Walker."

"Well, Justin, are you a homosexual?"

"No."

"Then what are you doing accompanying this known homosexual into a deep dark wood?"

"They're going to kill Stewart," I say.

The officer slaps me again. "Didn't I tell you to keep quiet?"

"I'm not a fag," says Justin.

"Oh, now, that's quite a homophobic word, isn't it? Especially in front of a known homosexual?"

"Jack's not a fag."

"Oh, but I'm afraid he is. Why don't you ask him?"

"Jack, you're not, are you?"

I look up at Justin. "It's true, I am."

"You tricked me!" Justin starts to struggle. "I hate AIDS-carrying fags."

"Trickery is typical of a homo, Justin. They only want two things: a hand in your pants and a cock up your arse."

"You bastard, Jack Moseley!"

139

I'm beginning to lose heart now. I look at Justin and see the anger in his face. I was almost sure he wouldn't react this way, but I suppose he's only thirteen and feels no different than Dan did when he first learned about me.

"Let him go, and let's see how much of a fag-hater he really is."

Justin is released and he strides over and kicks me in the ribs with his right foot. I grunt and slump to the ground.

"That was nice, very nice, and now there's just a couple more things for you to do, Justin, to prove yourself." The officer squats down and uncuffs me. "First, strip him naked..."

Both police officers hold me as Justin removes my T-shirt, trainers and socks. I struggle, but know there's little point. They've got me where they want me. Justin pulls off my shorts and boxers in one go, then they turn me over onto my back.

"Funny, that queers look exactly the same in the buff as normal people," the other officer says. All three laugh. I've stopped struggling now.

"Now, Jason... sorry, Justin... for your last public service we'd like you to give the homo an injection." Jowls sits on my legs and gets a hypodermic syringe kit and an ampoule of brown liquid from his pocket.

"I thought this might be difficult, but with our friend here it's turned into a piece of piss."

"I've never done this before," says Justin.

The officer puts on a pair of disposable vinyl gloves and fills a syringe from the ampoule. "The less expert you are, the more natural it will look – and the more painful it'll be."

"No, Justin!" I cry.

"Don't struggle, homo," the second officer says, tightening his grip on my wrists.

"Shut up, fag," Justin says to me. "It's only what you deserve."

"We'll make a police officer of you yet," says Jowls, handing the syringe over. He squats again, holding me by my ankles. "Now, just stick it in his biceps and inject one of those units at a time. Then, if there's no effect, inject another."

"Do you mean like this?" says Justin and he stabs the needle into the front of Jowls' thigh, pushing the plunger in at the same time.

"You cunt!" the officer screams. The empty hypodermic is still sticking out of him as he tries to stand. I kick out as hard as I can and he totters. Justin assumes what looks suspiciously like a martial arts posture and punches him on the nose. Blood starts to flow. He falls backwards.

The other officer lets go of my wrists. He doesn't know what to do. Justin takes a similar stance as before, but this time kicks out with his left foot, hitting him in the jaw. The man tries to grab Justin's leg, but I pick up my trainer and hit him across the head with it.

Blue jowls has risen to his feet again, but he's unsteady and the drug might be beginning to take effect. "Let's get out of here!" he shouts, pulling the hypodermic from his leg and throwing it like a dart at Justin. It misses by a mile. "I'll get you, fag-lover!"

His colleague is still dazed, and following an order is about the only thing he can do. They stumble away into the near-darkness. The glade is quiet again. Justin hands me my boxers and shorts. I pull them on, grab the phone from the shorts pocket and call for an ambulance. I explain it's probably a heroin overdose, and the fifteen-year-old victim is unconscious but still breathing. I'm told to put him in the recovery position and watch his respiration.

Justin, who has learned first aid at football training, unties Stewart and turns him onto his side while I collect up the rest of my clothes.

"Hey," says Justin, holding up the hypodermic syringe. "The needle must be still in that copper's leg."

"Good!" I reply. "I hope he gets blood poisoning and dies."

In the distance we hear a siren wailing.

"Let's get Stewy dressed. We don't want to have to explain why he's naked. In fact, we want to avoid explanations as much as possible."

By the time the paramedics arrive, we've tidied the glade and thrown the syringe into School Brook. We give them the minimum amount of information necessary and watch as our friend, wearing an oxygen mask and trussed up like a Christmas turkey, is carried away on a stretcher. It's been no more than fifteen minutes since I called them.

Justin looks at his watch. "Nearly half ten," he says and smiles ruefully. Now, as the adrenalin leaves our systems, we're both trembling, both scared shitless, both exhausted. For a moment we hold off, then we clasp each other in a hug and, being three inches taller and gay, I give him a kiss on the top of his head. He doesn't seem to mind.

"Thank you, Justin – you saved both mine and Stewy's lives tonight."

"No worries. I'm always saving the day at footy as well."

"Where did you learn to fight like that?"

"I did two years of *Kyokushin* karate."

"I didn't know."

"I got to yellow belt but I gave it up last October."

"You mean, because of football commitments?"

"Not really. Something else." Justin smiles and I know he doesn't want to say more.

"Had you already guessed I was gay?"

He shrugs disarmingly. "I was waiting for someone to tell me."

"Will you phone LB? I'll talk to Elspeth."

He nods and we set off back to our bikes.

***

44: Monday, 17th June. 11 p.m. 15 Leighton Lane.

JACK

I'm sitting up in bed still feeling shaky. LB has just brought me a cup of hot chocolate and a Jammie Wagon Wheel and wants to hear every last detail.

"When did you know Justin was acting?"

"When he booted me in the ribs with his right foot, not his left."

"Did it leave a bruise?"

I lift my PJ top. There's hardly a mark.

"He's good at those feints... for someone who's a cack-footed southpaw."

"He was the real hero tonight, LB. No wonder you two make such a brilliant combination."

"Not for much longer, though..."

"Hi!"

Mikey's standing in my bedroom doorway.

"Why aren't you in bed asleep, pestilence?"

"I was worried about you."

"Liar." I hold out my arm and he hops over and Dan lifts him onto the bed.

He puts his head on my shoulder. "Can I sleep with you tonight?"

"No, I don't want your cheesy feet in my bed."

Mikey giggles and lifts his foot. "Sniff!"

"They're nothing compared to Justin's," said Dan. "His are rancid."

"I haven't noticed."

"That's because you haven't been near him in the changing rooms after a match. Even Coach Brennan has commented on it."

"Can I have a Jammie Wagon Wheel?" asks Mikey, eyeing mine.

"No pest, they're for grown-ups." I decide to break off a piece of mine anyway and feed it to him. "Now you'll have to clean your teeth, again"

"That wasn't the jammy part," he objects.

"Little beggars can't be choosers." I break off a bit more nearer the centre and drop it into his mouth. "Now, scoot!"

LB lifts him down. "Wee, hands, teeth, bed," he says. "Go!"

I hand over my empty mug and wrapper. Suddenly my eyelids feel very heavy.

"I've set my alarm for tomorrow in case you don't make it," says Dan, adjusting my pillow.

"I've got to clean my teeth," I say and that's all I remember until the following morning when LB wakes me up.

***

45: Tuesday, 18th June. 7 p.m. Pear Tree Cottage, The Ropewalk.

ROBERT

Maybelle Crittenden cast her eye over the half-eaten plate of food in front of Robert.

He had been very quiet since his return from school that afternoon, and it was clear something was troubling him. Frank too eyed his son with something less than paternal affection. It seemed to him that his son had been showing a decidedly lukewarm response to the great mission of their church since they had told him about it.

"The sooner you go on Pastor Fisher's youth leader induction course, the better." He spoke his thoughts out loud, and couldn't help noticing the momentary frown that passed across his son's face.

"Are you sickening for something, hon?" said his mother.

I am sick, thought Robert – sick of all this. "No, Mom, I'm just not feeling so hungry tonight."

"You need to pull yourself together, then," said his father. "There is great work for you in the offing. Your soul should be filling with the Holy Spirit in readiness."

"Would you mind if I went out for a spell to get some fresh air? I've been revising most of the day?"

Maybelle reached across the table and patted his hand. "Maybe you'll feel better once the exams are over."

"Let us hope so," said Frank, "because he seems to have shrunk into something almost unrecognisable from the time when he'd uplift our spirits with his passionate love of our Lord Jesus Christ."

"Amen," said Maybelle.

***

Robert turned left along the Ropewalk then right onto Weymouth Road. His route was pre-planned, his breath of fresh air just another ruse to get him out of the house. He crossed over to the bus stop and waited. What had depressed him more than anything about the day was Jack's retelling at school of the events of the night before. The more he heard, the more he realised that it should have been him facing the dangers in Woolgrove Wood, not Justin Walker. It made him feel useless, almost a coward. When he had expressed these thoughts, Jack had brushed them aside, saying that he was needed on the inside, especially next Sunday. But playing the part of a fifth columnist was not something that came naturally to Robert. It was against his nature and made him feel unclean.

A number thirty-six bus came within five minutes. Robert paid the fare of £1 and ten minutes later he alighted at the top of Carisbrooke Drive, on which was the main entrance of Swanford Community Hospital.

"I've come to visit a patient," he announced.

"Children under the age of sixteen must be accompanied by an adult," said the receptionist, a woman with blonde highlights in her auburn hair.

Robert had not thought of that, and blushed.

"How old are you?"

"Fifteen."

The receptionist frowned and eyed him. "You're American, aren't you?"

"Yes, ma'am."

A glimmer of a smile passed her lips. "You could pass for sixteen."

Robert tried to look grateful.

"The patient's name?"

"Stewart Henderson."

She busied herself on the screen for a good number of seconds. "Stewart Henderson, Kingfisher ward. Down that corridor and turn left. I'll let them know you're coming."

"Thank you."

Most of the beds seemed to be occupied by very young children, but a friendly nurse took him down the ward to where the older boys were grouped together.

Stewart's eyes lit up as soon as he saw him. "Robert!" he called.

They clasped hands. "It's really good to see you, Stewy, and you're looking good too."

The American nodded at the woman seated on the other side of the bed, and she smiled back.

"This is my mum," said Stewart. "Mum, this is Robert Crittenden."

Robert reached across with his hand. "How do you do, ma'am?"

She shook it delicately. "Anne Waverly, and you must call me Anne. You're Jack's friend, aren't you?"

"Boyfriend," corrected Stewart. "Where is Jack?"

Anne stroked her son's arm. "Jack visited you earlier, do you remember?"

Stewart nodded doubtfully.

"He's having a few problems with his short-term memory," said Anne.

"Don't listen to her, I'm fine... Robert, you won't forget about Sunday, will you?"

The American sat down and drew his chair up close to the bed. "It's all in hand, don't worry."

"You boys are facing very real dangers and there's no one in authority to turn to," said Anne. "It doesn't seem possible in a supposedly civilised country."

"Who saved my life?" asked Stewart.

"That was Jack and Justin," replied Robert.

"Oh yes, Jack Moseley and Justin Walker. I must remember to thank them."

"When you get home, we'll invite all the members of the Famous Five to a thank-you party."

"Famous Five?" queried Robert.

"Yes, it seems appropriate for your gang," explained Anne.

Stewart looked around, frowning. "Why have they put me in a kids' ward?"

"Because you're under sixteen," said Robert. "They nearly didn't let me visit you because I'm underage."

"How long am I going to be in here for?"

"He's asked that twenty times already," said Anne. "Eight to ten days, until they're certain your brain is functioning normally."

"Stewy, would you like me to bring you something next time I come."

"Mandy."

Robert chuckled. "I'll see what I can do, though Max may not be happy."

"Jack said that Mandy was suspended."

"You see, he remembers that!" said Anne.

"Yeh, straight after the exam tomorrow until Monday."

"Why was she?"

"Because she swore at Patrick Johns in the canteen."

"Oh, yes!" cried Stewart with a grin.

"We've got a plan for when she comes back," said Robert.

"Some mischief?" enquired Anne.

"Civil disobedience," replied Robert. "Patrick Johns got off scot-free."

Stewart yawned. "Why am I in hospital?"

"Someone injected you with heroin," explained Anne, "and the doctors are having to get it out of your system." She looked across the bed at Robert. "I think he's getting tired."

As if on cue, a bell rang to signal eight o'clock, the end of visiting hours. "Would you like to come back to number forty-one, Robert? Jack will be there. He's doing a bit of baby-sitting for me and some revision for his exam tomorrow, and I can give you a lift."

"Thank you, I'd like that very much," replied the American. "Jack's spoken so much about the house."

"Robert, you won't forget about next Sunday, will you?" said Stewart.

"No, Stewy, it's all fixed. You just try to get a good night's sleep now."

After Anne said her farewells to her son, they left the hospital by a side door which was nearer the car park. As soon as they were outside, she allowed her veneer of cheerful composure to fall away, to reveal the tiredness and anxiety beneath. "He's having a CT scan tomorrow. I'm told it's routine," she said. "I don't know what's going to happen with his memory."

"It's a very worrying time for you, especially with moving and all."

"I'm wondering whether I'm doing the right thing bringing him back to Swanford, where his dreadful father seems to rule the roost. I don't know what I ever saw in that man!"

"Stewart is doing pretty well, considering."

"I have Jack and Justin to thank for that. They put their lives on the line for my son, while no one else seems interested that some bastards gave him an overdose of heroin and tried to do the same to his rescuers. I'm fairly sure that the doctors think that Stewart did it to himself. Honestly, Robert, the world is going mad!"

The American sent Jack a text saying that they were on their way back. The reply was *Yum,* followed by a line of exclamation marks which Robert hardly thought he deserved.

***

148

46: Tuesday, 18th June. 8.15 pm, 41 Westbury Avenue.

ROBERT

After being introduced to Elspeth, Robert went with Jack on a tour of the house, ending up in the kitchen. "This is like Mom's, only bigger," he said, "at least taller."

"You rich people don't know you're born," said Jack.

"We're not rich," insisted Robert, knowing that they had this conversation in some form or another every day. "What's through there?"

"Come on. I'll show you," said Jack.

They entered the white-walled room with the white floor tiles and white goods all in a row. "This is the utility room."

Robert looked round. "It's rather..."

"White?" suggested Jack.

The American nodded. "That's a good word for it."

"I think Elspeth's going to get a mat to stop her suffering from snow blindness."

"The rest of the house is like the old lady – very English."

Jack gently kicked the door shut, took Robert's hands and pulled him into an embrace. "You've been..."

"I know, out of sorts..."

"I can fix that."

"How?"

"With a snog," said Jack and planted a kiss on his lips.

Robert closed his eyes and felt the warmth of Jack's body close and desirable. His hand travelled down until it met the growing hardness between his boyfriend's legs.

"Ooo, naughty, in Elspeth's utility room."

The American withdrew his hand.

"I didn't say stop!"

Robert's shoulders slumped. "Jack, I'm no good for you; I'm no good for anyone. I'm beginning to hate my parents, and I already hate my church. I should be there for you, always, but I'm not!"

"You're talking about last night again." Jack stepped back, but held on to him. "Look, we've already had this out at school..."

"Justin Walker would make you a better boyfriend than me."

"Yes, but there are two basic objections to that: the first is he's straight, and second, though he's my hero at the moment and though he's very cute and though he has taken all my clothes off and though I did give him a little kiss, I don't love him like I do you."

"That's a lot of *thoughs*, though."

"Well, just leave out the *thoughs* and cut to the chase."

"I've made up my mind. Next Sunday will be my last attendance at church, and after that I'm going to see you when I like."

"Fine, and what happens when your mum and dad ground you permanently, especially as the summer holidays are coming up and a young man's fancy turns to swimming in Speedos and frisking in meadows?" Jack waggled his eyebrows.

"I want to be something more to you than your snog toy."

Jack began to laugh. "You what?" He took up Robert's hand and kissed it repeatedly. "But I love you, my precious little snog toy."

"Sap!" The American smiled despite himself. "Why can't I have a serious conversation with you for once?"

"You want me to be serious, then I'll be serious. Don't do anything that'll make life even more difficult for yourself. For the time being, keep being the dutiful son."

The door opened and Anne Waverly walked in, carrying a basket of dirty washing. "Oh, sorry, boys," she said. "I was going to put these in the washer."

"We've done our tour," said Jack.

"Then I think Elspeth would like to see you in the sitting room."

"Are we in trouble?"

She looked sideways at them. "I don't know. I'm only the hired help."

"Anne, would you like us to help you with your move tomorrow?"

"That's very kind."

"I'm sure Dan will help as well."

"Let me know how many are coming and I'll have a meal prepared."

***

"You wanted to speak to us, Elspeth?" said Jack, putting his head round the door.

"Oh yes, do come in and sit down. Anne has been kind enough to make us a pot of tea."

They sat together on the sofa facing the old lady while she poured milk, then tea. "Help yourselves to sugar," she said, handing out the cups. "I don't know whether you've noticed, but it's been a very lovely evening. I love the warmth and soft light at the end of the long June days. I would so very much like to enjoy a few more before I depart."

Neither Jack or Robert knew how to reply to this, and so they remained quiet. She sighed and smiled at them. "You boys are both homosexual, aren't you?"

Robert and Jack exchanged looks.

"There's no need to worry. I'm not going to bite you."

"Yes, we are," said Jack. "I just wonder if we'd be having this conversation if a boy and girl were sitting in front of you?"

"Indeed we would not; I find teenage romances extremely tedious with their repetitive conventionality and almost certain banality. Would you like a biscuit, Robert?"

"Thank you, ma'am. They're jammie dodgers, aren't they?"

"Oh, I don't know, Stewart bought them for me. You can dunk them if you like. Now, I want to talk to you about paradoxes and also give you a historical perspective on your

151

lives. I shan't insult you by quizzing you on your knowledge, and so you will have to forgive me if I am teaching my grandmother to suck eggs, as it were. Relax, Jack, this isn't the Spanish Inquisition."

"Sorry, it's as though we're at the beginning of a lesson in school."

"I don't think you will hear this at school, dear boy. Especially the way things are going."

"I'm probably more used to listening to my elders than Jack is," said Robert, giving him a nudge.

"You have to remember, Robert, that getting older doesn't give you natural insight into the human condition, nor is wisdom the prerogative of the aged. In this country, prior to 1967, the criminal law could be invoked for any kind of homosexual behaviour, and could result in a prison sentence. Even for thirty years after 1967, there were ways and means of prosecuting homosexuals if the police and magistrates so wished.

"When I came back to England in the early 1950s, there was a wicked Home Secretary, David Maxwell Fyfe, who instigated a witch-hunt against homosexuals, with the full backing of the Metropolitan Police and other police forces around the country. It saw many prosecutions, many lives ruined and many lives lost. Blackmail was rife, as was corruption within the police."

"Alan Turing," said Robert. "One of the girls at school talked about him."

"Yes, and he was just the tip of the iceberg. My husband was acquainted through his work with Sir John – you know?"

"Sir John?" queried Jack.

"Gielgud – one of our great Shakespearian actors, but before your time. He was prosecuted too. Now, boys, the first paradox. This very same Home Secretary, David Maxwell Fyfe, this ambitious Tory politician who had designs on the prime ministership, was one of the prosecutors at the Nuremberg war trials. The Nazis he was prosecuting for war crimes were responsible for killing, torturing and imprisoning homosexuals, facts which he clearly chose to ignore.

Now the second paradox. This same Home Secretary instigated the Parliamentary Committee's inquiry into homosexual offences under Lord Wolfenden, which eventually led to the Sexual Offences Act of 1967, which decriminalised homosexuality. An act which David Maxwell Fyfe, by now the first Earl of Kilmuir, voted against in the House of Lords. What he probably didn't know when he set up the Committee in 1954 was that Lord Wolfenden's son was a homosexual.

"Now, this is the third paradox, and possibly the one to bear in mind. David Maxwell Fyfe was responsible in large part for the drafting of the European Convention on Human Rights, an act which is oft quoted when the human rights of homosexuals are being abused. This is the legislation which many of those who want a return to the 1950s as far as homosexuality is concerned are anxious to see repealed."

"So, indirectly, this David Maxwell Fyfe did us a favour?" said Jack.

"*Indirectly* being the operative word. People of his class and background would not have thought that this sort of legislation was directed at them. More for the lower orders and Johnny foreigner, I suspect."

"But how does this affect us now?"

"Jack, I wish you young people were more politically aware. There are now so many means by which information is transmitted, and the ignorance of your generation astounds me."

"Oops," he said with a wry grin.

Elspeth shook her head. "I wouldn't be so sanguine, Jack. This new Parliament will repeal the act after the summer recess, and amend or repeal the Equality Act of 2010. When that goes and if they successfully reintroduce the 1988 section of the Local Government Act, this country will be in the same situation as Russia or any of the theocratic states in the world. Then, you will be thrown to the wolves."

"It's that bad?"

"The world can go backward as well as forward, Jack. Democracy, free speech and thought are always under threat."

"You seem very knowledgeable on the subject," said Robert, who had been listening carefully.

"My husband would now be considered to be bisexual," said Elspeth. "He was a very kind and loving man, and I did try to understand his needs – not always successfully, I have to say."

"Do you have children?" asked Jack.

"Alas, I have survived both my children. My son was killed in a car accident in the United States, Robert. And my daughter had breast cancer, something I have been mercifully spared."

"Sorry," said Jack.

Elspeth let out a deep breath and half closed her eyes. "I think it's almost time for bed now. And you boys have examinations to pass tomorrow. There is, however, one small matter which I would like to discuss with you, Robert, before you go."

"Do you want me to leave?" asked Jack.

"Of course not. Robert, I understand you lost your job when Mrs Annesley's Fruit and Flower closed its doors?"

"That's correct, ma'am."

"Are you looking for other employment?"

"I am."

"Well, I have a wholly neglected garden which I have been unable to manage for a good few years, and I can offer you employment as the head gardener and general handyman."

"Yes, ma'am! When would you like me to start?"

"Wouldn't you like to negotiate terms and conditions first?"

"Oh, I guess..."

"You won't find a better worker than Robert," said Jack.

"Your endorsement carries weight, Jack. I thought three and a half hours on a regular basis, say Saturday mornings, from 9.30 a.m. to 1 p.m., and the occasional shift at other times during holidays or long evenings. I think an hourly rate of £6 would be fair."

"That's more than I get!" exclaimed Jack.

Robert stood up and held out his hand. "Thank you, ma'am. I accept. Would you like me to start this Saturday?"

"The sooner the better."

***

47: Wednesday, 19th June. 9.30 a.m. Swanford Community School.

NOAH

In his wallet, Noah had two five pound notes, one given to him by his dad that morning, four one pound coins and forty-eight pence in change. *Only one pound, fifty-two pence away from the target. Then, it's off to Mars Colony to buy the vest.* He stood by his locker and counted again, while around him pupils spilled out of their form rooms and made for their first period lessons. Suddenly his hand was knocked and his change went flying up into the air.

"Hey, watch it!" he said, not realising that it had been done deliberately.

"Who are you telling to watch it, homo?"

But Noah was already down on his knees, trying to pick up the coins among the chaotic bustle. A foot came down on his hand. He looked up into Jason Spriggs' sneer. "I said, who are you telling to watch it, homo?"

Noah noticed Jason's brother, Lucas, picking up some of the coins. "Can I have those, please?" he said.

The pressure on his hand increased and Jason bent and snatched the wallet out of his hand. "You're not very polite, are you, homo? When a person asks you a question, it's normal to answer."

"I want my money, I want my wallet," said Noah, "and I want you to leave me alone."

The throng of pupils had almost dispersed now. Jason brought the full weight of his foot down on Noah's hand. Noah winced and groaned while the contents of his wallet were scattered across the corridor. Lucas showed him the pile of coins he'd collected, then threw them on top of the lockers. "Time to change your lifestyle, homo," said Jason, throwing the empty wallet down in front of him before releasing his trapped hand after one more press for good measure.

The Spriggs brothers sauntered away. Noah's hand felt big and heavy and his eczema itched like crazy. By the time he'd collected up the money and bits and pieces from his wallet he was already ten minutes late for first period. Now he only had £12.24, which meant he was short, even with the addition of this week's pocket money. Instead of going to class he went to the toilets and ran cold water over his hand until the pain had been numbed. Then he went to class.

"You've missed half the lesson," said Mr Graves, a short man with a pinched face who was not a bad English teacher.

Noah held out his hand, which was red, swollen and trembling.

"What am I supposed to do with that?" his teacher asked.

"It hurts, sir," said Noah.

"Aww, poor baby," murmured Jacob Lively, loud enough for most of the class to hear and cause hoots of merriment.

"Shut up!" shouted Mr Graves. "Noah, go and sit down and try to catch up."

"Yes, sir."

***

At break time, Noah decided to lie low just in case any more of his tormentors had plans for him. Spending twenty minutes in stall three of the science block toilets wasn't his idea of fun, but he consoled himself with thoughts of the dinner hour, when he could spend time chatting with his new circle of friends. He dared to call them friends, having managed to get up the courage to sit at the table without a specific invitation, and it seemed they had accepted his presence without comment.

That is, until he was warily walking along the corridor at the end of period three and happened to bump into Freddie Hall.

"See you at dinner," said Noah with a smile and a swish of his wrist.

Freddie blanched and looked around to see if anyone was watching. "Look, isn't it about time you went and sat on your own table again? You are a Year Nine, after all, and we're only Year Eights."

"Oh," said Noah, blushing. "I thought..."

"Ms Lane set all this up, you know."

"Did she?"

"We were meant to help you out for a while as a punishment, and now we've done it."

"I was a punishment?"

"Yes."

"Is that why she came over and said well done to Dan?"

"You got it in one."

The day had just got a whole lot worse. Noah felt as if he had been set adrift in a hostile sea. When the bell rang at the end of fourth period he all but ran out of the school, unable to face the embarrassment and possible intimidation of the canteen. For half an hour he hid on the bank near the tennis courts until he was moved on by Mr Peebles, the groundsman. He spent the rest of the dinner hour in the quiet room, where pupils could do homework under the watchful eye of a teacher. Today the unlucky man was Mr Joseph, who had recently returned from a period of sickness.

At the end of a lacklustre day, Noah waited for ten minutes before walking up to the cycle sheds, only to find his tyres had been let down and he had to go back into school to borrow the communal pump. Mr Harris, the school PE and rugby coach, kept it in his office, which smelled (just like the changing rooms) of sweaty feet and jock straps. Noah and Mr Harris were not natural soul mates. Mr Harris used Noah as an example of the physical specimen the boys might become if they didn't exercise hard enough. 'Limp-wristed Jessie' was one of his favourite epithets – but it was used sparingly and not when Ms Lane was around. Noah thought Mr Harris was on a different and lower evolutionary tree than *Homo sapiens*; in fact, just below *Homo neanderthalensis*. But there was no real hatred between them, because the teacher wasn't really any rougher on Noah than most of the other boys. In that he was consistent.

Noah cycled to his dad's shop, said hi to him and Mr Pullin, who was having his monthly trim, and then walked the three hundred yards to Savoy Flats. The lift had been out of order for so long that he didn't even think about it, and instead bounded up the four flights in block three, through the fire door and onto the landing.

His heart sank. Someone had spray painted, in bold red letters, on the door of flat 34b: *DIE FAGOT*. The fact that 'faggot' had been misspelled did not lessen his sense of vulnerability or dismay now that the haters had come right to the door of his home. Noah looked round, the skin prickling on his neck in fear that the perpetrators might still be watching or lying in wait for him.

The door of flat 34a opened and his neighbour Iris Green emerged. A widow of long standing, Iris was diabetic and her vision was less than perfect, but she was generally a kind soul, and she had lived in her flat for even longer than the Marshalls had.

"Is it German, Noah?"

He shook his head. "Did you see who did it, Auntie Iris?"

"Only their backs, when I opened my door."

"I hope I can clean it off before Dad gets home."

"If it's not German, what does it mean?"

"It means they want me to die, Auntie Iris."

"Surely not, luvvy. A sweet-natured thing like you? Surely not. Would you like a mug of tea? I'll bring it out for you while you work."

"Thank you. Do you think Cillit Bang will get it off?"

"You could try – it gets most things off."

***

48: Thursday, 20th June. 6.15 p.m. Ray's newsagent, Swanford high street.

JACK

Jack slung his empty bag down on the counter. "All done, Mr Ray."

"Tut, tut, tut. Jack my boy, what is the world coming to? I thought yours was a respectable school, not like that den of iniquity down the road, which fortunately they have now shut for good and all." Mr Ray looked up from where his head had been buried in page three of the *Swanford Mail,* and his moustache bristled. "I need advice as to whether I should withdraw my number-one son from a place of such disrepair." He turned the paper round for Jack to read.

More Trouble For School
Exclusive by John Little

A small group of homosexual rights activists tried to disrupt a peaceful meeting of Christians at Swanford Community School last Monday, I can report. It happened in the school canteen, said one of the victims, who has asked to remain anonymous. "We were standing around a table praying to our Lord Jesus Christ to forgive the sinners among us when a group of pupils began swearing and shouting at us. I recognised two as known homosexuals. They crowded round us, and such was their bullying tactics that we were forced to leave."

The headmaster was unavailable for comment, but the governors issued the following statement: "The school takes this type of incident very seriously and one pupil has been suspended. Religious freedom is of primary importance, and the ability to practise that religion is a basic human right and should happen without fear of persecution by a tiny vociferous minority."

There will be a peaceful protest outside the school gates next Tuesday afternoon by the town's Christian community, who wish to show solidarity with these young people.

"Mr Ray, if this article was judged on a scale of one to ten, with ten being the truth and one being lies, it would score minus ten."

"My number-one son, Sourajit, said as much not ten minutes past. He said he was eating his vegetarian cheesy vomit when this storm in a teapot arose and abated, which didn't warrant any purple prose. But here it is, in black and white."

"I think your son has got his head screwed on the right way."

"A very interesting term, which I shall commit to memory, Jack my boy."

"Mr Ray, a friend of mine has just started a new job and he's getting £6 an hour."

The moustache bristled. "You are still too young to understand the commercial delicacies, Jack my boy. For one thing, you have to take into account the great job satisfaction you get from delivering the news into people's homes and, for another, as your Bible says, money does not grow on burning bushes. Now, I have a young customer waiting to purchase some delicious Swizzels Lovehearts, so I shall see you tomorrow."

***

49: Thursday, 20th June. 6.30 p.m. 15 Leighton Lane.

__JACK__

"Mikey wants to show you something," said Pam.

Jack kicked off his trainers. "Don't I get any peace in this house?"

"Be nice to him."

"What's for tea?"

"Egg salad."

"We had a really nice meal at Elspeth's last night. *Home-made* fried chicken and chips followed by *home-made* strawberry trifle."

"Maybe you should go and live there, then, dear."

"Chance would be a fine thing. Did you know Elspeth owns a house in Hampstead which she rents out for – guess how much?"

"You shouldn't pry into other people's financial affairs. Go on, tell me!"

"£4,500 per week!"

"Oh my goodness!"

"She has to pay something for agents' fees and upkeep, but the rest..."

"How do you know this?"

"She told us she owned a property, so we looked it up on the internet."

"Elspeth is a lady, Jack; you must never betray her confidence."

Jack looked down and knotted his brow, registering the fact. He knew that tone of voice.

"Hmm," she continued, normality restored. "And she'll have a very nice doctor's pension as well. How the other half live – and here we are skimping and scraping to bring you three up."

"Yes, it's true, your children are a terrible drain on your resources. Maybe you should sell us into slavery."

"Now, there's a tempting idea..."

"Where's LB? You haven't sold him off already, have you?"

"Sophie called for him a little while back."

Jack pulled on the drawstring of his shorts. "Oh, they're having sex at her house tonight, are they?"

"I don't know why you have to be so common sometimes, dear. Now, hurry up, your father will be here in ten minutes."

After drawing a blank in the lounge and Mikey's bedroom, he traipsed along the landing to his own room, where he paused outside the door, which was standing ajar. "That's funny – I haven't been able to smell any disgusting cheesy stinks tonight," he said loudly.

There was a little giggle from inside the room. Jack pushed open the door to find Mikey standing in the middle of the carpet, a magic marker in his hand.

"And what is a little pest doing in my room without permission?"

Mikey lifted the hem of his shorts to emphasise the change.

"What is that?" asked Jack, pointing to the new blue boot-shaped cast.

"Will you sign it?"

"I might do." Jack scooped Mikey up and laid him on the bed. "But I've forgotten how to spell my name."

"J - A - C - K."

"Not so fast, clever dick. Shall I put an 'x' after it?" Jack sniffed and shook his head.

Mikey nodded affirmatively.

"All right, but it's not a sloppy one. Are you still on crutches?"

"Crutch," said Mikey. "Doctor says I've got to keep using it till my leg muscles are able to hold me up."

"Those skinny little things. It'll be never, then."

Mikey looked up with big eyes. "Jack?"

"What?"

"Can we play that monster game again?"

"What monster game?"

"The one where you play Israel Hands, I blow your brains out, but you come back as a zombie."

"Oh, that one. Do you promise to let me stab you first this time and you won't scream like a girl?"

162

Mikey nodded.

"I don't believe you," said Jack, lifting him off the bed and setting him down on the floor. "But you better get going, Jim lad, cos Israel is about to come after 'e!"

***

50: Friday, 21st June. 12.35 p.m. Swanford Community School.

<u>DAN</u>

"Where's Noah?"

No one spoke. Justin looked at Freddie, who looked away.

Sophie exchanged puzzled glances with Kate. "What are those two looking so guilty about?"

Kate shook her head. All eyes were now on Justin.

"Don't look at me," he said.

"What's going on?" demanded Dan, who felt he was being left out.

Justin sighed. "Time to 'fess up, Freddie, I think."

"What is going on?" repeated Dan, becoming annoyed. "Freddie?"

His friend spread his hands. "I just suggested it was time he went back to his own table..."

"You what?"

Freddie shrugged. "We've done our bit for him, and we don't need another girl on our table."

"Fuck you!" said Dan.

"What do you mean, we don't need *another girl* on our table?" asked Kate, insulted by the disparagement.

"I like him," said Sophie. "He's very dry."

"Sorry," said Freddie. "He is Year Nine; you'd think he could look after himself."

"Justin, did you know about this?" asked Dan, gritting his teeth.

"I only found out this morning. Freddie was too afraid to tell you himself."

"I was not!"

Dan glared at Freddie. "Why, what else has happened?"

"Why don't you tell him everything?" suggested Justin.

Freddie squirmed. "I told him that Ms Lane had made us do it. And I've heard since that the Spriggs brothers were boasting that they had found him with his wallet and threw all his money away, and painted '*die faggot*' on the front door of his house."

"You fuckers!" exclaimed Dan, meaning both Freddie and Justin. "How could you do this; how could you not tell me?"

Sophie put her hand on Dan's. "I don't think Justin's to blame."

"OK, I was wrong," said Freddie. "It's just that he makes us look bad, fluttering his hands and swinging his hips and flicking his hair with those blue strands in it..."

"You've been watching him closely, haven't you?" said Kate.

Freddie blushed. "What do you mean by that?"

"Where is he?" demanded Dan.

They all shrugged and shook their heads. "Haven't seen him today," said Freddie.

Dan stood up. "I'm going to see Ms Lane."

"I'll come with you," said Justin. "I've let you down."

"And we'll have words with Mr Hall about his attitude," said Sophie.

***

Ms Lane was sitting in her outer office eating salad from a Tupperware container when the boys walked in. She looked up at them.

"Teachers do eat," she said, seeing their expressions. "Close the door, will you?"

Justin shut the door quietly. "We've come about..."

164

"Noah, yes." She motioned for them to sit in the seats opposite her. "You can't look out for him all the time."

"It's not just that," admitted Dan. "We told him not to sit at our table any more; we told him what you said to us..."

"No!" stated Justin. "Ms Lane, Dan isn't to blame at all. It was Freddie who told Noah that, and when I learned about it, I didn't say anything."

Ms Lane put the remains of her salad down and took a sip of water. "Mr Marshall phoned this morning saying that Noah had fallen off his bike and wouldn't be in today. He also said that on Wednesday someone had trodden on his son's hand and some money was missing from his wallet. Intuition tells me that this is a small part of a much bigger picture."

"How badly was he hurt when he fell off his bike?" questioned Dan.

"Two sprained wrists, grazed knees, bump on the head, cuts and scrapes. Mr Marshall couldn't understand how the bike wheel got so badly buckled. Noah pushed it all the way from school to his shop on Victoria Street."

"Are you talking about Marshall's Barber Shop?" asked Justin.

"The same."

"My dad and granddad go there. I didn't know that was Noah's place."

"He doesn't live there; that's where they keep the bike. I don't suppose there's room in their flat."

"We don't know anything about him," said Dan.

"Mr Marshall is a single parent. He and Noah live in Savoy Flats."

"Jesus, the Allfours," said Justin.

"Yes, and when they got home last night they found that someone had urinated against their front door."

"It's the Spriggs brothers," concluded Justin.

"Probably not this time. They were both in detention for other offences."

"He gets free school meals, doesn't he?" asked Dan.

"I think it's safe to say that money is tight in the Marshall household."

"He's been rabbiting on about this vest he wants to buy for the summer. When he said it cost £16, I thought, well, why don't you just go out and buy it?"

Ms Lane smiled, something she was not apt to do too often. "I would guess that it would take him several weeks to save up that amount of money."

"What can we do to put things right?" asked Justin.

"The answer is simple," replied Ms Lane. "As I have already stated, you cannot protect Noah from this type of systematic bullying, and I'm afraid the school is not in a position to do so either..."

"What?" said Dan. "But the school has an anti-bullying policy – you told us so yourself."

Ms Lane sighed. "Dan, the school has adopted a new code that is popular in certain parts of America. It means, effectively, that gay people can be harassed if the motivation is religious conviction."

"But that's crazy," said Justin.

"Crazy or not, that's how things stand, I'm afraid." Ms Lane tapped her fingers on the desk.

"What can we do?" asked Dan.

"Well, if Noah had friends, real friends he could rely on and confide in, he wouldn't feel so unwanted, alone and unloved. So, if you fit that bill, fine – and if you don't, it's time for you to pull up anchor and move on." She blinked at them and picked up her salad to signal that the meeting was at an end.

***

51: Friday, 21st June. 5.55 p.m. 34b Savoy Flats.

NOAH

I am no longer the Creature from the Black Lagoon; instead I am the Mummy. Both my wrists are bandaged up, but the bandages also cover all of my hands except the fingertips, and go halfway up my arms. I'm supposed to keep them raised above my chest, so I'm sitting on our worn- out orange settee with the wooden legs and the bright flower print cushions, and my arms are stretched out on a pillow across our chipped yellow Formica table. I've got a bag of frozen peas wrapped in a towel to cool them down, and every four hours I take a couple of ibuprofen.

Someone knocked on our door at four o'clock, but I didn't answer, I just held my breath and hoped they'd go away. Why should a knock on the door make me feel sick with fear? It was probably only Auntie Iris from next door, anyway. She isn't really my auntie, you understand, but she used to look after me when I came home from school while my dad was still at work. Now I can look after myself, I don't go in there very much because it smells of cats – she's got two. That's another stereotype I've got to disappoint you with. I'm a gay boy who hates cats. Nasty, devious, slinky things. I would like a dog, mind you – not a small yappy thing, but a nice, big, soft-as-grease one that I can lean my head against while it fans me with its waggly tail.

Before he went to work this morning, our Dad brought me a mug of tea and a bacon butty to eat in bed. I love Dad's bacon butties, but now my bandages have got grease on them. I couldn't get dressed so I've been in my PJs all day. Not that I'm bothered. I've got nowhere to go and no one to see. I suppose I could have had a walk in the corridor, but I didn't want anyone to notice my bare feet. They're not bad feet; it's just that they're out of proportion with the rest of me, like a clown's feet.

My school clothes are ruined. The jacket's got scuff marks all up the front and on the sleeves, and my trousers are ripped. Did I say that the hospital bandaged my head and knees as well? They had more grit in them than my hands. I had an X-ray of both wrists, but the doctor thinks they're both just sprained. I'm supposed to have the bandages off tomorrow and start doing some mild exercises. I'm not sure, though, because they hurt like hell.

I'm glad my school clothes are ruined, because I don't ever want to go back there. What is the matter with people? Why can't they ignore me like they used to? My dad has to suffer because of me. He had to wash the floor and the door where the Lewis brothers had pissed on it, and throw our welcome mat into the skip. Can you imagine those two coming all the way here just to piss on our door? Someone must have put them up to it. Auntie Iris gave us a pretty good description, so I'm pretty certain it was them. They even had their school uniforms on.

I expect I'll be forced to go back to school, but they'll be sorry when they find me hanging by my tie from the banisters in the science block stairwell. Actually, they won't be sorry – they'll more likely dance and sing for joy, so I probably won't give them the satisfaction. In any case, I don't want to break our Dad's heart.

Ooh, that's his key in the lock now. It must be six o'clock, but I'm too lazy to turn round to check with the clock on the sideboard. Before he comes in here, he'll take off his shoes in the lobby and put on his slippers, then hang up his jacket on a coat hanger. It's like I can time him to the second.

He's just put his hand on my head. "Hello son, how's my best boy?"

"OK, Dad, I've got to take my peas off shortly. Have you had a good day?"

"Ten customers, and I sold a packet of BIC disposables."

That is a good day. My dad has to average eight haircuts a day in the week and five on Saturday morning to break even. If he doesn't, it usually means we can't have our week's holiday in the summer. That would be a shame. We usually go to Falmouth on the train and stay in the same B&B in Swanpool – that's a little way down the coast. It's nice there. Dad says given the number of times we've been, I should have learned to swim by now, but I just can't do it. I like splashing and paddling, though, and exploring the rock pools, and no one cares that I'm all out of proportion.

"Dad, I haven't been able to get tea ready."

"Don't fret. I just do my ablutions, then I'll get us something."

When dad says *ablutions* he means having a piss and washing his hands and face, and he knows it makes me smile.

"No sign of anything outside today?" I ask.

He shakes his head. "I don't know what this world is coming to. I've decided to have it out with that school of yours. They can't go bullying you like that and get away with it. Mr Beecher says I ought to sue, but where would I get the money for a solicitor?"

"I don't want you to worry about me, our Dad. I'll be all right."

There's a tap on the door – not a knock, a tap – and we look at each other as if to say that sounds suspicious. In any case, no one comes to our house except the postman, and he wouldn't come at six o'clock in the evening. The tap comes again, a bit louder.

"Maybe it's Iris," says Dad.

I shake my head. "Iris knocks; she doesn't tap."

"Right. I'll go and see."

My dad is hardly any more confident than me in a situation, despite being six inches taller and about a hundred pounds heavier. He disappears into the lobby and I stand up. I hear voices. My knees are knocking inside my PJs and I don't know what to do with my arms.

He comes back in, scratching his head. "There's two lads here to see you, Noah." He turns and beckons them inside.

I'm just about to shout *No, it's a trick!* when in walk Dan Moseley and Justin Walker in their socked feet. They've taken off their trainers in the lobby without being asked, which I know would impress my dad.

Now, I don't know why they're here, but suddenly I feel ashamed: ashamed of our poky flat; of the orange settee with the printed flower cushions; of the yellow Formica table; of the bag of everyday value peas; of my scrawny body, which is not big and strong like theirs; of my oversized bare feet sticking out of my PJ bottoms.

"Hello," I say and it sounds to me like the longest drawn-out whine. My bandaged arms flap in the air and my big bandaged head feels like it's going to explode with the humiliation.

Dan looks at me, sees this mess in front of him, and suddenly his eyes fill with tears. I take a step towards him, because I never want to see him cry, and he comes and gives me a hug and though it hurts, it's worth it because he's the most beautiful boy in the school, if not the world.

"I'm sorry, Noah," he says and those few words make me feel dizzily happy.

I'd like him to hold on to me forever, but he lets go and wipes his eyes on the back of his hand, and on him the gesture looks so masculine, whereas if I did it would be all pink and twirly.

"Right," says my dad, clearly mystified. "I'll go and do my ablutions. You lads make yourselves at home. Take a seat."

We sit down, Dan and I on the settee and Justin on one of our tubular metal dining chairs with the red plastic cushion, that were fashionable sixty years ago.

"Noah," says Justin, when Dad is out of earshot. "We didn't know until today. Freddie is such a dick. We want you back on our table. Kate and Sophie want you there too."

Dan draws out a piece of folded paper from the top pocket of his smart, white, cotton-rib polo shirt. "This is from Freddie. He couldn't come because his granddad's got cancer and he visits him in hospital."

I try to grip the paper but it's too awkward so Dan holds it up for me to read.

Dear Noah,
I'm sorry I was such a douche. I just panicked. Pls come and sit on our table again.

Luv,
Freddie.

"That's nice," I say and I mean it because it is.

"When do you have your bandages off?" asks Dan.

"Tomorrow, I hope. Dad's got me a double sling to keep my wrists up. I'm supposed to start doing exercises."

"We want to take you to the retail park tomorrow," says Justin.

I'm a bit puzzled by this. "What for?"

They look at each other as if I'm thick. "To get a new wheel for your bike, and that vest you wanted, of course," says Dan, as though it's obvious.

"I'd like to," I say, really meaning I'd love to. "But I haven't got the money."

"Oh," says Dan and he stands up and Justin follows suit. I think they're going to leave and I want to say *Please don't go, because I'll cry if you do*, but I'm too scared and I'm glad I didn't because they start emptying their pockets onto the table and it's all money. "We had a whip round at school. After we heard what happened."

"Dan's brother gave a fiver," says Justin, displaying the note with a grin.

"He's rich, though," mutters Dan. "Most of us gave a pound. Ms Lane gave us three, Mrs Parkin gave us two and Jack got Mr Colt and Mr Thompson to stump up as well, though they all told us it's strictly against the rules. We could have got more, probably, but we didn't have time."

Our Dad walks back into the room, having finished his ablutions, and he spies the pile of notes and coins on the table. "What's all this, then?"

Now, Dad is a very proud man and takes a dim view of anything he thinks of as charity, because it means to him that he can't support his own family.

"They did a collection for me," I say and it sounds to me like I'm bleating like a sheep.

Dan locks eyes with our dad and I can see he's going to be upset if it's refused. "We know Noah's being bullied at school, and because we didn't support him like we should have done, his bike wheel got buckled and he lost some money and we wanted to make up for it. All his friends have given a pound."

Our dad looks hard at Dan and I think he's taking his measure, then he looks down at me. "It's yours, son, you deserve it."

I hadn't realised I'd been holding my breath and I let it out, trying not to make it sound like a sigh of relief.

"We want to take Noah shopping tomorrow," says Justin. "Do you think he'll be OK?"

"If a couple of handsome young lads offer to take him out, I'm pretty sure he'll make himself OK."

Oh, my God! Did he just say that? I put my arms in front of my face. I can feel the heat coming off it. I'm going to die with embarrassment. Then I hear him again. "Are you lads stopping for tea?"

More cringing. "Dad," I whisper, "we haven't got anything."

"Oh," he says and after some thought continues. "I know. I'll get us all some fish and chips from Malin's. It's only a ten-minute walk."

I look through my hands and see that Dan's and Justin's eyes have lit up.

"If you're sure," says Justin. "We missed our dinner today."

"I haven't had proper chip shop fish and chips for ages," says Dan. "We usually have boring things like quiche and salad."

Ooh, I think, I'd love quiche and salad just once in a while. Perhaps I can persuade our dad... But no, if they called it cheese flan he might just go for it, but salad is for rabbits.

"The thing about Malin's fish," says our dad as he collects his ancient bucket-shaped leatherette shopping bag, "is that it's real cod, not that foreign stuff they dredge up from who knows where."

When he's gone, Dan and Justin grin at me.

"Sorry," I say, "that's our dad."

"He's great," Justin replies and sits down again. "I like this retro furniture."

Is that a joke? No, I don't think it is. They both send texts to say they won't be home for tea, then Justin begins to count the money on the table, stacking it into neat little piles.

"Shall I put plates to warm?" asks Dan, looking round for the kitchen.

I point to the door, hoping that the 1970s New World gas cooker won't give him too much aggro. "You have to light it with the yellow button in the centre," I shout.

"No problem," comes the reply.

As he's counting I notice Justin taking surreptitious glances down at my big feet. Each time he does it, he frowns to himself and I move them a little bit further back until they're almost under the settee.

"£48.50," he says at last, and begins to search his pockets. "Dan, I'm 50p short!"

"I don't think so," comes the reply, "Mr Colt gave £2.50."

Justin's look of relief is short lived as he stares down at my feet yet again and the frown returns.

"I don't know why they're so big," I gabble. "They've gone from size five to size nine in a few months. I look like a clown."

"I'm size nine as well, but mine are nasty. How do you get yours so nice and neat?" *Nice and neat?* He takes off his left sock, which is a dingy grey colour. There's an old plaster on his next to little toe; the nails are uneven and a bit discoloured, and there's more than a whiff of athlete's foot in the air.

"How often do you wash them?" I ask.

"I have a shower every day."

"But do you wash them?"

He shakes his head.

Dan is standing in the kitchen doorway. "Shall I butter some bread?"

"Oh, yes!" says Justin. "Chip butties. I was just showing Noah my feet."

"Noah, he's disgusting. They're worse than my little brother's feet, and he's got a cast on. Can you do anything for him? He won't listen to me."

"I'll try," I say. "The bread's in the bread bin."

Dan goes back into the kitchen and I turn my attention to Justin's problem. "You see, I've only got a bath, so my feet get soaked, which softens the nails and so they're easier to cut. Do you wear sandals?"

"Yeh, I wear them when my toes are trodden on in football."

"You've got athlete's foot."

"Yeh, I know. They itch."

I look at him. "They smell."

"You mean they stink!" shouts Dan from the kitchen.

"Shut up!" Justin shouts back then looks at me. "Go on..."

"OK, here's what to do. We'll get some athlete's foot cream tomorrow, right?" He nods. "Don't put a plaster on unless you have to, and if you have to, change it every day."

"Every day?"

"Every day. Wash and dry your feet properly every day as well and use a clean towel. Then put the ointment on. When your nails start getting long, soak your feet in a bowl until the nails soften, then take your time with the scissors, doing each one with one straight cut if you're able, and if you get any jagged edges use a nail file."

"A nail file!" he exclaims, as if I've just told him to wear a dress.

"Yes; the glass ones are really good. Change your socks daily and avoid nylon; wear sandals without socks whenever you can; and make sure your shoes and football boots are aired before you wear them again."

"That's a lot of work. But if I do what you say, my feet will look as good as yours, and Kate won't refuse to make out with me because she says I smell?"

"Yes." I try to sound confident.

"Cool!" says Justin with a grin, pulling his sock back on. "We'll start tomorrow. I've got to get things right before I go to the Academy."

"That's what he's really bothered about," shouts the voice from the kitchen.

Justin speaks quietly so that Dan won't hear. "I've got to go for a medical on 23rd July, and I don't want to put them off."

I'm still basking in the praise of my feet when there's a furious knock at the front door and I nearly jump out of my skin.

Dan pokes his head round the kitchen door. "Is that your dad?" he says in a low voice.

I shake my head. He motions for Justin to go with him into the lobby, while I follow not too closely behind.

"Look through the spyhole," I whisper.

But there's no need, because the letterbox opens and a voice shouts. "Noah Marshall, we know you're in there. Come out, or we'll piss through your letterbox." There's sniggering and the indistinct sound of two voices – one broken, the other not.

Dan beckons me forward and whispers in my ear.

"Go away," I say as instructed. "I'm not coming out."

"Get ready for the flood then, homo." There's more laughter and excited chattering from outside, then the letterbox is opened again. Dan twists the Yale lock and yanks the door open.

"Hello, Harry, your dick's hanging out."

Harry Lewis's mouth drops open.

"Smile," says Justin, who has been videoing with his phone.

"Shite," says Harry, pulling up his shorts and boxers. His younger brother Adam is with him, and he doesn't seem to realise his predicament. "Why are you with these homos, Justin Walker?" he asks. His shorts are still round his knees.

"Can't wait to upload this video," Justin says. "Do you think your parents will like it?"

Auntie Iris must have heard all the noise because she comes out of her flat. "You two dirty little boys are here again, are you? Get off with you or I'll have the law on you!"

Harry has got the message and bolts for the door. Adam hoists up his shorts but, when he tries to run, Justin grabs him by the collar. A short struggle follows, but Justin's hold is firm and Adam's swearing and cursing is brought to a sudden halt when Auntie Iris slaps him across the face.

"You disgusting, foul-mouthed little boy," she says.

"You can't do that to me!" he wails, and so Iris slaps him again, which quietens him considerably.

My *nice and neat* size nine feet are out and proud in the corridor, along with the rest of me. The younger Lewis, Auntie Iris and myself are about the same height; hobbits compared to Dan and Justin.

Justin relaxes his grip but turns Adam round so he's facing me.

"You're going to say sorry to Noah, aren't you?"

"No, he's a homo."

"What is a homo?" asks Dan.

Adam shrugs petulantly. "He's got a demon inside him who wants to bum me."

"Who's been filling your thick head with all that stupid nonsense?" demands Iris.

"I don't want him to say sorry," I say. "He's just a silly kid who wouldn't mean *sorry* even if he said it."

Reluctantly Justin lets him go. "If I catch you or your brother here again, I'll throw you down the stairs." He sounds as if he means it.

Adam gets to the fire door at the end of the corridor, pulls it open, then turns to us. "Fuck you all, homos. And, you witch, you're not allowed to hit me. I'll have ChildLine onto you!" Then he runs, and I can hear his feet clattering down the staircase.

"He needs a damn good hiding, him and that tall streak with him," says Iris, and we nod in agreement.

"Thank you, Auntie," I say to her.

"I'm glad you've found yourself a couple of nice young men, Noah; you deserve to be happy."

Dan and Justin exchange grins and my head goes the colour of plum jam. I wish adults didn't always jump to the wrong conclusion.

Our dad comes back three minutes later with his shopping bag full of cod and chips, and a carrier as well, because he's splashed out on some mushy peas and a bottle of Coke. I can't believe it, really; this isn't like Dad. I hope he has a good half-day in the shop tomorrow, or we'll be skint before the end of the month. Dan is back buttering bread in the kitchen, and Justin is laying the table. He did wash his hands, by the way. I told him when he brought in the tomato ketchup that our dad likes brown sauce, which he claimed to have never heard of!

During our tea, we tell our dad about the incident with the Lewis brothers and what Iris did, but we didn't say anything about the video. He said that when he was coming back from the chippy he'd seen a car drive off at speed, and he thought the driver had been a young woman. We had a really nice meal and I can see that dad has taken to Dan and Justin, especially when Dan fed me because I couldn't manage.

It's Friday and after tea Ken Roper calls to take our dad to the Star Inn – that's our local pub. They buy a round of bitter for each other and have a chinwag, and that's my dad's treat of the week. Normally he comes back about ten, we have a cup of hot chocolate, watch a bit of telly and then it's bedtime.

Ken is a bit wary of me. Dad calls him a man's man, and I think he was quite surprised to find Swanford United's Under-14s star players at our house. He knew who they were because he's a season-ticket holder, and sometimes goes to youth matches. Funny, he was chatting away to them while he waited for our dad, and he never even asked me how I came to have bandages on my wrists and head. I must have turned invisible.

Dad dresses in a cardigan and tie to go out. That's his version of casual. Dan and Justin volunteer to wash up, which really pleases him. I can tell Ken thinks it quite weird that boys should wash up, and I imagine his wife at home, forever in front of the sink while he's sitting in an armchair reading the newspaper.

The clean plates are stacked in the drainer, the table's been wiped free of sauce stains, and I half expect them to leave, but instead they sit me down and Justin pours out three glasses of Coke. "Right," says Dan, resuming his place next to me on the settee. "We've got a whole bunch of things to tell you, Noah, so prepare yourself because there's a monster load of shit going down."

"That sounds scary," I say. "Don't forget, I am gay."

They laugh and I know that whatever they tell me I won't ever again be as scared as I was before they came tonight.

I'm sworn to secrecy and I feel like I've just taken a blood oath. Then, as the story unfolds, I understand why I have been targeted, and that I'm just a small cog in the Swanford wheel. By the end I'm in a bit of a daze, but I know now that, even though I've got enemies a-plenty, I've also got friends who will help me, which is why I've got to buy a mobile phone when we go shopping tomorrow.

Dan and Justin have got this really solid friendship. There's a sort of telepathy between them which I suppose they developed on the football field, and their personalities complement each other so well. Justin is calm and quite reserved and thoughtful, while Dan is more intense and emotional and more often takes the lead. I love them both, but Dan is just so hunky and desirable. Still, I'm going to try my best not to spoil things by coming on to either of them, because Noah, *I think this is the beginning of a beautiful friendship*, as Humphrey Bogart said at the end of *Casablanca*. Ooh, I love that film, and it's one of our dad's favourites too.

***

52: Sunday, 23rd June. 8 a.m. 15 Leighton Lane.

JACK

Jack cut a banana in half and handed one part to Dan, who proceeded to slice it over his cereal. It was two hours before their usual getting-up time on a Sunday, and both were bleary-eyed.

"Toast?" asked Jack.

Dan shook his head.

"Tea?"

Dan nodded.

Jack got up and filled the kettle. "We might need a torch."

His brother looked out of the kitchen window sceptically. The sun was already well up into a near-cloudless sky.

"What are you two doing out of bed so early?" asked Pam, standing in the doorway in her dressing gown.

"What's the problem?" enquired Dan.

"There isn't a problem, dear, it's just noting an unusual occurrence."

"Duly noted, then," said Jack. "You can go back to bed now."

Pam frowned. "If you won't tell me, you must be up to something."

"We're going out," said Dan.

"Without telling your parents?"

"We were going to leave you a note: *gone out,*" stated Jack.

"And when will you be back?"

"Sometime late, I imagine," answered Dan.

"And what happens if your father and I have plans?" asked Pam.

179

"Permission to carry out your plans granted," said Jack, smirking at his brother.

"There's no need to be cheeky, Jack Moseley."

"Talking of plans," said Dan, "I've invited Noah for tea on Monday."

"Noah? I don't know a Noah, do I?"

"Now's your chance to get to know Noah, then," offered Jack.

"He asked if you wouldn't mind doing your *special* quiche and salad," said Dan.

"Are you being frivolous, dear?"

"Seriously," emphasised Dan.

"How old is Noah?"

"Fourteen – he's in Year Nine," replied Dan. "He's gay."

Pam looked at Jack, who was spooning sugar into two mugs of tea, then back at Dan. "Why are you inviting him and not Jack?"

Jack put a mug in front of his brother. "What's it got to do with me? He's LB's friend."

"Aren't I allowed to have gay friends?" questioned Dan.

"How do you know he's gay?" countered Pam.

"You haven't seen him," chuckled Jack, sitting down again.

Dan looked over at his brother. "He can't swim, you know. Justin and I are going to teach him as soon as he's given the all-clear."

"How were his wrists?"

"Swollen, painful and purply-yellow, but he can move them. We got him a new wheel, a mobile and his vest – all for under £60."

"Oh, the famous vest."

"Yeh, it's quite smart and very Noah, if you know what I mean, but it hangs off him a bit – no, a lot."

"Well, if he starts swimming, maybe you can build him up."

Dan nodded and gulped his tea. "We'd better be going, hadn't we?"

Jack looked at the clock. "You're right. I'll text Robert to tell him we're on our way." He looked at his mother and smiled. "Bye then, Mum. Have a good day."

"Yeh, we should be back for tea," confirmed Dan. "We'll let you know..."

***

53: Sunday, 23rd June. 8.55 a.m. The road leading to Folly Farm.

JACK

From the junction of the A998, it was about a mile up an un-signposted B road to Folly Farm. After half that distance, they began to look for a suitable place to hide their bikes. Between the narrow grass verges and the verdant hedgerows, there were overgrown ditches with a thin trickle of water in each. Mature trees had been allowed to grow up on the periphery of the adjoining meadows.

They stopped at a dilapidated five-barred gate overgrown with weeds on their left. A rusty chain attached it to a leaning fence post, but there was no lock.

"Shall we?" said Jack.

"As good a place as any," replied Dan.

They lifted their bikes over the gate and chained them to the firmest of the cross bars.

A light breeze rustled the leaves, but otherwise there was no sound but the background hum of distant traffic.

"Nice day," said Jack, stretching and gazing about him. "You nervous?"

"A bit," admitted Dan.

"Me too."

They both started as Jack's phone went off.

Alan and Derek not here. Good luck, R.

"Shit," said Dan.

"Two to one," said Jack. "It could be worse."

Only one vehicle, a tractor with a trailer full of second cut silage, passed them on their walk up the road. The driver waved as they stood back to allow it to pass. They rounded a bend and Dan signalled for them to slow down as they came within sight of the farm entrance on the right-hand side of the road. The upper storey of the house was visible, along with the shabby roof of the stables beyond.

The boys walked close in to the verge so they were concealed by the sparse hawthorn hedge interleaved with a barbed wire fence. The galvanised metal yard gate was open, supported on what looked like new concrete posts. The farm track led up to the right of the house, then curved away towards the stables. The nose of the white Ford transit was visible, having been backed in behind and at ninety degrees to the house. The driver's door was open, but there was no sign of Derek.

The front garden, if it could be called that, was full of builder's rubble, but had once been an apple orchard, as evidenced by the stumps and the four or five trees on the perimeter which had survived the chainsaw.

"This was good scouting, LB," said Jack as they squatted down just yards from the entrance. "It's the perfect place to keep someone prisoner."

"Well, at least if he's in there he's got entertainment," said Dan, indicating the satellite dish on the chimney stack.

"Weird," replied Jack. "Stewy never mentioned being able to watch TV."

"Perhaps Derek's a fan of Fox News."

"That wouldn't surprise me," answered Jack.

"Shall we make a move?" suggested Dan. "We can't stay here forever."

"OK, let's assume Alan is somewhere in the house. If Derek's in there too we've got to get him out, and if he's outside we've got to stop the psycho getting in while we're doing the rescue."

"Yeh, but..." began Dan.

"Yeh, I know. So I'll now rephrase what I said. If Derek's in there, I've got to get him out, and if he's outside I've got to stop the psycho getting in while you're doing the rescue."

"Agreed," said Dan.

"Right, get as close as you can without being seen and then wait till I've lured him away. If Alan's in there and I get caught, don't bother about me, just get him away." Jack smiled. "That's an order."

"Yes sir," said Dan.

They gave each other a hug, then Jack got up and sauntered through the open gateway. He walked up the dirt track until he was level with the house, where he paused to look round and listen. Then he heard the front door being opened. He ran towards the transit, not knowing if he had been spotted. The front door banged shut.

Jack turned to face the way he had come and leaned back as nonchalantly as he could against the wheel arch of the van. Derek rounded the side of the house and for a few paces didn't notice the visitor. When he did, he jumped, which for a moment amused Jack.

"Hello, Derek," he called. There was about twelve paces between them.

"What are you doing here, Moseley, you shirt-lifting poofter?"

"Charming. I'm here for my riding lesson."

"You stupid fuck."

"This is Folly Farm Stables, isn't it?"

Derek looked round. "I don't believe you're here on your own."

Jack spread his hands, noticing that Derek was edging towards him. "Who would want to come riding with a shirt-lifting poofter?"

"You know there's no way out of here except the way you came in."

"No, I didn't know, but thanks for telling me."

By now Derek was eight paces away. "I'm going to enjoy dismembering you, Moseley."

"Dismembering: that's a big word for a dim-witted psychopath, and I thought your speciality was raping boys, like your brother, Stewart..."

Jack didn't wait for a reply. He pushed himself off the wheel arch and fled, heart in mouth, up the track towards the stables.

***

54: Sunday, 23rd June. 9.20 a.m. Folly Farm.

DAN

I run across the gateway and push myself through the hedge, right by an old apple tree. They're still talking as I dodge round the piles of rubble and come to the front door.

There's a big hole in one of the glazed panels, and when I look through I see there's glass all over the floor and the nearest floorboards are discoloured with mould and damp. I put my hand through the hole and unlatch the door. Quietly does it. I enter the hall with the stairs facing me on the right and rooms leading off along the passage to the left. The house is dusty and dirty and hasn't been lived in for years. As I search from room to room, there's an old dresser in one and a heavy sideboard in another, and throughout there are the moth-eaten remains of carpets, but mostly it's pallets and old sacks and tarpaulins.

There's no sign of life down here, so I climb the stairs. A couple of the treads are loose, but don't give me any trouble. There's a dirty stained-glass window of a sailing ship on the high seas at the top. It's covered in thick strands of cobwebs, but at least it gives enough light to see by. I have a choice of five doors on the L-shaped landing, and open three of them onto empty rooms before I try the fourth. I find myself in a box room with a bank of computer equipment on a desk.

There's a heavy curtain over the window and the only light comes from one of the monitors. The screen is blank except for some writing: *Next session 11.00 GMT.*

I leave the room and come to the fifth door. It's solid and locked, and my chances of breaking it down are nil. For a moment I'm flummoxed until I notice a key hanging on a nail hammered into the frame.

I don't open the door in the normal way, but kind of throw it open – in case there's a trap. There isn't. There's just a boy standing against the far wall with a black bag over his head, wearing only a pair of dirty pyjama bottoms which are so long they cover his feet. His torso and arms have been flayed by what looks like a chain, and are criss-crossed with red and purple lacerations.

Except for the light from the door, the rest of the room is in darkness. So I look for a switch and find one of those half-spherical types that sticks out of the wall and has grooves in it and is made of metal. When I flick it, the room is bathed in a feeble yellow glow. The light bulb hangs from the centre of the ceiling, surrounded by a faded paper shade, and immediately attracts flies from elsewhere in the room. My brain barely registers the other cable coming down alongside the light with what looks like a high-tech connector on the end. I'm more concerned with the flies, which buzz excitedly: there's a really bad smell in here. The window has been boarded up and the room is small and completely empty except for an ancient metal bed with bare springs.

The boy is cowering against the far wall. I'm ninety per cent sure it's Alan, even though he's lost a lot of weight and I can see the outline of his ribs. Both his hands are behind his back and I assume that they've been tied.

"Alan," I call, "it's me, Dan Moseley."

This seems to really scare him, because he starts to shriek and shake his head, and the front of his pyjama bottoms is suddenly saturated with pee. I'm used to Mikey wetting himself, so this doesn't bother me particularly, though I can tell now that the bad smell is coming from him.

"Sssh, Alan, I'm not going to hurt you. I just want to get you out of here."

He slides down the wall until he's propped against it with his legs outstretched on the floor. He's moaning and it sounds like he's saying 'no' over and over and his whole body is shaking, and I don't know why, because I've said I'm not going to hurt him.

I go up to him and squat down and say, "It's OK."

I start removing the bag, which is fixed with a shoelace round his neck. It has a nose slit for him to breathe through, but none where his mouth is, and I wonder how long it is since he had any food or drink. His body slumps forward, like he's fainted, which in some ways makes it easier for me. I'm certain it's Alan now, and I'm pretty scared of what I might find when I take the bag off. I cradle him in my arms as I draw it off. His face is a mess. His lips are dry and cracked, he has two black eyes, and there's a gash across his nose, which looks like it's still got a stitch in it, though it's so swollen and purple I'm not sure. But it's only marginally worse than it was in the photo Ms Lane showed us.

Next I check his hands, and they're secured with one of those plastic self-locking cable ties and I've got nothing to cut it off with, which makes me feel stupid for not bringing any tools, not even a knife. At the same time I see that there are streaks of blood at the base of his spine and when I lift him slightly – and he's very light – I see there's a glutinous patch of reddy-brown liquid all around his bum, and this is where the stink is coming from.

I lower him back down and stroke his hair, hoping he'll soon come round. Then I notice his left pyjama leg is caked in dried blood, and there's a chain leading up inside the cloth. I look for the other end and see that it's attached by a lock to the bed frame. It's not a heavy chain, more like one that Mum uses for her hanging baskets, so it could easily be cut with the right tools. I try pulling on the PJs but his body starts to spasm, as though he's in pain.

I lie him down and roll up his pyjama legs one at a time. I do the right one first, and though his foot's filthy and there's some blood around the toenails it's not too bad. But when I roll the other one up, I nearly vomit, and have to take deep breaths to stop myself retching. I can feel my eyes getting watery at the sight of it. An inch back from the big and second toe, between the bones, someone has pushed a wire down through the flesh and out through the sole of his foot. Then the wire has been threaded on to the chain and the two ends bent into a loop and then twisted together. And I'm sure he's been dragged across the floor by it, because the flesh is torn and inflamed, and I think of the pain he must have endured when it was happening and I wonder what else they've done to him. I look back and Alan's eyes are open and he's staring at me, but now quite calmly.

"I'm dead, aren't I?" he states and his voice is still light, but a lot deeper than it was.

I shake my head.

"Then I must be dreaming," he says.

"No," I reply and smile.

Then I lift him gently by the shoulders so I'm cradling him again and stroke his brow. "Alan, I'm going to get you out of here, but I need to find some tools to cut you free."

"Are you really Dan Moseley?" he asks, and there's a kind of distance in his voice, as though he's only allowing himself to half-believe what's happening.

"Yes," I say and I give him a squeeze, but not too much in case I hurt him.

"Why are you crying?" he asks.

And I can't answer him, because I don't want to tell him how badly he's hurt. And he gives a little nod, as if he already knows, and closes his eyes and his body suddenly goes limp and just for a second I think he's died because he's so thin and they've done such terrible things to him.

And I want to stay with him, but I know I've got to hurry and get help or they'll be back and we'll all end up like Alan.

187

I get downstairs and phone Jack. He doesn't answer at first, but I keep ringing and at last he picks up.

"I've found him," I say "Where are you?"

"Running through some trees at the back of the stables. Derek's after me with a pissing air rifle. Is Alan OK?"

"No, he's pretty bad, and they've tied him up. I need some wire-cutters or at least a pair of pliers. Jesus, Jack, be careful – that guy is mad enough to kill you!"

"Yeh, I think you're right. Listen, there's a toolbox out by the van. Try that. Got to go, LB, he's catching up. I'll keep heading him away from the house, if I can!"

My heart's pounding. We've both put ourselves in danger and I'm not sure that the plan is workable any more. We expected Alan to be able to walk out, but that's just not going to happen.

I'm out of the door and up the side of the house in a trice. The driver's door of the transit is open and there's a bottle of water on the seat, so I take it and remove the keys from the ignition. The toolbox is nearby on the ground. I delve into the trays. There's a pair of expensive-looking side-cutting pliers which should do the job, but as I'm fishing them out I hear the crack of an air rifle and it's much nearer than I expected. Then my phone rings. It's a text from Robert. *They've left the church.*

I'm back in the house and up the stairs in about three seconds. Alan is tottering and limping about the room, and I can hardly believe the resilience of the little fellow. I unscrew the bottle and put it to his lips, holding the back of his head. He drinks, but doesn't gulp it as I expected, but savours it as though it is some special brew.

"Thank you," he says, incredibly gratefully, and I can't understand why I was so mean to him.

I show him the pliers and cut through the tie around his wrists with no trouble. There are deep marks where it's bitten into the flesh, and he flexes his hands and groans. Then he sits down and pulls up the pyjama leg and I snip the wire as close to the ball of his foot as I can. And he pulls it out without a second thought. My stomach turns over and I guess his does too.

But there's no time to dwell on it. "Hold on to me," I say, "and if you think you might pass out tell me and I'll carry you."

Once on the landing, I close and lock the door and put the key back on the hook, while he takes another drink. Then we start down the stairs. Just about halfway, stepping gingerly onto one of the loose treads, I see Derek's silhouette appear at the front door, air rifle in hand. He bends to peer through the broken panel. Alan moans. He has seen him too, and I give him another little squeeze and I know I'm going to protect him, whatever happens.

Then a brick flies through the other glass panel and I hear Jack's voice. "Derek Henderson, you psychopathic cretin, you couldn't shoot the backside off a barn door."

I almost laugh and Derek roars and turns away from the door and I hear the report of the air rifle again, and then a faint mocking voice. "You fucked up again, psycho-twat!"

"That's my brother," I whisper to Alan and this time he gives me a little squeeze and I begin to think he might be starting to believe this is real.

I carry him over the glass in the hall and, when I've seen that the coast is clear, he pulls the door open for me. Blood is dribbling from the sole of his foot and I'm fairly sure that the mess around his bum is getting worse too. My shorts are smeared with it.

Now we're outside, I can only think of one option: to get back to where our bikes are hidden and phone for help, but Alan has other ideas. "If the keys are in the van, I can drive it," he says.

"Not with that foot," I say.

"You can depress the clutch when I say clutch."

I am in three minds about this. My first mind is that Alan is badly injured and may pass out; my second is the memory of being nearly flattened by him; and my third is that it could work...

I run to the van and practically throw him in, then insert the key into the ignition. He pulls up his PJs until they're tucked under his thighs.

"The seat needs adjusting."

I look blank, and his little feet are swinging in mid-air.

"The bar..." He points down.

I lift the bar and push the seat and practically run him into the steering wheel.

"OK, get in."

I shut his door and run round to the passenger side. It's funny; Alan's taken charge and I'm glad, though my heart is thumping worse than ever and I know full well that we're both running on adrenalin.

"Push the clutch in and when I say, ease it off slowly."

As I aim for the pedal, I see his swollen foot. It's not pretty, and I wonder if this is such a good idea. Then I think about Jack and I look down towards the farm entrance. I shudder. Derek has just closed the metal gate and blocked our exit. I don't know whether he's seen us or not.

"Trouble," I say.

Alan glances down the track then turns the key in the ignition. The engine fires first time. Derek has heard it and he's running towards us now.

"Foot off."

I jerk it like a prat and the engine stalls.

"Fuck!" I say. "Sorry."

"Easy," says Alan. "Foot down." He clicks his door lock, puts the van back into gear, then retries the ignition. Derek is about forty feet away. The engine fires. I love Ford transits.

"Foot off, easy..."

My whole body is shaking. I can feel the pedal springs resisting. Alan revs, the pressure on my foot disappears, the clutch engages and we're off. Immediately, he turns the wheel and the van swings right onto the track. Derek is standing, his body in line with the front of the house. His rifle is aimed at the windscreen – at Alan. Something flies towards Derek from his left. He fires just as the projectile hits him on the side of the head. I hear a thud, then cracks appear in the windscreen, running in all directions from just below the driver's mirror. Derek drops the rifle, falls and jumps sideways at the same time. The van catches him a glancing blow and he's thrown onto the grass verge on my side. The van wheels crunch over the rifle. Jack is running down the track towards the gate. Alan slows.

"Clutch."

I obey and he puts the gear lever into neutral. The cracks in the windscreen are steadily becoming more pronounced, but the driver's vision is still good. Alan is very pale but his eyes are alight. I look back. Derek is sitting on the grass holding his head. The gate swings open. Jack comes round to my side. I open the door.

"LB," he says, "some fun. Hey Alan, how you doing?"

There's no reply and so he belts himself in, which I think is hilarious, then locks the door.

"Clutch," says Alan. I obey. He engages first gear.

"Clutch," he says and this time my foot rises smoothly off the pedal.

As the front of the transit passes out of the gate, a car turns in from the left, but we're not stopping. Alan accelerates, turns the wheel sharply right, but not so sharply that he misses the opportunity to deliberately clip the front of the incoming Volvo S80 with the tail of the van. We miss the ditch on the right by inches, trail along the grass verge for some twenty-five yards and then bounce onto the road. We're going the wrong way, but who cares, we're still going...

We go through the clutch procedure and Alan changes into second and then third, and I realise that this boy is a completely natural driver who could have driven from birth given the opportunity. No wonder he's so good on a skateboard.

"What about our bikes?" says Jack, ever practical.

Alan looks in the rear-view mirror to check we're not being followed.

***

55: Sunday, 23rd June. 9.40 a.m. The road leading to Folly Farm.

ALAN

I do a three point turn by backing into a lay-by. Already Dan is getting good at the clutch and I hardly have to say anything. I slow as we get close to the entrance to Folly Farm again, so we can see what's going on. The Volvo is up by the side of the house. I only catch a glimpse, but Jack says that my dad and brothers are clustered around it, and that there is a lot of steam, but whether it's coming from the car or the people he can't tell. I guess he's joking.

I stop the van by an old field gate so that they can pick up their bikes, but keep the engine ticking over. Because I'm not concentrating on driving, I begin to feel quite ill and sleepy, as if it's the van's energy that's keeping me going. They aren't long in putting the bikes in the back and when Dan returns to the cab he takes off his T-shirt and puts it on me, because he notices I'm shivering. You could fit two of me inside it.

When we start off again, Jack opens the window a little way and I know it's because I stink of pooh and wee, but neither of them say anything. I ask them where we're aiming for and they say 41 Westbury Avenue. I don't remember much else about the journey, except the van seems to be able to drive itself.

***

56: Monday, 24th June. 4 p.m. 15 Leighton Lane.

JACK

Jack watched his mother critically from his seat at the kitchen table. "Why are you hovering?"

"Don't be silly, dear, I'm not hovering, I'm washing the salad."

"I've been watching you. You've been pretending to scrub every lettuce leaf, radish and spring onion for the last fifteen minutes, but most of the time you're staring out of the window."

"I can't help it if I'm a little preoccupied."

"Are you worrying that LB will catch *gay* from Noah and not give you any grandchildren?"

"You do talk nonsense, Jack Moseley. I just don't understand why it is that your brother invites someone to tea who he's only known for five minutes, whereas he's never asked Sophie?"

"But she's got a standing invitation, hasn't she? Whereas Noah is a quiche and salad virgin."

"Oh my goodness, they're here. Oh, he's like a little matchstick man. Oh dear, he's got blue hair."

"He's got blue highlights."

"I thought you weren't allowed to dye your hair at school."

"The headmaster dyes his hair."

"That's not the same. Does he wear make-up?"

"Who, the headmaster?"

"Don't be obtuse, dear."

"I don't know if Noah wears make-up. But if he does I'm sure he'll give you a few tips."

"You never wanted to dye your hair or wear make-up, and neither does Robert."

"You don't know what Robert wants. I think I'd like him to have blue highlights in his ginger hair and a touch of mascara on his ginger eyelashes."

"Why don't they come in instead of standing chatting on the path?"

"LB's probably giving Noah a few tips on how to deal with the salad-washing gorgon."

At last the two boys entered the kitchen and Dan introduced Noah to his mother. Pam remembered not to shake hands because of his sprained wrists, which were still bruised and swollen.

"Hey Noah, welcome to the Moseley house of horror," said Jack.

Pam looked down her nose at her eldest son, then turned to her guest. "We have tea around six-thirty, Noah, when Dan's father gets home from work, so would you like a glass of orange and a biscuit to be going on with?"

"If you don't mind, I'd like to get changed first, Mrs Moseley. These trousers are so tight they're making my eyes water."

"Oh dear," said Pam, accompanied by her sons' chuckles.

"Foot up, Noah," said Dan.

Noah flicked his hair. "I'm such a baby. I can't even take off my shoes without help these days."

The two boys went upstairs to change while Pam moved the two pairs of discarded shoes to a safe place. "He's got big feet, hasn't he, for such a small boy?"

"And I've got small feet for such a big boy," said Jack unhappily.

"Why is he wearing such tight trousers?"

"Because when his bike was wrecked by the brethren of the psycho-church, he ripped his one good pair."

"I don't know why his father can't afford a second pair; he's a businessman."

Jack groaned and swallowed the last of his orange juice. "Well, I better be going, or Swanford's other billionaire businessman, Mr Ray, will be giving me the sack."

By the time he had put his trainers on, Dan and Noah had returned to the kitchen, both changed.

"Great vest, Noah," said Jack.

The boy beamed. "This is my first official wearing. I think it's a bit big."

"I shouldn't worry. You'll grow into it with all this swimming you're going to do."

"What?"

"I think he only bought it to show off his armpit fuzz," said Dan, reaching out and tugging at one of the tufts of dark hair.

Noah screeched. "Ooo, Dan!"

"Daniel Moseley, leave him alone," ordered Pam.

The sound of little hops coming down the hall caught Jack's attention. Mikey appeared in the doorway, ready to announce his arrival with his customary *hi*. His mouth opened, but instead of the high-pitched greeting he clamped his mouth shut, his eyes became like saucers and he blushed.

Jack eyed Mikey then shifted his gaze to the point that had transfixed him: namely, a twig-like boy in a multi-coloured sleeveless vest with blue highlights in his hair and a fringe that hid most of the right side of his face. He was chatting to Dan, one hand on his hip, oblivious to the attention he was receiving.

Jack looked knowingly at his mother who had also witnessed the extraordinary event.

Meanwhile, Mikey had moved sideways so that he was half-hidden by the door frame, though his attention hadn't moved at all.

"Michael Moseley!" his mother shouted.

The little boy jumped and his blush deepened, then he scurried away down the hall, his crutch tapping along the carpet.

"What's up with Mikey?" asked Dan.

"He's being foolish," said Pam.

On his way out, Jack put his hand on Noah's shoulder. "I think you've got a fan," he whispered.

***

57: Monday, 24th June. 8 p.m. 15 Leighton Lane.

NOAH

Mrs Moseley seems to have been on edge all night. I'm a bit worried that she doesn't like me. Dan told me to ignore her because she's going through the change. I asked him what he meant by that, and he laughed. Just because I'm effeminate doesn't mean I understand women, particularly mothers.

Mr Moseley has his hair cut at our dad's place, which is perhaps why he's more relaxed with me than Mrs Moseley. I told him about today in school, when we all gave Mandy Simpkins a standing ovation when she came in to assembly. Well, I say all – it was probably a third of us at least. Of course, a lot of people, especially in Year Seven and the sixth form, didn't know anything about it. The other good thing was that we earned ourselves a whole school detention on Wednesday, so even the likes of Jacob and Logan and the Lewises are included, even though they're in the enemy camp.

Dan was telling me about when he learned that his brother was gay and they had the biggest bust-up imaginable. It's hard to believe now, because they're so solid. In every look they give each other there's always a smile of encouragement or approval, or just plain simple love. I wish I had a brother like Jack, not because he's gay, but because he would make me feel special. Dan wants me to learn to swim, and he and Justin have offered to teach me. They want me to start this Saturday morning and be able to swim a length before Justin goes to Football Academy at the end of next month. That's a tall order. When we were in Dan's room, I told him I didn't have any trunks, so he rummaged through his drawers and found me an old pair of jammers that no longer fit him. I was too embarrassed to try them on, but they're a twenty-six-inch waist so they should be just right. I'm a bit worried I'll make a fool of myself – and I'll certainly look a fool beside them.

I loved Mrs Moseley's quiche and salad with wholemeal bread and butter. For afters we had ice cream with hot butterscotch sauce. Now that's what I call a tea. We've just been talking about the party we're all going to a week on Friday. It's at the legendary venue: 41 Westbury Avenue. I don't know why I've been invited, really. Our dad was really excited for me, because he knows that I love a party but don't normally get invited to any. What a sad person I am.

After tea, Dan took me up to his room again and I listened to some music on headphones while he did his homework. I'm still excused because of my wrists, which is about the only good thing about them. It didn't take him long, especially as I gave him some help with the maths problems. Then he told me all about the adventure he had on Sunday with his brother rescuing Alan Henderson. It was hair-raising. I would never be brave enough to be involved in something like that. I don't know Alan, but I have had dealings at school with his lard-arse brother Ben, who's a friend of Jason Spriggs. Dan says that Alan is completely different – which he needs to be if he's not going to be a total shit. He'll be at the party at number 41 too.

The old lady who owns the house is really rich and quite posh. When they parked up the Ford transit outside the house after the rescue, she phoned the police and told them that she'd seen three suspicious characters getting out of the van, but the descriptions she gave were of Alan's elder brothers and his dad. I'm not sure I'm going to fit in with all these goings-on. I'm totally useless at everything.

Which brings me on to the scary kid. His name's Mikey, and the way he stares at me is just weird. I'm not used to little kids, and don't know what they're about. So perhaps this is normal, but it is kind of freaky. I tried to say something to him earlier, like *hello, what's your name?* But he just kind of went rigid then ran away, like he was frightened of me. I can see that Jack finds this funny, so he obviously knows something that I don't. He said I had a fan in Mikey, but I think he must have been joking. I could see Mrs Moseley getting more and more annoyed with him and in the end she sent him to bed early, which made him carry on alarmingly. Dan told me not to worry about it because he was just showing off. One more thing about Mikey. He broke his leg and is hobbling around on a crutch, only it's not hobbling as he can practically climb walls with it. I hope he's not at the party on Friday week.

**

58: Tuesday, 25th June. 7 p.m. 15 Leighton Lane.

<u>PAM</u>

For once the house was quiet. Pam began to clear away the tea things. "Why didn't you go with Dan tonight?"

Roger looked up at her. "I'll come on to that when you've told me what's wrong. You were off last night as well."

"I wasn't off, and if I was it's because I think Noah is a bad influence on our family."

"What do you mean? He may be a bit effeminate, but he seems a perfectly decent lad to me, just like his dad."

"Look at the effect he had on Mikey."

"I think he was scared of Mikey, and who can blame him when the little horror was in full *Damien* mood last night?"

"That was Noah's fault. Don't you see?"

"Er, no."

"Jack saw what happened. Of course, he thought it was funny."

"In that case, get him to sort out his little brother. He usually can."

"Mikey was still in a mood today. That's why I sent him to your mother's, so the two moods could be together."

"OK, what else is Noah to blame for, besides Mikey's moods? Has he joined in a pincer movement with my mum against you? I'm told he's an expert military tactician."

Pam ignored the jibe. "I don't understand what Dan sees in him. They're completely different: polar opposites. Did you know that your son and Justin Walker are going to teach him to swim?"

"Pam, darling, you'll have to come up with something better than that if you want me to find fault with him."

198

"Our children are drawing away from us. They're becoming like strangers. Look at Sunday. They won't say where they're going, but when they come back they both look as if they've been through a hedge backwards and Dan has got blood on his shorts and T-shirt."

"My most vivid memory of Sunday was that they came back tired and happy, just like teenage boys should do after a day out."

"Roger Moseley, you're being obtuse, just like your eldest son is when I'm trying to have a rational conversation on important matters."

"If I'm being obtuse, Pam, it's because you haven't said anything to me that makes sense."

"What about Elspeth Chambers sending us an invitation to this party a week on Friday?"

"What's that got to do with anything?"

"It's a very strange affair."

"A few drinks and snacks in a nice house which you've visited and I haven't. What's strange about that?"

"The reason why our children are behaving in a peculiar fashion is to do with that house. That's where Jack is tonight and Dan's there almost as often."

"You told me it was like a palace inside with all the latest features and gadgets, and you're surprised our sons like to spend time there?"

"You're impossible sometimes, Roger Moseley."

"Oh well, if you think I'm impossible then take a look at this..." Roger took out a letter from his back pocket and threw it on the table in front of Pam. She frowned, picked it up and began to read:

Dear Mr Moseley,

Thank you for coming to the meeting on 13th June. This letter is to confirm the position we discussed.

At our meeting I gave you advanced warning that you are at risk of dismissal on grounds of redundancy. This situation has arisen through no fault of your own, but has come about because of outsourcing of the Environmental Department.

In these circumstances you may, if you wish, pursue alternative options...

"Roger!" Pam sat down at the table, clutching the letter.

"Yes – kind of puts worries about our children into perspective, doesn't it?"

"What's going to happen to us?"

"This is three months' notice. If I don't apply, or there isn't a job with the new private company, I shall be unemployed on 30th September."

Pam began to read the letter again, but found nothing different. "It doesn't mention anything about a new company. What new company?"

"New company means any group which has the money and means. The council is tendering at the moment. But you can be sure if I was to be redeployed it would mean a substantial cut in salary."

"Roger, can't your union fight this? You pay your subscription, so why don't they do something?"

"The union is us, Pam. You know the number of meetings I've attended recently. We have been fighting this for months, but we haven't got a leg to stand on. Social Services got their letters a week ago yesterday, and they were in uproar. They walked out for two hours, but it seemed to go completely unnoticed. Parks and Tourism get theirs next week. By the end of the year, all council services will be managed by private companies."

"What about redundancy pay? What about your pension?"

"Nine thousand pounds approximately, and the pension is frozen."

"Oh, Roger, why is this happening to us? Why are we getting this type of worry on top of everything else at this time in our lives?"

Roger shook his head and reached over and took both his wife's hands in his. "We'll just have to batten down the hatches and accept all the invitations to free meals we can."

"When are we going to tell the boys?"

"Let's keep it our dark secret for a while – there's no sense in worrying them."

***

59: Tuesday, 25th June. 7.30 p.m. Pear Tree Cottage, The Ropewalk.

ROBERT

The house telephone rang. Maybelle put down her copy of *Country Living* magazine and went out into the hall to answer it.

"Hello, Maybelle Crittenden speaking."

"Hello, Mrs Crittenden, this is Elspeth Chambers. I was wondering if I might have a word with your son."

"One moment, I believe he's in his room doing his homework..."

Maybelle put down the phone and went to the foot of the stairs. "Robert!" she called. "Robert!"

There was the sound of a door opening and Robert ducked his head into the stairwell. "Hi, Mom, everything all right?"

"Mrs Chambers would like to speak to you, hon."

"Oh, OK, thanks." Robert ran down the stairs in his socked feet while his mother returned to the lounge and her magazine.

"Hello Elspeth, this is Robert."

"Hello, my sexy snog toy."

"J—! Elspeth, I didn't quite catch that?"

"Can you come over now so I can have my wicked way with you?"

"I could come over tomorrow night, if you like?"

"Spoilsport. But I suppose it's better than nothing."

"What exactly do you have in mind?"

"Something very unseemly, of course."

"What time?"

"Seven-ish... I believe Elspeth has a couple of real jobs for you to do, so you might even make some money, you all-American hustler."

"Why, thank you ma'am."

"I've got to go and wipe Alan's bum now."

"How—?"

"He's still pretty incoherent, but physically he's getting there. LB is brilliant. Elspeth calls him her physician associate. The thing is, he really gets a kick out of all this medical stuff."

"I'll see you tomorrow."

"Kiss..."

Robert put the phone down and went into the lounge. "Looks like I've got some overtime work, Mom."

"As long as it doesn't interfere with your studies, dear."

"It won't."

"You say Mrs Chambers is eighty-three?"

"That's right."

"She sounds very sprightly for her age, and so very English."

"You should come round and meet her one day."

"Perhaps... Hon, I'm not sure you should be calling her Elspeth. In the South, a young gentleman would refer to her as ma'am or Mrs Chambers."

"She insisted, Mom."

"Very well, you must do as a lady commands, of course."

"When is Dad back?"

"I'm not sure, but I'm expecting a call later."

"I just wanted to tell him that I intend to speak to Pastor Fisher on Sunday about going on the induction course."

"I'm sure he'll be very pleased to hear that. I don't mind telling you, he was getting pretty riled by your attitude."

"I had a lot to think over, Mom."

Robert went back upstairs and attended to the rest of his homework, then he switched on his private phone and found he had an email from America.

Hi Robert,

Thanks for the picture of you and Mr Handsome English Boy. If they were all like him I doubt 1776 would have happened.

School's out in Tyree and I'm jetting off shortly to Bloomington for two weeks to stay with my favourite aunt and uncle. They have a boat on the marina, and we're going to spend a few days on Lake Monroe. I'm hoping my cousin Jeff will be going along – you'd like him, I'm sure!

Slut gossip. She's going as a 'trainee counsellor' to Church Summer Camp at Turner Falls for the whole of July. It'll be interesting to see what happens when all the 13–16-year-old boys come back with pus dripping from their dicks.

I don't believe English schools summer holidays! They're almost over before they've begun and don't get started till it's nearly fall.

Have fun anyway, and write soon,
R.

***

Hello Rosa,

Thanks for your email. Hope you have a great time in Indiana.

I have a new job: gardener. My employer is Elspeth Chambers, the rich English lady, and I'm now earning more than Jack. It's great because we can spend time together at the house.

There is a lot going on in this country which is really bad, and some of it is the fault of my church. It has a very long reach, and a lot of powerful allies here as well as overseas.

I'm due to attend a course on how to become a youth leader and mount an anti-gay crusade.

It won't be long before things come to a head. Wish me luck.

    R.

***

60: Friday, 28th June. 9.05 a.m. Swanford Community School.

<u>JACK</u>

Mr Colt was two minutes late, and even such a small delay was enough to unsettle form 4S, so rare was the occurrence.

"Something's happened," whispered Jack to Robert, though why he was whispering made no sense.

Since the class had grown unaccustomedly quiet with the non-appearance of their form tutor, the whisper carried even to the back of the class.

"What do you fucking know, Moseley?" retorted Mandy.

"Crikey, Manners, there's no need to shout," said Max.

"There is every need when Oracle Jack starts spreading doom and gloom. The man's only two fucking minutes late, for God's sake!"

"I think Jack's right," said Joan Field.

"He can't be right, he's gay," murmured Charlie Masefield, who had moved back a row and was now sitting next to his girlfriend, Barbara Carter.

A moment later Charlie was struck a blow across the back of the head. "Ow! That hurt."

"Well, keep your mouth shut then, you little cunt," said Mandy, going back to her seat.

"That's assault, that is," said Charlie.

"Serves you right, big man," said Barbara, smoothing his hair.

At that moment, Mr Colt walked into the classroom and as ever went quietly to his desk. Still uneasy, Jack looked hard at him to see if he could discern anything abnormal in the old man's mood. Two minutes later, his teacher looked up at the rows of expectant faces.

"I apologise for my unusual tardiness this morning," he began. "There was an unexpectedly lengthy staff briefing. There will be announcements made in assembly, I'm sure, but I think it is only fair to tell you, as I am your class tutor, that, as of the end of this school year, I have been offered early retirement. For those of you who are connoisseurs of the silver screen, I can say this was an offer I couldn't refuse..."

Jack rocked back in his chair, hardly noticing the noisy reaction around him. Hands started to go up. Mr Colt waited for the hubbub to die down. When there was no sound at all, he paused for a moment longer, then smiled. "Miss Simpkins, did you have a question?"

"Yes, sir. Why?"

"I believe the school wants to introduce new blood into the teaching staff. Miss Carter?"

"Do you know who your replacement will be, sir?"

"I do not. Mr Adams?"

"You would have been our form tutor next year as well, wouldn't you, sir?"

"That, as far as I know, was the accepted plan. Miss Woolley?"

"We don't want you to leave, sir."

"Thank you, that is a very kind thought, and may I say – without getting too sentimental – that it has been my pleasure to impart to you those few grains of knowledge which I possess."

"Something's not right," said Jack.

"Mr Moseley, I didn't see your hand raised."

"Sorry, sir, but it isn't."

"I would recommend you listen carefully to what the headmaster has to say on the subject during assembly. Now, I have one piece of good news to report, which some of you may already know. Stewart Henderson will be rejoining us on Tuesday next. I'm sure you'll make him feel at home again, as he has been through some particularly unpleasant times." Mr Colt waved away any further questions and took up his pen. "It is high time for the morning ritual of the register, otherwise our colleagues in administration will be accusing us of failing in our duty..."

***

61: Friday, 28th June. 10.40 a.m. Swanford Community School.

NOAH

Noah picked his way through the ragged lines of pupils waiting in the main hall for assembly to start. He sidestepped Jacob Lively's outstretched leg and ignored the *queer cunt* whisper from Logan Atkins, finally getting to the ranks of form 2S. It was never difficult to spot Dan Moseley and his friends, because they stood noticeably taller than most of their fellow year 8s.

"Hey," murmured Justin, "what brings you down to the lower orders?"

"You look shattered," said Dan.

Noah spoke in a low voice. "Auntie Iris, my next-door neighbour, she was taken to the police station last night and given a caution for common assault."

"You're joking!" said Dan, knowing that he wasn't.

"They came at ten o'clock and took her away in a police car. She didn't get back till midnight. They made her walk and she's diabetic and her vision is wobbly, especially in the dark."

"Bastards!" said Justin.

"Shut up, Walker!" shouted a passing prefect. "Marshall, get back to your own class."

Dan patted Noah on the arm. "See you at dinner; we'll talk then."

For twelve minutes the assembly followed its normal routine, including a lesson from the Bible chosen by Bronwyn

Hughes, the head girl. She chose Leviticus, chapter 27, which raised a few titters, and some tuts when it was revealed that a woman is worth only sixty per cent of a man. Heads turned towards the clock as the hands approached 10.55 a.m. Five minutes to break time.

The headmaster went to the lectern to read the notices.

"You may sit down, school," he said, causing consternation, because this normally meant an overrun. "I hope you learned your lesson from the whole school detention on Wednesday. It is unfortunate that the innocent are punished as well as the guilty, but one hopes that the responsible will now exert pressure on the irresponsible, so that we don't have a repeat of the juvenile behaviour we saw on Monday."

As the headmaster droned on, Noah yawned. His wrists were still causing him discomfort and that, combined with the upset of Iris's arrest, meant that he had not slept well the previous night.

"Marshall!" It was the voice of Patrick Johns, the head boy.

Noah woke from his doze with a start.

"Come and see me in the Prefects' Room after assembly."

"To conclude," said the headmaster, "I should like to take this opportunity to thank members of staff who will be leaving Swanford Community School at the end of the school year. There are just three and a half weeks to go before the summer holidays, and I am sure individual classes will want to make their own arrangements to say thank you to their teachers. I shall start with Mr Colt, who will be taking a well-earned retirement after some thirty years in the profession. Surely long enough for anyone..." There were gasps at this, and a ripple of conversation began near the back of the hall. "School, unless you want to be here for the whole of your break time, you will stop showing disrespect," continued the headmaster. "Three members of staff will be leaving to find pastures new. They are Ms Lane, our sometime equality counsellor and languages teacher; Mr Thompson, of chemistry fame, who I believe has already found a new post in Portsmouth, and our music expert Mr Williams, who is making a rather longer journey to New Zealand. This means the end of term concert that Mr Williams organises will be cancelled, and instead a special thanksgiving service will be held. We wish all four departees well."

The headmaster paused and became more animated. "Therefore, at the start of the new school year, we shall see some exciting new faces. The governors and education committee are appointing the replacements from overseas, and I am certain they will be warmly welcomed by pupils and staff in the great tradition of our school. I do hope they will be here to be introduced to the parents of our Year Tens and Twelves during our Celebration Evening on 17th July."

The classes filed out of the hall in order and made their way to break. Instead of going through the main doors in the lobby, Noah turned right, then left, down the near-empty main corridor. In trouble again, he thought, not looking forward to a meeting with Patrick Johns, which would entail a report to his form tutor, recommending a detention combined with a good dose of ritual humiliation. He went out of the main building and crossed to the science block where the Prefects' Room was situated on the first floor.

He tapped tentatively on the scuffed blue door, then rubbed his wrist.

"Enter," came the expected voice.

The prefects room had been the Year Seven and Eight library, but it had been laid bare some years back and now contained half a dozen old armchairs, a table and a kettle. A scattering of biscuit crumbs lay on the floor, along with stray crisp packets and stains from various drinks.

Patrick Johns was reclining in the least worn of the chairs, his leg over one arm like a character from *Game of Thrones,* while Bronwyn Hughes had seated herself statuesquely next to him. There were no other prefects in the room.

Noah shut the door behind him and, picking his way delicately through the debris, came to stand before his inquisitors, his right hand planted loosely on his hip.

"Can't you even stand like a man?" said Patrick.

Noah altered his posture to what he thought might be a more masculine pose.

"Tell me, Marshall, were you forced to become a pansy or did you decide for yourself?"

Noah was fairly used to this kind of disparagement, and had a number of stock replies. "I think it just sneaked up on me."

Patrick's face suddenly coloured. "You're trying to lure other boys into your web of sin with those disgusting tight trousers, aren't you?"

Noah glanced down at the relatively modest bulge that was the inevitable result of wearing trousers two sizes too small. "No, it's just that my new pair got ripped and I haven't got any others." And you shouldn't be looking, he thought.

"You fell asleep during the headmaster's address."

"That's true, but I can explain..."

"Go on, then," said Patrick with an affected wave.

"My wrists still ache from when I fell off my bike, and the police arrested my next-door neighbour so I didn't get a lot of sleep last night."

"You live in those rat-infested flats with the drug dealers, prostitutes and homosexuals, don't you?"

"Don't forget the paedos," said Bronwyn.

Patrick sneered "Paedos, homos, they're all the same."

"It's not that bad. Auntie Iris isn't any of those, but she is diabetic, and if there are any other gay people living there, I haven't met them." More's the pity, Noah thought.

"Why do you use that word to describe your perversion, Marshall?"

Noah shifted uncomfortably. "I'm as good as you are," he said quietly. Better, actually, he thought.

"I've heard nothing that mitigates your crime; in fact, you have only added to it by your insolence."

209

Noah flicked his hair nervously and began to fiddle with his shirt collar.

"Of course, I could be persuaded to be lenient, if you will cooperate..."

"What?" said Noah.

Bronwyn drew out her iPad and stylus. "Are you willing to cooperate, Noah?" she asked.

"How?"

"We want to know who all the homos are in your ring, and who in particular infected you. We already know Jack Moseley is a faggot, but what about his brother? Has he been infected?"

"And what about this boy?" enquired Bronwyn, showing him a picture of Robert.

"I don't think there are any ginger gays," said Noah with a straight face. "And I don't know anything about my ring, so I'd better just take the detention, if you don't mind."

Patrick put both feet down on the floor and sat up straight. "You know your days of mincing around are numbered, don't you?"

At that moment the door opened and Ms Lane entered in a cloud of pink and purple chiffon.

"Can I help you, Miss Lane?" asked Patrick.

"Ms!"

"Sorry, can I help you, *Ms* Lane?"

"We hear you're leaving the school, *Ms* Lane," said Bronwyn with undisguised pleasure, putting away her iPad and stylus.

"Yes, but not quite yet," she replied. "Noah, you may go."

"But I haven't finished..." began Patrick.

"Yes, you have." She turned to Noah and gave him a slip of paper. "This is a ten-minute pass. Get yourself out of this oppressive atmosphere and take a walk in the sunshine. There will be no further action concerning your recent cat-nap. Go and blow some of last night's cobwebs away on the playing fields."

"Thank you, Miss," said Noah, feeling like his fairy godmother had just appeared.

At the bottom of the stairwell, Dan and Justin were waiting expectantly.

"Did you?" asked Noah.

They shrugged coolly and in unison, then grinned at him and offered fists for bumps.

"Thanks guys," he said, bumping each of them.

"Swimming tomorrow," said Justin, looking strict. "We'll pick you up at ten."

I'm scared: scared of making a fool of myself and scared of how I'll look beside these two godlike boys. But I'm quite excited too...

***

62: An uncertain date and time. 41 Westbury Avenue.

ALAN

I thought it might be Mrs Warner but it isn't; this one's even older. She's examining me like she's a doctor, but doctors aren't that old, not even Doctor You-Know-Who. She says I need an injection. She asks me if she can examine my butt. My dad threw my book out of the window. Then he hit me, then Derek hit me, then John hit me. They put a bag over my head and pushed things with rough edges up my butt and made me bleed and it hurt, and the pain got worse the more they did it.

I don't care if she examines my butt as long as it doesn't hurt. I'm carried to the bathroom and sat on the toilet. I can't do it when they're watching, so they leave. I have a pooh and it feels like my insides are being turned inside out. I seem to spend half my time on the toilet. They wash me, they wash my butt. I hate everybody. I want them to go away and leave me alone. I want to be back in the detention centre with Mrs

Warner. She was my friend. She gave me the book by F.J. Camm.

They locked me up in a room with no windows. I had to watch while Derek pushed a wire through my foot. Dad and John held me and I screamed and they laughed and called me a fag. I'm not a fag. I killed Dan Moseley, ran him over and a little boy in a wheelchair. I didn't mean to kill him. I'm being punished for my crimes. I had a bag put over my head and they called me a dirty bum-fucker. But it wasn't me – it was them. And Derek pulled me across the floor by the wire and beat me with a chain and I screamed at him to stop, but he laughed and beat me harder. Then, when he was done, he chained me to the bed. Why don't they send me back to the detention centre? Why do they hate me? I told them I'm not a fag.

I was driving a 1934 Rolls-Royce Phantom II Continental and I couldn't remember whether it had whitewall tyres or not. So I got out and had a look and it went without me and Dan Moseley is driving now and he gives me a drink of water because I'm thirsty then he makes me take a pee in a bottle and I'm excited because he touches me down there. The old doctor takes a blood sample and she calls me a very brave boy. But I'm not a brave boy, because I have wet dreams about Dan Moseley.

Another woman, younger than the doctor, but still old – maybe a nurse? – came and told me that Stewart was coming home tomorrow. But I didn't understand. I think she meant my brother, but he's gone away and is probably dead because they hated him even more than me and doubtless stuck things up his butt as well. I asked them if my mum is in the house and the nurse dabbed my face and it was cool and I fell asleep, then someone came and gave me an injection in my arm.

When I woke up, it was dark, and I thought I was lying on the bed in that room with the flies, but then I realised it couldn't be, because I'd have been lying on bare springs which pinched my skin and I was better off on the floor. I hurt all over, but the inside pain is in my butt and in my heart. Why does everyone hate me? An older boy with red hair came into the room and I think I've seen him somewhere before. He was supporting me as I walked to the bathroom, and he asked me if I'd like anything and I said I'd like my book back which Dad threw out of the window. I might have told him the title, but I don't think he understood.

My brothers threw Jack Moseley out of the house and called him a fag, but he and Dan Moseley still rescued me from the room with the flies. Derek tried to shoot me with his air rifle, but he squashed a bird with his foot instead and I drove the Rolls back to the detention centre and Mrs Warner gave me a slice of chocolate cake and I sat on a seat in the sunshine and read *The Practical Motorist's Encyclopaedia* by F.J. Camm.

Dan Moseley isn't dead. He told me that himself, and neither is the boy in the wheelchair. So I wasn't in the detention centre for murder, after all. If I had killed him I would still be in the room with the flies because he rescued me. I dream about him a lot, and sometimes they're really faggy dreams, and other times they feel so real they're not like dreams at all. It worries me that some of the faggy dreams seem real, because if they were real that would make me a real fag. Then I'd deserve to be in the room with the flies and be hurt by being beaten with a chain and having things stuck up my butt.

This room isn't in the detention centre. I can see trees right outside the window and there's a lot more traffic noise. It's quite a nice room. I'm in a double bed and there's a sheet and a sort of duvet covering me. There are voices coming from below and laughter and for a second I think it must be Derek, but it's not cruel laughter so I don't panic. The pain isn't that bad any more. I lift the sheet and look at myself. I can see right down to my feet. The left one is bandaged and it hurts when I wiggle my toes, but the other one looks normal. I'm wearing a pair of shorty PJs, but they're not mine.

I'm woken by the curtains being opened. It must be morning because the light is bright. "What time is it?" I ask. I'm lying on my back and need a pee.

The person opening the curtains jumps at the sound of my voice. He turns and he looks like my brother Stewart, but his face is in shadow. "It's seven-thirty," he says and smiles and comes and sits on the bed and it is my brother and he looks happy to see me, which can't be right when I was always such a rat to him. He takes my hand and I let him because he's my brother and not because I'm a fag. "You're looking better," he says. "We were worried about you."

"Where am I?"

"41 Westbury Avenue..."

That rings a bell. Didn't I drive the Rolls-Royce here? No, that's not right. I've started to jiggle.

"Do you need the toilet?"

I nod. "Bursting..."

"Do you want a bottle, or I can help you to the bathroom?"

I'm not going to make it. He seems to read my mind. He picks up a plastic bottle from down by the side of the bed. He hands it to me, but I don't know what to do with it and any second I'm going to wet myself.

He pulls the sheet and duvet off me, tugs down my shorts, turns me onto my side, takes the bottle and tucks my thing into the neck. I notice I have quite a bush down there now. I let go. The relief makes me gasp. He chuckles. "You'll be able to do it yourself next time."

By the time I've finished, the bottle's half full. "That's a good lot," he says, holding it out. "That's a record for me."

I pull up my shorts and he puts the bottle on the side table and covers me with the bed clothes. "That was embarrassing," I say.

"I must have done it twenty times for you already. Dan Moseley says you get a stiffy when he does it..."

Oh no, it wasn't a dream! What if he thinks I'm a fag? What if I'm sent away to the room with the flies?

Stewart smiles. "Don't worry, it doesn't bother Dan at all. Nothing of that sort worries Dan. Elspeth says he should go to medical school."

"Elspeth?" I say, trying to put all thoughts of Dan Moseley out of my mind.

"She owns the house and was a doctor herself."

"Is she old?"

"Eighty-three... You know, this is the first time you've talked without rambling."

"How long have I been here?"

"Er, now, let me see. You were brought in the Sunday before last and today's Tuesday, so that's nine days. Would you like some breakfast?"

I look at my brother and he seems the same, only more grown-up. He takes my hand again and I think it's because he knows I feel sad.

"You're safe here, you know. You don't have to pretend."

What does he mean by that? I snatch my hand away, then wish I hadn't.

He carries on as if nothing has happened. "They're making me go to school today, so Mum will be looking after you."

"Mum! Is she here?"

"Sorry, I meant my mum. Listen, I gotta go, but she'll bring you some breakfast, OK?"

For some reason I hold my hand out to him and he smiles again and takes it. "Great to have you back, brother," he says. Then he picks up the bottle of pee and leaves. Half a minute later I hear the toilet flush.

***

63: Thursday, 4th July. 5.15 p.m. 41 Westbury Avenue.

ALAN

I'm lying in the garden on a sun lounger. It's made of white plastic with a padded cushion. The weather is warm and there are birds singing and I'm quite comfortable in my PJs and bare feet. So why don't I feel happy? Why do I feel that I would be better off dead?

The very old lady doctor spoke to me earlier, but she was talking about HIV and STIs and DNA and everything was initials and she could see I was struggling so she left me alone. Anne is Stewart's real mum and she has a little boy, Alex, who came out into the garden. He asked me if I wanted to play, but I was too tired and said maybe tomorrow. I was just fobbing him off.

I had a bacon, lettuce and tomato sandwich earlier and a strawberry milkshake, but nothing tastes right. I wish Mrs Warner was here to cook for me, then I might like it better. I asked Anne if there was a copy of *The Practical Motorist's Encyclopaedia* by F.J. Camm in the house. She went into the room with all the books to search for me, but they were either stories, or works on photography or paintings. So she bought me an F1 magazine and a drawing pad and pencil when she was out. I think I said thank you, but I'm too tired to read or draw. If I had a Nintendo, I might be able to escape from my thoughts.

I'm woken by voices coming from the house, but I can't see who it is because I'm facing the wrong way. In any case, I can't be bothered.

"Hey, buddy! Got something for you."

Dan Moseley's looking down at me. I don't understand why he's calling me buddy when I tried to kill him, then I remember he rescued me from the room with the flies and I drove the van.

He holds up my skateboard. It doesn't seem real. I don't think I want it. That part of my life is over. He puts it down by the side of the sun lounger. "Maybe tomorrow, eh?" he says.

I don't know why he said that. Maybe it was the way I reacted when I saw it. He's got a green first aid box with him as well.

"I'm going to change your bandage," he says, and takes out a fresh one and a pair of angled surgical scissors. "Don't worry – Elspeth's shown me how, and the one you've got on is an earlier effort by yours truly."

He squats down beside me. "Alan..."

I feel bad and can't look at him, though I like to look at him. "Alan, you're going through a really rough time at the moment. But it won't last; you will get better. You and Stewart should talk, because you had similar things happen to you."

I don't want to talk. I don't want people to be nice to me. "I want to be left alone," I say and I know the reason why. It's in case I cry because once I start I know I won't be able to stop and then they'll think I'm a fag and send me back to the room with the flies.

"OK, I'll do your bandage. You're clear of any infections, by the way." He waits to see if I've understood what he's saying, and I know he's told me in a sentence what the old lady doctor had tried to explain in a lecture.

He puts on a pair of gloves out of a packet and cuts the old bandage off in no time. Then he examines the injury. I don't want to watch, but I do.

Dan looks back at me and grins. "Elspeth says I can take your stitches out tomorrow if it appears OK – and it does. This bit of redness is normal, and they're very near the surface now anyway. Do you trust me?"

"Yes."

He cleans my foot with a wipe. "These nails could do with a cut, but I'll do them tomorrow as well, before the party." It takes him no time at all to put on the fresh bandage. "I enjoy doing this, you know," he says, and I think how much like a real doctor he is, only better – much better. Much better than you-know-who.

***

64: Friday, 5th July. 8 p.m. 41 Westbury Avenue.

NOAH

The party's in full swing and I've had a good time, particularly with regards to the food. Stewart's mother is a good cook, and even if everything isn't home-made, it's been laid out just like at a wedding. I had three hot mini sausage rolls and a lamb samosa with Waldorf salad, which by the way has walnuts and apples in it, but was all right. I tried these things called canapés which I'd never had before. Our dad would have been amazed. They were kind of like bite-size pizzas, only the toppings were different. The smoked salmon on cream cheese was a bit too much like smoky leather for me, but I did enjoy the Parma ham and mustard, and the egg mayonnaise. The best thing ever, though, was the home-baked Swiss roll filled with real strawberries and cream. That was treble ace. I haven't tried the raspberry trifle yet, I'll let the rest settle first. Sweet tooth or what?

I say I had a good time and not an excellent time because there were several pains in the butt. The first pain – and I know you'll think I'm a snake and you'll be right, because I really got the green eye – was when I saw Dan making out with Sophie in the garden. It gave me a pain in the pit of my stomach and I almost felt like crying. The trouble is, they're both really sweet to me, which makes it worse. My only consolation is that I think everyone loves Dan, so I'm not alone. I guess even Justin does in his own way. I'm really lucky to have Justin Walker as a friend. When it comes to loyalty he is it, and I don't mean in a doggy, unthinking way, but he's really thoughtful and trustworthy and kind – and he's hot too, but he's not so sexily hot as Dan.

Second pain: Mrs Moseley really doesn't like me. She tries to hide it, but her face says it all. Her lips kind of go thin and her eyes narrow when she sees me. I know it's because I'm girly with my hips and my hands, but I can't help it. She tries to be friendly, but she makes me feel awkward and the more awkward I feel the more swishy I become, and the less she likes me, etc.

Third pain. He's following me. I'm being stalked by a seven-year-old. I don't know what to do. Every time I look round, he's there. Even though I know I'm being irrational, it's unnerving. I wish they'd put him to bed or something. The thing is, I don't know what he wants from me. I'm in the hall at the moment, thinking where to go next to avoid him. There's a stained-glass window in the front door which makes the colours all mellow and muted. I love this house: you could fit our dingy flat six times over in it. It feels old because of all the dark polished wood, but it's got all mod cons as well. I think I heard the patter of tiny feet, so it's time for me to run upstairs.

I haven't been up here before. There are a lot of doors. I'm going to knock on one and see what happens. I don't want to burst in on Justin and Kate, or Jack and Robert, or Dan and Sophie. On second thoughts, though... no I'm not going down that route. There's no answer. Help! I think I just heard a creak on the stairs.

"Ooh, sorry," I say.

There's a boy lying, stomach down, on the bed reading a magazine. This must be Alan Henderson, who I should probably recognise from school, but I don't. The look he gives me isn't exactly friendly; mind you, it's difficult to judge because his face is still pretty mashed up.

"What are you doing here?" he says, which is strange really, because it means he must recognise me.

"Sorry," I say again, "I'm trying to avoid someone. I'll go if you want."

"Go or stay, I don't care." He casts aside the magazine and lies down flat, facing away from me. I see there are marks on his legs and one of his feet is bandaged.

I go to the door and listen for any noise, but hear nothing. It could be a trick. though, he could be just outside waiting for me. I decide my best bet is to stay and try to be friendly despite the frosty reception. I go round the bed and sit on a chair facing him. He's not moving but he's noticed me.

"You're Alan, aren't you?"

"Why have they sent a fag to talk to me?"

Charming, but I'll make allowances as I have invaded his space. "What?"

"I said..."

"I heard what you said. I'm not deaf. It's just a strange thing to say."

"Why do they think that sending a fag to talk to me is going to cheer me up?" His expression is antagonistic, but I see something else that I don't understand, but makes me feel sorry for him.

"First, I don't know who *they* are; second, no one's sent me; and third, insulting people by calling them fags, when you're being looked after by fags, when you were rescued by a fag, is pretty rich, even for a Henderson."

"Dan Moseley is not a fag."

"No, he's not," I reply. Unfortunately, I think. "But he's not the only one in the mix, is he?"

"What are you talking about?" I seemed to have got through to him, because his eyes have brightened, probably with anger.

"I'm not going to talk to you if you call me nasty names. My name is—"

"Noah, I know."

"Well, then?"

"All right, Noah, what are you talking about?"

When he talks normally his voice has a nice quality to it, quite deep and firm and even friendly.

"Jack and Robert are gay."

"Lying fag! They're nothing like you." Mister harsh voice is back. He picks up his magazine and throws it at me – well, he throws it in my direction because it plops down about a yard in front of me.

"Is that how you treat all your visitors? With a temper tantrum?"

I pick it up between finger and thumb and see that it's a very uninteresting magazine about motor racing, so I drop it again.

"Give it back!" he demands. Despite his bad manners, I can see the effort of throwing it has tired him so I decide to be kind and do just that, tucking it under his pillow.

"Well, I'd better be going," I say. "It's been nice."

"Shut up."

"Would you like me to visit you again?"

"What for?" he mutters. I think he's falling asleep.

"Well, now I'm up close, I can see you are quite cute." That was daring of me, but he is helpless, and it is kind of true.

His eyes snap open. "Fuck you."

"I'll take that as a yes, then."

I make my way to the door and gingerly open it. Relief, the stalker isn't there. But that doesn't mean he's not around. I think I need to find somewhere else to hide.

***

65: Friday, 5th July. 8.30 p.m. 41 Westbury Avenue.

JACK

Jack was seated alone at the big wooden table in the kitchen, eating a dish of trifle. The adults were monopolising the sitting room where all the food was laid out, and so the young people had spread themselves across the rest of the premises. The back door was open and intermittently he could hear either laughter or a snatch of conversation carried on the warm evening air from the outside where Dan, Justin, Sophie and Kate had arranged themselves on the garden furniture.

Max and Mandy, who were first-time visitors to No. 41, had been taken on a tour of the house by Stewart, who had particularly wanted to show them his new Kindle tablet – which had been bought for him, ostensibly by his mother, but in fact by Elspeth, who had insisted on upgrading both his and Anne's computer systems.

Approaching footsteps from the hallway made Jack look up. "Hello, my delicious ginger biscuit," he said.

Robert eyed him. "You've got cream round your mouth."

"Would you like to come and lick it off?"

The American walked up to him and kissed him on the forehead. "There, will that do for now?"

Jack made a face and wiped his mouth with the back of his hand. "Will they go with us tomorrow afternoon?"

Robert shook his head. "Mandy's not interested and if Mandy's not interested Stewart won't go and although Max wants to go he feels pressured by Mandy not to."

"Oh well, it's just us then."

"Maybe when Noah's sorted out and Justin's left, Dan will come with us again."

"It's because you want to race him, isn't it?"

"There may well be an element of competition in it, yes."

"You Americans – everything has to be dog eat dog!"

"That's what life's about," replied Robert breezily.

Jack reached up and took his boyfriend's hand. "I'd like to go on a bike ride with you into the country when we break up."

"Oh yes..."

"Somewhere we can be alone, properly, before you go on this mad crusade."

"I want to."

"I want to love you, Robert," Jack said quietly.

Robert took a chair and sat down right beside him. "And I want to love you too, though I'm more scared than you."

"We can just do as much as the other wants and no more."

"Let's go on the first Monday of the holiday."

"That's a date then, and I think I might know a spot where we won't be disturbed."

The American leaned over and kissed Jack several times on the cheek then drew him close and licked him on the lips. "There was still a bit of cream there," he said.

"I knew it! You just did all that smooching to get at my trifle."

The sound of a crutch advancing towards the kitchen from the hall diverted their attention. Mikey limped in, glowered at them then went and kicked the outside door with his cast-encased foot.

Jack exchanged amused glances with Robert. "Michael Moseley, come here this instant," he said.

Mikey stayed where he was, pouting and looking down at the door sill that had hurt his toes.

"Michael Moseley, if you do not come and stand before Robert and me this instant I shall get Elspeth to turn you into something unnatural." This allusion was to Mikey's overheard question as to whether the old lady was a witch.

The little boy moved towards them, shoulders hunched, eyes averted, brow knotted.

"Closer," said Jack.

Mikey took half a step.

"Closer," repeated Jack.

Another half step.

"Look at me."

The knot got deeper and the eyes stayed down.

"Look at me."

The eyes came up but the expression dissolved into unhappiness and large tears came out, accompanied by a whine.

Jack turned his chair round and opened his arms. Mikey came forward and Jack picked him up and sat him on his lap. "Now then, matey, tell ol' Jack what be the matter."

Mikey's whine reached a higher pitch and the tears came faster. "He doesn't like me!"

Jack held him and began to gently rock. "Who doesn't like you?"

"That boy."

"Ah! We wouldn't be talking about Noah, by any chance?"

Mikey nodded, shedding more tears.

"Why do you think he doesn't like you?"

"He won't say anything to me," sobbed Mikey.

"Is this why you've been Mr Moody for nearly two weeks?"

Mikey nodded again, leaned against Jack and went limp.

"Do you *like* Noah?"

"He won't talk to me."

"I asked you whether you *liked* Noah?"

The little boy moaned. "Yes."

"And is that why you've been trying to plaster your hair into a fringe for the last fortnight?"

Mikey's body stiffened as if he'd been found out doing something wrong. "I want my hair to grow long over my eye; I want my hair that colour!" he said defiantly.

"Shall I tell you two reasons why that's not going to happen?"

The little boy hung his head.

"I'll tell you anyway. First: Noah's hair is quite straight and yours is curly. Second: Mum is never ever going to allow you to have blue streaks."

"I want them," muttered Mikey.

"Right then, I want you to listen to me carefully now, OK?

"OK,"

"And I shall be testing you to see if you are listening, OK?"

The little boy glanced up at his brother and nodded. Robert handed him a clean handkerchief. "Wipe your eyes, little fella."

Mikey made a valiant attempt with the handkerchief, then gave it back to the American, who pretended to wring it out, making the little boy smile.

"Noah hasn't got any brothers or sisters," began Jack, "so what does that mean?"

Mikey frowned. "Is he lonely?"

"No, it means he's not used to having little pests pestering him all the time, understand?"

"I think so."

"So, when you first met Noah what did you say to him?"

Mikey thought for a while about this, but couldn't come up with an answer.

"When Robert came for the first time what did you say to him?"

"Hi?"

"Correct. So what did you say to Noah?"

"Hi?"

"No... You didn't say anything, you just stared at him."

Mikey's brain ticked over.

"And what should you never do to a person, especially when you first meet them?" Jack continued.

"Stare at them?"

"Correct! So why is it that every time you see him, you stare at him like a demented devil child?"

"Because he won't talk to me!"

"And why won't he talk to you?"

Mikey's face fell. "Because I stare at him."

"That is correct. You also follow him round and stare at him which is even worse."

"Everything Jack says is right, fella. If you want to be friends with someone, go up and tell them so." Robert thought for a moment. "Supposin' I went and found Noah now, and brought him here. Do you think you could handle that?"

Mikey became nervous and looked around him, as if searching for a source of courage. He slid off Jack's knee and took up his crutch. "OK, I'm ready..."

When Robert returned with Noah some minutes later, it was difficult to tell which of the two protagonists was more nervous.

"He was hiding in the toilet," said the American.

"Oh, shush," responded Noah.

Jack got up. "Mikey, this is Noah Marshall. Noah, this is Michael Moseley, known as Mikey. Shake hands and say hello to each other."

Noah offered a limp hand. Mikey grabbed it.

"Ow!" screeched Noah and Mikey giggled.

"You haven't said hello to each other," said Robert.

Noah cleared his throat. "Hello Mikey, you can let go of my hand now."

"Whisper," said Mikey in a secretive voice.

"Huh?"

"He wants to whisper something to you," explained Robert.

"Like in your ear," amplified Jack sarcastically.

"Oh." Noah got down on his knees and waited.

Mikey cupped his mouth with one hand and closed in on Noah's left ear. "I want my hair like yours."

Noah smiled, looked first at Mikey then at Jack, then at Robert then back at Mikey. "Can I whisper something in your ear?"

The little boy nodded and the reverse procedure followed. "Our dad does it for me. Would you like to come and watch next time?"

Mikey's face lit up with a beaming smile. He leaned in and gave Noah a kiss on the cheek.

"Mikey loves Noah," sang Jack.

Noah rose hastily while Mikey gave his brother the middle finger.

"Charming," said Robert, "and after all that Jack's done for you."

Dan walked in with two empty dishes. "Is there any trifle left, hogs?"

"No, we had a quarter each," said Jack, "but you can lick the bowl out if you like."

"I'm going to watch Noah have his hair done," said Mikey, proudly.

"Really?" replied Dan. "Have you told Noah you get a stiffy every time you see him?"

The little boy went very red and rushed at his brother, kicking him on the shin.

"Ouch!" exclaimed Dan.

Noah backed away. "Is this what having brothers is like?"

"Great, isn't it?" said Jack.

66: Saturday, 6th July 3.30 a.m. 15 Leighton Lane.

ROGER

A glimmer of pre-dawn light was filtering through the curtains when Roger woke, to find his wife just getting back into bed.

"What's up?" he asked.

"Just a touch of indigestion, go back to sleep."

"Well, you were certainly knocking back the sherry last night."

"I was not!"

Roger chuckled. "I wouldn't mind living there all the time. It was very comfortable and Anne is an accomplished hostess."

"Hostess!" exclaimed Pam. "what a word to use in the twenty-first century."

"But she is, and we were treated like royalty."

Pam pulled the duvet over her. "They were keeping us at arm's length, just like royalty do to their subjects."

"That's because you think there's some great conspiracy going on there."

"Did you notice that all the children had the run of the place as if it was their own?"

"I got the impression that's what Elspeth wants and that she is in full control."

"She seems to be able to control our children, when we can't!"

"Yes, she's just like Mary Poppins or perhaps the Pied Piper of Hamlin or the witch who lives in the gingerbread house in *Hansel and Gretel*."

"I can't have a serious conversation with you about this."

"Tell me something serious and I will."

"What was that boy, Noah, doing there, looking wild-eyed and sneaking about the place?"

"Yes, the poor lad spent most of the evening trying to escape from the clutches of our youngest son."

"Nonsense!"

"It's true, but at least they're friends now."

"What do you mean?"

"Didn't you notice how happy Mikey was when we left?"

"I put that down to stuffing himself with all the unhealthy food he could find there."

"You're the one with indigestion."

"You've got an answer for everything, Roger Moseley."

"Yes, and I was also correct in suggesting Jack would be able to sort out Mikey, which he did by the simple expedient of introducing him properly to Noah, with a little help from Robert."

"And you think that's a good thing?"

"One contented little boy makes it good enough for me."

"Noah is a bad influence and so is everyone in that house."

Roger sighed loudly. "No wonder you've got indigestion, fretting over non-existent problems."

"Mark my words," said Pam, "there'll be a reckoning."

***

67: Tuesday, 9th July. 9.35 a.m. 41 Westbury Avenue.

ALAN

My brother has given me his mum's old laptop, which is OK, I suppose, but I don't see why I should have other people's cast-offs when all my own stuff is at home. But it's not my home any more, is it? I'm never going back there. Does my mum know where I am? Why doesn't she come to visit me? I hate thinking about things; it just makes me feel worse. I don't know why I can't shut myself off, but everything keeps going round and round in my head. I don't suppose she even knows where I am or what's been going on.

I've got a feeling that she was kept drugged up by my dad. I wish I had some drugs now; I could smoke a nice spliff and forget everything, even though I'd cough and wake up with a headache. The only time I feel happy is when I'm asleep, and that's because I don't have to think. I wonder if there are any games on this laptop. I bet there's nothing decent on it.

Stewart has set up the Wi-Fi connection. The lady doctor is too old to have Wi-Fi in her house, isn't she? It's probably really slow. It's an Acer laptop with a 15.6 inch screen so maybe it's not so bad. I'll try later.

I like my brother much better now, but I can't talk to him. He's doing another exam at school today. Every day for two weeks, he'll be stuck in a room on his own doing them. I don't know why he bothers. There's no point to anything. Jack Moseley and the rest of his class have got the morning off. They call it self-study but I think it's just an excuse for the teachers to laze about as their classes have finished exams, and it's not far from the end of term.

I keep imagining that the fag is somewhere in my room, but I can't see him. He sneaked into my room the other day and said he'd visit me again. But he hasn't, which is typical of a sneaky fag. Wherever did he get that sleeveless T-shirt from? It hangs off him like a piece of rag because he's so skinny. I could see his nipples, they are so small – like little pink buttons – and he's got no definition at all. Jason Spriggs and his brother Lucas unscrewed his brake blocks then chased after him so he rode out of school too fast. That's when he hit the kerb and had to go to hospital. That's why his wrists are bruised and he's got a bump on his head, but he hides that with that stupid fringe which hangs over his eye.

Jack Moseley said they had a collection for him at school because he's poor, and got nearly fifty pounds. If they did a collection for me I'd get about 4p and I'm not a fag like him. Why does nothing good ever happen to me? They'll send me away when I get better and everything that happened to me in the room with the flies will happen again. I mustn't think about that or I'll start feeling sick.

I can have a shower now and wash my own butt, thank you. I don't know why I allowed those two to touch me in the first place. I didn't know for certain that Jack Moseley was a fag, though my brothers and my dad thought he was. He doesn't act like a fag, and neither does Robert. He's American, and doesn't really like me, I can tell, or maybe he's not such a good actor as the others and they all hate me. I hate myself, anyway, so I don't care that nobody likes me – in fact, I prefer it. How does a fag act? Yes, like that Noah. He is a real fag. He's got blue streaks in his emo hair and said he was going to visit me again, but he hasn't.

"Who hasn't visited you?"

That was Jack Moseley. He's been reading my thoughts, or did I just say that out loud? What else have I said out loud?

"No one," I say, but I'm going red.

"Do you mean Noah? He's got blue streaks."

"No!"

He's smiling at me now and I can see he doesn't believe me. Can fags read minds? "Is Robert your, you know... boyfriend?"

Why am I asking him this?

He gives me a look. "Who's been talking?"

So, it's true. "You rescued me, didn't you?"

"Dan rescued you, I just kept the baddies away."

He's calling my brother a baddy. My brother Derek. I can see his face. He liked to watch my face as he pushed one of those things with rough edges up inside me, then he'd pull it out quickly and push it back in and there was a sickening pain deep inside. Then he'd twist it as he pulled it right out next time and I'd scream and he'd laugh and he'd wipe his fingers over me and show me the blood and show me the thing which was streaked with blood, and my own brother, *my own brother* was the one being so cruel to me and the worst pain was in my heart. I don't ever want to see him again! But when I'm better I know they're going to send me back to Derek and my dad and they'll put me in that room with the flies again and... I think I'm going to be ill...

"Alan, are you OK?"

"Feel sick..."

I sick up all my breakfast into a bowl, which must have been in the room all the time. Maybe it's happened before.

"Finished?" he asks.

I nod and he gives me a glass of water. "Rinse."

I take a drink and spit it out into the bowl, then he takes both away and cleans my mouth with a wet wipe.

"I'll get rid of these," he says.

I feel dizzy. Why am I such a baby? Why are these people being kind to me? Maybe it's a trick. Maybe they're just doing it like in the hospital because it's their job. I don't know. I don't care. I'm feeling really tired again...

***

68: Wednesday, 10th July. 4.40 p.m. 41 Westbury Avenue.

NOAH

Stewart answers the door and takes me through to the kitchen, where I'm given a drink of Waitrose lemonade and a jammie dodger. Waitrose Real Lemon Lemonade is the best because it doesn't have artificial sweeteners in it and doesn't taste like the chemistry lab.

"Are you stopping for tea?" he asks. "I warn you, we're still eating leftover party food out of the freezer."

"Is there any of that raspberry trifle?"

"You can't freeze trifle. "

"OK. Can I take a doggy bag home for our dad?"

"I expect so. What's it like having a proper dad instead of a complete bastard?"

"I'm lucky, I suppose, even though we're not exactly millionaires."

"However well off we were, I'd swap mine for yours any day."

"Our dad loves his job, but it only pays peanuts. I worry really. He'll have to work till he drops, you know."

"You should find him a nice rich widow, like Elspeth," says Stewart and I watch his eyes twinkle.

"I don't think Elspeth would fit into my dad's comfort zone."

He nods at this. "How was your second swimming lesson, Noah?"

"I can float on my back and front now and keep my head underwater. I can manage a width of breast stroke in the shallow end and I'm trying to get the courage to do it in the deep end. But the crawl is a bit of a problem because I still haven't got the breathing right and usually end up with a mouthful of water."

"Sounds like you're doing really well."

"I've got two of the best teachers."

"You're blushing."

"I'd drown myself for them if they asked."

"Doctor Dan says your advice to Justin has already paid off in the Swanford United changing rooms, and he's more confident about his medical."

"Yeh, his feet are a lot better. At least I'm some use."

"Talking of which. Jack got the impression that Alan wanted to see you."

"I got the impression that he never wanted to see me again."

Stewart's face became serious. "He was always touchy, you know, and now he's feeling low, it's even less easy to get behind the brick wall he puts up in front of everyone. I thought I might be able to talk to him because of what happened, but he clams up on me just like everyone else."

"Where is he?"

"In his room, being no good to himself or anyone else."

"You got revision?"

"Don't mention that. It's not fair, everyone else getting days off and enjoying themselves while I've got to sit in a classroom by myself, slogging away at exams I've no chance of passing."

"Knuckle down like a fifteen-year-old should."

He looks at me, aghast, until he sees I'm joking. "It's all right for fourteen-year-old fairies who can flit about without a care in the world."

"I'd better flit upstairs then."

"If you can stick it out till six, we'll have tea, and Mum's made a lemon meringue pie."

"Now you're talking!"

***

I get upstairs to his room and walk in without knocking. He's lying on his side facing away from me, watching cars going round and round a track on his laptop.

"Hello Alan," I call out.

He jumps nearly two feet into the air then rolls over to face me. "This is a private room, you know – you can't just burst in when you like."

"Are we in a mood?" I say holding my hands together on my tummy.

"What makes you think I want you in here?"

I get down on my knees by the bed and put my palms together as if in prayer. "Please let me stay, I love being in your bedroom with tetchy old you." I try to wink at him but it goes a bit wrong because of my fringe which I decide to flick instead.

"You boss-eyed homo."

"That's more like it. Aren't you going to invite me to sit down?"

"I don't care what you do."

"Ooo, now that is an invitation." I sit down on the side of the bed and cross my legs.

"I don't have anything to say to you," he tells me.

233

"Good, I'll just sit here and gaze at your cuteness."

"Fag!"

"Actually, if I stay till six, Stewart says I can have tea."

"So you're just here for the free tea, are you?"

"Pretty much. That, and because Jack Moseley said you were dying to see me." I flutter my eyelashes at him and lightly touch his arm.

"Why do you have to act like some lady-boy?"

"Because I like being called a fag and getting beaten up, of course."

"You deserve to be..." He stops talking and a cloud of sadness descends upon him, which I guess means that he's just thought about what he was saying and what happened to him.

"None of us deserve that," I say.

He doesn't speak again for over a minute, but his eyes are moving continuously as if he's dreaming while awake. "You tricked me," he says at last.

"Did I?"

"You know you did."

"Shall we play a game?" I ask.

"What game?"

"I don't know; something that'll keep us going till teatime."

"Is that all you think about, your stomach?"

"Oh, yeh!" I say and show him how much room I've got in my vest.

"Why do you wear something that's three sizes too big for you?"

"They only do this one in large. Do you like it?"

"It sucks... No, it would be all right on someone who was a normal shape."

"Don't tell me, you think my head's too big for my body?"

"You haven't got a body, you've got a beanpole."

"Be careful with my ego," I say. "I do have a body image problem, you know."

234

He starts fiddling with the laptop. "Let's play hangman, and I'll whoop your little matchstick ass."

"Mmm, now there's a tempting offer," I say and he blushes.

I then proceed to thrash him five-nil at hangman, which we play online. Each time I win he gets more and more annoyed until he's hammering the keys and cursing his bad luck and swearing at me.

"Well, it must be almost six," I say after guessing P-H-A-N-T-O-M with only three letters: ?-H-A-?-?-O-?

"You fucking fag!" he shouts and tries to slam down the lid of the laptop.

"You forgot to say fucking *winning* fag..."

"Don't ever come back."

"OK, I'll see you on Saturday."

***

69: Saturday, 13th July. 6.35 p.m. 41 Westbury Avenue.

<u>NOAH</u>

I open Alan's bedroom door quietly and put my head round. He doesn't hear me because he's busy copying a picture of a racing car off the internet onto a piece of paper. Actually, it's not half bad. I decide not to make him jump and spoil it, so I close the door again and after a minute give two taps. Then, I open it and call out, "Hello, it's me, sweetie," just to annoy him.

I hear a groan, then he looks at me. "What do you want?"

I do a fem walk over to the bed, noticing that the laptop has been closed and there's no sign of the picture. "Aren't you going to invite a *laydee* to sit down?"

"You are so gross."

I sit down. "I went swimming today with Justin and Dan."

"Pity they didn't drown you."

"I thought you might like to come with us next week."

"No way, I don't want to be seen out with a fag."

"Why? Got something to hide?"

"Shut the fuck up!" he shouts and scowls at me and I just smile at him, because when I look at him like that his face always grows softer. "I haven't got any swimmers anyway," he says, "or any clothes for that matter."

"You could go naked; I wouldn't mind."

"Pervert."

"That's a date, then."

"What's that on your hands?" he asks.

"Eczema," I reply.

"What's that?"

"A skin disease."

He makes a face. "You're trying to give it to me, aren't you, like AIDS?" As soon as he says it, he remembers again and the shadow crosses over him and his eyes grow dim.

I look at the webs of my fingers, where the worst of it is. "It's not catching, it just looks foul, and sometimes it itches so bad I make them bleed with scratching."

It takes him a while to respond. "It's not that noticeable."

I chuckle. "That's the nicest thing you've ever said to me."

"Well, make the most of it."

"Shall we play hangman?" I ask.

"No! You cheat."

"Do not."

"Do."

"Not."

"Do."

When he realises that I've let him win, he pulls out the picture of the car from beneath the bed clothes and his hand is trembling.

"I drew this."

I take it from him. "Whoa, that is really neat. Where did you learn to draw like this?"

He looks at me, not certain whether I mean it. "It's a Mercedes AMG. I copied off their website."

"It's real skill. Can I have it?"

"If you want. I was going to give it to you anyway."

For once I am stuck for words, and there's a sudden ache in my heart. "Thank you," I manage.

"If we play hangman, can I choose the topics?" he asks with a sly glance.

I look sideways at him. "I suppose so..." I say doubtfully.

We play eight games, interrupted when Anne brings us up some refreshments. This time he wins five to three, largely because I get words like B-E-N-D-I-X S-P-R-I-N-G and worse I-N-V-A-R S-T-R-U-T P-I-S-T-O-N.

"That's really taking the piss-ton," I say when he reveals the word. He chortles at his triumph and I hope at my little joke. And I don't mind that he's winning because he's enjoying himself and making me laugh with his cheek.

I leave at 9.30 with my picture, which now hangs on my bedroom wall. Our dad looks at me when I get in and asks what's making me so happy, and I guess I can't really answer him.

***

70: Sunday, 14th July. 4.40 p.m. 15 Leighton Lane.

<u>PAM</u>

Pam hung the last item of ironed washing on the clothes horse and looked over at her husband. "Are we going to that Celebration Evening on Wednesday?"

"What Celebration Evening?" asked Roger, who was engrossed in surfing for cheap holiday destinations on his work laptop.

"It's for the parents of Year Tens." Pam propped the hot iron up on the kitchen table and folded away the ironing board.

"I suppose we ought to, then," said Roger without enthusiasm.

"The boys don't want us to go. Jack says the school's being taken over by religious crackpots."

"Sounds interesting for once."

"Yes, we should make the effort, shouldn't we?"

"Definitely." Roger looked up from his study. "Looking at this lot, I don't think we can afford a family holiday this year."

"Well, we've been away once already."

"Don't remind me of that!"

"Oh goodness!" exclaimed Pam, gazing out of the window.

"What's the matter?"

"It's that boy again! He's just propped his bike by the gate."

"Which boy?"

"Noah," said Pam, turning up her nose. "I wonder what he wants?"

"Oh, here's one. How about a week in Bulgaria on the Black Sea for £450, bed and breakfast?"

Pam did not reply as she was watching Noah's progress up the path. He had stopped half way to wave up at Jack's bedroom window, and was now in conversation.

"Well?" said Roger.

"Well what? Why does he wear that vest thing all the time?"

Roger closed the lid of the laptop with a sigh just as Dan entered the kitchen and made for the back door. "Noah's here."

"Yes, I know. I'm getting a running commentary from your mother."

Dan opened the door. "Hey Noah, what's up?"

Noah fluttered his fingers at him in greeting, then nodded a temporary farewell to the bedroom window. "I was looking for a favour, actually," he called flicking his fringe nervously.

"Come on in," said Dan, holding the door open.

"Thank you. Hello, Mrs Moseley. Hello, Mr Moseley, I hope you don't mind me calling."

"Of course not," said Roger. "It's always nice to see you, Noah. How's your dad?"

"Oh, he's all right, thank you. He had quite a good day yesterday. He's having tea with Auntie Iris this afternoon as she's not quite over her ordeal..."

There was a sudden noise in the hall and Mikey came into the kitchen pounding on his crutch. He rushed at their visitor and hugged him tight. "Noah! Noah! Noah!" he shouted.

"Ooo!" cried Noah, who had been slightly knocked back by the force of the embrace. He reached out tentatively to pat Mikey on the head.

"Pick me up," said the little boy, holding out his arms.

Noah looked round helplessly.

"It's all right," said Dan, "he won't break."

The first solo attempt was unsuccessful and so Dan lifted him up and put him into Noah's arms. Mikey beamed happily and began to stroke the fringe with its blue streaks. "When can I come?" he squeaked.

"I'm having it done next Saturday, after swimming."

Mikey looked innocently at Roger. "Daddy, will you take me for a haircut next Saturday?"

Pam, who had been watching the proceedings with mounting disapproval, snapped. "Michael Moseley, get down from there and behave yourself. You will have a haircut when I say, not when you want... Things have got to change round here, and one of the changes is not doing things just as and when you want – and that goes for all of you boys!"

Dan huffed. "Come on, Noah, let's go upstairs. We seem to be in evil stepmother mode down here."

"And don't you be cheeky!"

Noah lowered Mikey carefully to the ground.

"*Bloody* evil stepmother," muttered the little boy, a bit too loudly.

"What did you say?" exclaimed Pam.

Mikey grabbed his crutch and ran from the kitchen, with his mother in hot pursuit.

***

71: Sunday, 14th July. 5.05 p.m. 15 Leighton Lane.

DAN

"Cue for a lot of screaming and shouting," said Roger.

"Was all that really necessary?" asked Dan, shaking his head.

"Probably not, but your mum is under considerable strain at the moment."

"Send her to a shrink, then."

"Daniel, don't speak like that about your mother."

Noah was all of a tremble. "I don't think I should have come. I always seem to cause trouble wherever I go..."

"Nonsense," said Roger. "You two go on upstairs and forget about it. Noah, would you like to stop for tea?"

"What treats are in store for us?" asked Dan.

"I'm doing spicy beef salad with houmous and garlic bread and a Victoria sponge."

"Houmous?" enquired Noah, which sounded to him like humus from biology.

"Trust me, it's a gay boy fave," said Dan putting his arm protectively round Noah's shoulder.

Noah smiled shyly. "I'd like to, but I'll have to phone our dad."

On their way upstairs the boys passed the lounge, where there was indeed a lot of screaming and shouting, though it was clear that Mikey was doing the screaming and his mother the shouting.

"Are you causing trouble again, Noah?" called Jack from his room.

The two boys came to stand at his door. "Mikey called mum a *bloody evil stepmother.*"

240

Jack hooted with laughter. "Would you like to take the little one home, Noah? He'd be all for it, you know."

"I think small doses are best."

"LB says you're up for doing a length next week."

Noah's hands started to work nervously. "Well, I'm going to try, but I'm afraid of getting into a flap."

"You'll be OK," said Dan.

"I was wondering, that is if you don't mind, if I could invite Alan to come along?"

"Alan Henderson?" asked Dan with some surprise.

"Yes, if you and Justin don't mind. To be honest, I've already asked him. It would be a big step for him..."

"Yes, it would," said Jack. "So, you've become chummy with Alan?"

Noah blushed. "Sort of. He doesn't spare me the insults, but he did draw me a picture."

"What sort of picture?" asked Dan.

"A racing car."

"I didn't know you were into cars."

"I'm not, but he is. He's like a walking encyclopaedia on all things with four wheels."

"He's like Stewy with his photographs," said Jack.

"I'm not sure which he likes best, the really old or the really new. My picture says *A.H. F1 World Champion* on it."

"Very modest," laughed Dan.

"It's all front, you know. He's always very angry, but when I catch him off guard I can see how scared he is and he's lost all his confidence."

"You obviously care for him, Noah," said Jack.

"Of course he does. This is a good man," said Dan, clapping his friend on the back.

Noah swallowed. "Which is why I came round, really. I don't suppose you have another pair of swimmers that you've grown out of, like you gave to me?"

Dan looked doubtful, but then his face lit up. "I haven't, but I know a boy who has!" He took out his mobile and speed-dialled.

"Hey Dan," came a voice.

"Hey, Just, where are you?"

"Home, lazin'."

"Have you still got that pair of Zoggs your fat arse has grown out of?"

"It's not my arse that's got bigger, small fry, but yeh, they're upstairs somewhere."

"How about you and me donating half a bin bag of clothes each to Alan Henderson?"

"Sounds a plan. What, you mean now?"

"Noah's idea. We'll be round about seven-thirty."

"OK."

"See ya then."

"See ya."

Dan put away his phone. "Sorted."

It was twenty past six when Roger called them down for tea. Pam was already sitting at the table across from Mikey, who had half a glass of diluted rosehip syrup in front of him. His eyes were still red, but when he saw Noah he smiled and lightly tapped the table next to him.

"What's in the bin bag?" asked Pam.

"Clothes," said Dan, queuing up behind Jack to wash his hands.

"What clothes?"

"I've sorted some old stuff out for Alan Henderson."

"You can't just give away your clothes," stated Pam.

"Er, they don't fit me any more."

"You could save them for your brother."

Mikey wrinkled his nose in distaste.

"For five years?" said Dan, his temper rising, sensing his mother's ulterior motive.

"You could sell them," said Pam.

Dan managed to control himself, just. "It's not a month since you told me to have a good clear out and that I was selfish hoarding my stuff when I could give it to the charity shop to help the starving orphans!"

"Sit down, everyone," said Roger, calmly. "Noah, Mikey's reserved a place for you."

"Ridiculous!" muttered Dan, making more noise with his chair than normal.

Noah sat down uncomfortably, believing he was the real source of the discord. Mikey pulled on his sleeve and squeaked excitedly. "I'm coming to see you next Saturday."

"If you're good," said Pam, "very good."

Mikey came off his high just long enough to weigh up the chances of him staying good for a whole week.

"Maybe the pestilence should stop in bed for a week," suggested Jack.

Mikey stuck out his tongue.

"Huh, good start," said Jack.

"Don't tease," said Pam.

"So have we sorted out the clothes business?" growled Dan. "Am I going to be allowed to give away *my own clothes*, which no longer fit me, to who I want, rather than taking them round to the local pawn shop for 50p?"

"Hmm, porn," said Jack.

"Do what you want," said Pam. "I no longer have any say in the affairs of this house."

***

72: Monday, 15th July. 6.50 p.m. 41 Westbury Avenue.

NOAH

This bin bag weighs a ton. I didn't know clothes were so heavy. Mrs Moseley was acting very strangely last night. I know she doesn't like me, but there seemed to be more to it than that. Perhaps it is the women's problems that Dan was talking about. Still, I liked the spicy beef, but I have to admit the houmous was a bit gritty for me, even if it is a gay boy fave. Our dad said I was getting a taste for all this erotic food. I think he meant exotic.

It's taken me half an hour to get here. I've rested the sack on top of the gate post because my poor little wrists are aching. The things I do for that grouchy boy. Dan's were neatly folded but Justin's were all in a jumble. I had get out the iron on some of them. Actually, I really felt like keeping some of the stuff for myself, but that would make me out to be a real minger, especially if I was caught wearing something.

That's odd; they're all out on the driveway staring at the garage with those huge wooden doors. You could get a tank inside, by the looks of it. Perhaps they're thinking of knocking it down. I don't know what it's made of, but it looks like it's been there for a hundred years. Robert's seen me and he's grinning; he probably thinks I'm an old bag lady.

"Hello, Santa," he says, opening the gate for me.

The others are watching me now. Why are they all smiling at this sweat-stained, exhausted creature?

"Go straight up, it'll be a nice surprise for him," says Elspeth, and there's a sort of ironical tone to her voice.

Stewart makes a slitting-his-throat gesture and I've guessed by now that him upstairs is in a bad mood. So what's new?

I delve into the sack and bring out a pair of Karrimor sandals in a plastic bag and hand them to Stewart's mum. "Can you look after these?" I ask.

She nods. "You'll have to be very patient with him."

Oh, lord!

I reach the landing with the bag slung over my shoulder and I suppose I may as well go the whole Santa hog. It's funny that I always feel comfortable around Alan, whatever he says or does. Perhaps it's because he's so fragile, or perhaps it's something to do with me.

"Ho, ho, ho!" I shout, throwing the door open and entering unannounced and uninvited.

This time he ignores me completely, so I go up and dump the bag on the bed next to him.

"Hello, cuteness, have you put your stocking up for an early Christmas?"

He turns away and won't look at me or speak, so I reach out and stroke his head. He tenses and then for a moment seems to relax, but that doesn't last either as he hits my hand away.

"Get off me, I don't want your faggy skin disease on me."

"Naughty," I say, "when Noah's brought you some lovely things."

He closes his eyes and grits his teeth. "I don't want you here, and I especially don't want a homo-fag trying to be nice to me."

"I'm not *trying* to be nice to you, I am nice to you because I like you."

"I don't want to be liked..."

"I know, especially by a little homo-fag."

He burrows down into the bed, turns on his side, pulls the bedcovers over his head and shuts himself off. This is more difficult than I expected, and I wonder if I shouldn't go and come back another day, but then I have an idea and reach for the sack. I take out the clothes and sort them into neat piles on the bed while giving a running commentary. "Three button-up cotton T-shirts, one white, one green, one stripy; one blue cotton button-down polo shirt. Two pairs of chinos, one outrageous red, one boring beige. Five pairs of Vans crew socks, three white, two black. Ooh, three pairs of Dan's sexy boxers and two of Justin's very fetching Calvin Klein boxer briefs. A pair of preppy grey shorts with blue belt, and a pair of fluorescent green and orange cargo shorts, Dan's obviously..."

He hasn't moved, and so I go round to the other side of the bed and find that the sound of my boring, whiny voice has sent him fast asleep. And he looks so sweet and vulnerable, with his little face peeping out of the bedclothes with the scar across the bridge of his nose and the fading colours of all the bruises, that I've just got to draw up a chair and sit with him.

"Hey, fag!"

I open my eyes and blink. He's looking at me from his den under the bedclothes while I'm slumped in the chair, doubtless with drool running down my chin. I yawn.

"Ho, hum, sorry..."

Moments later, I yawn again and stretch. "I must have dropped off." I flick my fringe back into place.

"Pity you didn't drop off a cliff," he replies.

I can see that he's trying to stifle a yawn himself now. "You know, yawning is infectious."

"I don't want to catch any of your diseases."

He's obviously in a better mood. "Have you looked at your presents?"

"What presents?"

I go back round the bed to my neat piles of clothes and he turns himself over and hoists himself up onto one arm. "What's this?"

"I went round to Dan's house and got him and Justin to sort through the clothes which are too small for them."

"Cast-offs!"

"They're not cast-offs, otherwise they'd have thrown them out." I hold up the polo shirt. "You'll look so cute in this..." I put it down and hold up the grey shorts with the blue belt. "And sexy in these."

He sets his jaw and scowls. "I don't want them."

I smile at him disbelievingly and take the first pile over to the chest of drawers by the window. Once they're all safely put away, I return to the plastic sack. "I've got one more thing to show you..." I take out the pair of Zoggs black racer swimming trunks with curved white and orange stripes on the sides which used to belong to Justin. "These are for you on Saturday."

He starts to tremble. "I'm not going!" he shouts, and I know it's to cover the fact that he's frightened.

I smile at him. "Would you like to try them on now? I promise not to blush."

"You homo-fag pervert."

I shrug and go and put them in the drawer.

"Everyone will look at me," he says.

I sit on the bed again. "What's wrong with that?"

"I don't want people to see me like this." He pulls up his PJ top just enough for me to see the marks. They're fading now, but I can still make out the criss-crossed pattern of a chain over his tummy. I feel like crying, but I know I mustn't.

"I love your whirly belly button," I say. "Mine sticks out like a knot in a balloon." I pull up my vest for him to look.

"I don't want to see your scrawny fag body, thank you!"

Stewart comes in carrying two glasses. "I thought you could both do with a drink," he says in the same ironical tone that Elspeth used earlier.

"The homo-fag's just leaving," Alan says.

Stewart rolls his eyes and puts the drinks on the side table. "I don't know why you put up with him."

"He's lovely, really," I say. "And he's got such a cute belly button."

"Shut up!"

"I'll take your word for it." Stewart gives me one more pitying look and leaves.

I sit on the bed and take a sip of lemonade. "I don't know why I like you, when you're so horrid to me."

"Because you're a faggo-masochist."

"Could be, I suppose." I smile at him yet again. "I put the picture you gave me on my bedroom wall."

"Rip it up and throw it away."

"Will you show me how you draw like that?"

I can see he's struggling with himself, but I pretend not to notice. Instead I look round for his laptop, which I notice is tucked into his bedside cabinet along with a pad of paper and pencil. I sit on the edge of the bed and boot into Windows then wait a bit longer until the Wi-Fi connection completes. Then I'm onto Google.

"Can I watch while you draw *this* for me?" I say, turning the screen towards him.

"You homo-fag!" he cries.

"I love it, don't you?" It's a picture of Lady Penelope's pink Rolls-Royce. I hand him the computer and climb on the bed.

"What are you doing?"

"Snuggling."

Quickly he puts a pillow between us then takes up the pad and pencil. "Why do you wear those faggy black plimsolls with no laces?"

"Sorry," I say and slip them off. "They're cheap."

"You've got no socks on, either."

I wriggle my toes. "Justin says my feet are nice and neat."

"He must be a bit of a homo too, then."

"I'll tell him you said that."

He looks at me quickly and I smirk back at him. "Go on, then – draw..."

And now I've got two pictures of cars on my bedroom wall. FAB!

***

73: Wednesday, 17th July. 5 p.m. 41 Westbury Avenue.

<u>NOAH</u>

Now I know why they were staring at the garage. Someone's been busy painting those huge doors lime green. I expect it'll tone down in time, or we'll just get used to it. I hadn't noticed that there are four frosted glass window panels at the top, and whoever did the brushwork has done a good job of painting round them. Maybe Elspeth is thinking of installing an indoor tennis court.

Alan is sitting up on the bed like Lord Muck, his back supported by three pillows.

"Why are you here again?"

"Don't bitch," I say. "Elspeth asked me to take off those plasters. She says they've been on far too long."

"I don't want you to touch me."

"Why?"

"You know why."

"Well go on, say why."

"Fuck off."

I sit down on the bed near his foot. "Now hold still or it may tickle..."

He kicks me in the thigh with the ball of his right foot and it comes keen.

"Ouch!" I say and give him a pained look. He knows he's crossed the line and I can see him shutting himself down.

"I'm going to take them off now."

He looks away. "Do what you want."

I take off the top plaster to reveal an inch-long scar running back from between his big and first toe, then I look at the base of his foot and do the same. "There you go, all done. Don't you think I'd make a good nurse?"

He scowls at me. "I need new plasters."

"Elspeth says if the wounds have healed over you don't need them. So your nurse says you don't need them."

"Next time I want the organ grinder, not the monkey."

"I don't know whether I want to come again anyway."

He looks at me and there's a real sadness in his eyes, which makes my heart ache. "They'll send me back when I'm better," he says suddenly.

"Back?"

"Back to my dad, to my brother." He's trembling now, even his lips.

"No, they won't," I reply, having never given the possibility a thought.

"You don't know," he says, which is true.

"If that ever happens, you can come and live with me," I blurt out. "Our dad wouldn't mind."

He takes a second to take this on board, then snorts. "Living in a flat with a fag!"

"You could do worse."

"Not much!" He looks at me and I can see his mood has lightened.

"OK, you've got two choices now," I say.

"What?"

"You can either let me tickle your feet or send me back home..."

"You better go off to fag flat then, because you're not touching my feet."

"I already have."

"Piss off."

I grab hold of his ankle with one hand and run the tips of my fingers over the soles with the other and he half yelps, half screams, and his legs jiggle and his body shudders. "Get off me!" he shouts. "I hate you, fucking fag boy!" And I'm pretty certain he's not really angry because there's a sort of laughter in his voice. So I keep doing it till he's lying on his tummy beating his pillow with his fists and waving his legs in the air and screaming for mercy.

"There, I'll let you off now," I say at last.

He turns over and blinks at me. "Faggotard."

"Will you show me what you've been doing on your laptop today?"

"You're not interested in vintage cars."

"No, but it's a good excuse to snuggle up to you again." I take off my plimsolls and hop onto the bed next to him.

"Weirdo," he says, but this time he doesn't bother with the pillow.

I put my right foot next to his left and wiggle my toes at him. "My foot is bigger than yours."

"Yeh, and it's about the only thing that is."

"That's a naughty thing to say to a gay boy." I'm so close to him that I can feel the warmth coming off his body, and I have to catch my breath as I realise how nice it is.

He picks up his laptop and for the next twenty minutes babbles on incessantly about ancient Jags and Daimlers, Salmson French and Salmson British, and overhead cams and hydraulic this and twin carburettor that. Some of them look really cool, but by the end I just want to tickle his feet again.

"Can I tickle your feet again?" I say when he pauses for breath.

"You wouldn't dare!" he says.

"Oh, yes, I would!" I spring up and give his soles the full treatment, and he screams and shouts and kicks his legs and bounces about and calls me a fag and pervert, and his laptop nearly falls on the floor, but he just manages to catch it and then we start again and he tries to tickle my feet and I start to squeal and squawk and I'm having fun and I think he is too.

"Do you want me to come over again?" I ask when we're exhausted.

"No... Whatever."

"That's an improvement on *fuck you*."

"Fuck you."

That makes me laugh.

"Can I have this magazine?" I ask, seeing the copy of *F1* lying on the floor.

He looks over the side of the bed. "That's a man's magazine."

"It's for my dad's shop; he hasn't got many."

"What will you give for it?"

I smile sweetly. "A kiss."

"Ew!" He looks at me and just for a second his expression of disgust falters, then he buries his head in the pillow. "Quick, take it before I'm sick!"

When I get downstairs, Elspeth is waiting in the hall. "What was all that noise?"

"We were tickling feet," I say, thinking I might get told off.

"How wonderful," she says. "I assume his left foot has healed satisfactorily."

"Except for the scars, it's just like the right one."

"You're so good for him, Noah. He doesn't feel threatened by you."

251

I'm not sure that I feel particularly flattered by that remark, but I suppose it was a compliment.

"Come, I want your opinion on something I've been discussing with the others," she says. "I have a feeling that you are the person to see it through."

"Is it to do with Alan?" I ask.

"It is. You do like him, don't you?"

I think I'm blushing and have to flick my hair. "Yes, he's nice."

***

74: Wednesday, 17th July. 7 p.m. Swanford Community School.

<u>PAM</u>

The Celebration Evenings at Swanford Community School happen twice yearly, once in July and again in November. The July evening is for the parents of Years Ten and Twelve to meet with their teachers to assess the progress of their progeny, after which light refreshments are served. Then everyone assembles in the hall to listen to the headmaster make a speech about the great steps forward the school has made during the past twelve months. If there is also a guest speaker, the 'great steps' speech will be somewhat abbreviated to give the audience a chance to cope with more rhetoric before the boredom factor cuts in. The proceedings are interspersed with a showcase of the school's musical talents by the choir and orchestra, winding up with a rousing rendition of the National Anthem.

In the school lobby, Pam and Roger waited to enter the improvised booth where Mr Colt was ensconced behind a foldaway table, at this moment talking to Henry Allen's parents.

"Evening," said a voice behind them.

They turned to find PC Richard Masefield, known to close confidantes as 'Dickie', and his wife Vera standing behind them.

"Hello," said Pam. "You're Charlie's parents, aren't you?"

"That's right."

"We don't see as much of Charlie as we used to," said Roger.

"It always used to be Jack, Max and Charlie," added Pam.

Vera tried to smile, but it came out as more of a grimace. Richard, who was wearing a classic country shirt and cavalry twill trousers, was more successful in upturning his lips. "I suppose people grow apart. They choose a particular lifestyle and it doesn't accord with the norm."

"Pardon?" said Pam, not certain whether they'd been slighted or not.

"Such a shame. I suppose you must be very disappointed," consoled Vera.

"Disappointed?" questioned Roger "I don't understand."

"They've asked Dickie to become a governor of the school, you know – such an honour," confided Vera.

"An honour?" said Pam doubtfully. "I thought they were scouring the telephone directory looking for people."

"Not any more," replied the off-duty constable. "Only people with the right outlook are being considered."

Any further conversation was stalled by the emergence of Henry Allen's parents, closely followed by Mr Colt.

"Why, Mr and Mrs Moseley," he said, shaking hands, "A pleasure. Won't you come into my humble compartment?"

They followed their son's form tutor into the partitioned-off area and sat down in the chairs provided.

"I apologise for the rather cramped conditions. It reminds me rather of voting on election day. Do pull the curtain behind you if you so wish."

Pam turned and drew the curtain with a forceful tug, frowning reproachfully at the Masefields as she did so.

"You remembered us," noted Roger.

"I think it was more the familial resemblance, Mr Moseley."

"How is Jack doing?" asked Pam.

"The bare facts first. Given his mark in the mock examinations, I expect Jack to get an A in English Language and at least a B in Literature. Prior to the recent changes, you could have said A* and A. In a class of twenty-four he is in the top five in both subjects."

"Below Mandy Simpkins," said Roger.

"Mandy is a phenomenon and rather atypical of our students," smiled Mr Colt.

"And what about our son's progress overall?" asked Pam.

Mr Colt sat back and lifted his gaze. "There was a period earlier in the year when I was worried about Jack. Concerned both for his school work and his welfare. This was not confined to me, as all his teachers were voicing similar disquiet. It only became clear to me after the matter was resolved where the problem lay. That I did not understand what was happening and worse, in the first instance, drew the wrong conclusion was a failure on my part, which I regret."

"You were not the only one, Mr Colt, for we were even more culpable," said Roger. "But is everything as it should be now?"

"Since I am due to retire shortly I can probably afford to be a little more expansive than would be normal under these circumstances. Jack is progressing well across all subjects. I find him a joy to teach: he lifts my spirits and those of the whole class. His ready smile is as sunshine to our well-being. But whether this view is shared by my colleagues is something you will have to ask them."

"That's quite a glowing report, " said Roger. "If we told him what you said I think his ego would expand to fill the house."

"Superficially, perhaps, but I get the impression that your son is more level-headed than that."

"Hmm," said Pam. "I often think that we're losing touch with our boys, both him and Dan."

"I have some regrets that I shall not have the privilege of teaching your charming younger son."

Roger nodded. "I can see why Jack is so upset that you are leaving, Mr Colt."

"I'll be frank with you, Mr and Mrs Moseley. If there are any adverse reports about either of your sons from here on in, and from whatever quarter, do not take them at face value. Be alert and stay vigilant – and remember to give them unfailing support."

Pam and Roger left Mr Colt's booth, more disturbed than when they had entered. Not about their son's academic or social standing, but by his form tutor's closing words. As they drifted towards the tea urn and the plates of biscuits, they noticed Frank and Maybelle Crittenden in conversation with the headmaster. The dominating figure of Councillor John Henderson was another presence. He was talking to people they did not recognise.

It was as they were filling their cups that they were approached by a smiling woman in her mid-thirties with fair hair. "Hello," she said, "We meet again."

"Hello Anne," said Pam. "It's nice to see a friendly face."

"Some of them are a bit stand-offish, aren't they?" she says.

"Have you done the rounds of the teachers?" asked Roger.

She nods ruefully. "I got a few brick-bats about Stewart's laziness."

"That's not fair, you've only had him for five minutes," said Pam, realising not a moment afterwards that she had committed a gaffe.

"How did you find Mr Colt?" said Roger, trying to cover for his wife.

"Charitable," replied Anne. "He expects Stewart to get a C and a B in his GCSEs. Actually, with all the problems he's had, I think my son is a wonder."

"He's a very nice lad," said Roger.

"All of the No. 41 gang are," said Anne with a smile, though her eyes darted warily to where Councillor John Henderson was standing. "We were so pleased when your boys got Alan away from the clutches of that dreadful family," she said in a half whisper. She seemed on the point of saying more when she saw the blank stares of the Moseleys. "Oh, I don't think that was very discreet of me, was it?"

The bell rang, which meant that it was time for everyone to assemble in the hall. Anne excused herself quickly and made for the Ladies.

"Well one good slip deserves another," observed Roger.

"I knew it," said Pam.

"Knew what?"

"Those boys of ours – we never know what they're doing or what they get up to. They're controlled from that house. They need taking in hand, Roger. Their wings need to be clipped."

"If only you could hear yourself, Pamela Moseley. We should be encouraging good deeds, not clipping their wings. I learned my lesson with Jack, but you seem to have forgotten."

"Dan is only thirteen, he has no knowledge of the adult world."

"My advice is to keep shtum and let them find their own way. They seem to be doing all right to me, especially when it comes to the Hendersons."

"I don't know how you can be so devil-may-care."

"Probably because I was once a boy like them."

The bell rang again.

Roger took his wife's arm. "Come on, old girl, let's get in there before they shut the doors."

The stragglers entered the hall and found seats towards the back, including Pam and Roger. Anne hurried in almost last, and chose to sit in the opposite aisle to avoid any repercussions that might follow from her indiscretion. The ranks of teaching staff were already on stage, partially obscured by six of the school's best chairs arrayed along the front like miniature thrones. They were empty.

The conductor of the school orchestra, Mr Williams, the soon-to-be ex-music teacher, came out from a side door and took up his position at the upright piano to the left of the stage. The other members of the small orchestra, all pupils – three violins, double bass, two trumpets, clarinet, trombone and percussion – were already seated at their desks. A hush fell. The conductor raised his arms and a specially arranged version began of the slow middle section of 'Jupiter' from the *Planets Suite* by Gustav Holst.

Towards the end of the arrangement, the headmaster, along with Councillor Timothy Sullivan, the guest speaker, and four of the governors, filed on to the stage and took their seats on the thrones. Mr Williams ended with a flourish and the players stood up and received their deserved round of applause.

The headmaster began his address in lugubrious style, apologising for the lapse in moral rectitude that the school had suffered recently, before assuring his audience "that the ethos of our community, though essentially secular, would stay true to the tenets of the Bible. After all, we are a Christian country and we should not be afraid to say so..."

Roger leaned over and whispered to Pam. "What is the silly old buffer on about?"

"Sssh!" she replied, afraid that someone might overhear.

Having got that off his chest, the headmaster smiled and became more demonstrative. "In the spirit of our inspired evangelism, we Christians need to be even more confident and ambitious in improving our society and the education of our children. To this end, ladies and gentlemen, I should like to introduce you to our new members of staff who will be in post come the start of the new school year."

Three men, two white, one black, walked out on to the stage, to a scattering of applause. They were all formally attired in suits and ties and could easily have been mistaken for bank executives.

"The first gentleman I would like to welcome is the Reverend William Adeboye from Lagos in Nigeria. He will be our new RE Teacher and equality counsellor. He has a theological degree from Christ Alive Christian Seminary and University."

The headmaster shook the hand of the new member of the faculty, who gave a small bow to acknowledge the loud applause coming from a small section of the audience.

"The other gentlemen are both from the United States of America. First, I would like to introduce you to Bob LaPlante from the state of Montana. He will be head of the English department, taking over from our revered Mr Colt. Mr LaPlante has a postgraduate degree in English and Divinity from the Mountain States Baptist College."

Bob LaPlante stepped forward and thanked the headmaster in a strong Southern accent. He was a short, somewhat overweight man in his forties with a double chin and what looked very much like a wig. Pam put a hand over her mouth to hide her incipient chuckle.

"And, last but by no means least, may I introduce Todd Crozier from Omaha, Nebraska, our new teacher of science and a graduate of Grace University." From some sections of the audience, there were shouts and even whistles of approval, but most parents looked on in bafflement and a few with foreboding.

Todd Crozier shook the headmaster's hand vigorously and then walked to the edge of the stage and raised his fists above his head to celebrate his coming. A thickset man with a large head and very little neck, he sported a Van Dyke beard which had turned grey, in contrast to his receding hair, which was almost black.

Roger exchanged glances with his wife. "I've a feeling Jack may have been right," he murmured.

***

75: Thursday, 18th July. 6.45 p.m. 41 Westbury Avenue.

NOAH

I'm nearly blinded when I come down the driveway, because someone has given a second coat of lime-green paint to the garage doors. I press the bell and hear it ring far off in the kitchen.

"Hello," says Stewart, clearly surprised to see me.

"Aren't you going to ask me why I'm here?"

"I know why you're here – to see Alan," he says with a smile.

"Oh, am I that obvious?"

"Pretty much. I should go on up. Mr Mean and Moody could do with a visitor."

"Like that, is it?"

Stewart nods knowingly. "By the way, the big day is on for tomorrow. Robert's wrapped the parcel in the paper you provided. Do you do it deliberately to make him mad?"

I can't help grinning. "Yes."

He holds the door open for me and I breeze upstairs and waft into the bedroom. "Hello, sweets, it's me!"

There's a sudden scramble from the other side of the bed. He appears in some confusion, pulling on his PJ top and jumping onto the bed.

"You're not supposed to be here," he barks.

"You were having a wank," I say, and I can feel myself blushing even as the words come out.

"I was not!" he shouts, but he's also gone red.

"What were you doing, then?"

"None of your business. And keep your fucking fag fantasies to yourself, pervert."

I realise then what he was actually doing, and also the reason why. So I slip off my plims, jump onto the bed beside him and put my hand on his forehead. It's slightly damp and his little blond fringe is matted to it, but it feels nice. "Are you doing exercises, so you'll look beautiful for me?"

He knocks my hand away. "Why do you have to be such a fag?"

"Don't know," I reply. "Can't wait to go swimming on Saturday."

"I'm not going!"

"It'd be a shame, after doing all this exercising, not to show off your lovely muscles."

"Why do you have to be so clever?" he asks.

"Why do you have to be so gorgeous?" I counter.

"Shut up!" He looks away. "Don't say that sort of thing to me."

"Shall we prove it once and for all, one way or the other, whether you're gorgeous or not?" I say.

"What are you talking about now?"

"If you can remain silent for twenty seconds while I tickle your feet then you are not gorgeous. But if you're screaming like a girl after ten seconds, as I know you will be, then you are gorgeous. OK?"

He doesn't reply so I get down the bed and take hold of his ankle and put it across my knee. I haven't even started yet, and he's already shaking and flexing his toes in anticipation.

"Ready?"

He grimaces and I start to giggle. Then I'm off and within five seconds he's bellowing and laughing and bucking and beating the bed and I'm shouting "Who's a gorgeous boy, then?" And eventually he wrenches himself free and grabs my leg and grips my foot and starts on me.

"Say I'm not gorgeous," he demands, "and I'll stop."

"Never!" I cry, but I start to scream and jiggle and jerk, and I've nearly got to give in, but I'm saved at the last moment when Anne enters, holding a tray.

"Well, you boys seem to be having a good time," she says, putting the tray on the side table.

I wipe my eyes and we both compose ourselves. "Sorry," I respond, and fall back exhausted.

"Don't be," she says and starts to offload the tray. "There's ham and tomato sandwiches with pickle for you to share, a glass of orange and a Fruit Corner each, though you'll have to fight over who gets which flavour."

"Ooh, thank you," I say.

"Thank you," says Alan in his much more masculine voice.

She smiles at us. "You can bring the plates down when you're done, Noah. Alan, you've got to have a shower tonight so don't leave it too late."

Anne leaves us and we start on the food. I've already had my tea, but I'm quite hungry again.

"What are you smirking about?" he asks me.

"Well, it's either because I'm getting some more food or I'm thinking about your lovely body in the shower."

"How do you dare to say those gay sort of things to people?"

"Not people," I reply, "just you."

He shakes his head as he chews. "Why?"

"Because I feel comfortable with you."

"You think I'm a fag, don't you?"

I flutter my visible eyelashes at him. "A boy can dream, can't he?"

His face loses concentration. "They're going to send me back soon," he says. "I know it."

I shake my head. "Rubbish! How do you know?"

"Because I can hear them talking about me and when they realise I'm near they go quiet."

"Do you want to stay here?"

He gives me that look. "If I'm made to go back to them, I'll kill myself."

"No one is going to make you go back, ever!" I state, and I'm actually angry. "And if anyone tries to, they'll have to deal with me first!" We look hard at each other for a few moments and suddenly his face breaks out into a smile and then he giggles and then I giggle too.

"You think I'm just a weak little gay boy, don't you?" I say. I flex my bicep and nothing really happens; it's just flat.

261

He shakes his head. "You fag," he says, but his face is so smiley and friendly that I can't help grinning back like a loon.

***

76: Friday, 19th July. 5 p.m. 41 Westbury Avenue.

<u>NOAH</u>

This time it's Anne who opens the front door and she takes me into the sitting room, where Elspeth is snoozing, Alex is playing on the floor with a toy tractor, and Stewart has got his head buried in a book called *Lighting for Photography*.

"Hey," he says, looking up. "Exams finished. I'm a free man again."

"How did it go overall?"

He glances at his mum, then back at me. "We'll see," he says, giving me a look which could mean either an unexpected triumph or a monstrous failure.

"Is he upstairs?" I ask.

"In the garden," replies Anne, picking up the pair of sandals and handing them to me. "He'll need these on the driveway."

Elspeth opens one rheumy eye. "Hello, Noah, everything's prepared."

"Let us know how it goes, won't you?" said Anne.

"Yeh, we're standing back in case of more fireworks," said Stewart. "You know the one about the bull with the sore head? That's my brother."

I make my way out into no-man's land and saunter towards the sun lounger.

"Oh Alan," I say in a high-pitched voice, "it's me, little Noah."

He turns his head and glares.

I squat down by his side. "Why are you looking so miserable today?"

"Because you've come."

"You look very sexy," I say, noticing that the white button-up T-shirt and grey shorts with the blue belt fit perfectly.

"Shut up, homo."

"Summer holidays start next Wednesday."

"So?"

"I could come over more often."

"Who says I want you to come over?"

"I didn't say anything about coming over to see you."

He gives me that vulnerable look, which is like a knife being twisted in my heart. "I've brought these," I say, holding up the pair of sandals.

"I'm not putting them on because I'm not going anywhere."

"You're going swimming with us tomorrow."

"I'm not."

"You are. We're collecting you at ten. I want you to watch me swim a whole length."

"Huh! Only a length? That's what babies do."

"I could beat your sorry ass." I say, knowing that I couldn't beat the skin off a rice pudding. I look at him and can see that he's still fighting himself over the swimming and know how much courage it would take for him to go. "Right, forget that for now. We've got a nice surprise for you."

"Tell me what it is."

"No, it's a surprise. Do you want me to put these sandals on your ever so cute ticklish little feet?"

"Only fucking fags like you wear sandals and talk like that."

"They're an old pair of Dan Moseley's."

That shut him up. I go to strap them on, but first I look at him and waggle my fingertips very close to the soles of his feet. "Don't you dare!" he shouts, but his toes are already wiggling with anticipation.

"I think I'll save it for later," I say, letting him off for the moment.

I pull on the Velcro straps until they're tight and then he gets off the lounger and I think it's actually the first time I've been able to measure myself against him. We're about the same height, both shorties, but his proportions are more uniform than mine. Whereas my head is a bit like the one in that painting of *The Scream*, his is like a blond ball and much nicer.

"What are you staring at?" he asks.

"Your pretty little head," I reply.

"Fag!"

"Do you want me to hold your hand or will you just follow me?"

"What do you think?"

I lead him through the house and out of the front door, then hand him the key to the garage. It's has a really old-fashioned padlock made of brass with the name Chubb on it, and the key itself is like something from a castle dungeon.

"What's in here?" he asks.

I shrug. The hasp and lock have been freshly oiled and the hinges greased so that squeaking is now at a minimum. Alan swings open the right-hand door and I fasten it back for him. The lime-green paint has dried and doesn't look too bad really. He peers into the gloom. I flick the light switch and the interior is suddenly illuminated by two 150-watt bulbs set in reflector shades hanging from the roof apex. There's a large car, but its identity is concealed by what looks like a giant piece of curtain.

"Pull it off," I say. "It's really light, like parachute material."

I can see he's trying not to be interested, but failing miserably. When the cover is removed he stands and gawks at what is revealed.

"What do you think?" I ask.

Unconsciously, he strokes the polished black wing with the palm of his hand. "It's a 1950s Humber Pullman Mark III – or maybe IV. What's it got to do with me?"

"Show-off. Have a look at what's on the bonnet."

There's a parcel wrapped with pink paper and a sparkly pink bow. He looks daggers at me and I pout sweetly at him, but he unwraps it anyway. Inside there's a copy of *The Practical Motorist's Encyclopaedia* by F.J. Camm which Robert found on eBay.

And though he's turned away from me, I can see his shoulders are shaking and his head is bent and his hands are trembling. I know he's trying not to cry.

"Have a look inside the cover," I say in my most authoritative gay voice.

He has a bit of trouble opening it and then he kind of freezes because it says: *To Alan, from all your family and friends at No. 41. This car is your very own, for you to work on and make roadworthy. We hope it gives you many happy hours and that you will stay with us for as long as you want.*

And I can tell he's read it, because he begins to sob and he puts the book down carefully and covers his face with his hands and he looks so completely adorable that I've just got to go up to him and give him a cuddle. And when I do, he doesn't resist, and I hold him tightly in my arms and he puts his arms around me and lowers his head onto my shoulder and I can feel his warm tears on my skin and hear his heart beating.

And I'm going to whisper something in his ear because I can't help myself, and I hope he doesn't hit me.

"I think I'm in love with you."

And he turns his head and gives me a kiss on the cheek and now I'm crying too like a fag because that's what I am, and I hope that's what he is too.

***

77: Saturday, 20th July. 10.20 a.m. Prestleigh Leisure Centre.

ALAN

I've done a couple of easy lengths. Well, they weren't that easy because they tired me out, but now I'm sitting on the side of the twenty-five-metre pool, pretty much dead centre, with my feet dangling into the water. It's not one of the roped-off lanes, so I'm not interfering with anyone. In any case, this side is where the fag's getting his lesson from Justin and Dan. They've made him do a couple of widths at the deep end and now he's floating on his back with his arms outstretched. Every time they tell him to do something I can see the look of terror in his eyes, but he does it anyway.

It's funny. He's eight months older than I am, but he's probably only half an inch taller and twice as scrawny as me. He's like a drowned rat in the water; his eyes are all red and those big hands and feet flap about. He's severely uncoordinated. His wet hair doesn't fall over his face; it sticks out in all directions, and the blue streaks look like icicles. You can tell he's scared because his nipples have shrunk from dots to practically invisible. He's got a bit of hair on his legs, especially on the inside of his thighs, and in his armpits too. I suppose dark hair shows up more when it's wet. I haven't got any armpit hair yet, but I am catching up *down there.*

I looked at myself in the mirror just before they were due to arrive and got the sweats. I nearly had to call it off. But when they came up for me, they were so relaxed it kind of relaxed me, and I started to feel safe with them. They actually seemed pleased to see me – and I don't mean just him, but all three of them. I thought I was going to be scared meeting Justin for the first time since that incident at school, but do you know what the first thing he said to me was? *So sorry, Alan, I was such a jerk to you. Do you forgive me?* When I said *Of course,* he gave me a hug and I'm sure he meant it.

I was really nervous getting undressed in the changing rooms, in case anyone stared, but they were just normal. No, that's not true, he wasn't normal, he never is. He said I looked *so* sexy in my trunks. And he didn't say 'so' like Justin did, but in this exaggerated faggy way which made the others laugh. It was a good job we were the only ones in the changing rooms, except for three deaf old codgers down the other end and they don't count.

Yesterday, the fag said he loved me, but I don't know what it really means. I don't think even my mum has ever said that to me. He must be desperate if he loves me. I've never kissed anyone before, either – well, except my mum and my nan, but that was years ago, and now I've kissed a fag. It wasn't on the lips or anything gross like that, but it was still a kiss. I don't know where I'm going with this. I admit I like him, despite his faggy ways. I like talking to him. I even like him tickling my feet, and when he lies on the bed next to me – 'snuggles' is his faggy name for it – he makes me feel as though I'm not just a worthless piece of shit.

But I'm not a fag. I can't be a fag. And even if I was a fag, which I'm not, I'd go for someone like Dan Moseley, wouldn't I? He's the one I have faggy dreams about.

He's just come and sat down beside me. Really close, so that our legs are touching. "They've given me five minutes, then they want me to swim a length," he says in his gay, whiny voice.

I don't know whether I should move up, just to show him he shouldn't sit so close, but there's no one watching, so I stay where I am. He's really nervous; I can feel him shivering against me. His hands are clasped together over his scrawny chest and he's got goose bumps. I think I'd like to hold him – just to warm him up, you understand – but I mustn't.

"Your bony knees are knocking," I say and put my size six left foot onto his size nine right foot to act like a brake, and no one can see because they're underwater.

"Can I help you with your car?" he asks, probably to divert his thoughts.

I get butterflies in my stomach because I want him to. "It's man's work," I say.

He looks at me and smiles shyly. "I could polish the upholstery."

"Maybe, then," I say casually and we both know that means *yes*.

His face breaks out into a grin. "Hey! We could each get a pair of sexy dungarees to work in."

"You'll never be sexy!" I exclaim.

"I know," he says with a sigh. "I meant you, really."

"Noah, it's time!" It's Justin being strict with him, which is the only way to deal with a fag.

I don't look at him, but I ease my foot off the brake, then dab it back twice, which I hope he realises means good luck. As he gets up he brushes his lips against the skin at the top of my left arm and it's like a little jolt of electricity. I should tell him to keep his faggy lips to himself, but I don't because somehow it makes me feel good.

Dan is going to be his escort while Justin is supervising. They're all at the deep end now and he's in the water, hanging on to the side for dear life. I don't think he's going to make it. Justin counts him down and he's off. There's an awful lot of splashing and his stroke is somewhere between breast stroke and doggy paddle, and he's got his head way too far out of the water. I get up when he's about drawing level with me, but I can see he's tiring and beginning to panic.

"Come on, man up!" I shout, because I really want him to succeed, and I can see him smile and relax a little. So I decide to give him a bit of coaching. I walk along the side, keeping level with him. "Dip your head... raise your shoulders, not your head, breathe..." I keep repeating this on each stroke, and he seems to forget to panic and just listens to the rhythm and his strokes get longer and broader. Justin takes up his position at the shallow end to verify the length. Dan is just drifting alongside him now.

Noah touches home, and Justin gives him a thumbs-up. Now he's jumping up and down and whooping and you'd think he'd swum the Channel, not just a length of the poxy pool, his grin is so broad. He hugs Dan, then Justin jumps in and he gets a hug. Then he sees me, and gestures for me to jump in too. So I do, and he gives me the biggest hug of all. And we probably hold each for a bit too long, because Dan suggests to Justin that they get a crowbar.

***

JUSTIN

That was a real team effort, and it felt almost as good as winning at footy. Dan's just offered me a race, but I think I'll go and do a few lengths on my own to relax. I gave my goggles to the lifeguard so I'll have to walk back down to the deep end to get them. It's getting busier in here now and I can see the fast lane has already got four swimmers in it.

I have to admit, I had my doubts that Noah would make it this time. He was far too tense, but Alan seemed to relax him. If I didn't know better, I'd say there was something going on between those two. Noah is the world's number-one flirt. Not so much with me, but with Dan and even more so with Alan. I think he's got it really bad for him. The point is, Noah is such a down-to-earth little guy about most things, and when you get to know him there's a lot more to him than just the gay thing. For one thing, he makes us all laugh; it kills me the way he talks about 'our dad'. I hope he doesn't get his fingers burned over Alan. That guy must be seriously fucked up after what happened to him.

Imagine having that done to you by your own flesh and blood. Imagine having it done to you full stop. I suppose we're all capable of doing bad things, though – after all, I bullied Alan myself and made him cry. I felt really sick about that afterwards, and I know Dan did too. I hope he has forgiven me. It makes me cringe just to think about. It's only two months ago, but looking at him now it hardly seems like the same Alan that we pushed around in the shower. I guess he was just a little bit of a late starter. That was one example where I shouldn't have followed Dan's lead.

Everyone says I follow Dan blindly, and I have to admit it's not far from the truth. It's just the way our relationship has developed over the years. That's my main worry about going to the Academy. Dan won't be there. We were both surprised

269

that I got in and he didn't, but it's typical of Dan that it didn't spoil our friendship. It was more nearly spoiled by his rift with Jack. That was a bad period. I guess Dan is to Jack as I am to Dan, so I hope nothing ever comes between us.

"You were part of that foursome doing the length, weren't you?" That's the lifeguard speaking. I would guess he's about twenty.

I nod, and hope he's going to hurry up and give me my goggles.

"We've had a complaint." He taps his walkie-talkie.

I give him a *what?* look.

"Your friends were seen kissing."

I show him my palms as if to say I don't know what you're talking about, which is true because it certainly wasn't Dan and me, and if it was Noah and Alan then I didn't notice.

"A family in the gallery saw them."

I turn and look up to the entrance to the flumes, and who should I spy there but Harry and Adam Lewis, who are at the balustrade in their wetsuits, pointing and laughing at the crowd below. I suspect their parents are nearby too, but I can't see them.

"They're morons," I tell the guard.

"Well, just keep it down, will you?" he says and I look at him to see if he's into double meanings. His face is deadpan, so I nod non-committally and he hands me my goggles.

I do ten lengths of crawl then two more underwater; that is, without taking a breath except when turning. That's more difficult because you have to synchronise with the other swimmers in the lane, otherwise you'll run out of air.

When I'm finished, I go back to the changing rooms. Alan and Noah are already dressed and sitting together chatting about... a car or something, which is a bit of a surprise. I don't say anything about the Lewises.

"Where's Dan?" I ask.

"Shower," says Noah, with just the ghost of a smile.

"You fag," whispers Alan, shaking his head, and Noah nudges him.

"Better go and join him, then," I say and get my towel and gel.

They've taken the stalls down which used to separate the shower heads, because there was too little room, so now I can talk directly to Dan. I tell him about the Lewises and my little plan. He listens, nods and says, "Just be careful."

Ten minutes later I'm up in the cafeteria looking for the Lewises and at last I spot them, but only because elder sister Sarah is with them, looking like Miss Prim and Proper as usual.

"Mr and Mrs Lewis?" I enquire politely.

He stares at me through rimless spectacles.

"I thought you might like to see this." I put my phone down and touch play video. As they watch, I can hear Harry and Adam laughing and Harry saying, "Get ready for the flood then, homo."

The couple watch it in silence for a few more seconds then Mr Lewis picks up my phone, touches the trash button, deletes the video then drops it into his cup of coffee.

"Now where's your cheap and nasty video?" he says and laughs. "Gone, with your cheap and nasty mobile."

I'm paralysed not with fear, but incredulity that this seemingly normal man is in on his kids' dirty games. I want to tell him I've uploaded it onto the internet or downloaded it to my tablet, but of course I haven't, because I'm stupid. And my smartphone wasn't cheap and nasty – it cost nearly £200 in the sale and was bought for me last Christmas.

I try to fish the phone out of the cup. It takes two attempts, and I burn my fingers in the process. He sneers at me. "That's my coffee, you little fuck. Are you going to pay for a fresh one?"

I look at his wife, who hasn't said anything or reacted to what has just happened. Her expression is one of disgust and contempt, not with the video or her husband but with me. Then I realise that both of them not only know what their kids have been up to but also organised it.

Mr Lewis sees that he has won. "Just fuck off, you little shit-shover lover, before I call the police."

I turn away, but in the process deliberately knock the cup into his lap. It causes a commotion, but I'm gone before there can be any further repercussions.

I meet the others at the exit and explain what happened, but I still don't tell Noah and Alan the reason. I've already taken the battery out of the phone. Straight away, Dan is looking up *phones dropped into coffee* on Google. "It is salvageable, maybe," he says and shows us the screen.

"Iso-propyl alcohol," says Noah. "Our dad will have that and I bet we've got a bag of rice at our flat."

"I wouldn't know where to start," I say. "Can you do it for me, Noah? I don't want them to know at home. If it doesn't work I'll have to live with it."

"Course," he says. "I'll phone our dad to make sure he has some, then take it straight to the shop. I'm due to have my streaks renewed."

***

79: Saturday, 20th July. Noon. Marshall's Barber Shop.

ROGER

If Mikey still hadn't got the cast on his leg or if he was on his own, Roger would have walked to Marshall's Barber Shop. By cutting through side roads and pathways the distance was under a quarter of a mile. As it was, the drive up Leighton Lane, right at the high street and right again onto Victoria Street doubled that distance.

They found a parking space twenty yards down from the shop, near to the empty Orange Lounge Bar, and backed in just as a police patrol car glided slowly past. By the time his dad opened the car door, Mikey had already unbuckled himself from his seat.

"Hurry," he squeaked, pulling on his dad's hand as they walked up the street.

The little boy peered through the window and saw that Noah was already sitting in the big chair. "Quick, they've started."

The little shop bell rang and both members of the Marshall family turned their heads.

"Come for the demonstration then, young Mikey?" asked Alf.

"Can I have a blue streak in my hair, please?" asked the little boy.

"I only do blue streaks for special customers, like my best boy here." Alf looked over at Roger, who was already making himself comfortable on one of the chairs.

"This is new," said Roger, picking up the F1 magazine lying on the low table. "You never have any new magazines – even your newspapers are two days old."

"Now then," responded Alf. "That magazine was donated by my son. It belonged to his young man, who I hope to be meeting very soon."

Noah blushed. "Can I invite him over, Dad?"

Alf smiled and gave his boy's big head a hug. "Course you can, son."

"What about my blue streak?" said Mikey.

"That's up to your dad."

Roger was already engrossed in the latest spat between members of the Mercedes team. "Yes, go ahead," he said absentmindedly.

Mikey's jaw dropped and his eyes went wide. "Can I sit in the big chair with Noah?"

"You know it takes an hour and a half and you have to wear a cap," said Alf.

The little boy shrugged. "I don't care."

"Make room then, our son," said Alf, lifting him into the chair. Mikey laid his head on Noah's shoulder and smiled contentedly up at him.

An hour later, Roger was disturbed from a light doze by his phone ringing.

"Hello, wife," he said jocularly.

"Where are you? It's one o'clock!"

Roger yawned. "Won't be long."

"How long?"

"Half an hour yet," said Alf quietly. "He's been as good as gold."

Roger smiled proudly. "Well done, Mikey." He then turned his attention to the phone. "Pam, about half an hour or so."

"Half an hour! We have got shopping to do, you know."

"Yes, yes, everything is under control." The phone went dead and Roger closed his eyes again. Never had he had such a peaceful Saturday morning.

Mikey's curly hair had proved to be a bit of a problem for streaks, and so at Noah's suggestion Alf had made peaks of bright blue with dye and gel cement, having first bleached the areas. Now he removed the plastic shower hats from both boys and whisked away the white cloth.

"That's great, our dad!" said Noah, admiring himself in the mirror. "Just right for the summer hols. What do you think, Mikey?"

The little boy felt the stiff spikes and wondered at his image. "Wow! Better than streaks."

"I am now your official style guru," said Noah.

"What do you think?" Alf asked, turning the chair round so that it was facing Roger. "Your youngest is a real dedicated follower of fashion."

"Oh, God!" said Roger. This wasn't the restrained school-time colour, but a full-on, no holds barred, in your face electric blue.

Once they were out of the chair, Noah squatted down and gave Mikey's hair a final muss to give it a more natural finish. Roger mopped his brow and looked away, catching the movement of a patrol car as it drove past the window, the two officers peering into the shop.

"Police are busy today," said Roger, trying to forget about the confrontation he would have with his wife.

"I don't know what they're up to," said Alf. "Since poor old Tony was closed down, we haven't seen sight nor sound of them up here till this week."

"How much?" asked Roger, nodding towards his son.

"Oh, give us three. It's the cement that's expensive, you know."

He handed over four. "That's for keeping him occupied."

Mikey gave Noah a hug and a kiss, then grabbed his dad's hand. "Come on! I want to show Mummy and Jack."

"No hurry," said Roger.

***

80: Sunday, 21st July. 10.30 a.m. 41 Westbury Avenue.

ALAN

No sooner had I opened the garage doors than the fag rolls up on his bicycle. In his backpack is one of his dad's old white coats which he's brought to work in. By the looks of him, all his clothes are his dad's hand-me-downs. I stare disapprovingly at his emo fag hair and get one of his smiles from those pouty lips. Then he gives me a hug and I might just have wiped my lips across his cheek, which was a mistake, because it made him want to hold on to me for even longer. I told him to get his faggy hands off my body as there was work to be done, and he saluted me by putting two open fingers up to his one visible eye, which must be the faggiest gesture in the world.

We go into the garage. "Why hasn't it got any tyres?" he asks.

I shake my head in disbelief at his ignorance. "When a car's laid up for a long time you take the wheels off and put it on blocks."

He nods as if he understands, then I tell him that we're going to make a list of everything we need to get the car running. Elspeth said to present her with a costing, so we've got to do it properly. I hand him a pad and pen and he stands there in this white coat which comes down to his ankles, and makes him look like a snowman, and his big, black plimsolled feet are sticking out of the bottom and he smiles at me because he knows he looks an idiot. So I give him another hug and a peck on his cheek, just to keep him in line. And he tells me he loves me a lot and I tell him not to be such a fag and then we get down to work.

This car is immaculate, considering it's over sixty years old. It's a 1953 Humber Pullman Mark IV, which means it's a six-cylinder, four-litre, overhead valve engine. The bodywork is flawless, without a scratch on the black paintwork. It's not undersealed, but I can't find any rust at all. The Mark IV is supposed to be able to do 83 mph, though it would have to be in a following wind because it weighs over 2,500 kilos. It's not going to win prizes for performance either: 0–60 in 20.7 seconds.

Whoever put it up on blocks knew what they were doing: the fuel tank has been emptied, the engine and gear box have been drained of oil, and the sump is on the floor underneath. The battery has been removed, there's no water in the radiator, and though the hoses have perished it's otherwise looking good.

This particular model hasn't got the dividing panel between the front and back seats which separated the bigwigs from the chauffeur, though it could have been removed, I suppose. Six people will fit in with no trouble, and eight or even nine if the foldaway 'occasional' seats are down. At the back it has super-plush beige upholstery and thick pile carpeting, while it's real black leather in the front. The wood surrounds and dash are veneered in walnut and the whole car smells great, not musty at all. The gear box is only four-speed, but fully synchromesh, which was unusual in the 1950s.

"Where's the handbrake? Where's the gear lever? Where's the seat belts? Where's the heater, Where's the radio?" That's the fag asking questions, of course.

His mouth hangs open in shock when I tell him that wussy things like heaters and radios were optional extras in those days, and seat belts were only fitted in aeroplanes. He nearly falls over his white coat when I show him the gear lever on the steering column and the handbrake right by the door. I expect when he finds out that there's no power steering and you actually have to turn the wheel with your own strength he'll faint, especially when he experiences the cornering roll.

There's a toolkit, an instruction manual, a parts manual, a workshop manual, some useful spares and a full set of gaskets in the boot. They'll all come in handy. The garage has enough room to open the car doors wide on both sides, and there's a workbench along the length of the back wall and a window, but the outside is so grimy I can't see through it. Definitely a job for the fag there.

"What are these for?" he whines, looking closely at the louvres for the air conditioning that are low down near the back doors, and the cigar lighters in the arm rests. I explain, like he's a two- year-old, and he takes a drink from his bottle of faggy peach-flavoured water and grins at me and asks me if I want some. I take a couple of swigs but make sure I don't touch the bottle where his pouty lips have been, as I don't want to catch any of his diseases. Then he asks me if he can tickle my feet later. I tell him to concentrate on the job in hand.

The wheels and hub caps are on the shelf under the bench, along with the tyres and inner tubes. They're pretty far gone, which isn't surprising. Cross-plies, of course, 7.5×16s. I expect I'll be able to find a metric equivalent.

He's just bumped his head on the driver's door because it 'opens the wrong way'. I tell him to get a grip and watch where he puts his fat head. He gives me a sad look and asks if I can kiss it better. I decide I may as well, if it'll stop him whinging and whining about it.

The engine valves and seats will need replacing, and new guides fitted, if the car's going to run on unleaded petrol. You can buy an additive, but I'd prefer to be safe than sorry. There's so much space in these old engine compartments that there shouldn't be a problem stripping it down. We could even take the engine and gear box out, if necessary, because I've found a chain and pulley and there's a couple of RSJs holding up the roof to hang it off.

I've found him on his knees, the back door open, staring at the nameplate above the running board. "I thought this was a Humber," he says, and I know where this is going.

"It is," I reply, just the right amount of patient mockery in my voice.

"Why does it say 'coachwork by Thrupp and Maberly' then?" He gets up and pretends to hang his head in shame at his lack of education.

"The clue is in the word 'coachwork'."

"But it's not a coach, it's a car," he says, and smiles and bats his eyelids at me as though I'm going to be affected by his nonsense.

"The coachwork is the body, which fits onto the chassis."

He knots his brow as if trying to understand. "My head's still a bit achy," he whines. "I think I need a little snuggle." Which has nothing to do with Thrupp and Maberly and has everything to do with his faggy tricks. I sigh in exasperation and make him promise that if we do, he'll put his big snub nose to the grindstone afterwards.

Our first job will be to remove all the seats and carpets, because we're going to need access to the coachwork and chassis. In any case, if I leave them in place, the fag is bound to spill some of his faggy peach-flavoured water on them. I expect the best site to store the upholstery will be in the cellar, but it'll all have to be wrapped in plastic.

Some time later, Stewart comes out to the garage with Elspeth and smirks at the white-coated apparition. He says his mum is making us lunch and it'll be ready at one o'clock.

That's only fifteen minutes away. We've been working for over two hours and I hadn't noticed.

Elspeth asks me how's it going, and I'm hoping the fag's done a good job with the list because I haven't been checking, just calling out things. I thought I might be embarrassed at this point, but when I look, instead of the expected spidery, girly, twirly, faggy writing, I find it's really neat and readable – unlike mine, which is an untidy scrawl. Unfortunately, he spots that I'm impressed and so I suppose he'll be wanting another cuddle shortly, and maybe even a kiss.

I ask Elspeth how long the car's been in storage, because it only has 38,000 miles on the clock and I don't think it's been tripped. It takes her a while to count backwards, which I suppose is normal for someone who's nearly eighty-four. She thinks it was retired in about 1970 when her husband fell ill. In any case, they had a Morris Minor Traveller to knock about in during the 1960s, and she never learned to drive, which surprised me. They got someone from the local garage to decommission the Humber, but when I asked her which local garage, she shook her head. I expect it's long since closed.

I've just got time to play a trick on the fag before lunch. He's messing about in the boot, checking the contents of the toolboxes against the book inventory. So I'm going to call him and as he walks up to the front I'm going to switch the indicator on. On these old cars that's a retractable arm which fits flush with the coachwork between the doors.

"Fag, come here!"

I can see him through the driver's mirror. He's looked up and has a big smirk on his pouty lips. I'll soon knock it off.

"Come on!" I shout.

"All right, I'm coming!"

He's on his way. 3... 2... 1. Got him!

"Ooh, Alan!" he wails.

I open the driver's door and get out, shutting it behind me.

"What's wrong, fag?"

"Ooh, Alan, it nearly hit me."

"Heh! Heh! Heh! You should watch where you're pointing your big snub nose."

"What is it?"

"What does it look like?"

He's scrunched up his face, then he grins. "Choo, choo, choo." He's making train noises and doing faggy arm movements like he's Thomas the Tank Engine or something.

"It's the indicator arm for turning right," I say to cut off his silly antics.

"Ooh, I was nearly right." He prods it with his diseased finger.

"Careful!" I say.

He looks at me and lowers his head as if he's Princess Diana. "Alan, it gave me such a nasty shock that I think I need another little Thrupp and Maberly before dinner."

I'll give him Thrupp and Maberly. I just knew he'd use his faggy wiles on me and turn it to his advantage.

That reminds me – my brother's got a new camera, a late birthday present because of all that happened to him. It's a Nikon single lens reflex and didn't come cheap. He asked me if I wouldn't mind him taking a few photos. I told him it's OK, but to make sure he didn't get any of me and the fag in the same shot. More sad eyes, and so I agreed to have just one of the two of us. I tried to look serious but because of his faggy tricks we both ended up smiling and I've got my arm draped over his shoulder for some reason. We're standing in front of the open driver's door and you can see the Pullman badge. Stewart says he'll do a print for both of us, so I may have to put it up on my bedroom wall so as not to offend him.

***

81: Sunday, 21st July. 3.30 p.m. 41 Westbury Avenue.

NOAH

280

Our lunch was really like a dinner to me. Eggs poached in tinned tomatoes and a slice of fried bacon followed by fresh fruit salad. We usually get our fruit salad out of a tin. When we'd finished, Alan took me upstairs so that we could choose overalls on his laptop. Elspeth gave both him and Stewart a debit card and they get a weekly allowance put on automatically, with extra for special buys like now. Bibbidi-bobbidi-boo is all I can say to that!

I've noticed that the only room that's out of bounds to them is Elspeth's bedroom, and I don't expect they go into their mum's room much either. Actually, I've just said that wrong, because Anne isn't Alan's mum, though she might as well be, as she treats him like one of the family. Come to think of it, we're all treated like one of the family.

I asked Alan what size his manly chest was, and he told me off for checking him out. Then I said I'd need to measure him, and he told me I could, as long as I kept my faggy fingers to myself and didn't go near his inside leg. He has a lovely 33 inch chest – three more than me – and is ticklish under his armpits!

I love it when he's happy, and today he's been at his happiest since I met him. Just once or twice I've seen him start to drift off into the mopes, but he's managed to snap out of it pretty quickly. I can't wait to show our dad the photo of me and cutie-pie standing by the car. Stewart's camera takes amazing pictures. I shall have it framed and put on the wall next to my bed.

I showed him a pair of dungarees that I'd really like him to wear, preferably without a T-shirt because they're quite low-cut. He looked at me and called me a pervert and told me to choose something more sensible. Eventually we selected some quite ordinary ones, but they'll still set us back £70 for both pairs. I hope Stewart will take some more photos when we get them...

He puts the laptop away and says it's time to get back to work as I'm getting lazy. So I sit on the edge of the bed, look up at him, close my eyes and pucker my lips. He says he is never ever going to kiss my pouty lips because he isn't a fag, but if I'm good and work hard I might get a handshake later on.

We now have a list of thirty-eight items that we need to buy to get the Humber working again. Elspeth insisted we added seat belts to the inventory too, which I could tell Alan wasn't too happy about because he wants the car to be *authentic.* Some of the parts I've never heard of, like a clutch slave cylinder, but I'm not really a car person. This is going to cost a bomb. Alan said the price of the car was only £1,395 plus tax when it was new, but it's going to take four or five times that to get it running again. He said if the actual parts aren't available he would adapt others, but he wanted it as near to the original as possible. I love him anyway, but when his little eyes are all sparkly with enthusiasm it melts my heart.

It's been a really good day. I never thought I could get enthusiastic about a metal box on wheels, but I can't wait to see it drive out of the garage. I want Alan to get a chauffeur's uniform so that he can drive while I sit in the back and wave at the crowds lining the pavements on my Royal progress. In my dreams, he said, because he was having no fagginess in his car.

I'm just rolling up my white coat so I can put it back in my bag. It's 5.30 p.m. and I promised to be back by six because our dad and I have got our Sunday date at Wetherspoon's. When I get home I've got to check on Justin's phone, which is still buried in a bowl of rice. I think we managed to get all the coffee out with the alcohol, but I'll only know when I switch it back on.

Here, everything's been packed away, the seats and carpets are safely stored in the cellar, and the car has been put to bed under its cover. Alan is standing just inside the garage doorway looking at me suspiciously, because I keep casting smiley glances at him.

"I'm going, then," I say.

"Good," he replies.

"You didn't let me tickle your sexy feet."

"My body's off-limits to fags today," he says, which isn't true because we've already had six cuddles.

"Can we have a goodbye mega-Maberly?" I ask.

He shrugs and tries to look bored while he considers the request. "All right," he says and sighs as if he's doing me a great favour. "But not for too long and you'll have to come to me."

I know why that is, and it's not because he's playing hard to get. It's only five steps into the semi-darkness. I put my arms round him.

"Fag," he says and after a pause he adds casually. "Oh, yeh, and thanks for coming."

"I've loved it," I say, "almost as much as I love you."

He holds me at arm's length and looks at me as if deciding what to do next, then he leans in and gives me the lightest kiss on the lips. "That's only this once, mind," he insists. "Never again."

"That was so sexy," I whisper.

"Yeh, whatever," he says, as if he's done it a hundred times before. "Now get lost, fag, and be prepared for some hard graft the next time."

My day is complete. "Tuesday," I say and give him the fingers up to the eye salute which he pretends to be annoyed by.

***

82: Tuesday, 23rd July. 10.15 a.m. Woolgrove Wanderers Football Academy.

<u>JUSTIN</u>

Woolgrove is fifteen miles north of Swanford and is the county town. Not that it's much bigger; it just thinks it is. The Academy is a couple of miles to the west, pretty much in the country, which is why there was a lot of controversy over the use of green belt land when it was built. My mum, Monica – or

283

Mon to her friends – has brought me up for the medical and is now going shopping in town – at my insistence, as I don't want her hanging around trying to mother me and being an embarrassment in front of my prospective employers.

I said I'd phone her when it was done, which I can now do thanks to Gandalf the gay wizard of the mobile, Noah Marshall – plus *our* dad, of course. I hope the coffee I spilt over that Lewis guy's lap burned his balls off, so that he can't father any more of those Harry and Adam type brats.

Woolgrove Wanderers is one of those ancient football clubs that go back to the nineteenth century (as do some of its current players, ha! ha!). Like most old teams, their ground is slap bang in the middle of town, so there was no room for expansion there. My team, Swanford United, is a pup in comparison; 1924 is the date on the gate.

Having had its glory days in the Football League Division One (as it was in the 1950s), Wanderers is now an up-and-coming Championship League club with designs on the Premiership. This has been brought about by some serious money in the form of megabucks from some oil-rich zillionaires. Hence investment in a Category One Football Academy and yours truly – hopefully.

There are two full-size pitches here, one completely under cover on Astro-turf and the other outside, floodlit with an athletics track around it. Then there are various smaller pitches for the likes of me, but you have to walk further to get to them, boo! When I came for a visit earlier in the year, parts of it were still under construction, and there are still a few diggers and JCBs around the place.

I'm now in the reception area, waiting to be called into the medical room, which is down the corridor next to the gym. Everything smells new, and all the staff seem super-efficient. I don't mind telling you I've got a few butterflies, though I normally zip through medical exams. They said it would take about three hours altogether, so I don't know exactly what they're going to do to me. My little plastic bottle of wee has already been taken. It had to be the first one of the morning. Good job I didn't go drinking last night, ha! ha!

One thing I don't have to worry about now, thanks to Gandalf, the gay wizard of the feet, Noah Marshall (without *our* dad this time), is causing offence to sensitive noses. If I'd done something about my feet earlier, I might still be doing martial arts. Being told off in front of the whole class by my *sensei* for having stinky feet was terminally embarrassing for a twelve-year-old, and ended my short career in *Kyokushin* karate.

Well, that part's over and it took only half an hour of the three hours. After a few questions about my medical history, probably to see if I was awake, I was stripped down to my Calvin Kleins and the physio examined every joint and muscle in my body, even my fingers. After that it was the standard school exam with weight, height, cold stethoscope and two coughs, but then it got to be all high-tech. I was wired up to machines to check my heart, blood pressure and how much air I could blow into a balloon. I'm pleased to say I gave up smoking last week, ha! ha!

At the end of the medical, I got dressed, and one of the coaches, Bill Cullis, who I met on my original visit, took me along to a windowless room, where he asked me to sit in front of a touch-screen computer.

"Just follow the instructions on screen, laddie, and youse'll be fine," he said. I think he's Scottish.

The first instruction on the screen said *press START,* which I did. Then, for what seemed a very long time, I had to answer multiple-choice questions on maths, English, science, general knowledge and football, mixed up with all sorts of puzzles. There were quite a few questions on the history of Woolgrove Wanderers as well – oops!

Oh, I didn't mention that beforehand my mobile and other personal possessions, like my wallet, were taken off me by Coach Cullis and put in a basket, just like at an airport, except they were locked away in a cupboard.

The screen went off automatically after who knows how long, and by that time my head was spinning. I thought the three hours were up, but I was wrong because a dumpy man in a suit came in and told me that I had to fill in a questionnaire which he laid down before me, along with a Biro. Back to low-tech, I thought, and the man wasn't exactly my idea of a typical Football Academy staff member either.

"Take your time, son," he said. "There's no hurry."

The front page was for my name, address, date of birth, ethnicity and a listing of family members. It was only when I opened it that things started to get weird.

SECTION A

(Please circle the appropriate answer)

Question 1: Do you believe in God? YES NO

Question 2: What is your religion? Christian Islam Sikh Buddhist Jew Agnostic Atheist

Question 3: Do you believe in Heaven? YES NO

Question 4: Do you believe in Hell? YES NO

Question 5: Do you believe in Satan? YES NO

Question 6: Do you believe that demons are part of Satan's army? YES NO

Question 7: How often do you attend religious services: Daily Weekly Monthly Yearly Never.

Question 8: Do you believe that our Lord Jesus Christ is the son of God? YES NO

Question 9: Do you believe in the literal truth of the Bible? YES NO

Question 10: Do you believe in the Day of Judgement? YES NO

SECTION B

(Please circle the appropriate answer)

Question 1: Are you a homosexual? YES NO

Question 2: Are you attracted to members of the opposite sex? YES NO

Question 3: Do you believe that marriage should only be between a man and a woman? YES NO

Question 4: Do you believe that homosexuality is a lifestyle choice? YES NO

Question 5: Do you believe that those who follow a homosexual lifestyle go to Hell? YES NO

Question 6: Do you believe that homosexuality is caused by demonic possession? YES NO

Question 7: Do you believe that a demon can be exorcised in the name of Jesus? YES NO

Question 8: Do you have any family members who say they are 'gay'? YES NO

Question 9: Do you have any friends who say they are 'gay'? YES NO

Question 10: Do you know anyone who says they are 'gay'?
YES NO

I stared at this for at least ten minutes, going over and over each of the questions. I was tempted to write across it, *What has this got to do with football?* The dumpy man came back in and asked me how I was getting on. When I told him I couldn't do it, he told me that if I wanted to get into the Academy I must answer the questions as honestly as I could. There was no doubt in my mind that he was giving me an ultimatum, and that he had the power to pass or fail me. I was beginning to wish that I hadn't sent my mum away, or at least that I had my phone back so that I could get some advice on this crap. I may not be the brightest button in the box, but I knew this was not a run-of-the-mill test for prospective football players.

I started on section B, as that seemed easier, but then I realised I didn't know the answer to some of the questions, and really wanted a *don't know* box. In fact, when I say 'some', I really mean most, and more specifically numbers three through eight. Numbers nine and ten I could deal with. Jack Moseley is gay and so is Noah Marshall, and I would call them friends. Robert Crittenden is, but I don't know him well enough to say he is a friend. I'm not sure about Alan Henderson, but I wouldn't be surprised. Anyway, I circled those two questions as *yes* and then noticed some words at the bottom of the page.

Please turn over.

Now I broke out in a sweat because it was becoming clear to me what the real purpose of the questionnaire was.

SECTION C

If you have answered yes to Questions 8, 9, or/and 10 in section B, please provide the names and addresses of the individuals concerned, and as much information as you can about them.

The rest of the back page was blank, ready for me to spill the beans on my friends. I sat there for the longest time, not knowing what to do. At length, Bill Cullis came back into the room and told me that my mother was waiting for me in the reception area. It gave me the excuse I needed.

"I haven't had time to finish all the questions."

He went to the cupboard and retrieved my belongings. "I know. We were watching you on the monitor." He pointed to the camera in the ceiling.

I hadn't noticed it, and now feel stupid. "What do you want to know all this stuff for?"

"It's not fer me to say," he replied. "My job is to coach young talent to become the future stars of the beautiful game. But our new masters are concerned about the decline in moral standards and they think that football is so important it deserves their attention."

The dumpy man appeared in the doorway, unsmiling, and looking intently at Coach Cullis.

"I'm sorry I couldn't complete the questionnaire," I said, though I wasn't sorry at all about that. I just felt sorry for myself, having blown my chances of joining the Academy.

"Would you like to see him oot, Mr Maitland?" Coach asked the dumpy man.

"I will leave that duty to you, Bill," he replied.

"I've blown it, haven't I?" I said as we walked back down the corridor.

"I wouldnae hold yer breath, laddie. Pity ye didnae come a while since."

In the car, Mum wanted to know first why I had been in there for so long and, second, why I was so despondent. I told her it had been a long morning's work and I was just tired. Whether she believed me or not, I'm not sure, but it was after three o'clock when we got back to Swanford.

***

JACK

Justin looked at Jack and smiled resignedly. "So there we are... That's the story of my trip to Woolgrove Wanderers."

Dan, who was sitting next to Justin on his brother's bed, turned to him. "I'm glad you came over to tell us, Just, and didn't just text. It's unbelievable."

"I had to tell someone, and who better than my oldest and best friend and his wise old bro?"

"And friend, Justin," said Jack. "I don't think many people would have sacrificed their career like you just did."

He had never seen Justin so upset about anything, and even now the younger boy was remaining stoically calm. "It just didn't feel right."

"Moral courage," stated Dan. "That's why the scouts picked you for the Academy in the first place."

"You mean not for my dazzling ball skills?"

"Tuh! A cack-footed southpaw? Hardly," replied Dan.

"We'll see about that at practice tonight," said Justin.

"You're still going?" questioned Jack.

"Why not? A good knock-around will take my mind off it."

"Those fools at Woolgrove Wanderers don't know what they're missing."

"Jack, the people who matter there are not interested in the game at all."

"I wonder what Coach Brennan will make of it?" mused Dan.

"I doubt it'll bother him much. He couldn't understand why I got picked instead of you, Danny boy."

"And he'll be pleased to be keeping his dynamic duo at Swanford United," said Jack.

"Your dad won't let it rest until he knows the exact reason why you failed the medical, will he?" said Dan.

"No, but he won't know I've failed until the letter comes in a couple of days."

"You could tell him," said Jack.

"I could do, but I'm not going to. We can have it out when I get it, but I know he won't understand why I've given up something so important for what he would see as such an unimportant reason."

"What if they were just trying to frighten the information out of you and it won't make any difference to you being accepted?" suggested Dan.

"In all honesty, I'm not sure I'd want to go back there now. It's kind of spoiled it for me."

"But the Academy is just a stepping stone, Just, not the be-all and end-all."

"I know, I'm still trying to make some sense of it." Justin got to his feet. "Well, better get back..."

"Are you going straight home?" asked Jack.

"Got to get my kit together."

"I'll ride with you, then," said Jack. "Mr Ray will be twirling his moustache if I'm not there soon."

"Don't forget your ointment, Just," said Dan.

Justin grinned at his friend. "Huh! Ointment? I don't need ointment any more. I may as well let my feet slide back into stinkiness."

Dan got down on his knees and put his hands together. "Have mercy on us, oh great one. Let not the curse of the cheesy toes be upon us again."

Justin put his hand on his friend's head. "Arise, Sir Danny, your nose is safe. I've decided to enrol for *Kyokushin* karate again, which requires sweet feet."

***

84: Wednesday, 24th July. 10 a.m. 41 Westbury Avenue.

NOAH

First day of the summer holidays, and here I am ready to work. But the garage doors are locked, the house is quiet and I'm beginning to worry. When Stewart answers the door, he looks at me with that expression which tells me His Majesty is out of sorts.

"He had another nightmare – a bad one, I guess. I didn't hear, but it woke Mum."

"So, what's with him now?"

"You know about the bear with the sore head? Only worse than usual..."

"You mean, won't speak, won't eat, won't get out of bed."

"Correct about the last two, but only half-right about the first. That is, for 'speak' substitute 'shout and swear'. *Fuck off, leave me alone* being about the extent of it."

"Better go up, then."

Stewart nods and pats me on the back. "Good luck with that."

On the landing I meet Anne, who's been cleaning the bathroom. "Hello Noah, come to brave the beast in his den?"

I can tell she's a bit miffed, and I almost feel like apologising for him.

"Don't worry, it's just that his breakfast ended up on the carpet."

"Oh."

"Yes, 'oh'. I have to admit I did tell him off, which is just what he wants. I'm only pleased that Elspeth doesn't have to deal with him when he's like this, otherwise I think she might show him the door."

I know I'm only fourteen, but I'm a bit sceptical about that because it strikes me that Elspeth is the toughest one among us.

Anne gives me a tired smile. "If you need anything, including help, just call." Then she takes her bucket and mop downstairs, leaving me standing outside his room. Well, better get on with it.

I open the door quietly and close it just as quietly behind me. He's lying on his back under the duvet, staring up at the ceiling. Beside the bed is a wet patch where the 1001 has been used to clean the carpet.

"Hello, cutes! Isn't it time we got to work?" I make him jump as usual.

He turns to look at me, and his eyes are all puffy and he looks pale and drawn. "Sling your hook, homo," he says. "You're not wanted here."

"That's a nice picture," I say, noticing our photograph hanging on the wall above his bed. Stewart has mounted it in one of the 6 × 4 frames he found in the cellar and has made a good job of it.

"You can take your faggy picture and stick it up your arse."

"Like they did to you?" I say. Possibly not the most tactful approach, but it just slipped out.

"You fucktard!" he shouts, and reaches up for the picture, takes it off the wall and throws it at me. Fortunately I manage to duck, but unfortunately the photograph is mounted behind glass so that when it hits the wall near the door it shatters and the frame disintegrates and falls to the floor.

"That was close," I say, shaken. There's no reply and he just stares into space, his jaw set.

"Do you want me to go?" I ask.

He keeps staring at nothing. "Yes, fag, I want you to go and never come back."

I step neatly over to the bed and, in as near as I can get to an American accent, say, "Tough, cos I ain't goin' nowhere."

Slipping out of my plims, I get into bed beside him. "Snuggles time," I say, half ready to be attacked. But he doesn't attack or shout or swear, he just lies down and turns away from me. So I spoon into his back and slide one hand under him and the other over and hold him gently. And he doesn't react in any way, but his heart is beating ten to the dozen, he's hot and damp with sweat, and very tense, so I blow lightly on the back of his neck and quietly rock him back and forth. And I just love the feeling of being so close to him, and soon I start planting soft kisses on the back of his lovely, blond, cannonball head.

***

85: Wednesday, 24th July. 12.05 p.m. 41 Westbury Avenue.

ALAN

I wake up and there's a big snub nose and a pair of pouty lips about five inches away from my face, and his hair is all messed up and so I can see that both his eyes are closed. He's in a half-curled position and I can feel his knees against my thigh. I lift up the bedclothes. He's wearing his oversized vest and a pair of shorts and I can see his big flappy feet on the end of his skin-and-bone legs.

I know I don't deserve him; I know I don't deserve to be in this house being looked after by people who treat me like I'm part of their family. I deserve to be chained up in the room with the flies waiting for Derek to come and hurt me with one of those things with the rough edges.

His eyes have opened and he's watching me. I don't want him to see how weak I am, and that I'm no good to anyone. And he's just told me that he loves me more than anything and that I'm gorgeous and that he's dying for me to kiss him on his pouty lips again because it's the best feeling ever. Then he brings up his faggy, diseased fingers and wipes the tears off my cheeks, which have appeared from nowhere, and then he smiles at me and kisses me on the nose and then on both cheeks and then on my lips. If I was a fag I'd probably fall in love with him then and there, and maybe I am in love with him already, because he's sweet and kind and sexy – and maybe one day I'll be able to tell him how I really feel.

***

86: Wednesday, 24th July. 3 p.m. The front garden of 15 Leighton Lane.

JACK

Jack pumped vigorously but the tyre refused to stay inflated. Working under the hot sunshine was making him sweat, despite wearing just a T-shirt and shorts. He paused to take stock of his old bike, seeing the rusty chain and back cogs, the worn-out saddle, the bent spokes and now the puncture as well.

"See you later, Jack," called his mother, who by the time he looked round was already out of the front gate.

He turned back to the bicycle, unscrewing the pump hose connector from the valve. The first day of the summer holidays had been anything but the laid-back affair he had been expecting.

"Hi!"

"Ugh!" A bad afternoon just got worse. "What do you want, pest?"

"Mummy says you've got to look after me because she's gone to have her hair done."

"Can't you go to Nan's like normal?"

"Mummy says Nana Moseley is being awkward – again."

"Why don't you go to mad Mike's?"

"He's in the doghouse."

"Where's LB?"

Mikey grinned. "Sexing Sophie."

"I'll tell her you said that – and you won't be her darling any more."

The little boy made a face. "Why can't I have a bike like you and Dan?"

"I don't know." Jack stood up and stretched. "I've got my paper round in an hour."

"Mummy says you've got to take me with you."

"Oh, Jesus Christ!" exclaimed Jack, looking skyward. "Right, you, fetch me a couple of old newspapers from out of the shed while I get a bowl of water and the tools."

"Why?"

"Just do it!" snapped Jack, making the little boy jump.

Mikey scurried off towards the shed, while Jack went to the kitchen to get the puncture repair outfit, the bowl, a cloth and a can of bike oil.

When he returned, Mikey was standing in the middle of the lawn, his head bowed and two yellowing copies of the *Swanford Mail* in his hand.

"What's the matter with you?"

Mikey looked up and his lips trembled. "You shouted at me."

"I know, I'm a very bad brother. Spread the papers on the grass while I get the bike."

Jack wheeled his bicycle onto the lawn and inverted it onto the sheets of newspaper, which his little brother had laid out surprisingly neatly. As he got to work with the tyre levers, his eyes fell on a photograph on one of the inside pages of the paper. He stopped to have a closer look, then took his phone from his pocket.

"Hey Justin, it's Jack. Are you at home?"

"Yeh, man – lazin' on a blanket in my shades and shorts with a bottle of suntan cream and a chocolate milkshake."

"You bastard."

Justin chuckled. "I take it you're not?"

"I'm sweating over a puncture with a pesky brother who I've got to cart round on my paper round, which is in less than an hour."

"Sounds like you need to take a lesson from young Justin and chill."

"I've got something interesting to show you, if I can come round in half an hour?"

"No probs. Do you know where I live?"

"Gainsford Crescent."

"Yeh, *número dieciocho*, or eighteen to you non-linguists."

"See you soon, Señor Andador."

"Hasta la vista, baby," laughed Justin.

Jack put his phone away and picked up the interesting sheet of newsprint, carefully folding it and putting it in his pocket.

"Right," he said. "How do you fancy a chocolate milkshake at Justin's?"

Mikey nodded.

Jack looked at his brother. "Do you forgive me?"

Mikey nodded again and a small smile crossed his lips.

"Good, so get to work, slave, and mend this puncture."

***

Jack and Mikey walked down the patio steps of 18 Gainsford Crescent onto the lawn, where Justin was stretched out on an orange-and-white striped blanket exactly as he had described.

"We've come to visit the sun worshipper," said Jack.

Justin took off his sunglasses, yawned and sat up, getting hold of his toes with both hands.

"You're all shiny," said Mikey.

"That's because I'm in rude health," answered Justin.

The little boy giggled. "Justin's rude."

"Didn't Mum offer you a milkshake?" he asked.

"She's going to bring them out to us. She asked me to call her Mon."

"That's because you're old," said Justin.

Jack pulled off his trainers and sat down beside him, while Mikey dropped cross-legged onto the blanket in front of them.

"Take that grubby sandal off, peasant," ordered Jack. "Justin doesn't want dog muck on his blanket."

"When are you having that blue boot off, shrimp?" asked Justin.

"Next week," said Mikey, "but I don't need it any more." He kicked out his leg, as if in affirmation.

Monica Walker arrived with two milkshakes in proper milkshake glasses, complete with straws, and a top-up for her son.

"Here you are, boys," she said, "and here's a plate of homemade brandy snaps."

"Oh, we are living the high life," said Justin.

"Has Justin told you about his interview at the Football Academy, Jack? We're all so proud of him."

"Yes, he has," replied Jack levelly.

Justin crunched on a brandy snap. "You can't be that proud; it hasn't happened yet."

"Whatever the outcome, Justin is still a star," added Jack, exchanging a glance with him.

Monica Walker gazed askance at them both. "You boys always give the impression that you're involved in some plot which your parents aren't allowed to share. Your mother said just that, Jack, when I was in the post office the other day."

"They'd much prefer us to be *normal* teenagers and take drugs, make girls pregnant, raid cash machines and stab people," said Justin. "Just like they did at our age."

"Oh, I'm not stopping to listen to any more of this nonsense," said Monica. "One day you'll learn..."

They watched her until she had disappeared through the French doors. "She's all right, really," said Justin. "She's just dreaming of having a second home in Barbados and a private jet, courtesy of her son."

"What happens if the letter actually says you've passed?"

"I'll fall down dead with shock, so it won't matter."

Jack fished out the folded page of the *Swanford Mail* and handed it to Justin. "Take a look at the photograph on page three – and remember, it was taken two years ago."

"So that's why they call it the yellow press," said Justin, taking the sheet and sitting cross-legged, like Mikey. A moment later, he nodded. "Oh, that's him all right. *Promotion for local officer. Swanford Police have a new Detective*

298

Inspector, David Rains, seen here with Councillor John Henderson and newly elected Police and Crime Commissioner Kenneth Anderson... Less double chin, more hair, no needle in his leg. Where did you find this?"

"Mikey found it," said Jack, pointing at his brother. "A couple of years ago, Dad started hoarding newspapers in the shed when he went through a gardening phase."

Mikey crawled over and looked at the photograph. "They're ugly mothers," he said.

Jack sucked in a mouthful of milkshake. "He likes saying that."

Justin continued to read. *"John Henderson, one of the first United Kingdom Majority Party candidates to be elected a councillor, said that Detective Rains was a much-needed new broom who will sweep away the cobwebs in the Swanford Police and make fighting crime a priority – instead of the laissez-faire, community policing which is in vogue at the moment.*

"My granddad calls him Councillor Hermann Göring to annoy my parents, who think he's God's gift to Swanford."

"Well, that balances things out quite well, because according to our religious leaders I'm Satan's gift," said Jack, putting down his empty glass. "Right, Just, time the little pest and I were off. Places to go, people to see..."

"Adiós, amigos," said Justin, returning his sunglasses to his face and settling back down on the blanket. "Have fun, come back."

***

87: Thursday, 25th July. 9.30 a.m. 41 Westbury Avenue.

<u>ALAN</u>

I'm lying on my bed trying to read through *The Humber Pullman Owner's Handbook* for 1953 while referring to *The*

299

Practical Motorist's Encyclopaedia by F.J. Camm for detailed explanations.

"Did you throw your breakfast on the carpet today?" he asks.

"Fuck off."

"That's a nice picture," he says, looking at the 10 × 8 photograph above my bed.

"I didn't want any more of your faggy sad eyes," I reply, giving up on the handbook for now.

Stewart did me a new print of *that* photograph and mounted it in another frame from his collection in the cellar. He said that every time I broke one, the next time it would be printed one size bigger, up to 24 × 16. When I look at the enlargement now, it's worse than I expected, because not only is my arm draped over his shoulder but his faggy hand is around my waist – as if he's my boyfriend or something!

"Guess what I've got?" he says with a huge grin.

"AIDS," I say.

"Don't be mean," he answers and picks up the parcel he brought in and draws out two pairs of blue denim dungarees. "No T-shirts allowed," he insists, and he's practically wetting himself.

I said sorry to Anne and promised to do extra chores today, so before I start work on the car I've got to clean the front windows. There's a really old wooden extension ladder in the garage which I'm going to check out. Of course, he's volunteered to help me, but I expect that means just wringing out the sponge.

In the end we did the whole house from top to bottom. It took us nearly two hours and we finished by cleaning the garage windows, including the really grimy one. Now we're in the garden drying off on a pair of sun loungers.

"If we had straw hats, we'd be just like Tom Sawyer and Huckleberry Finn," he says.

"Which one of those is the fag?" I ask, which makes him smile and I smile back.

"My feet are soggy," he says, wiggling his toes.

That's because I accidentally on purpose kept splashing a lot of the water from the window cleaning bucket down onto him while he was holding the ladder. He said he wanted a go at the top of the ladder too, so I told him it was man's work and being my deputy at the bottom was about all he could hope for.

"Can we have a little Thrupp and Maberly before we start work?" he asks.

"No," I say, "and what are you staring at?"

"Your beautiful, manly, thirty-three inch, naked chest and your cute little size six feet sticking out of your ever-so-sexy dungarees."

I tip him out of the sun lounger onto the grass and he screams like a girl, then we have a wrestle and I pin him down with my knees and he looks up at me and grins and puckers his pouty lips, so I bend down and give him a kiss on his forehead and tell him to be satisfied. He gives me his faggy salute and we set to work.

I got him some beeswax polish for the woodwork. Unlike spray polishes, this takes time and patience, but it's worth it because you get a really deep, long-lasting shine. Meanwhile I've been studying the lubrication chart at the back of the owner's manual and I'm going to oil and grease everything. There are six different types of lubricant mentioned in the handbook, and some of them aren't made any more, so I had to look online for their modern equivalents. There's over sixty points that need some type of oil or grease, which means that I'll be lying under the car on my lilo for the rest of the day and probably all of tomorrow as well.

"Alan!"

I thought it was too peaceful to last. He's supposed to be inside the car, polishing.

"Alan!" he whines again.

"What?"

"Will you come to our flat for tea tomorrow?"

"No."

His head appears and it's even more ridiculous than usual because it's upside down. For some reason, probably hair gel, his fringe has stayed over his right eye. I shine my workshop light at him, which I'm using to examine the underside of the car, and the blue streaks reflect back, making me squint.

"I'll cook for you, sexy eyes," he says, "then we could go to the Roxy, and it'll be like a real date."

"What will you cook?"

"Anything you like. Egg, beans and chips or fish fingers, beans and chips."

"Is there anything that doesn't include a lot of farting?" I ask.

"We could have sausage, egg and chips," he says hopefully.

I haven't been away from the house on my own since I got here. In fact, except for swimming last Saturday, I haven't been anywhere full stop. Going out. The thought scares me, but I can't stay here forever.

"I'll think about it," I tell him.

It's 5.30 p.m. and he's getting ready to leave because he's promised to get his dad's tea. He's only done about a third of the woodwork, but I have to admit he's made a really good job of it. I inspect it thoroughly then nod. "Hmm, not bad for a beginner," I say and he looks as pleased as punch.

"You're not coming here tomorrow, then?" I ask, trying not to sound disappointed.

He's standing by the garage door. "I promised our dad I'd help in the shop in the morning then go and do the supermarket shopping in the afternoon."

"And you want me to come to the fag flat for tea?"

He smiles and his eye lights up.

"All right, but I'm not sure about the cinema."

He gives me a sly look. "Our dad goes down the pub on Friday nights, so we could make out on the settee instead... maybe get naked?" His face has gone scarlet.

"In your fucking dreams, boy!"

"I wish I could be in your dreams," he says, and he's wearing his serious face.

"What do you mean by that?"

"So you wouldn't get those nightmares," he explains.

"You in my dreams would be my worst fucking nightmare," I say.

"What happens?" he asks.

"What happens when?"

"What happens in your nightmare?"

I can feel thin ice beginning to melt beneath my feet. "Nothing happens," I say.

I'm standing by the Pullman's bonnet and he walks over and puts his arms around me. "Is it the same one every time?"

I nod slowly, but don't look at him.

"And is it in that room where Dan found you?"

The ice is breaking and I'm beginning to fall, but he is still holding on to me, so if I tell him maybe I won't go under. "I've got a bag over my head so I can't see anything, yet I know I'm in that room. I'm chained to the bed and the chain is pulling on my foot. It's a needle-like pain and I can smell the shitty, bloody smell and hear the flies, and the bulb in the ceiling is casting a yellow glow. And then I hear footsteps approaching... and I told you – nothing happens because I always wake up just as the door is opening..."

My face is buried in his shoulder and he's stroking my head and telling me he loves me, and I really want to tell him how much I love him too, but I can't.

"It's me," he says at last.

"What's you?"

"At the door. It's little Noah coming to tell you that tea's ready."

I have to smile at him. "You and your tea."

He grins at me and gives me one last kiss on the cheek before he gets on his bike for the ride home.

I open the gate for him.

"See you tomorrow 'bout quarter to six," he shouts and gives me that salute.

"Fag!" I shout back and watch him pedalling up Westbury Avenue until he's gone from my sight.

88: Friday, 26th July. 10.30 a.m. The Cedars, off Swanford high street.

ROBERT

The third day of the summer holidays had dawned with a packet of heavy showers blown in on a blustery southerly wind. By the time Robert was abroad, however, the wind had eased and the pavements were merely damp, with puddles left in the uneven surfaces. With a surprisingly light step, but holding tight to his folded umbrella, Robert walked towards the house of Pastor Gerald Fisher and his wife Alison. The pastor lived at Sherwood Lodge on the Cedars, a quiet tree-lined residential cul de sac which at its north end joined high street.

Not as grand as No. 41, he thought, ringing the bell on the outside wall. The porch had been enclosed with a white uPVC doorway into which he was beckoned by a smiling Mrs Fisher when she appeared at the interior front door.

"The pastor is waiting for you upstairs. It's the door at the end of the landing."

Robert slipped off his shoes and leaned his umbrella against the porch wall. "Thank you, ma'am," he said. It was the first time he had spoken to Alison and he wasn't sure that he recognised her accent.

His first impression of the room upstairs was of a small military command post. The window had been covered by a blackout panel, and illumination was provided by a strip of overhead spotlights. There were maps of the UK and continental Europe at various scales and a wall-mounted screen, now rolled up. Five steel-framed chairs had been neatly stacked away in one corner, along with a projector and computer equipment, as if a previous briefing had only recently finished.

"Good morning, Robert. Exciting times, eh?"

304

"Yes, sir," he replied, not certain yet what was so exciting.

"Here is a list of what you need to pack. It's just standard things like a toothbrush, underwear, socks and soap. You won't need outer garments; those will be supplied when you get there." Pastor Fisher hoisted an ex-army rucksack onto the table behind the door. "This is yours. It already contains items such as mess tins, cooking utensils, lighters, sewing kit and rope that you're not likely to have at home. This is the only bag allowed, so make the most of the space."

"It sounds like I'm going on a hiking expedition."

"It's all part of the training, son."

Robert picked up the rucksack and slung it over his shoulder. It didn't feel too bad, though it was only one-third full and who knows how heavy it would begin to feel after a day in the field. "Have you got a date yet, Pastor?"

The man smiled at him. "I thought you'd never ask. This very Monday. A car will call for you at 6.30 a.m. to take you to the airport."

Robert's head went into a spin. This Monday? But what about his trip with Jack?

"Airport?" he exclaimed.

"Indeed. We have a special training facility in Europe. Maybe one day we'll have one in this country as well, but for now our recruits will be trained abroad."

"But how long, sir, and do my folks know?"

"Your parents are fully aware of the itinerary, if not the exact timetable, Robert, and it's for you to inform them of the date. You'll be away for as long as is necessary, until you are a true Soldier of Christ, ready to lead your forces into battle against our enemies."

"I wasn't expecting it to be quite so soon."

"Tomorrow I want you and your mother and father to come to a day of contemplation and prayer at the church. It will be the start of your spiritual rebirth, which I would like them to share."

***

89: Friday, 26th July. 11 a.m. 18 Gainsford Crescent.

JUSTIN

Justin picked up the letters from the hall carpet and took them into the dining room, sorting through them as he went. A circular from Virgin, another from Lloyds Bank addressed to his father, Simon Walker, and a letter addressed to him from the Woolgrove Wanderers Football Academy, their logo emblazoned in the top left-hand corner of the envelope.

"Has it come?" asked his mother, who was ironing bed sheets.

Justin put the other two letters on the sideboard. "Yep," he said.

Simon put down his newspaper and looked up at him from the armchair. "Well, aren't you going to open it?"

Justin sighed and slit open the envelope with his left index finger. There was a single sheet of headed A4 notepaper inside.

"Read it to us then," his dad requested excitedly.

Dear Justin,

Thank you for attending the recent medical and general fitness examination at the Academy on Tuesday.

The Woolgrove Wanderers Recruitment Committee has reviewed the results carefully and has concluded that, though your physical health is excellent, the results of your aptitude test fell some way short of what is required.

While you presented yourself extremely well and impressed us very much, I regret that we are not able to offer you a place at the Academy at this time.

Thank you for the interest and enthusiasm you have shown, and we wish you all the best for the future.

Yours sincerely,

Graham R. Maitland
Head of Academy Recruitment (Designate)

"You knew, didn't you?" said his mother, placing the iron down on the rest.

Justin sniffed and wiped his nose with the back of his hand. "Pretty much," he said.

"No," said his father, rising from his chair. "This is not right. I've a good mind to phone them up now."

"I don't want to go, Dad."

"You don't want to go?" Simon narrowed his eyes at his son. "Your mother said you were out of sorts when you came out of that place. Something happened. Did someone make a pass at you, or worse—?"

"No, Dad."

"What, then?"

"They asked me questions I didn't want to answer."

"That's what you and Jack Moseley were being so secretive about the other day," said Monica.

"What questions?" persisted Simon.

"Stupid religious questions, and whether I had any gay friends or not."

"But you don't know anyone like that."

"I do."

"So you answered yes to the question, and then they rejected you? That's discrimination!"

His mother frowned. "Who do you know like that? You shouldn't mix with people of that persuasion; you'll get a bad reputation."

"If you'd have answered no, none of this would have happened," snapped Simon.

"It would have been a lie," said Justin calmly.

"So?" said his father.

Justin chuckled humourlessly. "When I talked this over with Dan and Jack, I told them exactly what you'd say, and I was right."

"You shouldn't talk about your parents behind their backs, Justin," said his mother.

"You always taught me to tell the truth and shame the Devil – now you're saying I should have lied?"

"Your future is more important than a white lie," retorted Simon.

"They wanted to know the names and addresses of my gay friends," said Justin, flatly.

"Why would they want to know that?" enquired his mother.

"You tell me," replied Justin. "But the whole thing creeped me out."

His father looked hard at him. "You threw away your career, and the possibility of fame and fortune, for the sake of a couple of poofs?"

"No, Dad, I did it for the sake of a couple of good friends – and my own self-respect."

"And who are these good friends that you value more highly than your profession, your vocation, the sport that you excel at, and your gateway to a fulfilled and happy life?"

"There are at least a million other things I can do when the times comes."

His mother picked up the iron again. "You aren't really very academic, Justin, you do better with your feet and hands than you do with your head."

"You mean I'm thick?"

"No, that's not what I mean and you know it."

"I give in," said his father. "It's your future. Waste your talent, go to work as a shelf-stacker in Aldi."

"OK, I'll put in my application tomorrow."

***

90: Friday, 26th July. 11.10 a.m. Swanford high street.

ROBERT

"Jack!"

"Hey, Robert! Good news – Dan won't need his bike on Monday"

"I've got to speak to you now."

"I'm in the house."

"Can I come over? I don't care who sees me."

"No problem. There's only Dan and me here. Mikey's having his cast taken off today!"

"I'll be there in ten minutes."

"Where are you?"

"On the high street."

Carrying his pack and umbrella, Robert ran the one-third of a mile to 15 Leighton Lane, stopping only twice to recover his breath. The door was already open and he fell into Jack's waiting arms in the kitchen.

"They're sending me away – abroad – this Monday!" he sobbed.

Jack said nothing, but held him close and kissed him gently while he recovered.

Robert held on to him as if for dear life. "I'll not see you again before I go..."

"Oops, sorry," said Dan, walking in from the hall and promptly turning on his heel.

"LB!" called Jack. "Don't go. Could you make us some tea?"

"That's what I came down to do," the boy replied.

Five minutes later they sat round the kitchen table, drinking mugs of tea while Robert told his story.

"I can't stop long," said the American when he'd finished. "Dad's home, and they'll get suspicious and start asking questions." He wiped his eyes with his handkerchief and blew his nose, making Dan smile.

"And you've no idea where they're sending you?" questioned Jack.

Robert shook his head. "I don't even know which airport I'm flying from."

"Maybe there's something in the pack that'll give you a clue," suggested Dan.

"I've looked – it's just camping equipment."

"Listen, Robert," said Jack, taking hold of his hand. "This is important. Make sure your phone's fully charged, and keep it switched off and secret till you get wherever it is you're going, then let us know."

The American nodded. "I was so looking forward to Monday."

Jack squeezed his hand. "It's just a delay. And we'll both have something to look forward to when you come back."

"Better go..." said Robert, rising to his feet.

Dan stood up and offered his hand. "See you soon, big man, and keep in touch like my brother says."

They shook hands, then Jack rose and wrapped his arms around his boyfriend. "I'll miss you so much. Just promise me you'll keep yourself safe and you won't do anything mad."

"I promise that I will do my best. I love you, Jack."

They shared a kiss, then walked together down the path to the gate where they embraced for one last time. Then, with his backpack slung over his shoulder and umbrella in hand, the American made off down Leighton Lane.

*****

91: Friday, 26th July. 5.30 p.m. 41 Westbury Avenue.

ALAN

They all know how nervous I am, but none of them say it out loud. Anne offered to drive me, but I said no. That would make me out to be a real wuss. Stewart has lent me his hoodie just in case one of my brothers is passing by. It's only half a mile to the fag flat anyway, which is what? One thousand paces. I could count them off to keep myself from stressing.

If I was at school, they'd laugh at me and call me names for being so afraid. I was never afraid before, and I was out all the time on my own. But that was because I didn't have any friends. In any case, people have always called me names because they don't like me. I've got a feeling that I'm really dense about some things, especially how to deal with other people. Is it normal not to know how another person is thinking? I wish I was a telepath like Charles Xavier.

I'm sure the fag believes I'm his boyfriend, and maybe he's right. But I'm not getting naked with him, though; that's unthinkable. I'll never get naked with anyone like that. In any case, I don't know what he sees in me. I'm useless and nasty. Damaged goods, that's what I am. He says he's going to cook for me: sausage, egg and chips. Sounds good. I could probably do that myself. Maybe I should invite him round and cook for him one day.

I've closed the garden gate behind me and I'm ready to set off. They're all standing at the front door like I'm going away for years, and they wave at me so I wave back. There's quite a bit of traffic because it's rush hour, but the road has dried out completely after the rain. I wish I was driving the Humber, then I'd get to the flat with no trouble. I've got my mobile and Stewart's told me to phone him if anything goes wrong. I know what he's getting at. If I'm halfway there and can't move because I'm too afraid, I'll ring him. But I want to do this on my own. I've got to do it on my own!

I'm almost at the top of Westbury Avenue now. That's two-thirds done and no mishaps so far. I'm just by the church that does all the anti-fag stuff. They've got scaffolding up and some of it is covered in green sheeting. I expect they're going to clean the stonework, because it is pretty black. There's balloons outside and streamers too, so it probably means they've sacrificed another fag on the altar.

I know his dad owns the barber's shop on Victoria Street, and they haven't got much money. All his clothes are old, except for his faggy vest, which he wears all the time. It never smells of armpits though, so he must wash it pretty well every day. In that case it's likely to fall apart soon. I'd like to buy him another. Actually, I like the way he smells. A lot of boys smell like strong deodorant, but he doesn't. Perhaps he doesn't wear deodorant because of his faggy skin disease or something. He smells more like soap, probably one that's specially made for girls. Maybe I should take him to the cinema – I mean, pay for him. At least I wouldn't have to get naked then, but if I did pay for him, he'd probably think he was my boyfriend. Would it matter if I had a boyfriend even though I'm not a fag?

I've crossed the high street and the flats are in view. They're called Savoy Flats, but everyone calls them the Allfours because they're laid out in a square pattern. 'Savoy' is too posh for these concrete dumpsters. A white transit van went by a second ago and it's given me the shakes. The police towed away the one I drove from No. 41, but I don't know what happened to it after that. If I see a bronze Volvo S80 I'll probably die of fright.

I'll have to get used to calling him Noah if his dad's there. I don't expect I'd get many brownie points for addressing him as 'fag'. Why do I get funny feelings when I think about him? And I don't mean *down there*. They're kind of in my tummy and chest, like a tightness, and I have to catch my breath. That's when I want to be with him, which is where I want to be now.

I think this is the block. They live on the top floor, but I'm not going to try the lift because a) it'll stink of piss, and b) I'll probably be sharing it with the Allfours Junkie Axe Murderer. At least the stairs don't smell too bad. Here we are – Flats 34a–34d. Why am I out of breath and why does this fire door seem so heavy? Because I'm still weak, that's why. I hope we go swimming again tomorrow. I really enjoyed last Saturday.

This is the fag flat, 34b, but that's funny – the door's open. I've knocked and called out, but there's no reply. Perhaps he's popped out for the chips, but I'd never leave my door unlocked, never mind open, especially round here. I'm in their little hallway, but there's no sign of life, and I am getting a bit scared. I push open the door and go through into the living room. Huh! The furniture looks like it came out of the ark. Noah's ark! I just made that up.

"Hello!" My voice is all quavery.

I'm in the kitchen now and there's two plastic bags of groceries. One is half unpacked, but nothing's been put away. There's some Lidl sausages lying on the worktop and some frozen peas. They've starting to melt. His phone's here too. Perhaps he's in the toilet.

I've searched everywhere. I've even been in his bedroom. It's really small. I knew it was his bedroom because it's full of faggy things and our picture's on the wall by his bed. I'm worried about him. If he's playing a joke on me, I'll kill him!

There's an old woman standing in the hall doorway. She made me jump. I don't know if I did the same to her – probably not.

"Are you Noah's young man?" she asks and I go red.

I've got a feeling this must be Auntie Iris that the fag keeps talking about. She's half-blind through diabetes.

"Yes," I reply. "Are you Auntie Iris?"

"That's right, love. They've taken him, you know," she says.

"Who've taken him?"

"Social services."

"Why?"

"His dad's been arrested."

"Why?"

"I don't know, love; they wouldn't tell me."

I feel faint. I don't know what to do. "The door was open," I say. "Do you know where they took him?"

She shakes her head. "You look as if you need to sit down."

She's right. I sit down on the orange settee and she fetches me a glass of water. "I'd better put those groceries away," she says. "And just when I thought things were looking up for the poor little mite."

I phone Stewart and explain what's happened. I know he can hear the panic in my voice. He tells me to hang on and

313

he'll get his mum to come and collect me. Most of the time Anne keeps her car on the grass verge outside the house. It's not legal, but everyone does it.

Fifteen minutes later they both arrive and the first thing I do is burst into tears. What a fag! Anne gives me a hug and tells me it'll be all right, but I don't think so. Stewart looks more anxious than his mum, and I've got to find out why. Iris comes into the living room and is happy to repeat the story she told me. She even offers to make us all a cup of tea, but Anne tells her we have to get back. Then she locks the flat up, we say goodbye, and I return to No. 41, worrying myself sick about my ridiculous, beautiful, sweet fag who's been taken away from me!

***

92: Saturday, 27th July. 9 a.m. 15 Leighton Lane.

<u>JACK</u>

On 95.3 FM this is Radio Swanford, your local station, guiding you through the day with news, traffic reports and music. It's 9 a.m. and here is the Saturday News Briefing with Melanie Ashton-Humphrys.

Good morning, Swanford, but it's not such a good morning for our moral well-being, folks. In a series of overnight raids at addresses in the town, police have arrested a number of people who are suspected of being part of a paedophile ring. Among them is thought to be Sarah Heath, Member of Parliament for the Woolgrove constituency.

I have just interviewed Police and Crime Commissioner Kenneth Anderson, who told me that a number of boys had been taken into the care of social services following the raids. You can hear the full interview in about ten minutes' time...

"I don't want to hear any more of that on a Saturday morning," said Pam, putting down her toast and flicking off the radio. "I can't believe people can be so wicked."

Jack exchanged glances with Dan, then looked at his mother. "There's no need to believe it, because it's just the usual load of garbage."

"Oh yes," said Roger, "and when did you attain the power of omniscience?"

"Trust me, he's right," stated Dan. "All lies... Is there any more toast?"

"So *both* my older sons are omniscient now; how wonderful."

"If they really were omniscient, surely they would know how to make toast," commented Pam.

"Even we X-Men are flawed by that ancient artefact you call a toaster," said Jack.

His mother was about to make a comment about their financial status when there came a hobbling noise from the hall and Mikey appeared in the kitchen doorway. "I can't walk," he said with a pained look.

"How did you get from your bedroom to here then, doofus?" asked Dan.

"I limped."

Jack chuckled. "Good answer, pesto."

"Will one of you take Mikey swimming today?" requested Pam. "The doctor said swimming will be good for him."

"Drowning would be better," said Dan.

"Maybe the chlorine will get rid of those ridiculous blue spikes as well." Pam looked daggers at Roger, who smiled back benignly.

"I'm not going," said Mikey.

Jack looked at Dan. "We could go this afternoon, LB – it might do Alan good too."

"That means taking him with us this morning. Which means bus fare."

"Yeh, but it's Alex's birthday today so it could be the best option. We'll get a card and a bag of sweets from Mr Ray's and we can all sign it. That'll kill all the pests with one stone, which will leave us free for the serious stuff."

Roger put his mug down and beheld his two sons. "Why is it that you two are always scheming and planning as though you're involved in some secret operation?"

"Pretty close, Dad," acknowledged Dan. "Good guesswork."

"Yes, he'll be working at Bletchley Park before we know it," added Jack.

"I would have enjoyed working there," said Roger, "with people of similar intelligence."

"Yeh, whatever," responded Jack. "But your sons have got Mission Impossible coming up so we'll see you later. Pestilence, go and get your Speedos and your turtles towel and you can wear a bathing cap like Robert if you're bothered about your spikes."

"OK," said Mikey, who hurried from the kitchen, forgetting to limp.

"Time was when our children enjoyed the company of their parents," said Pam.

"I don't suppose you've noticed we no longer wear nappies," said Jack.

"It's called growing up, Mum," said Dan. "Get over it."

***

93: Saturday, 27th July. 11 a.m. 41 Westbury Avenue.

ELSPETH

Elspeth sat in her armchair supporting her chin in one hand. Next to her on the occasional table sat a cordless telephone which was still warm from use. Stewart, Dan and Jack were settled on the sofa, while Alan was perched on a padded stool by the fireplace, looking lost and forlorn. Anne entered and took the remaining armchair. "Sorry to keep you waiting. I think those two will be all right in the garden together."

"Another day, another outrage," began Elspeth. "Conveniently for the people involved, the social services department is not open at the weekends; however, from what I have learned from my erstwhile colleagues, twelve boys have been taken into care, all aged below the age of sixteen, all either homosexual themselves with single parents, or the children of homosexuals." Elspeth paused to gather her thoughts. "This time, they have targeted the most vulnerable, such as Noah and his father. Easy pickings for the police and no sympathy from the public. But to what purpose, other than to ruin innocent people's lives, no one seems to know."

"Does there have to be any other purpose?" questioned Anne.

"In my experience, the people we are dealing with will always seek some empirical justification for their actions, however irrational the premise."

"You said *this time*," said Jack.

Elspeth regarded him. "I did, and after the summer recess when Parliament resumes and new legislation is brought forward and old legislation repealed, we could see more raids like this."

"And it could be my family next time, because of me."

"Not because of *you*, Jack; because of *them* and their perverse mindset. And once new legislation is passed into law they won't need the excuse of paedophile rings or whatever."

"But what about Noah?" murmured Alan. "I want to know where he is."

"I am sorry, that is a question I have been unable to find an answer to. Normally people taken into the care system are either put into residential establishments or fostered out. But of course, the majority of these boys are homosexual and that is the sole reason why they've been extracted from their families."

"You don't think they're going to be hurt, do you?" asked Dan.

Alan moaned and covered his face.

Jack gave his brother a nudge.

"Alan, come and sit with us," said Stewart, shifting over.

The other boys did the same. "You're not on your own, you know," said Jack. "We're here and we want to find Noah as much as you do."

Disconsolate, Alan moved to the sofa and sat down between his brother and Dan, who whispered *sorry* to him.

"The question may not have been posed in the most tactful manner," said Elspeth, "nevertheless it is relevant to what we face. These are dangerous people, who have gained positions of power within the state apparatus. Maybe they are testing the water with this one to see how much the general public will accept."

"Justin ought to be here," said Jack. "His name is mud with some very dangerous people."

"He's gone over to the summer fete at Fairacre with Kate and their families," Dan replied. "But I'll fill him in tonight."

"Ah!" said Elspeth. "A village fete; that reminds me of times long ago and far away."

***

94: Saturday, 27th July. 1 p.m. 41 Westbury Avenue.

ALAN

Jack Moseley came up to my room and told me to hurry up and get my swimming kit together, as if he's the boss or something. Then he asked me point-blank whether Noah was my boyfriend, because I certainly acted as if he was. I should have told him to mind his own faggy business, but instead I started to cry like a fag.

Then he spent the next half hour telling me everything I already knew about the difficulty for a boy of accepting that he's gay, especially when he comes from an intolerant household. Blah, blah, blah, it went on and on, as if I was in fag school or something. I decided to get a plastic bag from the utility room to put my stuff in, and he followed me around still talking and I was answering with *yeh, well, whatever* and *s'pose*. In the end he smiled at me and called me a chump, like he was a hundred years old.

Dan Moseley is going to take over Robert's job while the Yank is on his religious anti-fag army kick. Fancy a fag agreeing to do something like that. I suppose it's because he's a Yank. Elspeth said that I should move into top gear with the car; I don't know if she was being funny or not. Dan Moseley said that Justin Walker liked to work on mechanical things and would I like some help? I said he couldn't be any worse than the fag and then I nearly cried again. That's when he gave me a hug and I agreed to everything.

My brother Stewart is a crap swimmer. If anything, he's worse than Noah, because he doesn't even try. He stays in the leisure pool with Anne, Alex and Mickey and plays on the flumes. I had a few races with Dan Moseley, but he beat me hands down. That's only because I'm not up to full strength yet and he's two months older than me. So in two months' time I'm going to be as built as he is now, like with a six pack, though I probably won't be as tall.

Mickey Moseley is a weird kid. I asked him why he'd got blue spikes in his hair and he said it was because Noah was his style guru. Where does a seven-year-old kid pick up language like that? He said his best friend Mike was trying to persuade his mum to let him have blue spikes too. If you ask me, Swanford is turning into Fagsville.

After swimming, we went back home and Alex had his fourth birthday party. It took the little dork three goes to blow out the four candles on his cake. Why can't he get some friends of his own age? Then we teenagers wouldn't have to sing 'Happy Birthday', which is the most embarrassing song ever. I suppose the talk I had earlier with Jack Moseley was all right, but I'm not admitting I'm a fag, not even to a fag.

95: Monday, 28th July. 5.45 a.m. Pear Tree Cottage, The Ropewalk.

<u>ROBERT</u>

Hi Rosa, I'm off and I can't tell you how much I DON'T want to go. Cells not allowed at our Spiritual Awakening camp, but I'll keep this one secret. Will try to stay in contact. Give me a smile with tales of the 'Counselor's' exploits. R.

Dear wonderful Jack, my final text before I get to wherever I'm going. Pastor Fisher calls this my Spiritual Awakening. But I shall never be spiritually awake until we're together again. Missing you already. Try not to feel as sad as I do now. All my love, Robert.

Robert switched off his phone and plugged in the USB charger. It was just a top-up, as it had been on charge all night. The haversack stood filled to capacity on his bed. In one side pocket there was a bottle of Coke and a bar of chocolate, and in the other a King James Bible presented to him by Pastor Fisher on Saturday, during their Day of Prayer.

"Good morning, son," said Frank. "I couldn't resist getting up earlier than usual, both to see you off and knowing that your mother is cooking us a special breakfast."

"Good morning, Dad," replied Robert, feeling sick to his stomach and not hungry at all. Before sitting down, he put the company mobile and his house keys on the mantelpiece. "A little less weight to carry," he said.

Frank nodded approvingly. "I'm glad you remembered."

His mother entered the lounge carrying a dish in her oven-mitted hands. "Baked cheese grits, hon," she said. "Just right to send you on your way."

Maybelle followed this with a bowl of sausage gravy and a plateful of biscuits, all to be washed down with Community Coffee served from a silver pot. Robert did his best, knowing that it might well be the best meal he would get for some time. At 6.25 a.m., after they had said a final prayer together, he went upstairs to clean his teeth and collect his belongings.

By the time he got downstairs again, a white Ford Mondeo had pulled up outside the cottage and his father was talking to the driver.

"Put your luggage in the trunk, Robert, it's open," called Frank.

Once it was stowed, he came round to the front passenger door, where his mother was waiting. "Goodbye, darlin'. I know you'll come back a fine upstandin' boy, ready to do Christ's work." Robert nodded and gave his mom a hug and kiss.

His father held out his hand. "Our thoughts and prayers will be with you, son."

"Thank you, Dad," said Robert, beginning to feel emotional despite himself.

They shook hands and Frank looked him in the eye. "I want you to put all that has happened in this country behind you, son. I know at times it hasn't been easy for you. I understand what temptation is, but to do God's work is never easy: it means overcoming the sinfulness within and letting the Holy Spirit into your heart. Your mother and I are confident that you will come back as a true Soldier of Christ, ready with sword and shield to put to flight the minions of Satan."

Robert tried to open the passenger door, but found it locked. Without looking, the driver, who was in a chauffeur's uniform, indicated with his thumb that he was to get in the back. The engine was already ticking over and the moment Robert slammed shut the door, the car pulled away leaving him time for only a perfunctory wave out of the side window. He turned to look through the back. Frank and Maybelle were still standing on the pavement, watching the receding car. He waved again, even knowing that they wouldn't see him through the tinted glass.

The Mondeo turned left onto Retford Road and gathered speed. The chauffeur was wearing ear pieces in both ears and it seemed to Robert that the man was in no mood to talk. The drive continued on A roads for almost an hour before they joined the northbound carriageway of the M1 near Milton Keynes. Another twenty minutes passed before the chauffeur pulled into Watford Gap Services and parked close to the main entrance.

"Do you need to piss?" he asked, looking in his rear-view mirror.

"How much further?"

"About an hour."

"Where are we headed?"

"I asked you if you need to piss."

"Might as well."

"Well, hurry up then."

"I need my wallet out of my pack."

"You don't need a wallet to take a piss. Now move."

Robert decided not to say anything further to the driver and when he returned he got quietly into the back seat and closed the door.

At 8.50 a.m., after an uneventful journey, they left the motorway at Junction 23A, and shortly after arrived at East Midlands Airport. Robert expected the chauffeur to take him to the main entrance, but instead they went down a side road, passing a Royal Mail depot, and came to the first of two barriers. The driver swiped a card through a reader and the red-and-white boom rose. The Mondeo moved forward and the boom lowered behind them. They were now inside the airport. The second barrier was manned. The attendant was given a document from the glove box and, after scrutinising it, proceeded to inspect the interior of the car, including the boot and the engine compartment. When satisfied, the man went into his hut and the barrier swung open.

A one-lane concrete road led them directly to a parking area for small and medium-sized aircraft. There was one plane there, a Gulfstream III, a twin-engine jet, liveried in the black and red of the Burnoco Oil Corporation. The cabin door was open and the chauffeur drove to within a few yards of the passenger boarding stairs.

"Well, what are you waiting for?"

"My luggage."

"It's open."

Robert collected his pack and made for the stairs.

"You haven't closed up!" the chauffeur shouted through his open window.

The American turned. "Close it yourself, you ignorant oaf."

As he started up the steps, he heard the driver get out of the car and say in a low but perfectly audible voice, "Fucking queer ginger cunt."

The remark made him stop and shudder, but he steeled himself not to look back. Instead he gazed around at the sunlit airport as if taking in the sights. To his right a Boeing 787 Dreamliner was taxiing along the main runway, ready for take-off. Overhead vapour trails criss-crossed the sky. A middle-aged man appeared above him in the doorway, dressed in a green jumpsuit and carrying a walkie-talkie slung on his belt.

"Robert Crittenden?" he said.

The American heard the Mondeo's boot lid being slammed. "Yes."

"Your passport."

"It's in my bag."

"Well, get it out then."

The steps made this procedure awkward, but eventually he handed over the blue document and glanced behind him. The Mondeo was moving away towards the exit on the concrete road. It seemed to be only the size of a toy.

"This will be returned to you when you leave," the man said cryptically.

"Am I the only one on the flight?"

"You're the first to arrive."

"Are you the pilot?"

"The pilot is doing the more important job of checking that the plane works. I am the co-pilot, and doing the less important job of checking the passengers." The man raised his hand to forestall any further questions. "You are in seat 9A, the last one on the starboard side, but first stow your luggage in the compartment at the back."

There were nine bucket seats up each side of the plane, with an aisle between, plain but not uncomfortable. He took out the Coke and chocolate, slung his pack at the rear of the aircraft and went to sit down. The advantage of his position was that he was directly in front of the partitioned-off area of toilet and wash basin. The disadvantage was that the nearest window was forward of his position and therefore his view was restricted.

Just sitting soon got boring. Robert looked at his watch. 9.25 a.m. The man in the jumpsuit had disappeared into the cockpit, and so he thought about getting out his mobile, but resisted the temptation and instead sucked a square of chocolate.

At 9.40 a.m. he happened to look across the cabin and saw, through the portholes opposite, a minibus approaching. The man came out of the cockpit and spoke into his walkie-talkie, receiving a garbled reply. He took up a clipboard and pen which were hanging on a hook by the door and stood waiting by the entrance.

Minutes later a group of boys were queuing up to enter the plane. Each one had their name ticked off on the clipboard, after which they were allocated a seat number. As they filed down the aisle to claim their places, Robert watched. A few glanced disinterestedly in his direction. Two or three seemed familiar. He guessed their ages varied from ten to fifteen. All but one looked pale, confused and frightened, the exception being an African boy whose demeanour could only be described as thoughtful. Like the rest, he had his hair clippered short, and wore a plain white T-shirt and jogging bottoms. No one showed the excitement or anticipation one might have expected from new recruits into the Army of Christ. None had any luggage. There were eleven in all.

Then Robert noticed that one boy near the front hadn't taken his seat and was staring directly at him. When their eyes met, he realised it was Noah Marshall, barely recognisable without his trademark fringe.

"We're in the shit," the boy mouthed.

A chill went up Robert's spine. He gave the merest nod to acknowledge that he had understood.

A man and woman followed the boys onto the aircraft. The man was powerfully built and beetle-browed, dressed in a black tracksuit which heightened his intimidating presence. He sat down in the front seat on the port side and folded his muscular arms. The woman walked halfway down the aisle, where she stopped and looked round. She was not tall, but made up for this by an authoritative bearing. She had a helmet of blonde hair and was dressed in a crisp white uniform belted tightly at the waist. Robert noticed that she wore a blue-bordered name tag, with *Sister Margaret Hopkins* on it, with *Lambda Healthcare* printed in smaller letters beneath. She carried a case which was attached by a chain to her wrist.

"Now listen up," she said. "We shall be taking off in ten to fifteen minutes, and will be travelling for approximately three and a half hours..."

"Where are we going, Miss?" a voice quavered.

"There are to be no questions. There will be no talking. You will remain in your seats at all times unless given permission to move. If you want to ask permission, you will put up your hand and wait to be acknowledged."

The woman's eyes fell upon the American. "You are Robert Crittenden?"

"Yes, ma'am."

She strode forward, opened her briefcase and took out an envelope. Without speaking further she handed it to him, then turned to address the other boys. "Shortly after take-off, you will be given your Bibles – the only reading matter that you will be allowed. I suggest you read, mark, learn and inwardly digest the annotated passages. Now fasten your safety belts." She sat down in the seat directly across the aisle from Robert and began to primp her hair.

The American recognised the handwriting on the envelope immediately, and with trembling fingers opened the flap.

Dear Robert,

Your mother and I have known for some time now that you have been lying about your feelings, not only towards your family but also to your church and community. You have chosen to go against nature and God in search of your own gratification; to hate the good and to love the malign.

We have always tried to instill in you the virtues of clean living and self-respect that, combined with the boundless love of our Lord Jesus Christ, would protect you from Satan's influence.

Instead, you chose to turn away from the path of righteousness onto the stony, barren ground of homosexuality. Sinfulness writ large, deceit and treachery. All hallmarks of Satan's hold on you.

You let the demon into your heart and turned against Our Lord, Robert. Your immortal soul is in danger, and because of our love for you we have had no alternative but to employ a little subterfuge of our own.

You must be helped to exorcise the demon of homosexuality that has become your master. And once the demon has been eliminated, you must be purged of that sinfulness in your nature that allowed it to enter.

Fortunately, through the auspices of Burnoco Oil and the Russian Federation, a treatment center for your condition now exists. That is where you are being taken. There you will meet two distinguished scientists, Professors Igor Zaronovich and Dmitri Salkorov, who will guide you through the treatment program at their new institute. Life there will not be easy. It is not meant to be, but through physical exertion, therapy and religious instruction I know you will be made whole again.

These are hard lessons for you, Robert, and your mother and I cannot be absolved completely from blame. We are praying for you and doing penance, as directed by the church.

Rest assured that our love for you is undiminished. We hope that by the new year the treatment will have been successful and that you will return to us, restored and invigorated, with the shining light of our Lord Jesus Christ in your eyes, ready to take up arms against the very demon that has enslaved you.

Your loving father,

Francis R. Crittenden

The End
of Book 2

SATAN'S LEGIONS

INDEX OF CHARACTERS BOOKS 1 and 2
(in alphabetical order)
(Ages and status are as they were at the beginning of Book 1)

** Major character, narrator
* Major character

C

Barbara Carter............................ *Charlie Masefield's girlfriend, in class 4S*

Elspeth Chambers**................... *lives at 41 Westbury Avenue; born in Calcutta in 1932*

Miss A. K. Chawner .... *school secretary*

Dr Clarke.................................... *doctor, Swanford Medical Centre*

Ralph E. F. Colt*........................ *Jack's form tutor; English teacher*

Muriel Colt................................. *Mr Colt's wife*

Neil Cunliffe.............................. *a classmate of Alan Henderson*

Alice Crabtree............................ *pupil in Jack Moseley's class, 4S, and Sam's sister*

Ilona Crabtree............................ *co-proprietor of the Jewel Café; Alice and Sam's mum*

Richard Crabtree......................... *co-proprietor of the Jewel Café; Alice and Sam's dad*

Sam Crabtree............................... *Year 13 pupil, Alice's brother, waiter in the Jewel Café*

Aaron Crittenden......................... *Robert's brother (died age 7)*

Francis Robert Crittenden*.......... *Robert's dad*

Maybelle Crittenden (née Page)* *Robert's mum*

Robert Crittenden**.................... *aged 15, born on 7 November*

Todd Crozier............................... *science teacher from USA*

Bill Cullis.................................... *head coach, Woolgrove Wanderers Football Academy*

D

Sophie Dale.................................. *Dan Moseley's girlfriend*

Fred Dunn..................................... *pastor in the church in Tyree, USA*

E

James Edison............................ *Bible study pupil, small-time drug dealer*

Edith... *church congregation and friend of Patty*

Adam Ellis................................. *Year 11, drinker in the Orange Lounge bar*

F

Joan Field.................................. *pupil in Jack Moseley's class, 4S*

Gerald Fisher............................ *pastor and evangelical Christian*

Alison Fisher............................ *Gerald Fisher's wife*

Chris Foster.............................. *aged 16, Robert's church friend, Tyree, USA*

Katie Foster.............................. *aged 14, Robert's church friend, Tyree, USA*

G

Mr Graham................................ *history teacher*

Mr Graves................................. *English teacher*

Iris Green.................................. *Noah Marshall's neighbour*

Mr Green................................... *Swanford Resident (no relation to Iris)*

Mrs Gutteridge......................... *maths teacher*

H

Freddie Hall.............................. *Dan and Justin's friend and classmate*

Megan Hall................................ *Freddie's sister*

Arthur Hammerton.................... *Inspector, Chief of Swanford Police*

Mr Harris............................... *PE and rugby teacher*

Simon 'Si' Hazeldene............. *gym instructor at the Swanford Fitness Centre*

The headmaster...................... *Swanford Community School headmaster*

Sarah Heath............................ *Member of Parliament for the Woolgrove Constituency*

Alan Henderson**................... *aged 13, born on 4 December*

Ben Henderson........................ *aged 15, born on 20 March*

Derek Henderson*................... *aged 18, the heir apparent to the Henderson legacy*

John Henderson*..................... *councillor, head of the Henderson household*

John Henderson Jnr................. *aged 16*

Lisa Henderson*...................... *Alan's natural mother and wife of John Snr*

Stewart Philip Henderson*...... *aged 14, born on 15 June*

Margaret Hopkins*.................. *nursing sister at Lambda Healthcare*

Dr Howell................................ *doctor, Swanford Medical Centre*

Bronwyn Hughes......................*Year 13 pupil*

Mike Huntley........................... *Mikey Moseley's best friend, born on 16 October*

Mrs Huntley............................ *Mike Huntley's mum*

Lawrence Hyde........................ *UKMP potential candidate for the Woolgrove Constituency*

J

Abbie Johns .... *a pupil at Mikey's primary school, sister of Patrick*

Patrick Johns .... *head boy, Swanford Community School*

Callum Jones........................... *Bible study and Morcross school pupil*

Mr Joseph................................ *geography teacher*

L

Ms Helen Edith Lane*.............. *languages teacher, equality counsellor*

Bob LaPlante........................... *English teacher from the USA*

Anne Marie Leonard .... *Year 9 pupil*

Adam Lewis.............................. *Year 7 pupil, brother of Harry and Sarah*

Eve Lewis................................. *mother of Adam, Harry and Sarah Lewis*

Harry Lewis.............................. *Year 8 pupil, brother of Sarah and Adam*

Nigel Lewis.............................. *father of Adam, Harry and Sarah Lewis*

Sarah Lewis.............................. *Year 12 pupil, sister of Harry and Adam*

John Little................................. *reporter on the* Swanford Mail

Jacob Lively.............................. *Year 9 pupil, Joanna's brother*

Joanna Lively............................ *Year 10 pupil, Jacob's sister*

M

Sandy McKellan........................ *pastor at the Baptist Church*

Graham R. Maitland.................. *Head of Recruitment, Woolgrove Wanderers FC Academy*

Carol Manning........................... *pupil in Jack Moseley's class, 4S*

Alf Marshall*............................. *Noah's dad and proprietor of Marshall's barber shop*

Noah Marshall** .... *aged 13, born on 16 April*

Charles Edward Masefield*...... *Jack's friend, Barbara's boyfriend, in class 4S*

Richard 'Dickie' Masefield........ *Charlie Masefield's dad, Police Constable*

Vera Masefield.......................... *Charlie Masefield's mum*

Colin Messom............................ *pupil in Jack Moseley's class, 4S*

Bruce Miller.............................. *Rosa and Tammy's father, Tyree, USA*

Pearl Miller............................... *Rosa and Tammy's mother, Tyree, USA*

Rosa Miller*.............................. *aged 14, Robert's friend, Tammy's younger sister, Tyree, USA*

Tammy Miller*........................... *aged 16, Rosa's elder sister, seductress, Tyree, USA*

Daniel Moseley**....................... *aged 13, born on 26 September*

Jack Moseley**.......................... *aged 14, born on 14 February*

Michael 'Mikey' Moseley*......... *aged 6, born on 2 February*

Nana Moseley............................. *Roger's mother*

Pamela Moseley**...................... *Jack, Dan and Mikey's mum*

Paul Moseley............................. *Uncle Paul, Roger's brother*

Roger Moseley**....................... *Jack, Dan and Mikey's dad*

Walter Moseley.......................... *Granddad, Roger's father (deceased)*

N

Sally Nunn.................................. *a friend of Dan Moseley*

Nicholas Ntagali......................... *Burnoco Oil representative to the government of Uganda*

Sally Nunn.................................. *a friend of Dan Moseley*

P

Una Page*................................... *Robert's aunt on his mother's side, Oklahoma City, USA*

Mrs Parkin................................. *Spanish teacher*

Patty.. *church congregation member and friend of Edith*

Mr Peebles... *head groundsman, Swanford Community school*

Dora Penny... *Swanford town councillor*

Peter.. *Archbishop Benn's assistant*

Mr Pullin.. *Swanford resident*

R

David Rains**.................................... *Detective Inspector, Swanford Police*

Satyajit Ray*...................................... *proprietor of the newsagent's shop, Swanford*

Sandip Ray.. *Mr Ray's no. 1 son, Year 11 pupil*

Sourajit Ray.. *Mr Ray's no. 2 son, Year 7 pupil*

Jonathan Read..................................... *Swanford town councillor*

Kimberley Robinson........................... *Ben Henderson's girlfriend, Louis's elder sister*

Louis Robinson................................... *Swanford United Under-14s player, Kimberley's brother*

Ken Roper.. *Alf Marshall's drinking buddy of a Friday night*

S

Barney Sanchez.................................. *Tom and Una's child, aged 4, born on 20 August, USA*

Catalina Sanchez................................ *Tom Sanchez's grandmother, Oklahoma City, USA*

Susie Sanchez..................................... *Tom and Una's child, aged*

3, born on 28 December, USA

Tom Sanchez...................................... *Una Page's partner, Oklahoma City, USA*

Kieran Scott...................................... *Bible study and Morcross school pupil*

Max Seddon*.................................... *Jack's friend, Mandy's boyfriend, in class 4S*

Paul Sharpe...................................... *Year 9 pupil*

Gregg Simmons............................... *aged 18, Robert's church friend, Tyree, USA*

Mandy Simpkins*............................ *Jack's friend, Max's girlfriend, school, class 4S*

Bryan Smith..................................... *a solicitor in Basingstoke*

Jason Spriggs................................... *Year 11 pupil, brother of Lucas*

Lucas Spriggs.................................. *Year 10 pupil, brother of Jason*

Timothy Sullivan............................ *Swanford town councillor*

Ian Sullivan.................................... *UKMP potential candidate for the Woolgrove Constituency*

T

Mr Thompson................................. *science teacher*

V

Andy Venables............................. *aged 17, born on 2 April, part-time waiter (Jewel Café) and barman (Orange Lounge)*

W

Justin Walker**............................ *aged 13, born on 26 October*

Monica Walker............................ *Justin's mum*

Simon Walker.............................. *Justin's dad*

Mrs Warner.................................. *Archbishop Benn's housekeeper*

Alexander 'Alex' Waverly.......... *aged 3, born on 27 July, Anne's son, Stewart's half brother*

Anne Waverly (née Baxter)........ *Stewart Henderson's natural mother, mother of Alex*

Mr Wilkinson .... *Swanford Community School deputy headmaster*

Mr Williams .... *music teacher*

Dennis Wills............................. *Detective Sergeant, Swanford*

Linda Woolley.......................... *pupil in Jack Moseley's class, 4S*

Deirdre Wren........................... *Police Constable, Swanford*

www.ingramcontent.com/pod-product-compliance
Lightning Source LLC
Chambersburg PA
CBHW070206260626
47160CB00002B/462